Foodchain

Jeff Jacobson

FIVE STAR
A part of Gale, Cengage Learning

GALE
CENGAGE Learning™

Detroit • New York • San Francisco • New Haven, Conn • Waterville, Maine • London

GALE
CENGAGE Learning·

LIBRARY OF CONGRESS CATALOGING-IN-PUBLICATION DATA

Jacobson, Jeff (Jeffory)
    Foodchain / Jeff Jacobson. — 1st ed.
      p. cm.
    ISBN-13: 978-1-59414-820-0 (alk. paper)
    ISBN-10: 1-59414-820-1 (alk. paper)
     1. Hunters—Fiction. 2. Vendetta—Fiction. 3. Ranchers—Fiction. 4. Exotic animals—Fiction. 5. California, Northern—Fiction. I. Title.
PS3610.A356756F66 2010
813'.6—dc22   2009046966

First Edition. First Printing: March 2010.
Published in 2010 in conjunction with Tekno Books and Ed Gorman.

For Dad

ACKNOWLEDGMENTS

I would like to gratefully thank the following for their support and inspiration:

All the wonderful folks in the Columbia College Chicago Fiction Department, particularly the wisdom of John Schultz, John Helfers, Tiffany Schofield, and the rest of the crew at Five Star, Mark Ferguson at Hard Boiled Records, Jen and House Domonkos, Dave Chichirillo, Christian Behr, Trent Haaga, Arlene Wojtalik, Clay Jacobson, Mom, Craig Christie, David Morrell, Gil and Linda Hibben of Hibben Knives, Dr. Janice Prunsky, and the one and only Mort Castle.

Special thanks to Deb. I love you, little one.

And a headbangin' thanks to 3 Inches of Blood, AC/DC, Amon Amarth, Bad News, Black Sabbath, Chrome Division, Deadbolt, Dethklok, FEAR, Gwar, Himsa, Immortal Souls, In Flames, Insomnium, Iron Maiden, Judas Priest, Lard, Motörhead, Rammstein, Searing Meadow, and Slayer for the music that fueled the writing of this novel.

DAY ONE

In the sudden silence that filled the trunk after the engine died, Frank heard strange cries and howls. The other guy locked in with him started whimpering again. Frank got the feeling that the guy, a little man with a billion freckles, had been out here before, but the guy hadn't said much, just sobbed damn near the whole ride. Frank fought the urge to kick him to shut him up.

They'd been in the trunk of the long, black car for hours and when it was finally opened, the light from four piss-yellow floodlights made Frank squint. Empty cages and bare concrete slabs surrounded a gravel parking lot, as if a primitive roadside zoo had been abandoned halfway through construction.

Sergio and Giulio, the quiet gentlemen who drove the car, stepped away from the trunk and jerked their heads. Frank and Red climbed out awkwardly; their hands were bound with plastic zip-ties. Frank wore a short-sleeved button-down shirt, boxers, and one sock. The gravel felt warm under his bare foot.

Red recognized the place and made a hurt sound through gritted teeth. He said, "Please. Just listen to me. I'll pay Mr. Castellari. I'll pay, okay? Please. I've stashed enough money away—you need to listen to me."

It didn't look like the quiet gentlemen were listening. Frank didn't know if they were related to Castellari in some way, maybe his nephews, or God forbid, his sons. They looked like him, no necks, not really, just muscle; the bottom of their ears damn near brushed the shoulders of their black suits. But unlike Castellari, Frank didn't think they would change their expressions if he set their black hair on fire. No anger. No impatience. No joy, either. No nothing. It was as if all their emotions had been sucked out by an especially enthusiastic abortionist who had jammed his hollow knife into the back of their skulls and vacuumed out all feeling. They marched Frank and Red into the dead zoo, following a line of flickering floodlights.

Red sniffled harder, breathing in hushed, staccato hisses. "You gotta listen to me. Please. Please. I'll take you right to it. All you gotta do is drive there, you understand? Please." The pleading broke down into sobs, tears, and mucus dripping onto his stomach and the plastic cuffs.

Sergio pulled out a tiny cell phone, extended one stubby finger the size of a plump hot dog and hit a button. Frank wondered how he managed to hit just one button, considering the size of that finger. Giulio jangled the keys in the left pocket of his suit and checked his watch.

"We're here," Sergio said, in a clear, polite voice, his first words all day. He nodded, and held the phone out to Frank.

That's when Frank realized that he was a dead man. This was a goodbye call.

If tonight was simply a warning, then Enzo Castellari would have waited. He would have left Frank wondering what the hell was going to happen all the way out here, out in the middle of nowhere with all the weird animal howls. Castellari wouldn't call, he wouldn't say anything. He'd just let Frank sweat it out, scare the shit out of himself, all on his own. Then, after seeing something, a demonstration, maybe something having to do with the other poor bastard stuck in the trunk, and after Frank got so scared he was ready to piss himself, then Castellari would talk to him.

But to talk to Frank before he even had a chance to see what could happen, before his imagination had a chance to run screaming into the night . . . Frank knew his time was up. Castellari simply wanted the satisfaction of saying goodbye. So Frank gingerly took the phone with the heavy realization that no matter what Castellari said, no matter what kind of salvation was promised, every word was a lie.

"Yeah," Frank said.

"Hello, Frank." Castellari's voice was smooth, polished; it slithered into Frank's right eardrum, curling itself up and making itself at home. "I imagine right now you're a little . . . worried. Wondering where you are and all. That's understandable."

Frank didn't answer right away, just waited until it became apparent that Castellari wasn't going to say anything until he acknowledged the question. Or was it a statement? Frank wasn't sure. So he just said, "Yeah."

"Take a good look at the man with you. Take a good look."

Frank shifted the phone slightly, tilting it away from his ear, and hit the volume button with his pinkie. The voice continued, getting just loud enough to catch Red's attention. Red stopped sniffling, his eyes meeting Frank's and getting bigger by the second.

Castellari said, "There's a man who can make numbers dance and sing, make no mistake. No matter how foul my financial excrement smelled, this man could sift those numbers through that magnificent, devious brain of his and it would always come up smelling like roses. Always." A plastic sigh, full of resignation. "Trouble is, this man apparently felt I wasn't valuing his services . . . appropriately. So, while it was true that he could make the numbers dance and sing, they were still out of tune."

Castellari was always a melodramatic sonofabitch, but Frank made sure Red was getting it. And boy oh boy, he was getting it, all right. He'd frozen altogether, staring at Frank, at Frank's

11

right hand, at the phone.

"Now, this man was warned. Make no mistake about this. He was given every opportunity to rectify the musical numbers. But some men simply do not listen, no matter how loudly you speak, no matter how much effort you put into . . . *impressing* upon them the significance of the matter. I trust you're listening, Frank?"

"Yeah."

"This man has been in your shoes. He's been here before. He knows what awaits him." Castellari took a deep, patient breath, enjoying himself. "This man has seen God. He's seen God, up close and personal. Unfortunately, this man was not . . . impressed with God." Castellari paused. "Few men need to see God twice."

Air hissed out of Red's nose like it was escaping a tiny hole in a balloon.

"So. Now you're in the position of trying to understand the significance of this matter. You watch and try to learn something. Are you listening, Frank?"

Frank didn't say anything. Let the sonofabitch wait *this* one out. "Okay, Frank. Okay." It took him a while to realize that Castellari had hung up.

They passed rows of dead carnival rides. Tangled metal, twisted spires, and dusty bench seats with safety bars stuck upright were collected together in a spiderweb of gathering shadows and faded colors that seemed to suck the light out of the air instead of reflecting it. Frank recognized a few rides from his childhood. The Whizzer. The Tilt-A-Whirl. The Mangler. The Ferris wheels looked like giant wagon wheels, leaning against each other, remnants of failed pioneer trips to the promised land of California.

A flashlight flickered over Frank and Red; another man was

waiting for them. Folds of pale, hairy flesh spilled out from around a leather apron and erupted around his chin. Tiny, dull eyes gazed out from between snarled eyebrows and blackheads. Loose rubber boots rose almost to his knees. A metal tube dangled from his belt. He carried the flashlight in his right hand and a large plastic bucket in his left. The bucket was full of fresh bones. Plenty of gristle. Chunks of meat, some covered in gray fur, swimming in blood.

They walked. The zookeeper led the way, picking his way through rows of cages, sweeping his flashlight back and forth in the dusty air. Many of the cages were secured on flatbed truck trailers. Animals started to appear. Most were dead. There were a lot of big cats. A lion sprawled on his side, all four legs splayed away from his swollen stomach. A dead leopard, his head wedged between two bars. Flies crawled over its gray tongue. The flashlight kept checking cage locks and doors, nailing cringing animals into corners, scattering the black shadows under the flatbeds.

They passed a cage that ran the length of a flatbed. A huge animal stood motionless inside. Four ancient, sagging pillars rose into shoulders that crested at nearly six feet tall. The creature was over thirteen feet long, covered in a heavy, wrinkled gray skin that seemed at least twice as big as the bones underneath. It reminded Frank of a horse, with a long, sloping skull that tapered down to a rounded snout. Black eyes reflected the flashlight. Two flat, smooth spots, like stumps of trees, dominated the top of its nose.

Frank realized that he was looking at an old rhinoceros, standing ankle deep in its own shit. Its horns had been cut off. Flies, sluggish in the cool air, covered the entire cage like a buzzing black blanket.

A tiger paced incessantly along thin bars, rumbling low in his throat. Several lionesses lay in separate corners of one large cage, tails flicking at sluggish flies. At the sight of the zookeeper and the bucket, they pulled themselves to their feet and snarled. It sounded like old muscle car engines, old 454 V-8s, sounds that made your teeth vibrate and shake your fillings loose.

The entire zoo erupted in more snarls, howls, screeches. It was feeding time and everybody was hungry; but Frank knew this went beyond simple hunger. He could count ribs on nearly every animal; they were slowly starving to death. This was where circuses came to die, where animals too old, too tired, too unpredictable, finished their lives, in a carnival junkyard, refugees from dying traveling zoos, unprepared private owners, and cancelled casino shows. It was a waiting room for the damned, as if hell was simply too full at the moment.

The zookeeper strolled from cage to cage, reaching into the bucket and tossing scraps of bloody meat through the bars. Frank recognized leg muscles, paws, and other pieces of dogs from the meat in the bucket. The cats pounced instantly, growling, snarling, snatching the chunks, ripping the morsels away from each other.

They reached the last cage in the row. It held a huge male lion, nearly ten feet long. He jammed his massive snout against the cage door, straining the thin bailing wire that had been twisted around the bars, securing the door. A very deep, very drawn sigh hushed out from his chest. He tilted his head and roared, shaking the matted mane and exposing teeth bigger than the quiet gentlemen's fingers. The sound reminded Frank of a jet taking off. The roar held enough authority to quiet the rest of the zoo, at least for a few seconds.

Frank noticed the zookeeper didn't get too close while tossing the meat into the cages. He may have been fat and lazy, but he wasn't stupid. Frank took a long, hard look at the bailing wire holding the door shut. It looked like it had been there for a long time; most of the wire had rusted together.

The zookeeper pulled a greyhound's head out of the bucket, holding onto the slim ear. He tossed the skull into the cage. The lion seized and cracked the greyhound's skull between those giant teeth. It sounded like small branches being snapped for kindling.

Red started crying again, really sobbing. His nose dribbled more mucus, then suddenly erupted with blood. The thick liquid bubbled out of his nostrils, sheeting his upper lip in crimson snot, and kept spilling down, across his bottom lip and over his chin. Frank wondered if the accountant had discovered the wonderful world of cocaine; if so, that might explain Castellari's financial concerns. Frank almost felt sorry for the guy.

The zookeeper looked at Red like he'd just scraped a plump white bug out from under his toenail with a pocketknife. He snorted, coughed up a thick ball of phlegm, and stuck it in his bottom lip, saving it for later. He grinned. "Didn't think you would be back. Thought you were smarter."

Mucus bubbles swelled in Red's nostrils and popped. "Hey," Red croaked. "Hey. You guys listening? I can make you rich. Rich. Oh Jesus, I've got so much money stashed away, you have no idea. Please. Just listen to me. Please."

Frank tried to tune out Red's bleating and focus on the quiet gentlemen. Overpowering them was out of the question. They just stood there like goddamn Buddhist statues. Although these guys were about as Asian as John Wayne when he pretended to be Genghis Khan in that movie where he'd worn some kind of goofy wig and heavy goop over his eyes to make him look Oriental. Frank wondered if they were anywhere near where they made that movie, because it had been filmed a tad too close to a nuclear test site, and as it turned out, as the whole cast, the whole crew, everybody really, had grown themselves nasty, awful *lively* cases of cancer, just like Frank's mom, who in the end couldn't do a whole hell of a lot more than bark sticky clots of blood out of her charbroiled lungs onto wadded balls of Kleenex as he helped her apply lipstick even as her wig slid off and—*FUCKING CHRIST*—

Frank bit the side of his tongue. Not too hard. Just enough to draw blood. Just enough to snap things back into focus. The fear had his mind on the run; it kept racing, looping, straying back into tangents, slipping back into his past. He shifted gears, skipping down through the spinning teeth in his mind, and tried to focus on the moment.

Acting like he thought they were on the move again, Frank took two steps forward and collided with the zookeeper. The fat man flinched, jerked away. The bucket hit the ground and toppled over. Blood and meat spilled out into the dust.

Frank stepped back and mumbled, "Sorry," aware of the blood seeping into the dirt, watching the lion's nostrils expand and contract.

The zookeeper shoved him, holding the flashlight against Frank's throat. The metal tube came out of his belt and made a crackling sound as he held it up to Frank's face. "Just what exactly is your fucking problem, retard?" he asked. "I'll fry your brain like goddamn scrambled eggs."

The lion roared again and slammed into the bars, eyes narrowing into slits, nostrils flaring.

A lone flatbed blocked the path. It looked like some kind of tank, at least thirty feet long and ten feet high. Narrow metal stairs had been secured to the side, rising from the ground and clinging to the side of the tank for about twenty feet before descending back to the ground.

The zookeeper stomped up the stairs; the rusty metal shuddered and groaned. He sidled along the catwalk, flinging the remaining blood in the bucket over the tank. After dropping the bucket next to him, he looked down at the men and said,

"Awright then. Make 'em strip. I ain't fetching any more clothes out this time. It ain't good for 'em, fucks 'em up." He shook his chins. "They puke out that shit for days."

Red dropped to his knees, keening, "Please, please, please," over and over and over. Blood seeped down from his nose, down his chin, down his shirt. Frank blinked and Sergio had a knife. One moment his hands were empty, the next, he held a wicked-looking six-inch blade. It was like a magic trick. Frank wondered if Sergio had learned it from one of the magicians in the casino shows.

Sergio brought the knife down and effortlessly split Red's shirt in half, from the back of the collar down to the small of his back. Red suddenly found his feet and herked and jerked his way up the stairs.

Sergio reached out and caught the back of Red's khakis. The knife came down again, splitting the fabric covering Red's bony ass. Red fell forward, grunting and spitting blood, and crawled out of his shredded pants.

The zookeeper said, "Take off your shoes."

Giulio stepped closer to Frank, nodding at Frank's clothes. Frank started to unbutton his shirt. He glanced up over Giulio's broad shoulder into the pale yellow darkness. Snarls, screeches, and howls echoed off the cages, flatbeds, and carnival rides, but he didn't hear what he wanted—metal on metal.

Up on the catwalk, the zookeeper said, "Take off them socks."

"Oh God, please. Just listen to me a minute. Just for a—"

The zookeeper jerked out his cattle prod and cracked it across Red's forehead. "I said, take off them fuckin' socks."

Sergio started up the stairs and Frank hoped the catwalk wouldn't support their weight. The metal moaned a little, but held. Red curled into a ball, drawing his bony knees up to his pale, hairless chest and covering his head with his freckled arms.

"Jesus humpin' Christ. You pussy." The zookeeper thumbed

the switch and the cattle prod crackled like bitter laughter. Without hesitation, he jabbed Red just under the armpit. Red flopped and wriggled for several seconds, making "Uhhhh-uhhhh-uhhhh" sounds. A dark stain spread across the front of his white underwear and urine ran across his hip, his thigh. Sergio, apparently familiar with the effects of the prod, held off on grabbing Red until the zookeeper withdrew it. He caught hold of Red's calf and the six-inch blade snickered through Red's green sock.

But Red wasn't giving up easy. He kicked out with his other leg and caught Sergio square in the balls. Sergio exhaled harshly, took half a step backward, then leaned back in and slammed the blade into Red's thigh, driving it deep, all the way to the hilt.

Red's scream even shocked the monkeys into silence.

Then Frank heard what he'd been waiting for—a distant, twanging, metallic snap. It didn't look like the zookeeper had heard it. In front of Frank, Giulio allowed a flicker of impatience to flash across his emotionless features. He fixed his dead gaze on Frank and pulled out his own knife. Frank didn't want to get stuck like Red, so he quickly yanked his shirt off, tearing the buttons over the plastic cuffs. He curled his big toe into the top of his one sock and dragged it off.

Up on the catwalk, Red wouldn't stop his high-pitched screaming. Sergio plucked the knife out of Red's thigh and grabbed hold of Red's bleeding nose with his other hand, pinching the nostrils shut with his huge thumb and forefinger. He held Red's head very still and wiped the blade clean in the red hair. He cut off the other sock with his newly cleaned blade and sliced Red's underwear in half at the hip.

Giulio nodded at Frank's boxers. Frank took a deep breath, slid his boxers down to his ankles, and kept watching the darkness under the cages.

Red managed one more *"—please—"* before the zookeeper and Sergio lifted his naked, bleeding body and dropped him into the tank with a dull splash.

Above and behind him, Frank heard quick, savage movement. A desperate, gurgled shriek. Brittle leather scraped over wet iron. Water, thick with algae, splashed over the rim, slid down the outside of the tank, and dripped onto the top of his head, trickling down the back of his neck. It felt warm, like a used bath.

The zookeeper and Sergio turned to stare down at Frank. He tried to breathe slow, easy, and found that he couldn't even take a breath. His exposed balls felt cold and shriveled in the night air. He curled his toes, felt the sand and grit underneath. It was time to make his move. He'd stalled long enough. He had to try something, anything. Trouble was, nothing was coming to him. Nothing was left inside. Nothing except the urge to simply bolt, to spring naked between the cages, to flee shrieking into the night.

But the quiet gentlemen would catch him. And they'd make his death last for days. So he started up the stairs, legs feeling weak, like overcooked spaghetti, head down, hands cupped over his dick and balls. It was a funny time for modesty, but ingrained habits died hard. Giulio followed him up the stairs, snicking the knife away.

The surface of the water seethed and boiled as if it was alive. Frank caught a flash of white, a belly maybe. Whatever it was, it wasn't Red. A flat, tapered tail slapped the surface with eagerness. Something dark rolled several times and disappeared in the roiling water. Bubbles, silver in the yellow light, popped and fizzed. The zookeeper bent over and banged the cattle prod several times against the side of the tank.

Shadows rose to the surface. They were large, maybe eight, ten feet long and nearly two feet across.

Frank finally realized that the tank was full of alligators.

Freezing terror scrabbled up his spine and sunk its fangs into the bottom of his brain. His knees quivered, threatened to collapse completely. He should have known. Should have known that the tank would be stuffed with some kind of goddamn squirming nightmare. He hated reptiles, alligators especially. Ever since he was a little kid in East Texas, playing on the sloping lawn that dropped abruptly into that black canal.

Frank didn't trust anything that didn't generate its own body heat.

A single word, "Please," erupted in his throat like the silver bubbles in the tank and nearly popped in his mouth. But he choked it down. He'd be damned if he started begging now. For a moment, under the gassy, rotten smell of the water, he suddenly smelled his father, the sickly sweet smell of his shaving lotion.

"Go ahead. Shoot me. Get it over with," he said.

The rubbery folds in the zookeeper's face split into a smile. "Fine. Shoot him then."

Sergio shook his head. "We can't. Mr. Castellari gave specific instructions."

"Just shoot me. C'mon, you spineless fucks. You fucking wop *motherfucking cocksucking—*" Frank's voice got high and tight, like an overstrung violin, and he screamed, "Shoot, you greasy motherfucking—"

But instead Sergio and Giulio curled their thick fingers around the muscles above Frank's elbows, and the sudden sense of being powerless, of being *forced,* slithered into his mind and squatted above the gleaming fangs of terror, enveloping his consciousness in a white, blurry haze of shock.

And just as the two quiet gentlemen started to tilt Frank forward, forcing him to topple face first into the alligator tank, just as all the strength left his knees and he felt his own warm, humiliating piss run down the inside of his left leg, just as the zookeeper played his flashlight over the rolling black water, catching the awful black eyes of the alligators, the lion leapt.

Later, Frank could only guess that the lion had been driven into a frenzy by the smell of the blood and raw greyhound meat in the dust, maddeningly just out of reach, and had somehow forced its cage door open just enough to slip out. After gulping down the few pieces and licking up Red's vomit, he must have followed the drops of nose blood and the pure, uncut scent of panic, obeying the oldest instinct of all, older than fear.

Hunger.

Frank sensed, rather than heard, the roar behind him, felt the impact of the lion hit the catwalk like a five hundred pound wrecking ball. The lion came down hard on Sergio, claws slicing through the tasteful suit like a plow breaking through the last frost of winter.

Frank grabbed Giulio's left wrist with both hands as he fell forward and pulled the heavy, quiet gentleman down. They toppled into the tank together, Frank fumbling for the car keys in Giulio's suit pocket. Frank's bare feet hit the slimy bottom and he instantly kicked out, driving his heels into Giulio's chest, pushing himself back toward the catwalk. He heard nothing but a rush of bubbles and the thin, staccato beat of his own heart.

The lion's back feet, claws outstretched like lethal grappling hooks, caught the bottom rung of the railing. As the front legs bounced off the catwalk, the ungodly massive shoulders rolled with the impact. The back legs tensed, pulling the giant cat backward. Sergio dropped to his knees, his eyes popping open as shock ratcheted into his soul.

The zookeeper stumbled away, fumbling with the cattle prod, and fell backward down the stairs.

Sergio managed to get his .38 clear of the holster just as the lion's front left paw swung through the air like a scythe and sent the quiet gentleman's arm, fingers still clenched around the taped gun handle, sailing out over Frank and the alligator tank. The arm spun, spitting a fine mist of blood into a rainbow above the black water and yellow light. The hand muscles twitched and the gun flinched, firing a round into the night sky.

The lion rolled his back hips over the railing with a fluidity that matched the surface of the water and stalked forward, inch-long splintered claws slipping into the gaps in the steel mesh.

Sergio took one solid, confident step forward. In his mind, he raised the .38 and squeezed off three quick shots.

The lion struck faster than a rattlesnake, clapping his great stretched paws on Sergio's shoulders and crunching his skull between his jaws like a walnut under a hammer. The cat shook his head once, twice, and raggedly ripped Sergio's head off.

Down in the tank, Frank gathered his legs under his chest and shoved down as hard as he could manage, throwing himself onto the catwalk, just under the flicking tail. The steel mesh chewed into his chest like a cheese grater, but he thrust his elbows down, pulling himself out of the water.

Sergio's headless, one-armed body sank to its knees, as if he had finally given up completely, and toppled backward, bounced down the stairs, and landed heavily on top of the zookeeper, who was scrabbling away when the limp sack of bones and flesh slammed him into the dirt.

Frank rolled under the bottom rung of the railing as two quick explosions shattered the water's surface. Frank didn't know if Giulio was shooting at him, the lion, or the alligators; he didn't care. His bare feet hit the dust and he broke out into a flat-out run, ignoring the sharp edges of gravel, cuffed hands swinging, elbows flailing in the cool night air.

The lion shivered, shaking his head, crunching those giant teeth together. The pieces of skull cracked into splintered fragments, dribbling blood over the black lips and tawny fur of his bottom jaw. Elegant drops clung to the long, thick whiskers like heavy dew on a spiderweb. The tufted tail flicked happily back and forth. The taste of blood had jump-started his other senses; smells suddenly gained new dimensions of texture. Every sound became crisp, clear. Even the quick snick-snick of the .38 being cocked.

Frank ran. Behind him, gunfire popped. The lion roared.

The shooting lasted for a long time and as the thunderous, almost numbing sound of gunfire continued to ring in Giulio and the zookeeper's ears, neither heard the engine of the long, black car start as Frank stomped on the gas, plowed through the front gate, and shot into the night.

DAY TWO

He hadn't meant to kill the horse.

No, that wasn't right, Frank corrected himself as he steered the long, black car along the high desert highway. That's not exactly being honest. He'd meant to kill the horse, all right, just not then, not that way. He braced his naked knees against the steering wheel and reached over with his cuffed hands to turn on the heat. Soothing, warm air exhaled softly over his white skin.

The grooms called him, *"El Caballo Susurrero."* The Horse Whisperer.

After Frank and his mom moved away from East Texas, away from the ghost of his father, they settled in the industrial wasteland of suburban southwest Chicago. Mom told Frank that she was a waitress, but he found out later she was a stripper.

Frank found work at Hawthorne, a nearby horse racetrack. For a long time, Frank worked alongside the little Mexican guys who found their way north riding in the backs of trucks. He cleaned stalls, shaking and sifting the shavings until nothing remained, no horse shit, no soiled hay, nothing except wood shavings. He tacked up the thoroughbreds, preparing the snorting, dancing racehorses for their morning run, and washed them after their workouts.

He may have made a good jockey, but genetics betrayed him. Mom was damn near six feet and his father was at least six feet five inches. But his father's height was never impressive; he looked like a scarecrow that had seen too many hard winters.

In the barns, Frank hung back, always helping, always watching. When he spoke, it was quiet, but people started to listen. And listen hard. By the end of that first season, he'd been driven up to Arlington to watch the horses there. His observations about the horses and his race predictions were eerily correct. The big money boys, the guys that watched the races from behind great walls of air-conditioned glass, took notice. It wasn't hard to pull an eighteen-year-old into the fold.

They paid for college. Frank went to school nights while working at the track during the day. Two years away from a veterinary degree he saw his mom cough blood. She was washing dishes. He'd come down from his bedroom and saw her back hitch a little as she gripped the side of the sink. Little flecks of crimson suddenly appeared within the bubbles. She whipped at the water in the sink with a wooden spoon, as if stirring in some exotic herb into a frothy soup. Frank put a frozen burrito in the microwave and his mom asked him if he was going out that night and neither one of them mentioned it again.

The next day Frank was bent over, wrapping the front left leg of a five-year-old filly nearing the end of her career, trying to focus on the job but thinking of all those flecks of blood in the soap bubbles, when a groom tried to bring a notoriously twitchy colt under the lead line connected to the filly's halter. Any other day, it probably would have worked, but the colt was spooked by the sound of a pitchfork being tossed into an empty wheelbarrow. It reared and kicked, and the next thing Frank knew, he was vomiting uncontrollably in a hospital bed. The doctors spoke in clipped, officious tones, throwing out terms like "brain damage" and "limited recovery" as if they were simple math equations.

Once the pain went away and the vomiting stopped, Frank

didn't feel much different. Except for two things. He'd been kicked in the left side of the head, and the muscles on that side of his face didn't work very well. They'd respond halfheartedly, like a tired, petulant ten-year-old being ordered to wash the dog. Other times, they'd constrict, as if they were trying to climb right off his face. Most of the time, though, they just hung there like heavy, wet curtains. The right side worked just fine.

The second thing was, for some reason he never did understand, he couldn't get his brain to decipher numeric representations. He could read a traditional watch with an hour and second hand, understood it on a core level, but a digital readout looked like a series of random LED slashes.

The college board wanted to know how he would read textbooks, medicine bottles, syringes. Frank demonstrated that he could count just fine, as long as the numbers were written out as words, and he could mark on the measurements on a bottle or syringe, but they wouldn't give a definite ruling. His employers told Frank not to worry, that the school had to make sure they couldn't get sued, either way. Weeks dragged into months. Frank's mom moved into the hospital and didn't come out. Yet, there was still hope.

Until the day Frank beat a man to death with a fistful of aluminum horseshoes.

The defense successfully argued that the man had been treating a racehorse with exceptional cruelty, and what with Frank's past as a promising young veterinarian, dedicated to preserving these animals' health and safety, combined with his recent devastating brain injury, he couldn't be held responsible for his actions that tragic day. He had to visit a psychiatrist one day a week, and his career as a vet was over, but that was it. No jail. No hospital.

Later, Frank wished he'd been locked away somewhere instead.

The men who'd paid for his aborted education wanted to know how and when he was going to pay them back. The nature of Frank's work changed. He decided which horses had potential, which horses could stand another round of injections, and which horses would make more money if they died from insurance claims. Once in a while he would hear the grooms whispering about him in halting flurries of Spanish and English, as if it was safer to talk about a man like that in a deliberate blurring of language. A rumor started that if he visited a horse, held up his finger to his pursed mouth, and said, "Shhhh," that horse ended up dead.

His mom never came out of the hospital. The men paid for her funeral.

And so Frank became the guy you'd go to when you needed a horse dead. At least he killed the horses humanely, with drugs so they'd just slip away, just go to sleep. Not like that sonofabitch who'd slide lubricated wires into the horse's asshole and then connect the wires to a car battery.

Frank kept the needle around sixty-five and shifted on the gray leather seat, rolling his head, easing the kinks in his neck. Long, black hair hung in his face; the left side of his mouth was pulled down by an unseen fishhook. He had to find some clothes. It didn't matter what he told the cops, if he got pulled over, that was it. They'd take one look at his nakedness and the handcuffs, and he'd be spending the night in jail. Waiting, no doubt, for more quiet gentlemen to show up. Castellari had connections everywhere. Frank probably wouldn't last more than a few hours in jail. They'd bail him out and drag him off to a garage in the middle of nowhere and go to work on his flesh.

Clothing was the first priority. Well, that and the goddamn

cuffs. He slowed the long, black car to twenty miles an hour, scanning the side of the highway. Luckily, he hadn't seen anyone way out here yet. He found a wide, level spot and pulled the car off the highway and steered it deep into the scrub brush.

Two weeks ago, he'd gotten a call from Mr. Enzo Castellari. Ten minutes before the Breeder's Cup at the Arlington Racetrack, Frank pretended to pat *The Elizabeth Dane*'s flank affectionately, but he was actually shooting fifteen ccs of his own special cocktail into her bloodstream. Mom had worked as a magician's assistant in one of the riverboat casinos for a while, and she taught Frank a few tricks. Mostly sleight of hand. He used a latex bulb syringe, used for cleaning babies' ears, a curved needle, and a length of surgical tubing that snaked up his sleeve.

As the drugs slipped through the horse's circulatory system, eventually hitting specific nerve endings in the brain, it was supposed to gradually stimulate her into a frenzy of strength and speed as she went charging out through the race, winning by several lengths. Then, while the insurance was quietly changed, significantly raising the coverage, the horse would slip into a coma and die in three or four days. The insurance companies were in on the scam as well, they had business insurance, and everybody just kept ripping everybody else off up and down the ladder.

But a group of animal rights activists had stormed the racetrack, delaying the race for an hour. Once the race finally got started, Castellari's horse burst out of the pack early in the race and seemed a sure bet, until blood burst from her nostrils and she collapsed in the soft dirt in a tangle of long, impossibly thin legs and leather reins, flicking the tiny rider away. The other horses simply thundered around the body as the jockey, who knew that the horse had been poisoned, got caught on camera stomping at the dead horse.

The Elizabeth Dane was supposed to slip away quietly, out of the spotlight. Instead, she died on national television. Frank knew Mr. Castellari wouldn't give two shits about his excuses and so he ran, ran out into the parking lot, out of Chicago, out of the Midwest.

There was a pair of wraparound black sunglasses, half a roll of Tums, and a cassette tape of Herb Alpert and Tijuana Brass in the glove compartment, but that was it. The car was clean, so clean he couldn't even find dirt in the plush carpeting.

Frank killed the engine and sat for a moment under an empty sky. Then he got out. He found two crisp black suits, neatly folded and pressed, still snug in their dry cleaning bags, in the back seat. Blinding white shirts too. He figured the suits might have been just in case the two quiet gentlemen got any blood on their clothing while feeding the animals. There were even two pairs of gleaming black shoes.

At first, he didn't think the trunk key was going to work. He gripped it tight, ready to shove the key through the lock, through the metal, through the goddamn back seat if necessary, but forced himself to calm down. If the key broke, he'd have to walk back to the highway and take his chances.

After a few moments of restrained wriggling, the key clicked over, the trunk popped open. The whole thing was lined with plastic, but under that the carpet was as clean as the rest of the car; the whole thing probably got washed and detailed at least every other day. He yanked at the bottom of the trunk, pulling up the floor, something he'd been unable to do when he'd been locked back here with Red. A black leather bag lay nestled within the spare tire. It held a screwdriver, a jack so tiny it was pretty much useless, and a tire iron, one of those condensed tools, shaped like an L. At the bottom of the L was the shell for the lug bolts; the other end was flattened to a dull blade.

He looked at the screwdriver. It was a Phillips and utterly useless for the cuffs. That left the tire iron. He held the top half of the iron between his wrists, wedging the blade against the plastic strip, while bracing the bottom half of the L against his chest. Then he slowly forced his wrists toward his chest, willing the plastic to snap. It didn't work. So he settled his hands on the bumper and leaned over, using his weight to increase the pressure on the cuffs. At first, he felt a little awkward with his naked ass sticking out in the chilly night air, but gradually, the pain in his wrists replaced the embarrassment, and nothing mattered but breaking the plastic.

It took a while. In the end, both wrists and the center of Frank's chest were bleeding, but the plastic finally split, sending the blade into the soft tissue of his left palm. He barely felt it. He threw his head back and hissed in triumph, spreading his arms wide to the glittering stars.

He lived in hotels for six days, never really sleeping. The windows always drew him. It didn't matter if he could see the flat, alien mountains of the west or a view of I-80 and a couple of neon casinos, he'd turn off the lights and the TV and sit at the little round tables in those stiff, narrow chairs in the faint light from the parking lot and stare, watching the long, black car in all that neon, just watch all the lights and finish a bottle of Jamaican rum.

Until finally, inevitably, he went to answer the door, expecting pizza, and found the two quiet gentlemen instead. They wore expensive suits. Frank was wearing boxers and one sock.

He carried a half-empty bottle of Appleton Estate.

They carried revolvers.

Both suits were roughly six or seven sizes too large. Frank felt like a ten-year-old dressing up in his father's clothes. Although, he reflected, this wasn't really at all like his father's suit. His father had been tall and painfully thin, like Abraham Lincoln, except slouched and without the beard; his father shaved twice a day. He was a preacher and he *believed;* every moment on this Earth was a test from the Holy Spirit.

His father had handled swamp rattlesnakes in a large shack filled with half-burnt pews stolen from other churches, sliding his hands slowly around, caressing two or three snakes at a time, as more rattlesnakes and cottonmouths slithered around his feet. A bunch of desperate people surrounded Frank's father and the snakes, all of 'em leaning into it, clapping too quickly, eyes wide and dull, singing kinda' low, while Grandma slapped her upright piano and moaned a little now and then.

He found a map under the driver's seat and figured out he was in the high desert mountains of central Nevada. He headed north. The shoes didn't fit any better than the suit; in fact, they fit worse, so Frank drove barefoot. News of the zoo would have probably reached Castellari by now, so he couldn't head south, back to Las Vegas. They had his picture, and in Las Vegas you couldn't stick your hand in your pocket to scratch your balls without two or three surveillance cameras catching you. He couldn't head west either; California was full of lying fucks who would happily call Castellari for the slightest hint of a reward.

Frank hit I-80 with an empty stomach and an emptier gas tank. He turned west, toward Reno. Nearly four hours had passed since he'd gone for a dip in the alligator tank. He needed cash. Quickly and quietly. Gas stations and convenience stores were out; that was for guys with brain damage, guys with PCP habits bigger than Texas, guys who thought shooting the camera would wreck the videotape.

More than anything, he needed rest, so he took the next off-ramp. It curled down into a low gully filled with tumbleweeds.

He followed the narrow road until a sagging pole barn loomed up ahead in the darkness. He found a dark place to park behind the barn and killed the engine. For a while, he just sat still and listened to the dull roar of the freeway, watching the distant headlights scatter shadows across the hills.

Frank had been to Jamaica once, with a filthy rich widow who owned dozens of racehorses. She'd wanted a "friend" to go along. What the hell, she paid a lot. He fell in love with the island, and all he wanted out of life was to simply make enough money to buy himself a little concrete shack, right off of a palm-strewn beach, maybe pick up a sweet and sassy little Jamaican honey. A place where he could lay in the sun, swim in the ocean, and quietly drink himself to death in peace.

He bounced around the radio for a while, but couldn't concentrate on anything. He closed his eyes, but the surging, boiling water of the alligator tank kept leaking out. Teeth slammed together, tails slapped metal, and segmented white bellies flashed in yellow light as they rolled and rolled and rolled—

Something clamped itself around his right ankle.

Frank screamed and flinched awake in the driver's seat of the long, black car and found his ankle wedged underneath the brake pedal. He jerked his knees angrily up to the steering wheel and sat up. His stomach growled impatiently. But he could handle that. It was the irritating, thirsty itch in the back of his mind that really bothered him.

He headed west again. He needed a place to clean himself up. He pulled into a nearly empty rest stop and parked at the far end. The place smelled of diesel and dog shit. An open area full of maps, brochures, and pay phones split the building in half;

the women's room was on one side, men's on the other. He counted three trucks in the parking lot and no cars.

He waited a while and was just about to meander on over to the building and see if they had any vending machines with food when a semi hissed itself to a stop in the truck lot. Frank kept still, watching through the rearview mirror. A man jumped out of the cab, stretched, and walked slowly to the men's room.

Twenty minutes later the guy was still inside.

Frank got tired of waiting. Maybe the guy had stomach flu or something. He slid the tire iron up the inside of the suit's right sleeve, up along his forearm, and curled his fingers around the lower half of the L.

He climbed out of the car, tire iron hot and tight in his fist. He clomped across the parking lot as fast as possible in the loose shoes. It would have been easier barefoot. But he didn't want any unnecessary attention and since a guy wearing an ill-fitting black suit and oversized shoes didn't seem as strange as being barefoot, he slogged forward, keeping his toes flexed so the shoes wouldn't fall off.

Frank stepped into the light in the middle of the building, scanning for food. There was a vending machine for soda, but that was all. No candy bars, no chips. Not even those bags of fake health mixes, with chunks of petrified nuts and dried fruit that tasted like horse shavings. He stopped for a moment, watching the snoring trucks and listening intently. Except for the fast food wrappers dancing in the wind, nothing moved.

Frank stepped inside the men's restroom.

Searing white fluorescent light stung his eyes. Bleached gray tiles covered the floors. The stalls waited on his left. On his right, the sinks and reflective metal mirrors. Two air hand dryers. The place smelled burnt, not only through the temperature from the desert air and those hand dryers, but chemically as well.

One of the stall doors was shut.

Frank skied across the tiles to the nearest sink. He twisted the handle, and as water hit the porcelain, he bent over to see what waited under the closed door.

A pair of gray snakeskin cowboy boots.

Frank splashed water on his face, then bent and drank deeply. The water tasted foul and smelled of sulfur, but since he hadn't had any liquid at all in over eight hours, he didn't mind. He gulped it down, pausing only to suck in a quick breath now and then.

The stall door swung in, slowly. A voice, rough and low, whispered, "Hey, man. Hey. Look at me."

The guy on the toilet was close to Frank's age, maybe low thirties, sandy beard, wearing a Mack Truck cap and a plaid western-cut long-sleeved shirt. His jeans were bunched around his ankles, and his right hand was stroking his erect dick.

Frank slowly straightened, wiping the water away from his lips with his left hand, keeping his right hand with the tire iron hanging loose at his side. "I'm sorry?"

He stepped out of the black shoes. The tile was cold and clammy beneath his feet.

"Look at this, man." The breathing and stroking grew faster. "Look at it. Yes . . . you like it, don't ya? You like my cock. I can tell."

"Yeah," Frank agreed as he took three quick steps toward the stall and brought the tire iron down on the trucker's head before the man could even let go of his dick. The iron bar hit his skull with an unsatisfying, brittle thud. So Frank hit the guy again, cracking the corner of the L into the trucker's nose. The guy finally let go of his dick and instead of protecting his head, went for his jeans. Frank cracked him a few more times and the guy twitched and flopped for a second or two like a fish on a flat rock, but eventually he stopped trying to move at all.

Very little blood hit the floor. Most of it was running down the guy's face, down his neck, soaking into the plaid shirt. The guy's eyes had rolled up, showing nothing but white slits. His mouth hung open. His hands hung straight down on either side of the toilet, arms more limp than his dick. Frank left the guy's jeans down around his ankles and snagged the wallet. Eight crisp twenties waited inside.

Frank shook his head. His luck was making him nervous. The trucker had a fistful of pills in a plastic baggie in his shirt pocket. Frank tried the boots. They fit much better than the shoes, a little tight, but not bad. The suit legs were so wide that the cuffs nearly obscured the snazzy snakeskin; Frank felt like he'd just stepped out of some seventies exploitation movie.

Frank slipped the large black shoes on the trucker's feet, re-arranged the limp arms in the man's lap, and locked the stall door from the inside. Frank slipped under the door and backed away, scrutinizing the closed door. It simply looked as if the trucker, with his jeans down around his ankles, draped over some large black shoes, was simply taking a long, unhurried shit. Maybe he was reading the paper. It would have to do. Frank tucked the money and baggie of pills away in the inside pocket of the suit jacket, flexed his toes in the boots, and left.

He hit Reno an hour later and headed north, rising suddenly into the Sierra Nevada mountain range. He came around a hill and nearly had a heart attack when he saw the border station. With much of the state devoted to agriculture, California had established permanent roadblocks around its borders, stopping every car that crossed over into the state, asking everyone if they were bringing any fruits or vegetables across. But the officer, a young woman with a face as round and smooth as one of the state's peaches, hadn't shown the slightest interest in Frank. Even before he shook his head to her question, she was already waving him through.

He bought a bottle of rum and spent an hour in a tiny town called Milford. It wasn't exactly Appleton Estate, but it would work. He parked near an old cemetery full of genuine gunfighter skeletons, sipped from the bottle for a while, and finally slept.

His dreams were dark, full of slippery shadows and galloping hooves on tight sand.

The midmorning sun hammered through the windshield like the stern gaze of God and left Frank sweating and confused. The bottle, half-empty, sat upright in the passenger seat as if waiting to be seatbelted into place. He screwed on the cap and threw it under the seat. That was fucking smart, leaving an open bottle in plain sight within the vehicle. Sucking at the sweet and sour film on his teeth, he found an empty campground near Honey Lake and took a shower. It felt good to scrape off the slime from the alligator tank, not to mention the piss on his leg.

Frank slid back behind the wheel, feeling clear and level. He decided the bottle could wait. He wasn't sure what to do. The long, black car had half a tank of gas left. The urge to keep running still seethed through his veins, so he decided that he needed more ground between him and the zoo.

He followed a rough two-lane road northwest, through vast plains of sagebrush and patches of bleached, gray husks of trees, scorched long ago by forest fires, still standing guard like silent ghosts. The pavement curled out through lava-strewn hills, eventually spitting the long, black car into a narrow valley. To the southwest rose the steep, forbidding Sierra Nevada Mountains. To the west and north, more mountains. To the east there was nothing but the high desert wasteland beyond the few low foothills.

He spotted the water tower first, a dying Martian crouching

over a cluster of white buildings and a few scattered homes. The green, bullet-specked sign read, "Welcome to Whitewood. Home of the Wildcats." The population was three figures; he figured that might be a generous estimate.

Frank pulled into the gas station on the right side of the highway at the edge of town. Behind the gas station, there wasn't much but empty desert and rolling foothills. He stopped next to the pumps, remembering this time that the tank was on the passenger side of the car. The place only had two pumps, no roof, just a tiny store next to the one-car garage.

Frank climbed out and nearly went to his knees in the heat. "Good fucking Christ," he blurted in venomous surprise as two hours of air-conditioning bled out of the car. The air smelled dry and full of lead.

A three-story farmhouse with a wraparound porch sat directly across the street from the gas station. The house looked old, hurt. The wood may have been painted green once, a long time ago. Somebody had started nailing up aluminum siding along the north wall, but gave up after a while. Chunks of shingles were missing. Most of the windows were covered in flattened cardboard boxes, swollen and splotched from rain. The place looked like it was suffering from a serious case of gangrene.

The surrounding yard wasn't much better. Ten or twelve cars had been eviscerated in the patches of dead weeds and smooth dirt. Amongst the tires, car doors, bumpers, and broken glass, was a rusted horizontal freezer. A pair of lawn chairs flanked a gigantic satellite dish, nearly eight feet across, perched awkwardly at the edge of the yard like some fat vulture, and looked like it was capable of picking up signals from one of the moons of Jupiter. Frank got the feeling it was some kind of shrine.

A leafless oak tree, gnarled and twisted in slow-motion agony, rose from the center of the yard, rising into stumps of limbs nearly forty feet in the air. It took him several seconds to realize the dead tree was full of children.

Frank froze, holding the gas nozzle in midair. The children's silent stares made him powerfully uneasy. Still keeping his eyes on the tree, he jammed the nozzle into the gas tank and squeezed the handle. The clicking tank behind him made him feel a little better, but not much. He had a little over forty dollars left, more than enough for the gas, but while looking at the deserted streets, he'd been thinking of breaking one of his own rules, seriously considering robbing the gas station. But now that was out of the question.

One of the kids had a slingshot.

The kid, a boy with a flattop that may have been trimmed about three or four months ago, raised the slingshot. It had some kind of brace that came out of the bottom of the handle and wrapped around the kid's wrist. He was seven or eight, wearing shorts that hung to his calves and a #54 Chicago Bears football jersey. He stretched the elastic surgical tubing back, straightening his left arm, pulling his right hand back to his jaw, and let fly.

Something popped into the rear window, about a foot from Frank.

Frank tried hard not to flinch, but knew he was too late. Then he got pissed. He knew from hearing the deep crunch that it had left a small crater in the window. He left the clicking tank behind and started across the empty street. Weeds grew from cracks that zigzagged across the pavement. He put his hands in his black suit pockets to hide them in case he suddenly had to curl his fingers into fists. He just wanted to talk to the children, not scare them. Not yet, at least.

Frank stopped in the middle of the road feeling like he'd just stepped onto a cast iron skillet that had been left on the campfire for too long and wished he hadn't left the sunglasses on the dashboard. "Hi there."

The children didn't say anything. They stood on limbs, leaning against the trunk or quietly hanging from the branches with both arms. In the vicious afternoon light, the kind of light that carves shapes into greasy slivers of silhouettes, it looked like the burnt husk of a tree full of skeletons. To Frank's sunblasted eyes, the tree looked like it was still on fire.

He shielded his eyes from the glare and tried again. "Hey there." He realized he didn't know what the hell to say.

"Nice boots," a girl's voice sniggered, as the kid with the slingshot fired another projectile at him. Frank heard the rock or whatever it was whistle past his head and thwack into the car.

Suddenly, nearly every boy produced their own weapon. Most of them had slingshots, but a couple had BB guns, long narrow pistols, and skinny air rifles.

Frank took a step forward, no way in hell that he was letting a tree full of children scare him away, and heard hissing snaps as the kids began pumping the BB guns, priming them to fire.

A low growl prickled the hairs on the back of Frank's neck. He faltered, stopped as a dog wriggled slowly out from under the porch and padded silently through the junk, stopping just short of the pavement.

At first, he thought it was a pit bull, but the dog was larger than any pit bull he'd ever seen. It had the wide head knotted with clumps of muscles so large around the jaws that it looked like it had the mumps. The short bluish hair was shot through with flecks of gray. The teats hung loose and low. One eye was gone, leaving just jagged folds of scar tissue. She looked like she'd happily chew on the rusted engine blocks all day and fire sharpened nails out of her butt.

Frank found out later the dog's name was Petunia.

★ ★ ★ ★ ★

Petunia fixed her good eye on him and growled again.

With a sinking, numbing certainty, Frank realized that his gift with animals, his ability to somehow calm them, even talk with them, wasn't going to work with this particular dog. He jammed both hands back in his pockets and clenched his fists and weighed his options. He could either keep walking forward to the dead tree, which meant almost certainly facing the dog, not to mention the onslaught of slingshots and BB guns, or he could back away and pretend nothing had happened.

The gas pump stopped clicking.

Frank didn't like it much, but he backed across the street.

The girl laughed. "You fuckin' pussy."

Frank suddenly wished he had one of the quiet gentlemen's guns, just one, so he could shoot a couple of the boys out of the tree like goddamn pigeons. He just wanted to pay for the gas and get the hell out of here. As soon as he reached the car, they fired. Rocks, marbles, BBs, and grapes struck the car and the pavement in sudden, crackling, popping sounds, like Drano poured into Rice Krispies. Frank didn't turn around, refused to even look back across the street. He replaced the gas nozzle and went into the small convenience store.

It was a little cooler inside, but that was like saying that stepping into a Port-A-Potty would get you out of the sun. The place wasn't a whole lot bigger than a Port-A-Potty either, with two aisles filled mostly with junk food. A plump, middle-aged woman leaned over the counter. "Those kids giving you a hard time?" she asked eagerly under bangs so red they hurt Frank's eyes. Her hair looked stiff, brittle, as if it would shatter if he looked at it crooked.

He shrugged, shook his head. "Nah. They're just . . . kids." He flattened a twenty on the counter.

"Bunch of savages if you ask me. They're downright vicious, I'm telling you. Believe you me, I know what I'm talking about. Sit here all day, every day; I could tell you plenty. They didn't hurt your car, did they?"

Frank shook his head again, hoping that she would just take the money and give him his change. But the woman ignored the money and glanced back out the grimy front window. "Half of 'em aren't even related." She flashed him a look with raised eyebrows, lips drawn tight, nodding. "Them two women, couple of . . ." She dropped her voice, as if someone could hear her outside. "*Lesbians*. Them two women," in case Frank wasn't sure who she was talking about. "Don't know how many times they been married, see? Just up and decided one day they liked women." She shook her head again, looking as if she'd just chewed up and swallowed a bug and couldn't decide if she liked the taste or not. "This was after they had all them kids. All different fathers, of course. So when they got together, it's all one big happy family. Kinda' like the Brady Bunch." She giggled, startled at her own wit, and raised a hand to her mouth, then finally took the twenty.

"Yeah," Frank said.

"All them boys, they're a bunch of holy terrors. Sometimes," she said in a confidential whisper, twenty clutched tight in fingers that tapered off into inch-long purple nails, "things get kinda slow around here, I'll just call the cops on 'em, just to see what happens. But I try not to do it too much, you know?" She jabbed one of the purple nails at the cash register. "It's better when I got a legitimate reason. Like just now." The drawer sprang open with a tired *ding* and the purple nails scratched at the change.

"I'm sorry?"

"The deputies. Olaf and Herschell. They don't take any crap from that family, I'm telling you."

"You . . . already called the cops?"

"Of course. I watched those kids give you a hard time out there and thought . . ." She looked up into Frank's face and didn't like his attitude. "I thought . . . I thought that that's what you would want. *Decent* people appreciate it when you try to help 'em out." She slammed the change on the counter. "You sure weren't gonna stop 'em, make 'em pay for what they did by yourself." The woman drew back. "No sir. Didn't take you long to come runnin' in here."

Frank didn't say anything. He didn't want to look at the woman. He scooped the change off the counter and was outside before she finished. "Thought I was doing you a favor," she called.

He had just reached the long, black car when the police cruiser suddenly appeared on the highway and his stomach rolled and flopped. He forced himself to move in slow motion as the cruiser slid to a stop in front of the satellite. He realized the cops had been there plenty of times, parking in the same spot every time, because the giant satellite protected the car from the slingshots and BB guns in the dead tree. Still moving nice and easy, he nodded at the cops and opened the driver's door.

But just as Frank was about to slip into the long, black car, one of the deputies held up a finger, wordlessly telling Frank to sit still, to just wait a minute. The deputy had a flat, squashed face pinched in the center by a pair of mirrored aviator sunglasses. He pinned Frank with an eyeless stare and parked his hands on his hips. Frank nodded back, polite, just a regular citizen. Still, he settled himself into the driver's seat and slipped the key into the ignition.

The other deputy, a short young guy with a crew cut so severe he was damn near bald, fastened his round hat over his skull. The deputies ambled out past the safety of the satellite dish, all casual and patient. They tilted their heads and quietly regarded the children for several moments.

Hot, stinging sweat trickled down the back of Frank's neck.

The older deputy, the one with the face that looked like he'd kept it mashed against a brick wall for thirty years or so, finally called out to the tree. "Thought we made it real clear last time. Thought it was understood that you and us were gonna have some serious problems if we had to come back over here."

The girl's voice shouted back, "We didn't do *nothin'!*"

The deputy nodded. "Is that right? Then why are we here then?"

Nobody answered. The deputy asked, "Your mom around? Either one of 'em? No? They out at the auction yard? Heard one of your brothers was fightin' this time."

"Ernie. And he's gonna kick *aaaasssss*," the same girl called out.

The deputy chuckled. "Yeah. He oughta, that's for sure, that's right. But still, that don't have nothin' to do with what we got going on here."

The younger deputy slowly made his way over to Frank. He touched the edge of the round brim. "Howdy." A brass bar identified him as "DPTY HALFORD."

Frank nodded back. "Hi." He grinned, easy, smooth, and loose.

"They give you a hard time?" Halford tilted his head at the dead tree.

"No, not really," Frank said.

Halford's gaze slid back to the pockmark in the glass. "Looks like they cracked your window some."

Frank felt his crooked grin slipping off his face like the pair of oversized black shoes. "Aw hell, I think that might of already been there. I think the lady inside was just trying to look out for me."

They both looked at the grimy window and found the woman glaring back at them. Halford laughed. "Yeah. Myrtle can get a little fired up sometimes. She don't like that family much. To tell the truth," he lowered his voice, just a bit, "Hell, neither do I. Them kids, they're . . . they're a handful."

Frank nodded back, Mr. Agreeable.

Across the street, the older deputy was wrapping up his lecture. "Now you listen, and listen good. If I gotta come back here, you're gonna wish you never, ever met me before. You got that?"

The kids were smart enough to stay quiet. Frank thought, *Oh yeah, those kids have got it.* They looked scared to death, all right. He figured the deputies would be lucky if they made it back to the cruiser without getting cracked in the head with something hard and sharp.

Halford asked suddenly, "You in town for the rodeo?"

Busy sifting through possible responses in case the deputy asked for his driver's license, Frank just said, "Yeah."

Halford nodded. "Thought so. Tell you what, we're heading out there, you just follow us."

"Thanks. Appreciate it."

"No problem. Just follow us." Halford and the older deputy climbed back into the patrol car. Frank pulled the long, black car out of the gas station and followed the cruiser into town.

Whitewood was nearly as dead as the oak tree. Frank saw a few pickups here and there, parked in the center of the wide streets, one or two people on the wooden sidewalks, but that was all. Nearly all of the businesses facing the wide main street sported squared-off false fronts and plywood over the windows.

Frank thought of the wasps he used to kill. He'd wait patiently on the warped steps of the church until a wasp landed at the edge of one of the pools that collected in the knotholes after a thunderstorm. Slowly, slowly raising the softbound Bible above his head, he'd slam it down, smashing the wasp into the soft pine woodgrain with the whipcrack sound of a .22. But no matter how quickly he brought the good book down, no matter how hard he smashed the insect into the plank, it never died quick. The wasps always twitched for a long time, fighting death with every fiber of their doomed bodies, waving the segmented limbs around in agony, always trying to crawl away, and always, always curling their abdomen, thrusting that vicious dripping stinger into the air at the unseen attacker, a last stab at vengeance.

This town was like a wasp. It didn't have sense enough to know when to die.

They passed a small park, anchored at the four corners with oak trees and covered with brown, dead grass. The town's only stoplight waited at one corner, hung from wires strung from telephone poles. The deputies didn't bother waiting for the light and slid right through the red.

For a moment, Frank panicked. He didn't know if he should stop and wait for a green signal, or just slip on through like the cruiser. In the end, he slowed to nearly a full stop, then gunned the long, black car quickly across the empty intersection. The deputies kept going.

They led him into a large gravel parking lot a quarter full of pickups at the fairgrounds. Frank parked and climbed out, remembering the sunglasses this time. They were decades old, thick, with squared corners, like something an old man would consider cool from his youth, but didn't have enough fashion sense to know or care they were outdated. He put them on, feeling a little ridiculous, and waved at the cops, pretending to head into the fairgrounds. Halford tipped his hat at Frank as he pulled in a tight circle and steered the cruiser back into town.

Frank's steps faltered and stopped. He took a deep breath of the dry, hot air. Even his short, squat shadow, weirdly textured on the rough gravel, looked like it wanted out of the sun. He glanced back at the long, black car. It had nearly a half of a tank of gas left. His wallet held a little over thirty dollars.

The way Frank figured, he had two options. He could climb back in the car and keep heading north, take his chances on the road, hoping that the money would last a bit longer, and the cops wouldn't see him. Or he could simply stay, lay low for the afternoon at least. Weariness settled over his head like a thick wool blanket, and he wondered if there might be any gambling possibilities inside the gates. A horse was a horse, it didn't matter if it was running a mile in seventy seconds or trying to shake off some fool clinging to its back.

For a moment, Frank wondered what the trucker's pills might do to a horse.

Frank passed a rusted steam engine and the coal car stranded on a strip of railroad track just 100 feet long. He followed quaint little street signs that directed him along narrow streets, lined with tired trees and dead flowers. The asphalt felt soft beneath the boots.

Just inside the fairground gates, a greasy guy with loose skin sagged against a stool, wearing a mustache so thin it looked like a drunk old woman had drawn it on with an eyebrow pencil. Frank nodded at the jagged mustache and kept moving, acting like he'd just stepped out for a smoke.

The guy snapped his fingers. "Five bucks, pal."

Frank wasn't happy, but he paid. The guy slid the money into his pocket and scratched a tiny slash mark in a notebook even greasier than his hair. He jerked his head.

Frank asked, "No program?"

The guy squinted at Frank for a moment, unsure if he was joking. He looked as if he sure as shit didn't want any goddamn city cocksucker making fun of him, but he also didn't want to offend anybody important. In the end, he just shrugged and stared off into the distance. Frank went on in.

It wasn't much of a rodeo. The heat had thoroughly baked the energy out of every living creature. The calves wouldn't run; they simply stood still, rooted in place, tongues hanging dry and purple in the searing sun. Barrel racers cantered and trotted instead of galloping. The announcer's voice, crumbling apart in slivers of static, sounded half-asleep. Even the wild broncs bucked and kicked in a bored, listless fashion.

The small stadium stand rose fifty feet; twenty-five benches slanted up to the rippled aluminum roof. Twenty or thirty people, mostly older couples, were scattered across the wooden benches. Frank kept his face down and climbed the creaking stairs. When he hit the shade near the top, he sank onto a bench. The stands overlooked a dirt racetrack that encircled nearly five acres. The center was full of grazing fields, paddocks, and chutes that surrounded the center rodeo ring like a blocky spiderweb.

Frank lasted a half-hour before visiting the beer garden in the back, under the stands. He stood in the shadow on the north side of the stands and sipped his beer, listening to the knots of men that had gathered in the shade. The men talked weather, crops, sheep, cattle, fishing, hunting, and their boys, whether they were playing Pop Warner football, riding the bulls, or in the fights.

Frank got another beer, watching his cash slip away. He knew it was stupid to be wasting money, but it was goddamn hot. He kept his eyes open, but couldn't see any money changing hands. Nobody seemed to really care what happened with the rodeo, one way or another. He decided he'd rest until nightfall, then get back out on the highway.

He ducked into the men's room, under the stands, next to the concession booth, and for one particularly anxious moment, he almost wished he had his tire iron. But the place was empty. As Frank was taking a leak, the door opened and a little man came inside. He was short, but that wasn't what Frank caught out of the corner of his eye. It was the long cattle coat the little man was wearing in the heat; he looked like a dark, oiled canvas traffic cone.

He stepped up to the opposite end of the trough confidently, like he meant business, marking his territory. He reminded Frank of a little dog. In vet school, Frank had encountered plenty of dogs. There's three kinds of little dogs. There's the kind of little dog that barks and yaps nonfuckingstop and nine times out of ten that little shit will try and take a tiny bite out of you. Then there's the kind of little dog that's dead quiet, and flinches if you blink at it. And then, once in a while, there's that little dog that only looks dead scared until you aren't watching it closely. And there's nothing tiny about the bites that dog will take.

The guy in the long coat was maybe in his late fifties, it was hard to say. He took off his cowboy hat with his right hand and slid his forearm across his forehead. He was bald. Actually, he went beyond bald. There wasn't any hair on his head at all. No five o'clock shadow. No hair in his nose, his ears. His skull looked like a dry eyeball. A puckered scar ran from one ear to another, curving around the back of his head in a skeletal smile. Frank fought a sudden, irrational urge to draw a couple of rolling, insane eyes above the smile.

The man caught Frank looking at him.

Frank nodded hello, willing a small, manly grin to grow on his face, as his heart hammered wildly away inside the oversize suit.

The little man just stared at Frank. His eyes, startlingly naked under hairless eyebrows, were the color of frozen granite. He wore a revolver, some kind of cowboy six-shooter, in a holster on his right hip.

Frank zipped up and tried not to hurry as he washed his hands.

The little man stepped up to the sink next to Frank, staring at himself in the heavily graffitied reflective metal. His cowboy hat was back on. It had a flat brim, pulled low over his face. Frank splashed water on his face. Drying his hands on the inside of the jacket, Frank nodded at the little man again and headed out.

A high, wild laugh crackled over the loudspeakers. Frank peeled open one eye. Down in the ring, a rodeo clown, wearing a foot-high rainbow Afro and a pair of shredded overalls, leaned out of the announcer's tall booth and shouted into the microphone. "It's *that* time again, boys and girls, friends and neighbors. Grab your men, grab your women, grab your ass, grab whatever you can and hang *ooonnnnnnnn.* You folks are about to witness the biggest, the baddest, the meanest bulls that ever roamed this here land. They spit poison and shit fire! And that ain't no bullshit! No sir! It's fun for the whole family. You're about to witness the most dangerous, most deadly sport right here in the U.S. of A.! I give you . . . the bulls of Whitewood!"

Polite applause. The crowd had grown slightly, and semi-filled the bottom of the stands. Frank shook his head, rubbed his eyes, and sat up. He wasn't going to make any money here. It was time to climb back in the long, black car and hit the road.

Two more rodeo clowns jumped into the ring as the opening chords to the Scorpions' "Rock You Like a Hurricane" reverberated into the stands. The clowns energetically threw themselves into a dance routine, all spread legs and thrusting hips. Frank figured they had to have been drinking heavily and that reminded him of the rum in the front seat. He stood, stretched, and headed down the stairs.

The original announcer came back on, still drowsy. "Thank you, uh . . . Mr. Spanky, for that . . . spirited introduction. But he's right, you folks are in for a real treat here. These bulls are the real deal. Voted meanest bulls four years running in the North Valley Circuit. And first up is young Bartholomew Wilson, a sophomore at Whitewood High School, trying for his second tournament championship this year."

Frank was nearly at the gates when one of the closest clowns, wearing green mop strings over his head, shouted at another clown, "You ain't got enough sense to pour sand out of a boot if the instructions were printed on the bottom. I got a twenty that says Wilson is gonna eat dirt in less than six seconds."

"Then you're as dumb as you look. You got it," the second clown, wearing a red cape, shot back. Frank wasn't sure, but he thought it was the same guy from the front gate.

Frank's steps slowed and he changed direction, heading for the fence. The gate across the ring sprang open and two thousand pounds of pissed-off bull muscles jumped and twirled across the soft dirt. The kid on the bull's back, Wilson, hung on as best as he could, but his fifteen-year-old muscles were no match for the backbreaking spinning and popping, and he was flung off into the dust.

"Three seconds, motherfucker!" Green head shouted.

Red cape shrugged, pulled out a twenty from his costume, and flicked it into the dust in the ring. "It's all yours, dickhead."

Frank turned away from the gates and slowly ambled around the ring, past Green head, past the announcer's booth, until he could see the loading gates. He took his time, peering at the wild bulls, noting their body stance, their breathing, their eyes. He surreptitiously pulled the remaining twenty from his pocket, folded it over, and kept it curled in his fist.

Several riders tried their luck. Nobody lasted more than five seconds. The clowns thrived on leaping into the ring, catching the bull's attention, and outrunning the animal.

Finally, Frank found a bull he liked. He ambled slowly back and got two beers. He brought them both over to the ring and leaned against the fence next to Green head. "Howdy." Frank nodded.

The clown nodded back, scratching at his scraggly beard. It had been spray-painted orange. Frank suddenly noticed his second beer. He held it out. "Thirsty?"

"That's goddamn white of you." They clinked the bottles together through the bars and drank. "Who are you, some kind of junior G-man?" the clown asked, eyeing the black suit. He laughed, raised his hands above his head. "Don't shoot!"

Frank forced a chuckle, let a few moments pass. "Say, I happened to overhear you laying a little money down on a few of these riders. Thought I'd see if you might be interested in any other wagers."

"Could be, could be. What are you thinking?"

"I think this next rider's gonna hang on for a solid eight seconds."

"You think so, huh? Okay. Just how sure are ya?"

"Twenty bucks sure. For starters."

The clown scratched at his beard, then his wig. "What's the bull?"

"Uh . . . it's called Chopper, I think."

"Who's the rider?"

"Kid named Garth Ennis."

The clown nodded. "Could be close." He watched the gate for a moment, as the Ennis kid settled on Chopper and the names crackled out of the loudspeakers. Finally, "Okay. You got it. Twenty bucks. Deal?"

"Deal." They shook on it.

The gate burst open. Chopper spun and kicked and bucked, but his heart wasn't in it. It looked like the bull was tired, tired of the heat, tired of the dust, and tired of jumping and twisting. Eight seconds later, when the buzzer sounded, Ennis was still on Chopper's back.

"I'll be damned. Be right back," the clown said, dropping from the fence with the other clowns and scrambling at the bull. They got Ennis off safely and lured the bull back through the gate. Green head came back, wiping at his face. Sweat trickled down through his white makeup, leaving streaks of tan skin.

"Not bad. Not a bad call at all. How'd you know?" He pulled a twenty from his oversized shorts.

"Lucky."

"Lucky, huh?" Green head leaned back and took a second, closer look at Frank, this time noticing the slack, dead left side of his face. He slapped the money into Frank's palm through the fence. "Maybe so, but it don't matter. You still won."

"Appreciate it," Frank said. He went back to the stands and treated himself to a beer. The place suddenly didn't seem so bad after all. He gulped down that beer, ordered two more, and took them back out to the ring. He handed one to Green head.

"Name's Pine Rockatanski," the clown said.

"Frank Winter." He bit his tongue as he realized, too god-damn late, he'd given his real name. He blamed it on the beer and the heat.

Pine chugged his beer and sprinted out into the ring with his ambling, bowlegged gait as another teenager got bounced into the dirt. Afterward, he asked, "In town long?"

"Not really. Just passing through, you could say."

"Well, if you're gonna be around tonight, there's gonna be some more gambling opportunities, case you're interested."

"Depends. Mostly, I just stick to the horses. What's the game?"

Pine grinned and spit. "You're gonna like it. Trust me. You a drinking man?"

Frank looked out over the ring, watching as the dust hung in the still air. "Sometimes. I like to drink a six-pack before it gets warm."

Pine laughed. "Let's roll."

Frank met the rodeo clowns in the fairground parking lot at six.

A late-model diesel pickup roared through the empty parking lot. Just as that pickup slowed to a stop, a second pickup appeared, immediately followed by a third. They hit the entrance fast, rear tires sliding, and raced each other to Frank's car. He'd finished the rum earlier and flung it at the fence.

The two pickups slid past the long, black car in a storm of dust and flecks of asphalt. Frank walked over to the first pickup and introduced himself.

"You the one that took twenty off Pine?" The guy behind the wheel came across as a cowboy in an old cigarette ad. Sure enough, a fresh cigarette jutted from underneath a handlebar mustache, bobbing at the side of his mouth as he talked. He was the guy that introduced the bull riders, the guy in the rainbow Afro.

"Yeah," Frank said, almost apologetically.

"Good. Dumbshit deserved it. Anybody that couldn't see old Chopper was damn near dead was too goddamn dumb to look." He stuck out his hand. "Jack Troutman. Pleased to meet ya."

Pine climbed out of the second pickup, yelling at the guy in the third. "Pay up motherfucker! That was all mine and you know it." Without the clown getup, which made him look sort of mischievous, now he looked like he was two steps short of starting a cult. He still had the beard and most of the orange had been washed out, but instead of continuing up into his hair, it stopped dead in a thick tangle of sideburn at the top of the ear. The rest of Pine's head was bald. The back part looked particularly shaved, as if the hair had gotten confused, and instead of growing on the back of the head, it was growing on his chin. Pine made the best of it, overcompensating, embracing it, as if growing a heavy beard was somehow superior to having a long tangle of hair, like Frank.

"I got a better idea," the other guy yelled back. "Come on over and lick my ball sweat instead." He was the guy that had taken the money off Frank out front, and had worn the red cape at the rodeo. His pickup was at least twenty-five years old and looked as if it was being slowly eaten alive from the bottom by a fungus-like rust.

"That dipshit over there is Chuck," Jack said.

They congregated near Jack's tailgate as he broke out a twelve pack of Coors and a bottle of Seagram's 7. Jack and Pine might have been brothers, all sharp angles of lean bone. Plenty of scars. Cowboy hats. Cowboy boots. Wranglers, tight around the hips, several inches too long, bunched around the ankles. Belt buckles the size of a baby's head. Their knuckles were scabbed, swollen. Calluses and ragged fingernails. Tattoos. Bad breath.

Chuck ignored Frank and glared at Pine. "You still owe me ten bucks." Chuck was stockier than Jack and Pine, but his skin looked slack somehow, like it was several sizes too large. He had a flattop and acne scars dotted his flabby cheeks. Wore work-boots instead.

Everybody ignored him.

Jack's twelve pack was gone in about twenty minutes, but it wasn't a problem. Chuck had a case of warm beer in his pickup. They took turns pissing in the gravel and telling stories. They boasted about women. Card games. Fights. After a while, the clowns got all nostalgic and proud and took Frank on a tour of their hometown.

Jack drove, Frank rode shotgun as guest of honor, and Pine and Chuck rode in the back and chimed in once in a while through the open back window. They drove past the high school; Jack was the only one who graduated. The town had three bars, empty, depressing places. They hit all of them, then drove up to the Split Rock Reservoir Dam, where Jack and Pine had lost their virginity, both to the same girl. Jack and Pine teased Chuck about still being a virgin, something that Chuck loudly and repeatedly denied.

They drove past the house with the dead tree and the giant satellite dish. The children were gone. "Fuckin' Gloucks," Jack snapped at the disintegrating house. "Worse than fuckin' garbage." He hit the gas and wandered aimlessly up and down the quiet streets, and Frank pieced the history of the town together.

Whitewood had seen better days. The valley used to be rich, renowned for its wild rice. Exported it all over the world. But after a flood several years back, the rice started dying, as if the soil itself was diseased somehow. The rice would grow for a bit, under the protection of the irrigation water, but then it just slowly started to rot, until all that was left was the flooded fields chock full of muddy water and decomposing rice stalks.

Jack spit into a flooded rice paddy. The water was utterly black under the stars. They had stopped to take a piss by the side of an empty strip of blacktop that cut through two rice fields, each the size of several football fields. "See them lights?" Jack nodded at a cluster of yellow lights at the base of some dark hills to the south. "That's where our boss lives. Horace Sturm. His great-grandfather started the town. He's a good man."

"A damn good man," Chuck echoed.

The others agreed and raised their beer cans. Frank raised

his as well, eyeing the lights.

"He's dyin' though," Jack said.

"Don't say that," Chuck said. "He's fightin' it."

Pine turned to Frank and said, confidentially, "Cancer."

"Fuckin' brain tumor," Jack said. "You can only fight that so much."

Frank thought of the odd, fierce little man in the restroom at the fairground.

"Doctors took it out, but they say it'll probably come back. Bigger," Pine said. "He went through a shitload of chemo. I mean, a shitload. Doctors wanted him to stay in the hospital, but he said, fuck that, I'm goin' home. If I'm gonna die, then it'll be at home. Not the hospital. And he's been home, so far."

"How long's he been home?" Frank asked.

"A month," Jack said, proud. "He's gonna beat it." They all took a drink, watching the lights across the black water.

The auction yard squatted at the top of a low hill on the north side of town. The large building rose to a steep crown in the center, its sharply angled shingles a glossy green in the moonlight. Heavy stones anchored the walls into the earth, giving way to dark slats of oak. The rest of the building sloped off to either side, long and low. Frank couldn't see any windows. The parking lot was full of pickups.

He caught the faint, guttural roar of a crowd.

They parked near the end of the parking lot. The clowns pointed out where they lived—a large gooseneck trailer at the edge of the property. They finished the bottle of Seagram's and cracked open one last beer. "No alcohol inside," Pine explained. "We work auctions four days a week. Saturday nights, usually, we got dogfights. Tuesday nights, Sturm rents the place out to the spics for cockfights. Tonight . . . tonight only comes once a year."

The roar reverberated out of the building again.

They went inside. The floors were stone, the walls dark wood. The main room was large, with high ceilings. Five sodium vapor lights hung over the circle in the center of the room, bright enough to bleach the color out of skin. Stadium seats surrounded the center, aluminum slats that echoed with a shrill, hollow sound as cowboy boots dragged across the metal. The seats were full of men; ranchers and farmers and fieldhands. Frank smelled sawdust, sweat, and underneath it all, the sour, yet tangy aftertaste of a steak that's just a shade rare—the smell of spilled blood.

Eight gates formed an octogon in the center of the room. The clowns marched right on down and leaned against the gates. On the opposite side, one of the gates was open, leading to a tunnel under the stadium seats. Off to the side was a large chalkboard, displaying a round robin–style elimination. It only had last names. The last three spaces were vacant.

Underneath the chalkboard, a plank lay over two sawhorses where a guy sat in front of a ledger and a chipped metal cash box. A second man stood at the chalkboard, carefully writing names across the last two lines. The last two names were Glouck and Sturm.

Frank hung back from the clowns and made his way over to the table. "What're the odds?"

"No odds here. Just even money," the guy sitting at the table said.

"I'll be back."

The guy shrugged. "I wouldn't wait too long, mister. Window closes in . . ." He peered up at a clock enclosed in steel mesh above the chalkboard. "Three minutes."

Frank nodded. "I'll be back."

The other guy walked over until he was standing above the tunnel. He held up a bullhorn. Reading off a sheet, he spoke in a flat, emotionless tone. "Welcome to the one hundred and fourth annual summer fights. In the championship fight, we have thirteen-year-old Ernie Glouck at one hundred and fourteen pounds . . ." There was a smattering of applause but the clowns started booing, drowning out the applause. "Versus thirteen-year-old Theodore Sturm at one hundred and twenty-three pounds." There was a lot of cheering for Sturm. The clowns went nuts, applauding, whistling, shouting.

The fighters appeared. Theodore Sturm had his blond hair cut short, but it looked expensive, too perfect, as if the artful spikes had been shaped and gelled by a professional hairdresser. His lips were drawn in a thin slash. His nostrils were wide and pumping, eyes flat and hard. Well-defined muscles wriggled up and down his arms. Frank figured the kid had been hitting the weights for five or six years solid. Theo's taped fists popped the air in a flurry of combinations, right, right, left—left, right, left, left. The kid was quick; Frank gave him that much.

The man behind Theo was the same little guy from the rest-room at the fairgrounds. Horace Sturm hung back, dark and squatting in the shadows, a goddamn midget Grim Reaper in that black, flat-brimmed cowboy hat and ankle-length duster. Frank watched closely, then checked the clock. Two minutes left.

Ernie Glouck followed Theo. Ernie had a severe buzz cut, so short Frank could see worms of scar tissue like mountain ranges on a relief map, exclamation points of pain across the kid's skull. Like Theo, he wore shorts and a T-shirt. But while Theo's shorts looked like expensive boxing trunks, maybe even silk, Ernie's were oversize jean cuttoffs. They hung below his knees, drawn up tight around his narrow hips with a length of extension cord.

His two moms followed Ernie. They looked like somebody had put two shapeless housedresses on a couple of dull and pitted hatchets and walked them around. Five or six older brothers darted between the two mothers, offering strong words of advice and thumping the scarred skull. Ernie flinched easy. Too easy, Frank figured.

He pulled out a twenty, flattened it on the bare plywood, and said. "That's twenty on Ernie Glouck."

"Twenty on Glouck. Name?" the guy at the table asked.

Frank said, "Winchester."

The guy wrote down the name and slipped the twenty into the box. Frank headed up the stairs to a nearly empty bench at the top. Just as he sat down, the rest of the men rose to their feet. Their right hand came to a rest over their hearts.

Frank finally realized that they were looking at the United States flag that hung vertically above the sodium lights just as everyone started in a slow, jagged rhythm, "I pledge allegiance, to the flag, of the United States of America. And to the republic, for which it stands . . ." Frank got to his feet and mumbled along. It had been a while, and he couldn't quite remember the words. ". . . with liberty and justice for all." Everybody sat back down. All talking stopped. The hollow sound of hard leather soles scraping ridged aluminum ceased. Nobody breathed.

Theo and Ernie walked into the ring, eyeballing each other. The gate closed behind them. They backed into opposite corners, Theo bouncing on the balls of his feet, Ernie rolling his head on his neck.

Horace Sturm approached the ring, eyes cloaked in the shadow from his hat. Several silent moments crawled by, until finally the guy with the microphone held up a large bell and hit it with a hammer.

Frank could only hear the rustling of the boys' bare feet in the sawdust and their quick, shallow breathing as they slipped away from the gates and approached the center of the ring.

Neither wore boxing gloves, just medical tape that bound their fingers into tight fists. They circled each other for a few seconds, bobbing and weaving, feinting and rolling their shoulders, sizing each other up. Ernie threw a half-hearted jab with his right, easily blocked by Theo.

Pine shouted, "Knock his fuckin' head in the dirt, boy!"

Horace Sturm shot him a look. Pine got quiet.

The two boys kept circling, throwing short, cautious jabs.

Then Theo got impatient and went for it. He stepped in close, faking with his right, all the while lowering his left shoulder, preparing to bring his left fist up. Ernie saw it coming. Frank saw it coming. Everybody saw it coming. Ernie flicked in close, jabbed Theo in the nose. Surprised blood popped out of Theo's nose. His head snapped back as his left uppercut went sailing through empty air.

Ernie hit Theo in the nose two more times before dancing away.

Theo shook his head, spraying blood over the sawdust. Ernie came in from the side, cracked Theo in the left ear. Theo back-pedaled, holding his taped fists up over his bleeding face. But Ernie stayed right with him, slamming his fists into Theo's stomach, doubling the rich kid over.

For the first time in his life, Theo panicked. And without thinking, he tried to kick Ernie in the balls.

The room froze for a split second in a glacier of silence, then erupted in shouting and stomping. Ernie's brothers leapt onto the gates and screamed up at the two men under the chalkboard. In response, the clowns jumped off their seats and climbed onto the gates that encircled the ring, shouting at the Glouck family. The rest of the crowd rose, as one, to their feet.

But Ernie, after years of getting kicked and kneed in the crotch, was used to this trick, almost expecting it, blocked Theo's clumsy kick easily. He retaliated by savagely punching

Theo in the face. Theo stumbled back, desperately trying to block the relentless pounding. He hit the gates near his father and doubled over, protecting his head. Ernie didn't let up; now he could take his time, gritting his teeth, slamming blow after blow down, cracking his taped knuckles across Theo's skull.

Horace Sturm never moved.

Finally, Theo crumpled and he fell, curled up, drawing his knees tight against his chest. Ernie rested for a moment, arms shivering, then started kicking Theo. He stopped just long enough to spit on Theo's back.

The clowns leapt over the gates, swarming Ernie. Instantly, the Glouck brothers flew over the gates and attacked the clowns. For a moment, chaos reigned inside the ring. Grunts, shouts, blows, and curses filled the room. Frank lost track of who was fighting whom. He glanced up, beyond the ring, at Horace Sturm.

Slowly, calmly, Sturm pulled that six-shooter out of its holster and held it tight against his leg. And just as Frank realized that Sturm might just shoot somebody for the hell of it, a gunshot shattered the air and a blue cloud of gunpowder erupted from around Sturm, rolling through the ring like ground fog. The clowns and the Gloucks stopped fighting. Reluctantly.

As the smoke cleared, Frank saw that Sturm had fired directly into the ground, just an inch from the outside of his right foot. If it had been anyone else, it would have looked as if the person had fired the revolver by accident, arm straight down, aiming at the floor, but by the look in Sturm's eyes, it didn't look as if he was the type to do anything by accident. Especially around firearms.

The two sides parted quickly and suddenly froze, as if unable to admit the gunshot had caught their attention. They backed away from the center of the ring, out of the light. The Glouck boys pulled Ernie back. The clowns helped Theo to his feet.

Sturm stepped forward, fingers still tight around the revolver's handle. He eyed the men in the ring, his son, and then the crowd, taking his time, letting the silence gather and build. The crowd stood still, afraid to even sit down. Finally, Sturm spoke. "This fight is finished." His voice was low. "I declare Ernie Glouck the winner, by default."

The Glouck family erupted in shouts, screams. Everybody else was silent, nobody even moved.

Sturm reholstered his pistol, speaking slow. "My son . . . my son will regret this night for the rest of his life. These fights are over."

DAY THREE

Frank didn't advertise the fact that he'd bet on Ernie Glouck. The clowns were pissed and wanted to go raise some hell. They wanted to get back at the Gloucks somehow, but nobody suggested actually going on over to the Gloucks' house, although Pine and Chuck wanted to go collect their shotguns and at least shoot the shit out of that satellite dish. But Jack wouldn't let them, pointing out that Sturm would be pissed. In the end, they stood around their pickups in the auction yard parking lot, drinking some more, bitching about those goddamn Gloucks, and chucking the occasional rock out into the night.

Finally, around three or four in the morning, the clowns passed out. They had offered a bunk to Frank, but he declined. Something was itching, gnawing at the inside of his skull like a trapped, hungry rat, and he knew he wouldn't be able to sleep. Jack offered to give him a lift back to the long, black car at the fairgrounds, but Frank decided to just walk, see if he couldn't figure out what was eating at him.

He headed back, along dark, quiet streets of abandoned houses and dead lawns. The air felt mercifully cool. Thanks to the beer and Seagram's, Frank felt pretty good. Confident. Even almost optimistic. His sense of humor was back. But even in that condition, he had to admit to himself that the possibilities of a future safe from Castellari were getting slimmer.

Maybe that's what was bugging him. The sinking feeling that he would be looking over his shoulder for the rest of his life.

But he wasn't sure. It didn't feel right; that didn't seem like that was the little tickling thorn in his brain. Maybe it was the alcohol, dulling the effects of fear.

He kept walking, through the center of town, down buckled sidewalks along a Main Street wide enough to fit four or five lanes of traffic. He couldn't remember the last time he'd been in a town this small, and the silence surprised him.

An honest-to-God tumbleweed bounced lazily along the curb. To Frank's eyes, it seemed small for a tumbleweed, maybe only two feet straight through, but it didn't matter, not really. It was a sign.

An overwhelming sense of being in the West washed over him, stopping him short and leaving him weaving slightly in the center of the wide street. It wasn't just the geographical sense of being in the West either, it was more like stepping into a land of myth and legend. A landscape that never truly existed, except in dreams. This was a land of possibilities, a land where someone quick, someone sharp, someone willing to do whatever it took, this was a land where someone could make something of themselves. The wave of civilization had crested out here, to be sure, but it hadn't crashed yet, hadn't flattened out and receded, settling everything into place. Everything was still topsy-turvy; the silt was churned and the waters muddy. A man could establish himself in the murk, where people couldn't see clearly, and when the waters did calm, and the silt finally settled, that man would have something to stand on. He'd be ready. Frank nodded to himself, flush with the drunken importance of a heavy philosophical realization, and started walking again.

Nearly every building was empty, either gutted and hollow, or had large sheets of particleboard over the windows and a "For Rent" sign nailed to the front door. Apart from an ancient grocery store, the only other place still in business had a carved wooden sign, hanging motionless in the still air, that read

"Dickinson Taxidermy."

Frank stopped for a moment, cupping his hands on the dusty, cobwebbed windows and peering inside. A long workbench stretched along the right side, under a wall full of various knives and hatchets. A sign had been tacked up in the back, "You shoot it, we'll stuff it." Large boxes littered the rest of the room. And the heads. Deer, elk, antelope, and boar. Some complete, hung up on the left wall, frozen in an eternity of blank, open staring. Other heads were in a reversal of decay; after being stripped down to the bone, they were being built back up, antlers bolted to skulls, hide tacked to frozen backbones, glass eyes popped back into sockets.

The itching thorn was suddenly yanked from his brain as an idea hit him.

Frank held the thorn, all sharp and glistening in the starlight, up in front of him. A sequence of possibilities clicked into place like the tumblers of a padlock, and suddenly the future didn't seem quite so tight. He started moving again, not seeing the street anymore, instead sifting through the variables, the difficulties, and the risks. Deep down, he didn't think it would work. He made his way to the fairgrounds and crawled into the backseat of the long, black car and watched the stars slowly fade into the sky as morning broke.

He drove back to the gas station and brushed his teeth with his finger, tried to straighten out his hair a little, shaved using a disposable razor and spit, and put on the fresh suit from the trunk. Then he followed the highway out north of town, past the fairgrounds, past the auction yard, out into the flooded rice fields, watching for the cluster of buildings that he'd seen last night. It took a while, but he finally found the driveway.

It was more of a private road, really, lined with towering palm trees. Frank suddenly remembered that he was still in California.

The driveway stretched for over a mile. There had to be more than a couple hundred palm trees; they were sixty or seventy feet tall at least, rising above the walnut and oak trees that surrounded the rice fields.

Eventually, the road split in half around a huge lawn. The house loomed behind the half acre of perfect grass, two stories, in a strange amalgamation of styles. Southern pillars out front, flanking the front door. Farmhouse windows, sunk into stuccoed walls. Red clay shingles, Mediterranean-style. Frank pulled around to the right and parked the car in front of the door.

He climbed out and felt like someone was watching him, but the windows were blank mirrors, reflecting the morning sun. He buttoned the top two buttons of the suit jacket and walked briskly up the front steps. He pushed the doorbell and stepped back from the large, wooden double doors to show respect. The sun climbed higher, and sweat collected in his sideburns, rolled down his armpits.

The right door opened and Theo glared up at Frank. He had a split lip and two black eyes. One nostril was swollen shut. "What do you want?" It sounded like he was trying to talk and swallow melted cheese at the same time.

"Your father home?"

"Why?" Theo's breathing sounded painful.

"I'd like to talk to him."

"Who are you?"

"I'm the guy who wants to talk to your father."

Theo glared at Frank for a while but eventually said, "Wait here." He shut the door and Frank respectfully stepped back, off the front porch, and prepared himself.

After a few minutes, the door opened again, wider this time. Theo tilted his head. "He's in his office. C'mon."

Frank followed Theo into a modest foyer. Carhart jackets hung from an oak coat rack. Cowboy boots lined the walnut-paneled walls. Theo glanced at Frank's feet. "Take off your boots. Dad don't like outside boots inside."

Frank didn't want to, but he pulled off the snakeskin cowboy boots, settling his bare feet on the smooth, warm wood floor.

Theo watched Frank a moment. "You got something against socks?"

"Yeah."

Theo shrugged, then led Frank through a gigantic kitchen. The house was silent, save for the slow, deep ticking of a grandfather clock. They went down a long hall that ended abruptly at a closed door. Theo knocked quietly, then opened the door.

The first thing that hit Frank was the books. Thousands of them, lining the walls, stretching from the wood floor to the wood-paneled ceiling. Sounds seemed to sink into the pages and vanish. Dozens, possibly hundreds of small picture frames surrounded the window. Frank couldn't see what was inside the frames because brutal sunlight sizzled into the room, slicing through the dancing dust motes and falling full upon Frank's sweating face. He blinked several times.

"Something I can do for you, mister?" Sturm's voice sounded tired, raw.

Frank made his way over to two antique chairs. They faced an oak desk large enough to bury four people comfortably. Sturm waited behind the desk, his back to the window, fingers loosely clasped on the bare wood. His skull reminded Frank of a bare bulb in the sunlight.

Frank wasn't sure if he should sit or remain standing. He chose to stand. "My name is Frank Winter." He took a step forward, extending his hand. Sturm didn't rise, but grasped Frank's hand in a quick, perfunctory shake. Frank marveled at the size of the man's hands; they seemed disproportionately large, as if Sturm's hands and head belonged to another, bigger body.

"I am here under . . . unusual circumstances."

Sturm's face remained in silhouette, except his eyes, as if they were lit from inside by a cold fire. Frank's prepared speech crumbled and fell to pieces around his naked toes. He would have rather tried to talk to the Gloucks' mutant pit bull, Petunia. "And uh, with that in mind, I, uh, would like to offer you a business proposition."

Sturm leaned back. "Is that so. Well, then. Guess it would depend on these special circumstances."

Frank nodded, pinned like a dead moth under the weight of Sturm's hairless stare. Either he told the truth, confessed his sins, or he thanked Sturm for his time, climbed back into the long, black car, and kept running. "Mind if I sit down?"

"I'm a busy man, Mr. Winter. 'Case you haven't heard, I don't have much time left."

"I have heard, and I appreciate your, uh, situation." Frank sat. "In fact, that's why I am here today. I may be able to help you."

"I have cancer, Mr. Winter. Unless you got a cure for one fat brain tumor, I'm afraid you can't help shit."

"No, sir. I don't claim to have the cure for cancer." Frank met Sturm's glacier eyes. "But I might just have a way to make the days you have left around here," Frank made sure Sturm understood he was talking about the town, "a bit more enjoyable. Maybe even more . . . worthwhile. Respectable even." Frank knew he was pushing it.

"Spit it out, son."

Frank sat. "I am, well, used to be anyway, a vet. Horses, mostly. I worked on a few racetracks for, well, let's call 'em businessmen. Businessmen that didn't like to lose. They didn't see much sport in racing thoroughbreds. They just saw . . . opportunities. And, well," Frank shrugged, "I don't get around so well anymore since I got kicked in the head. It didn't help my finances. So I helped these gentlemen take advantage of these opportunities."

Sturm clasped his thick, stubby fingers in front of his chest and waited patiently.

"Anyways, one of these opportunities didn't work out." Frank looked down at his bare feet on the wood floor. "It didn't work out at all." He looked back up, met Sturm's eyes again. "In a place not too far from here. A place with a lot of animals. Exotic animals. Lions. Tigers. Monkeys. Even goddamn alligators.

"Now," Frank leaned forward, "you seem like a man who can appreciate the finer things in life. I'm not talking about material things. No. I'm talking about things like skills. I'm talking about things like the relationship between a predator and its prey. I'm talking about instinct. I'm talking about hunting. I can provide you with an opportunity for the hunt of a lifetime. A hunt like this town has never seen. A goddamn safari in your own backyard. A chance to hunt—and eat—and mount—lions. Tigers. Monkeys. A rhinoceros. And all the gators you can shoot."

Frank leaned back, crossed his legs. "But I don't want any misunderstandings here. These animals aren't for sale. We'd have to go in there . . . and take them."

Sturm didn't say anything for a while. "So . . . basically, you're talking about a, a heist? Is that it?"

"Basically, yeah."

"You're asking me to break the law."

"Technically, yeah. But, and this is the important thing, this, this heist, is unnaturally safe. There's no law enforcement involved. None at all. There's only one man. One man that feeds the animals. And I'll take care of that element. Of him." Frank realized he wasn't talking in complete sentences anymore, but he didn't care, he just wanted to spit it out, to get all the details on the table. "All you gotta do is go pick up these animals. And they're yours."

"And what's in it for you?"

"Finder's fee. A safari'd set you back ten grand, easy. I'm looking for ten percent." Frank figured a grand would get him to Canada.

"So, you want one thousand dollars, just to point me in the direction of these animals."

"And to make sure the zookeeper doesn't bother you."

Sturm watched Frank for a long time. Finally, he lowered his steepled fingers. "Son, you're either telling the truth or you're so full of shit it's about to start dripping from your ears."

Frank didn't say anything.

Sturm drummed his fingertips on the desk. "Roy Rogers used to say he never met a man he didn't like. I'd say he never got out much." He barked out a harsh, quick laugh.

Frank stood. "I'm sorry to have wasted your time. Good day and good luck with the time you have left."

"Now hold on just a minute, son. Didn't mean any disrespect. No, sir. None at all. Just a little short on patience since my boy fucked up the fights this year. But that don't mean I got to take it out on everyone." He stood as well, and looked up at Frank. "You say you're a horse doctor?"

"Yeah."

"Then come with me. Afterward, maybe we'll talk about this hunt of yours."

Sturm led Frank through an elaborate garden. Frank couldn't see any weeds, not even a tip poking through the rich black soil, as he passed through rows of tomatoes, squash, and corn. But the plants themselves were wilted and dying. The squash looked like used condoms and the tomatoes like raisins. They went through a white picket gate at the far end and walked up to a bright red barn.

Inside, a tired, still horse waited within a spacious stall filled with pine shavings. "This is Sarah." Sturm fished in the pocket of his jeans and pulled out a peppermint. He crackled the wrapper, catching the horse's attention. The horse was old. She was a deep red quarter horse, appearing startlingly thick and stocky to Frank, who was used to the lean, long-limbed thoroughbreds. Sturm gently stroked the horse's neck as he popped the peppermint free from the wrapper. He expertly caught the clear plastic wrapper between his thumb and forefinger and rolled the striped candy into the center of his palm as he offered it to the horse. Sarah tenderly took the peppermint in her teeth, crunching it, then bouncing her head slightly in pleasure.

"This horse is going to take me to my family's cabin where I am going to die." Sturm spoke evenly, giving each word careful consideration, but without emotion. "It's an eleven mile ride, due west, straight into the mountains," he indicated with a nod of his bald head, "and I want to make sure she can make it back. See," he turned his attention from the horse and focused his frozen eyes on Frank, "I plan on dying in that cabin. I know I don't have much time. I'll be goddamned if I'm going to die in some hospital. No. To hell with that. I'm going to die on the land of my forefathers, like a man. Not like a . . . a failed lab experiment. And what I want to know is, is she sound enough to make the trip back? She's damn near twenty. It's bad enough that one of us has to die on this trip. I don't want to be responsible for her death as well."

"Eleven miles? What kind of terrain?" Frank knelt. Under his breath, he whispered soothing words to the horse as he gently curled his hand around the slim bones just above the right ankle.

"Mountains. Soft dirt. Logs. Rocks. It ain't pasture, or racetrack, if that's what you mean."

Frank carefully prodded the protruding bones just above the

Jeff Jacobson

hoof, then repeated the movements with the left leg. He stood, bent over, and slowly coaxed Sarah into lifting her front right leg, gently flexing it.

Frank tested the other leg. "She's flexing a little sore, but nothing major. Rub her down with some DMSO, wrap her legs at night. Got any magnetic boots?"

"No. No new age bullshit around this barn."

"Then just wrap her at night. Keep these ankles warm." Frank stepped back. "It's hard to say. I'd have to see her move."

"Then let's take her for a walk." Sturm clipped a lead line onto Sarah's halter and said, "C'mon girl. Let's see how you walk." Frank followed the stocky horse and the short man out of the stall, into the aisle, and outside into a large paddock. He watched closely for any hitches, any hesitation, any signs that the horse was reluctant to put weight on any of her legs. Sarah moved stiffly, but without any apparent pain.

"She looks good, but to be absolutely sure, I'm gonna have to do a flex test," Frank said. "You know how it works?"

Sturm nodded, then said, "I ain't feelin' up to run today." He hollered at the house. "Theo! You got three seconds. One! Two!" The back door banged open and Theo came sprinting out.

"You mind watching the clock?" Frank asked Sturm as he pulled Sarah's front right leg up, curling it against itself, cradling it between his chest and thigh. Sturm counted off sixty seconds, Frank released the leg, and Theo took the lead line and trotted the horse straight across the paddock. Frank watched with a critical eye. Then they repeated the procedure with the three remaining legs.

Afterward, Frank said, "She's old, she's stiff, and yeah, she's a little sore. But she shouldn't have a problem. Up there and back, not really. Not if she takes it easy."

Sturm nodded and almost smiled.

72

Sturm made Frank point out exactly where he thought the zoo was on a map before he made his decision. Frank leaned over crisp folds of the highway map, laid over a well-oiled butcher block, and traced until he hit the third rest stop, then followed the next highway south. "Somewhere in here."

Sturm said, "Okay. But understand this, and understand it well. You fuck with me, I will kill you quick. I got nothing to lose."

Frank said, "Yeah."

Sturm didn't pack much. A rifle, some beef jerky, an old milk jug full of water left in the freezer, a pair of binoculars, and a pair of walkie-talkies. Theo loaded everything except the rifle into a small black backpack.

They didn't talk at all during the drive. Sturm didn't even turn on the radio. Frank had to sit with his knees spread wide, wedged up against the dashboard, since Sturm had the bench seat moved all the way forward so his feet could reach the pedals.

It was nearly dusk when they reached the zoo. Sturm drove slowly, eyeballing the place. Frank felt a squirming, itching panic surge through his chest as he wondered if the quiet gentlemen waited on the other side. The place looked dead, not much different than three nights ago. Now, in the daylight, he could see the garish paintings splashed haphazardly across the rippled metal. Bright slashes of blood dripped off oversized teeth and claws, massive snakes curled around buxom, silently screaming women, alligators ripped and tore at pith-helmeted white explorers. The front gate had been wired back into place and locked. A small "Closed" sign was slung over the top.

"I can't see shit," Sturm said and goosed the pickup back up to seventy. A mile west of the zoo, they spotted a dirt road, nothing more than an old logging trail really, but Sturm shifted into four-wheel drive without slowing down and they lurched and bounced through the brush along a low ridge.

"There's a pair of binoculars in the glove box," Sturm said. He took his foot off the gas, letting the pickup slowly roll to a stop on its own. "Don't need a goddamn cloud of dust against the sun advertising us," he explained.

Frank handed Sturm the binoculars and they climbed out. Sturm came around to the passenger side and settled his elbows on the softly ticking hood, forming a steady tripod as he peered into the binoculars.

Frank watched the zoo with his naked eyes, hands in his pockets, as the desert wind billowed the suit against his frame like hanging sheets in a hurricane. He couldn't see a whole lot of detail. The huge compound, maybe fifteen or twenty acres, was spread out like a prickly fungus in the desert. Thin roads meandered through piles of scrap metal. They were too far away to even hear the animal cries. "See anything?" he finally broke down and asked.

Sturm took his time before answering. "Nothing moving. Lots of cages, though. Can't tell if anything's in 'em."

Frank glanced back at the setting sun. He figured he had maybe a half-hour of daylight left. He grabbed one of the walkie-talkies and some beef jerky off the front seat. "Give me an hour."

Sturm nodded. "I'll be waiting."

Frank eased himself down the shifting, sliding slope of shale. He heard the pickup door open and shut. Sturm's dry voice floated down. "Hey, son."

Frank looked back up at the short silhouette. Sturm said, "You get yourself into trouble, you best get yourself out of it, understand? Don't look to me for help. I won't be here."

"Yeah." Frank kept going down the slope.

★ ★ ★ ★ ★

He reached the chain-link fence just as the sun sank below the mountains. The fence was bound tightly to heavy steel poles, sunk deep in the dirt and anchored in concrete. There were no gaps. Above him, the piss yellow lights flickered sporadically to life, and Frank hoped that they were light sensitive, and someone hadn't turned them on. They provided enough light for Frank to follow the fence east to the far corner, then south.

Once out of the line of sight of Sturm's binoculars, Frank felt a little better. He kept following the fence until the monkeys' screeching sounded the loudest, then he used the wire cutters he'd stolen from Sturm's toolbox. After snipping a four-foot gash in the chain links, he peeled it back and slipped inside. He tucked the heavy tool into the small of his back and double-checked the tire iron was carefully secured in his right sleeve.

He moved slowly through the deepening shadows. He didn't have a plan. Part of him wanted to wait until the zookeeper opened one of the lion or tiger cages for feeding, and then shove the sonofabitch inside and lock the door. But the zookeeper was too cautious; he never opened any of the doors.

So Frank crouched in the gloom under an empty flatbed truck and waited.

Twenty minutes later, he knew the zookeeper was on his way because the animals started in with their symphony of savage hunger. And before long, he saw the swinging light and the waddling zookeeper carrying a bucket full of pieces of dead greyhounds. Frank squatted lower, curling his fingers around the tire iron, but strangely, he felt no fear. He just felt tired. The zookeeper shuffled past, wheezing like a gutshot tractor.

Frank still didn't have a plan. He'd thought about maybe skirting ahead of the zookeeper and opening one of the big cat cages, but figured he'd never be able to open it far enough in advance. The cats would almost certainly stalk Frank instead.

He followed at a distance, waiting for some kind of opportunity to present itself. The zookeeper shambled down through the lanes, never getting close to the cages, flinging chunks of meat at the animals. Soon the bucket was empty. Frank's fist got tighter and tighter around the tire iron, but he never moved from the shadows until the zookeeper was a long way down the road.

He followed him back to a small house trailer sitting at the edge of a quarter-acre clearing. A dusty La-Z-Boy recliner waited next to a fire pit as if waiting for its turn to be burned. The fire was lit, cracking and snapping happily at an iron bar erected over the pit as a makeshift spit. Thick wooden tables flanked the trailer. Frank realized that if the zookeeper made it back into the trailer, that was it. He'd never be able to get inside and keep the man from making a phone call. And Frank had no way of knowing what kind of weapons were stashed inside the trailer.

The zookeeper dropped the empty bucket near one of the tables. He bent over, opened a battered red and white ice chest under the table, and pulled out a cut of meat wrapped in white butcher paper.

Frank circled around the clearing, then dropped to his knees and wriggled under the trailer. He had to pick his way over tangles of barbed wire, fence posts, and rolls of chain-link fence. The only thing he could think to try was to maybe get close enough to the zookeeper while the man's back was turned and crack him across the skull with the tire iron. It had worked for the truck driver.

As Frank crawled closer, holding his breath, watching the trunks of the zookeeper's legs walk back and forth from the table to the fire pit, his left hand came down on something heavy. In the flickering glow of the pale yellow light and the flames from the fire pit, Frank saw that it was a T-square fence post, a thick red steel one, six feet tall, with raised notches along the length for wrapping wire, and two flat blades two feet from the bottom for anchoring it into the earth.

Frank waited for a moment, watching the shuffling legs kick up dust as they approached the table. He tucked the tire iron back into his sleeve, and gently slid the fence post forward. He rose a little, waiting to see if his knees would crack. They didn't, and he watched the wide legs amble back to the fire pit. Frank burst smoothly and silently from under the trailer like a white shark snatching a sea lion from the surface, whipping the fence post up and over his head.

As the zookeeper stood facing the fire, squeezing ketchup onto a plate of steaming lion steak, Frank brought the fencepost down like he was splitting open a stubborn chunk of firewood. He buried the blade three inches into the man's skull, driving the jawbone into the collarbone, blowing out all of those chins like an underripe zit.

The zookeeper wobbled a moment. The lion steak landed in the dust. The paper plate drifted into the flames. The zookeeper dropped to his knees and fell face first into the fire. Blood boiled and popped.

The body shivered and twitched for a while. Frank left the fencepost stuck in the head and collapsed into the La-Z-Boy. He knew he needed to drag the body out of the fire; the smell of burning flesh would get the animals' attention, and Frank didn't want any of them getting loose like last time. The zookeeper's ears were burning now and creamy blue smoke curled around the fencepost as it rose.

Frank left the burning man behind and went into the trailer. When he came out, he was holding a bottle.

"Hell, son." Sturm's voice came from the shadows. "I'd say that you killing horses is an understatement. You got yourself a genuine talent for killing damn near anything alive to start with."

"Yeah." Frank wasn't surprised to hear Sturm. He tilted the bottle and drank for a solid fifteen seconds, then sat down heavily on the trailer's steps. The smell of burning flesh filled the air, sweet and rotten at the same time, reminding Frank of a can of frozen orange juice concentrate about a year on the wrong side of the expiration date.

It was Sturm's idea to feed the zookeeper to the animals.

They dragged the burnt corpse out of the fire and hoisted it onto one of the tables. The clothes and the rubber boots went into the fire. The butchering didn't take long, only about half an hour to chop the zookeeper into pieces no bigger than a football. It helped that the tools had been well maintained, kept sharp. They dumped the pieces into the five-gallon buckets; the fatty meat filled seven of them.

When they were finished, Sturm handed Frank two buckets and said, "Here. Go feed them animals. They could use it. I got a call to make."

Frank took it slow. He'd ease up to a cage, talking in a relaxed, low voice. "Easy, that's it, easy does it. Easy girl." He called all the animals "girl" whether they were female or not.

The big cats watched him warily from a distance, but their flicking tails and attentive noses gave away their hunger. Frank would spear pieces with a long BBQ fork and gently flick the meat through the bars and watch as the cats snatched at it with scary speed and accuracy. Then they'd settle into the darkest corner of the cages and rip at their chunk.

When Frank got back to the trailer, he found Sturm in the La-Z-Boy, talking on the cell phone. Frank wondered if he was the only person in the west without a cell phone. He kind of wished he hadn't tossed out the one he found in the car.

Sturm looked up. "Any suggestions for a tranquilizer?"

Frank thought for a moment. "We used Acepromazine at the track. If it'll calm down a goddamn thoroughbred, it should work here. Ketamine, too, if you can get it."

"How much?"

Frank shrugged. "As much as you can get."

Frank returned for the last bucket. Sturm was waiting. The cell phone had disappeared. "Have a seat."

Frank tossed the bucket under the table, but remained standing. Sturm leaned back, folded one leg over the other, adjusted his jeans, and clasped his hands across his groin. It looked awful prim and proper coming from a guy in a black Stetson. "So. What should I call you? Mr. Winter? Or maybe Mr. Winchester?"

"Call me Frank."

"And how am I supposed to know what's true here?"

"The name I gave you is my real name."

"Is that so."

"Look, there's some . . . people after me. Some *connected* people, if you follow. Men with friends. Powerful friends. A lion, from here, killed one. Another went into the alligator tank. I don't know what happened to him. And this," he nodded at the last bucket, "is the rest of the men who knew I was here. When I was at the fight, at the time, I didn't think it was smart to give my real name."

"Hell son, you can call yourself Mary fucking Poppins for all I give a shit. When someone makes money off me—I don't give a flying shit how much it is, twenty bucks or twenty thousand—I'm going to know how. And why. I make it my business. All I really want to know right now is why you bet against me and my son."

Using the fencepost, Frank arranged the logs in the firepit into a pyramid shape, then jammed the end of the post into the center of the fire. "Well. You have to understand that it was nothing personal. I'm not exactly from around here."

Sturm waited patiently.

As he talked, Frank heaped more wood, solid chunks of oak, onto the fire, keeping the fence post in the very heart of the fire. "Your son, he looked liked he worked hard, that's for damn sure. But it looked like he'd spent a lot of hours in the gym, instead of . . ." Frank took a deep breath, and shoved the end deeper into the fire. "That other kid, he looked like he'd spent a lot of time getting the shit kicked out of him." He twisted the fencepost slowly, and deep in the fire, the blades slowly broke away. "You have to understand, when I got to the fight, I didn't know anything about you, anything about this town. Didn't know any history."

Sturm nodded and glanced over his shoulder at the animal cages. "So all that time you were drinking and driving all over God's creation, them boys never said anything. Okay. Fine. So all I want to know is *why.*"

Frank shrugged. "It looked like the other kid knew how to fight."

Sturm looked pained, as if each word was a tooth being pulled out slowly with a pair of pliers. "So what you're saying is, if I'm understanding this right, from an outsider's point of view, it looked as if that little Glouk pissant was tougher than my boy."

"I don't know about tougher. It looked like he'd been in more fights, yeah."

Sturm looked like he might throw up. "Jesus humping Christ."

Frank kept twisting the fencepost, sinking it deeper and deeper into the fire, ignoring the heat that seared his face. The fire burned hotter and the silence grew, stretched thin. But neither said anything else.

Sturm walked with Frank to empty the last bucket. When the meat was gone, they stopped for a while, watching two lionesses gulp it down. Sturm took off his hat and held it at his side as he crept slowly up to the cage. He breathed out long and slow, letting the cat smell his breath. Her ears flicked. "Whoooeeeee," he said, a low, awed voice. "Look at her. Just look at her. You know the thing about lions? The females? They're the ones that hunt. Males don't do shit. They just sleep and fuck. The females, they're the tough ones. They're the ones that deserve respect, the ones to watch out for." Sturm reached out, put his hand flat against the bars. The lioness snarled, suddenly vicious, ears flattened, head low.

Sturm laughed delightedly. "Goddamn. Goddamn! Look at them teeth. That's something." He cocked his head. "Those canines, oh boy, they're bigger'n your thumbs. That's something all right." He glanced back at Frank. "Did you see them teeth back in my office?"

Frank thought of all the picture frames that surrounded the large window and shook his head.

"When we get back, I'll have to show you 'em. Just got a whole set of Moray eel teeth. Goddamn needles. Vicious. Mean, you know? Not like these." He nodded at the lioness. "These are . . . I don't know. Honorable. Proud." He stepped back and replaced his hat. "You can tell everything about an animal by its teeth. How it lives. What it eats. Anything." Sturm was excited. "They tell us everything about evolution. God's plan. Those with the biggest teeth dominate. See, you being a vet and all, you oughta understand this."

"Her teeth are bigger than mine. Yet she's in a cage and I'm out here."

"Don't mean shit. Her being in a cage. That's missing the point. *Physically,* she has bigger teeth, yes. But I'm talking about the bigger picture here. Your opposable thumbs there, those're nothing but longer, sharper teeth." Sturm nodded again, then shrugged. "We're nothing but predators. That's all there is to it.

We're nothing special. We're just like them. Oh sure, we're at the top. But it's a tenuous hold, make no mistake. Long as we got our thumbs using tools, we're set, but take those tools away, and we ain't shit. Makes me sick sometimes, the arrogance I see. People thinking that humans are some kinda' higher life form. That we're meant for some kind of enlightenment. Bullshit. We're just efficient eaters. That's all. And we're just gonna keep eating and killing every goddamn thing until something else comes along and takes our place at the top."

Frank wondered just how big that tumor in Sturm's head had gotten.

The cell phone rang. It was the clowns, and they were on their way.

DAY FOUR

"That's one big pussy," Chuck said when he saw the tiger.

Sturm was giving everyone the grand tour. The three clowns and two other drivers, quiet Mexicans that worked at the auction yard as well, had brought damn near every truck in Whitewood. Frank counted three semis with livestock trailers, plus Chuck's pickup. Frank was kind of surprised it had managed to make the entire trip. They even brought the tow truck, just in case. The only large vehicle that Frank could think of that wasn't here was the ancient fire engine that rested in the park in the center of town.

While the two Mexican men smoked cigarettes and kept an eye on all the trucks that were parked along the narrow, twisted road that ran through the center of the zoo, Sturm introduced the clowns to all of the animals, providing a running commentary on the strengths, predatory instincts, and pretty much anything else that popped into his mind. Frank was impressed with the depth of Sturm's knowledge. Those books back in the office hadn't been just for looks.

Sturm had even found places in the zoo that Frank hadn't seen. Frank was surprised and sickened to find out that two chimps also lived at the zoo, locked away in a cinderblock storage shed. The door was a length of chain-link fence, stretched sideways. Black shit coated the walls. The two chimps huddled together in the far corner and watched the men through heavy-lidded eyes. Much of their hair was worn down to white skin pockmarked with seeping, open sores, like infected blisters that had finally popped.

"Shit, Chuck. So this is where you been hiding them sisters you keep telling us that you fucked last year," Pine said.

"That's fuckin' funny. Absofuckin' hilarious, cuntwipe." Chuck leaned over, peering at Pine's piss-poor excuse for a mustache. Unlike his chin, Pine's mustache was sparse, sprouting in embarrassed fits and starts. Chuck kept going. "Considering whatever the hell that is on your lip there. Fuck is that? Pubic hair? Looks like you're the one's been smoking monkey dick."

"Ape dick," Sturm corrected, and nobody was sure if they should laugh or not. "Those in there are apes, not monkeys. Monkeys got tails, see?"

In addition to being educational, Sturm had also been thinking ahead. He instructed the clowns to bring raw hamburger and bananas. During the ride, Pine had injected Ace into the bananas and soaked the hamburger in the drug. And as they'd wandered through the zoo, they'd doled out the hamburger to the cats and bananas to the monkeys. When they walked back, they found the monkeys dropping out of trees. The clowns went around picking them up by the long, sinewy tails and dropping them into gunnysacks.

The whole loading process didn't take nearly as long as Frank had expected; once the tour was over, he was impressed with how serious the clowns acted. There was no horsing around, no calling each other names, no laughing, and no drinking. The animals were sluggish after their extra meal, and the tranquilizers didn't hurt. The cats got most of the drugs. They tied the sleeping cats' front and back paws together with duct tape, and wrapped it around the cats muzzles for good measure. Then two of them would hoist a cat onto their backs and, walking stiffly, legs moving in unison, they carried the cats out to the cattle trailers and laid the unconscious animals gently in the thick straw. It took four of them to carry the tiger.

As the sun rose, Frank got the rhino into the first truck by himself; he held a flake of hay and loaded the majestic, sad creature into the trailer. The head, bigger than an engine block, swung toward Frank and she heaved and puffed for a while before taking a step forward. It took the old girl a while to make it up the ramp. Sturm said, "Son, you take all the time you need with that animal. It'll be something special, to put this one down."

Before they left, Frank set the zookeeper's house trailer on fire.

He rode in the truck that carried the rhino. Jack was driving. They were second in line, just behind Sturm's pickup. The other three trucks followed, with Chuck and the tow truck bringing up the rear. Although it was now early morning, the sun was already hot and hellish.

Sturm reached the front gate, got out, and opened it. As he drove on through, the CB crackled with his voice. "Chuck, close that gate behind you. No point in advertising nobody's home."

As Jack eased the massive semi through the narrow gate, Frank caught a glimpse of a dark smudge, far down the highway. "Hold it," he snapped and jerked the binoculars up.

But instead of a squad car, Frank stared at a turd brown station wagon that had been manufactured sometime during the Carter administration. Someone had jacked it up into a four-wheel drive, and now the doors sat nearly four feet off the ground. It looked like some six-year-old's idea of a really cool Matchbox car. Frank was suddenly acutely aware of the black smoke he could see in the semi's side mirror. The smoke bled up into the nearly white sky, growing thicker and darker by the second as flames consumed the cheap insulation and press-board of the house trailer. "Shit. Somebody's watching us."

"Who? Cop?" Jack asked.

"No. Some kind of four-wheel-drive station wagon."

Jack snatched the CB from the cradle as Sturm pulled out away from them, picking up speed on the blacktop. "We got a problem here, Mr. Sturm. Don't know how, but them fucking Gloucks followed us. They're watching."

Brake lights flashed on the back of Sturm's pickup.

Pine's voice broke in. "Those fuckers. Let's go say howdy."

Jack nodded slowly, watching the car, maybe a mile distant. "Might be a good opportunity here, take care of that goddamn family once and for all," he said into the mike. "Nobody's around."

Chuck agreed. "Fuck yes. Let's go settle them right now. Nobody'll know."

But Sturm's voice came back, quick and harsh, "No. Leave 'em be. We got these animals to get back home. Worry about them people later. They'll get what's coming to 'em. Don't you worry. Now let's go home."

And with that, the pickup accelerated, and slowly, slowly, the convoy followed, gathering speed as they rolled through the desert. For the first time, the zoo was quiet, empty except for the alligators. Frank hoped the starvation took a long time, until they finally started to turn on each other, boiling the tank in the frothing madness of hunger and blood.

They followed the highway north, along Frank's original route, without incident. Once, they had spotted a sheriff's car, coming the opposite way, but it had sped past without slowing. Frank was glad once they hit I-80, because of the extra traffic. A few semis with livestock trailers would blend in with the blur of all of the other trucks. Around noon, Sturm's right blinker began to flash, and the convoy took the off ramp, pulling into the same rest stop where Frank had cracked the trucker in the head.

"Why are we stopping?" he asked, keeping his voice level and unconcerned.

"Can't cross the state line in daylight," Jack said. "We're gonna have to stop here and wait it out. Soon as its dark, we'll cross."

They parked all over the place so as not to make it obvious the trucks were traveling together. The place was busier than last time, full of semis, tourists squeezing in one last trip of the summer, and students headed for college. Frank hoped the tranquilizers would hold; he didn't want some family in a mini-van getting curious and one of the big cats chewing off a toddler's groping hand.

Frank got out to stretch. He slowly walked along the line of rumbling semis, easing the kinks out of his back and shoulders. There was a sharp, twisting pain in his right side and he wondered if he'd pulled something while whipping the fence post over his head. It didn't feel serious, but it was enough to make him catch his breath.

He squatted in the thin shade of a few dusty trees and looked back at the semi. Heat waves danced on the trailer's roof. Frank realized the temperature inside the trailer had to be over a hundred and ten. Maybe a hundred and twenty.

He found Jack eyeballing a carload of sorority girls. "We gotta cool these animals down somehow," Frank said. "They're gonna cook."

The girls giggled and cast tentative glances at Jack, eyes full of lust and fear. Jack never looked away from their car. "Then take care of it. You're the vet."

Frank couldn't argue with that. He should have known better. He walked the length of the grassy area on the outskirts of the parking lot and found what he needed. After grabbing a wrench, a hammer, and a screwdriver from Sturm's toolbox, he had the automatic sprinklers on in under a minute. Like machine guns, the sprinklers spit arcs of water out in precise bursts, first spraying the grass, then the trucks once Frank adjusted their aim.

The cats weren't happy. Still not fully awake, they pressed themselves into corners, turning their faces away from the water. Except one. It lay sprawled near the back and never flinched even as drops of water rolled down the matted fur. Frank watched the sharp ridges and valleys of the cat's rib, but it wasn't breathing. "Shit," Frank whispered.

He went looking for Sturm and saw the poster instead.

It was up near the vending machines, tacked up over the maps. Frank recognized the trucker's face from over fifteen feet away. Glancing around, he saw that the posters had been put up everywhere. Something cold grabbed at his heart. People pushed past, ignoring the poster and Frank. He went and stood next to it, pretending to study the map. Above the stark red "INFORMATION WANTED" was a grainy, black and white picture of the trucker's face, apparently from his driver's license. Below, it read, "Please contact the Nevada State Police with any information regarding the death of Randall James Stark, 32, murdered on August 13." There was a phone number, but Frank had turned away, ice spreading throughout his body despite the sizzling midday temperature. Three men in three days.

When he finally looked up, he saw Sturm, on the far side of the rest stop, taking down one of the posters, carefully folding it and stowing it safely away in the inside pocket of his duster.

Someone yelled. Frank heard honking and saw a woman wave a chicken nugget toward one of Sturm's trucks at the far end of the parking lot. The two chimps were scrambling across the top of the trailer in their swaying, bowlegged run. They swung down from the exhaust stack, nimbly scurrying away from a diving tackle from Jack, and darted across the parking lot before disappearing behind another truck.

Frank half-jogged through the vehicles and met up with the clowns. The chimps had taken off in a loping run through the sprinklers and across a dry field beyond the rest stop. Chuck burst around the corner of the trailer, panting, holding a rifle. He jerked it to his shoulder, but Sturm stopped him with a sharp whistle. They turned, and saw Sturm standing at the edge of the parking lot, maybe thirty yards away. He shook his head, patted the air in front of him.

Chuck mumbled, "Shit," under his breath and lowered the rifle, looking around to see if anyone had seen him. But everyone's attention was focused on the bounding figures, now just hazy specks in the distance.

Frank inspected the trailer doors. One was slightly ajar, but the rest of the monkeys were still sleeping soundly, bound in their canvas sacks. He had no idea how the chimps had managed to get the door open, and he wondered how pissed this would make Sturm. And even if it did affect his final payment, Frank was glad the chimps had escaped. He wished them luck as he refastened the wide doors. Pine didn't waste any time jumping in the cab and pulling away, just to avoid any questions. He'd wait for the rest of the trucks farther down the road.

The rest of the afternoon and evening passed quietly. Sturm went and picked up some burgers and fries and brought them back for the clowns. A flask was surreptitiously passed around, scratching the itch in the back of Frank's throat. He even managed to forget about the poster of the dead trucker in Sturm's pocket for a while.

Around ten that night, they started leaving in fifteen-minute intervals. Somewhere before the border, the trucks left the freeway and followed a series of dusty gravel roads that cut through farm fields.

Frank felt exhaustion creeping through him, filling his pores like spongy seaweed that was revealed at low tide after the high, surging adrenaline-filled waters had receded. He stared out at the moonlit fields, watching the sprinklers, giant wheels, each connected by a long, thin axle, slowly rolling across the alfalfa fields, feebly spitting out warm water, turning slower than the second hand of Sturm's pocket watch. Frank's head bobbled with the rhythm of the dirt roads, and he finally fell into a deep, dreamless sleep, sleeping even through the twisting, turning logging roads where the trucks crossed over the mountains.

Day Five

Frank finally woke around noon, still slumped in the front seat of the truck, steeped in sweat that smelled bad enough to bring tears to his eyes. It felt as if he'd spent the past few months jammed tight inside a greasy garbage can. Gingerly rolling the kinks out of his neck, he crawled out of the sweltering cab and shielded his eyes from a merciless sun that hung directly overhead. After spending a few moments unpeeling the suit from his damp skin, he realized that he was alone in the auction yard parking lot. He was glad the clowns had let him sleep, even though the inside of the truck had become an oven.

Thirst hit him like a sledgehammer. He found a coiled hose along the wall, but the water that came out was damn near scalding. After a few minutes though, he got to the water that had been waiting under the heavy stone foundation, and it gradually turned crisp and blissfully cool. Frank tried not to gulp at it and in the end just held it over his head. To hell with the expensive suit. It wouldn't take long to dry in this heat; besides, he knew he would have to find some new clothes soon.

The cold water shocked his system like lightning striking Frankenstein's monster, causing him to gasp involuntarily and left him with a big, stupid grin on his face. He kept chugging the water, alternating with letting it cascade down his skull and his back, until finally, he was afraid that if he drank any more he'd just vomit it all back up.

A long deep howl, from somewhere deep in the building, rose

into the still air, then silence.

Frank put the hose back and went looking for the clowns.

He didn't have to go far. They were sitting in front of their trailer, under the awning, at a wooden picnic table that the clowns had stolen from the rest stop. A couple of neon beer signs hummed listlessly in the still air, hung against the trailer between cheap mirrors that bore large cigarette logos. The duct-taped cooler was stowed in the shade under the trailer. Jack was the only one moving, methodically building a pyramid of charcoal briquette in a round BBQ.

"Thought you might be half Indian, way you were sleeping in that cab like it was a kind of sweat lodge," Pine said. It sounded like he was trying to be friendly, but it came out flat and tired.

Frank grabbed a beer. He sat next to Chuck, decided he couldn't wait for Jack to finish building the fire, and ate a raw hot dog. With the cold beer, it almost tasted good. "So what's happening?"

Jack shrugged. "Nothing. We got the animals inside and locked up. Sturm said to let you sleep. We're supposed to meet him at the fairgrounds, soon as it's dark. Just to make sure the animals were safe and sound, and to hang tight."

Pine spit into the dust. Frank watched the saliva roll into a dusty glob and quiver like jello. Heat made the gravel shimmer and dance. They drank slowly, making the beer last, and waited silently. Even Chuck kept his mouth shut. The men watched the shadows slide across the ground, listened to the big cats hiss at each other, and did their damndest to move less than the lizards.

Frank had never seen anything like it. Sturm had invited the entire town, even the Gloucks, out to the fairgrounds where he barbequed the lioness that had died on the journey. At least a hundred people showed up, all carrying something. The women carried food, most of it sacks of potatoes, while the men lugged coolers full of chicken and beer. The children brought water pistols and homemade get-well cards, flaking glitter and raw macaroni shells. Sturm had paid the carnival to stay open an extra day, and so the air was filled with clanking rides, happy shouts and screams, the sickly sweet smells of cotton candy, and wisps of sharp smoke from barbequed meat.

Everyone gathered around a gently curving string of wooden picnic tables under canvas awnings that covered cool concrete slabs. Beyond the shallow semi-circle of tables was a dry creek-bed, maybe thirty yards across; useless farmland, overgrown with star thistles, lay on the other side.

The monolithic BBQ, built of solid, blackened brick, rose at the far end of the strip of tables. Sturm had built the fire at dawn, using a combination of eucalyptus and oak at the beginning, building a massive bed of glowing hardwood coals, and added green apple branches, four inches thick, just before the meat was slapped onto the chain-link grill.

Sturm saved the heart for himself and Theo, frying it up in butter in a cast-iron skillet and eating it with biscuits and gravy. Everyone else at least got a taste of the rest of the animal, either leg muscles or ribs, served along with the food that the town had brought. Food like blackened chicken legs, breasts, thighs, wings. Boiled hot dogs. Gallons of baked beans. Giant tubs of coleslaw and potato salad. Enough French bread to build a fence around the picnic tables. Sturm even cut the tail off the lioness and gave it to the Mexicans for stew.

Frank hadn't eaten much in several days, and he wasn't about to pass up this chance. He loaded his plate with chicken, mashed potatoes and gravy with chicken drippings, potato salad—made from baked potatoes, onions, mayonnaise, sweet pickle relish, black olives, and hard boiled eggs—and fries from a deep fryer. Even a corn dog, just for the hell of it. Sturm set aside a special cut of the lion for Frank, something resembling a filet from the chest. It was the only thing he didn't enjoy; it tasted sour, overcooked.

When everyone had eaten, and the crowd had thinned, drifting off to the carnival rides and games, Sturm and Frank sat together in the gathering twilight, watching the glowing coals slowly fade. Frank felt the heat from fifteen feet away. Sturm instructed Theo to bring him an envelope from his pickup.

Sturm handed it to Frank. "You earned it, son. This is a hell of a thing here, thanks to you."

Frank murmured, "Hell, happy to help," as he glanced inside the envelope. His heart tripped over itself for a second. "Wait . . . there's more . . . more than we agreed on." He quickly added the bills, guessing there was nearly ten grand in the envelope.

Sturm grinned as the rolling, spinning lights from the carnival reflected in his eyes. "Yep. I know. Figured you deserved it."

"Hell, I don't know what to say."

"Don't say anything, son. Like I said, you earned it. Use as best you see fit." Sturm glanced back at Frank. "I know you got yourself some pressing personal problems, and I understand if you have to keep moving. But here's the thing. Our vet took off last winter. If you want it, there's a position available here, for as long as you want. I could use a man like you. Got some plans for them animals. We're gonna have some fun. This, this here," Sturm gestured at the tables, the stands, the carnival. "This is just the beginning."

Frank sat back, feeling something close to warmth in his chest as he watched the women cleaning up all the food, the knots of men, smoking and drinking, the children running about in the dark with flashlights and glowsticks. He felt strangely affectionate toward all of them, as if they were all animals in his care and they needed his guidance, his skills, his love. He was surprised to find himself smiling.

"Yeah," he said. "I'd like that."

Sturm clapped him on the back and said, "First thing in the morning, we're gonna have to get you some decent working clothes." They both laughed, and sat for a while, sipping from their beers, watching the people, and enjoying the slight cool breeze that had come up.

Sturm saw Petunia first. "Hell's that damn dog doing here?" he muttered, crumpling his tenth or eleventh beer. Frank glanced over, saw the dog nimbly hop up onto the top of one of the picnic tables and help herself to the leftovers. The three people still at the table suddenly found some urgent business somewhere else.

The Gloucks followed Petunia.

They came out of the darkness, a ragged, seething group of boys, ebbing and flowing around the two mothers in a surging amoeba of bodyguards. The two women, the two mothers, Edie and Alice, walking purposeful and unhurried, headed straight for Sturm, chins up, like the proud, sticklike birds with dagger beaks that strutted through the flooded rice fields. Folks got out of their way.

Two girls, holding hands, trailed the group. One was seven years old, the same little girl that had hollered at the two deputies from the dead tree several days earlier.

The other was nineteen. Her name was Annie.

Frank saw her immediately. She wasn't plump exactly, just filled out; lots of curves in all the right places and she moved like a racehorse, smooth, graceful, strong.

The boys spread out in feral, scuttling movements, spilling around Frank and Sturm and fading back toward the tables. They wore long, baggy shorts, oversized basketball tank tops, hats turned sideways. They'd been watching too much MTV off that gigantic satellite and were doing their damndest to look like wannabe hip-hop thugs that carried nine millimeters of handgun next to their dicks. But instead of nine millimeters, these kids were packing air pistols and BB guns and slingshots.

Alice extended a flat dish that steamed in the cool air, a gift for the potluck. She stopped just short of giving it to Sturm as Edie shouted back at the boys, "Git that dog off that fucking table. We're guests, goddamnit." She gave them a meaningful look. "There will be no ruckus here tonight."

The boys nodded. Annie smiled, gave her sister's hand a squeeze.

The mothers turned back to Sturm, still pissed at their boys but at the same time, deferential and respectful to Sturm, ignoring Frank. The food was a thin, burnt husk of something. It smelled of BBQ sauce, onions and garlic, maybe some Tabasco, and something else, some kind of meat, something different underneath.

"Well, thank—" Sturm started.

"We'll need that dish back," Edie said. Her left eye seemed glaringly fake, a ping pong ball or something, some kind of cheap movie monster from the '50s, staring at the stars somewhere over Frank's head. She fixed her good eye on Sturm, moving her head as if on a thousand ball bearings, utterly smooth, like a rattlesnake on opium.

Alice leaned in, smiling, and bumped Sturm's chest with the potluck dish. Sturm tried to talk, to take the dish, anything, but couldn't manage anything but licking the inside of his lips. "Uh, well . . ."

Frank stepped in, very smooth, very diplomatic, and took the dish.

Sturm finally managed, "Thank you," and stiffly held up his hand, shook Alice's hand. The mothers were very pleased. They all stood around grinning at each other as if they'd been friends for years. Finally, Sturm couldn't take it anymore and gestured at the tables. "Please, please, make yourselves welcome. Eat."

The boys hit the tables like crabs going after a dead whale. "Thank you very, very much." Alice took Sturm's hands with both of hers. She bowed her head and the mothers descended upon the tables, a couple of egrets joining the crabs.

Frank wasn't sure if the dish in his hands was supposed to be meat, pasta, or vegetable. It smelled scarily of fish. He put the dish on the table in the center of the half circle of tables, between a carrot cake and cookie sheets heaped with blackened chicken. The mothers watched him.

Edie coughed.

"Hell, son," Sturm said. "Don't be shy. Go on ahead. Try some." He tapped his skull and gave a sad smile. "I would, but . . . afraid the doc's got me on a restricted diet. Smells delicious, though."

Frank reluctantly tried to scoop out a little piece, but snapped the plastic fork instead. He took a nearby spatula and had a hell of a time cutting himself out a few bites. He dumped a few crumbs on a paper plate, got a new plastic fork, and scraped a little into his mouth and just as he realized it was the worst thing he'd ever tasted, he heard Annie's voice from somewhere close. "You like it?"

The bite from the potluck dish tasted like a deep fried turd. Frank tried to swallow, turned, tears burning his eyes, his gag reflex threatening to explode.

Through the stinging tears, he got a closer look at Annie. She wore cutoffs; white, dangling threads accentuated her strong, tan legs. Her flip-flops were nothing more than flat strips of rubber that used to be neon orange, smudged with grime. Silver toe rings glittered. One of them bore a grinning skull. The bottom of her feet were black, darker than dirt. The white halter top had risen, revealing a sliver of a round brown belly. Heavy, full breasts strained the fabric; the raised buds of nipples were clearly visible in the night air. She had straight black hair that hung just past her earlobes and a round face made for smiling.

Frank swallowed the bite of potluck without tasting it anymore and nodded dumbly, head itching maddeningly under his long hair, suddenly hyper-aware of his surroundings, of everyone around him, as if a brilliant spotlight had focused on his lanky frame, and he was the center of attention, stared at by the mothers, Sturm, the clowns, even the quiet gentlemen somewhere deep in the shadows. "S'good," he said, but couldn't quite suppress the coughed gag that escaped from his mouth.

Annie's smile just grew wider. The dimples grew deeper. "You want to go on a ride with me?"

The creek bed and scrub beyond exploded in light and for the briefest moment, Frank wondered if he had died. But it was just the massive klieg lights that had powered on with an impact that made everyone jump in mid-conversation. The smart ones were expecting it, and already had their shooting glasses on, tinted yellow, gold, or blue.

Shotguns appeared. Frank followed the curve of the tables that weren't only meant for eating; now he could see that they were arranged around a shooting range. In the harsh glare of the field lights, there was a square concrete bunker that even now had started flinging clay pigeons out into the sky above the farmland. Shotgun blasts split the night with flat, booming thunder.

"If you don't want to go on a ride, that's okay. I understand if you don't want to go with me."

Frank suddenly remembered Annie. "Um, hell no. I mean, yeah. Yeah. Let's go. Let's go on a ride." He found himself smiling back at her. He nodded at Sturm and the mothers as he slipped the plate onto the table, let Annie link her arm through his, and they slowly moved off toward the carnival. As they walked away, he heard one of the mothers say, "Now what's all this we hear about all these new animals at that auction yard of yours?"

Annie leaned in close and said in a loud stage whisper, "Sorry you had to eat that. Mom made it for Sturm special, if you know what I mean."

Frank shrugged. "You didn't make it?"

Annie shook her head. "No. Not sure exactly what all went in there, but I know for a fact that the main ingredient was a raw catfish that Ernie caught out of the ditch last week." She thought that was funny. "Sturm and my moms got a little feud going. They're unbelievable cooks, and Sturm knows it, but he's scared to try anything they make, because he doesn't know what they'll put in it."

"I don't blame him."

Frank and Annie took it slow, wandering through the carnival, through the garish lights, the shouts and screams, the smell of egg roll on a stick, dunked in sweet and sour sauce. Frank caught a quick glimpse of Theo a couple of times, dashing from one ride to another with a few of his buddies, but the Glouck boys were nowhere to be found.

"This one," Annie said, and squeezed Frank's arm.

"This one?"

"This one."

It was called "WHEEL OF SCREAMS" and was just a large, flat disc, about thirty feet across, with a six-foot wall around the outside. They went up the steps, walked out onto the disc, painted in a giant spiral circling out from the center, and found a couple of open spots on the wall. "Stand there, with your back up against the wall, and grab hold of those bars," Annie instructed. There were no straps, no safety bars that went across your hips and held you in place. Just vertical bars along the wall, like playground bars. At the last minute, Theo and his followers jumped on and found places along the wall opposite of Frank and Annie. The operator said, "Y'all have fun," and slammed a bar down, shutting the ride off from the outside world. Frank started to sweat, nervous, worried that he would puke up the potluck dish, the chicken, the potato salad, the corn dog.

The disc began to spin, slowly. Frank swallowed and exhaled through his nose. Annie's hand found his on the bar between them. The world revolved; Frank saw the carnival worker, rolling a smoke on the front steps, then the big bouncing balloon castle with its segmented floor and walls, always leaning slightly over, as if a corner had split open, the Corn Dog and Egg Roll trailers, the distant startling white lights of the shooting range, and the carnival worker again, but just the back of his head this time, as he walked down the steps.

Annie gripped his fingers tighter as the machine gained velocity. Frank felt himself slowly pressed back into the wall as the ride spun faster and faster. With a lurch that sent Frank's stomach scrabbling queasily up onto the back of his tongue, the disc started to tilt. One edge rose and rose, until Frank realized the whole disc was on some kind of arm, resembling more of a wheel than a disc. It kept rising, until the wheel was almost completely sideways, holding its passengers in check through centrifugal force.

Something deep inside Frank relaxed its clenched fist just a bit, and he found himself grinning, almost enjoying the rush of wind, the powerless feeling of watching the pavement slide past, followed by the jet black darkness of the night sky, the ground again, giving way to the sky, the ground, the sky. He uncurled his fingers from the bars, letting the ride take him, giving up control. Annie whooped, raising her own arms, fingers spread wide. Frank closed his eyes, opening his palms to the stars and neon lights.

He couldn't remember the last time he'd felt this good.

As they staggered slightly away from the Wheel of Screams, still feeling the effects, Frank wanted to ask Annie if she'd like to try another ride, but just as he was about to speak, they both watched Theo fling an empty beer bottle at Ernie Glouck's head.

The bottle missed, and by the time it had shattered against the pavement, Ernie had launched himself at Theo. They went down, Theo tearing at Ernie's Laker jersey, Ernie slamming punches into Theo's midsection. The rest of the Glouck boys swarmed the two fighters while Theo's friends slipped through the crowd and ran.

For the third time that night, Frank wondered where the clowns were, but didn't have time to wonder long because Annie was no longer standing next to him. She stormed into the circle of teenagers, grabbing her right fist in her left hand, twisting and turning like a pissed-off tornado, jabbing her elbows into anyone who came close. Her brothers, both by blood and by marriage, had enough experience with their oldest sister to get the hell out of the way. She came upon Ernie, hanging onto Theo's hair and T-shirt, kneeing the bigger kid repeatedly in the left kidney while Theo kept slamming his bleeding knuckles into the back of Ernie's head and getting nowhere.

Annie planted her back foot and kicked Ernie square in the small of his back. Her brother spasmed and released Theo before rolling over onto his side, flailing as if in the grip of an electric current. Theo backed off for a second, let his eyes wander over Annie, then turned back and punched Ernie in the face.

"Little boy, what is the matter with you?" Annie asked, walking toward Theo, slow, taking her time, rolling those formidable hips like an expensive, wide yacht in calm waters.

Theo started to yell something, but Annie kicked him in the balls before he got a breath. She turned to Ernie, cursing quick and quiet. "Stupid dickbrained motherfucking pieces of garbage . . ." She kicked him again, this time in the muscle of his thigh, enough to seriously hurt him, but nothing permanent, nowhere near a joint like the knee. "Get home. Now." He broke off into a run. "You better pray I calm down before I get home!"

Theo had just about straightened from the kick when the little Glouck girl expertly flipped a rock the size of a cell phone at his head, not particularly fast or furious, just hard enough to smash his ear against his head, splitting the cartilage and skin. He went back to his knees, suddenly realizing that the entire Glouck family, except for the mothers, had surrounded him.

"Get on home to Daddy, little boy," Annie told Theo. "It's past your bedtime." Theo didn't run like Ernie, but he moved fast just the same, knees never straying far apart in an uncomfortable shuffling dance, back toward the shooting range. Annie shooed her family away. "Rest of you trigger-happy fucks get home too. Now." They didn't argue, just broke into a jog toward the parking lot.

She came back to Frank, shaking her head. "Boys, boys, boys," she said with a grin. "I'd better go too." She cocked her head. "Are you going to be in town long?"

"I don't know. Maybe."

"Maybe?"

"Yeah."

"Then maybe I'll see you around." She smiled at him again and Frank felt that warmth, as if everything inside of him, floating free after the ride, had settled down into a safe place for a comfortable nap. She turned and waved, just once, on her way to the parking lot. Frank wasn't even aware he was waving back until he caught his hand in the air.

Frank was far from a virgin; the horse world was full of women that gladly rode any horses or men within reach. Still, when Annie had touched his hand on the ride a shock wave of lust had ricocheted through his chest and groin. It surprised him. He had no idea that he was even capable of a need that intense, especially after the events of the past week. Maybe facing death just added fuel to the fire.

Frank drove back to the auction yard, planning on sleeping in the house trailer with the rest of the clowns, but found the place empty. The animals were gone too. Frank hoped they hadn't escaped. It didn't look like it, though. Everything was locked down and clean. Just empty.

He walked back up the low hill, still lost in the rushing sensation of the Wheel of Screams and Annie in those shorts to worry about the animals or the clowns. At the trailer, Frank helped himself to a warm beer from the ice chest under the picnic table. He was considering taking a quick look through the trailer, rifling through the cupboards for a bottle of something stronger than beer, when Chuck pulled up.

"Been looking for you. Heard you accepted the job." Chuck jumped out of the truck and shook Frank's hand vigorously. "Glad to fuckin' hear it, believe me."

Frank wasn't sure what Chuck was talking about.

" 'Bout time this town had itself a new veterinarian."

"Oh. Yeah."

"Hop in. We got it all set up."

"Okay." Frank climbed into the passenger side. "You got anything to drink?"

Chuck laughed, tossed Frank a bottle of Seagram's 7, and turned the truck toward town. "How was the barbeque?"

"Good, good." Frank took a long pull off the bottle. "Cooked a hell of a lot of chicken on that coal bed you built. Ate 'til I thought I might bust." Frank took another long drink. "Lotta people there, even that crazy family, Glouck or something."

"No shit? Those goddamn fucks had the balls to show themselves? They eat much?"

"Yeah, the boys did, all right." Frank passed the bottle to Chuck and leaned back, feeling good, feeling like he was a part of something, like he belonged here. The air from the open windows felt cool, and looking out over the landscape, watching the moonlight reflected off the water in the rice fields, the atmosphere was almost tropical. "Went on a ride with the oldest girl," Frank said. They passed a gas station, an abandoned burger joint, then into the heart of the dark town. "Pretty sure her name was Annie."

"No! No! No shit?" Chuck shouted, gripping the steering wheel with both hands. "Holy fuck, that didn't take long." He laughed, grinned hugely at Frank. "So . . . how was it?"

"It was . . . good. Nice."

"Nice. 'Nice,' he says." Chuck shook his head. "Fuck man, she's the best. The absolute champ. None better. None. 'Nice.' You fucking kill me, man. How much did she charge you?" Yard after yard was stuffed with overgrown dead grass.

"What?"

Chuck turned left at the end of the street, filled with more empty houses. An orange tree grew in the occasional yard. "How much money did you spend?"

"I dunno. Not much. Enough to get on the ride."

Chuck giggled. "Enough to get on the ride. Classic. Fucking classic. Last time, I paid twenty bucks. Far as I know, that's what everyone's paying. So what did you pay? More or less?"

"What?"

"How much did you pay, man? I know she'll blow your mind, but come on, spill. She give you any kind of discount?"

"Uh . . . we went on a ride. I didn't pay her anything."

Chuck's face went slack. "Wait a minute. Wait. You're telling me, you, you didn't give her any money?"

"No."

"Holy fucking Christ. She gave you one for free? Goddamn."

"She didn't give me anything for free. We went on a ride," Frank said. "Then she, well, she kicked the shit out of Ernie and kicked Theo in the balls, and well, that was it."

"Wait, hold on. She kicked Theo in the balls? That fucking bitch."

"Well, he had it coming. See, he—"

"Wait, just fucking wait. You're telling me she never, she didn't . . . you didn't get a blowjob?"

"A blow—what? No, no." Frank shook his head hard. "No. Not at all. She . . . she gives blowjobs for money?" The muscles in the left side of his face twitched.

"Shit, where you been? Of course she gives head for cash. How the fuck you think she makes a living?" Chuck shook his head. "She's sucked damn near everybody's dick in town."

Chuck pulled into a dark parking lot, a rippled sculpture of dry mud, all cracks and dips and curves, and killed the engine. They sat in the darkness for a moment. Frank got his first good look at the veterinary clinic. The building sat apart from the rest of the houses on the street, at the far end of an empty field full of star thistles and puncture vines. The clinic was roughly the same height as the rest of the ranch houses in town, but shaped like a large U, and swallowed by ivy. There was a small barn in the back. The grass looked well watered but hadn't been mowed recently. A radio tower rose a good fifty feet, tucked into a corner of the building. It looked as if one good strong gust of wind would break it in half, send it toppling to the ground.

"If I was you, I wouldn't mention Annie," Chuck said and

climbed out. "Jack and Pine . . . they don't wanna hear about her."

Frank followed him and crossed the yard, mindful of needles. He knew that vets worked on horses anywhere and dropped the syringes if the horse turned mean. He'd seen people forget this; they'd be walking and give a sudden, quick hop, clutching at their feet. Usually they just ended up with a needle in the bottom of their foot, but sometimes, the medicine inside would find its way into the bloodstream. Sometimes, they'd end up with heavy-duty horse tranquilizer in their system, and spend the rest of the day sleeping comfortably, or worse, they'd yank the needle out of the wrinkled flesh where the big toe meets the rest of the foot and realized that the syringe contained some kind of steroid or stimulant. Some just rode it out until they crumbled after six hours into a fog of tequila, some curled up in the shower, shivering, puking, shit running out in thin streams. A couple of folks simply fell down, their heart clenching itself tight and refusing to let go.

The back door opened into an examining room. As near as Frank could tell, the room was prepped and ready for nearly anything. There was a stainless steel table in the center of the room, a refrigerator, a wide stainless steel sink off to the left next to a cabinet full of medicine, bandages, tools. To the left was the front desk and waiting room. Off to the right, the far end of the room led into another intersection.

Frank took a left at the intersection at the end of the room, and saw small cages, set up for cats at the top, dogs at the bottom. To the right was an operating room, sealed in sterile tile, with more cages, where they isolated puppies with Parvo. Tonight, though, they were filled with stoned monkeys.

Straight ahead was a thick wooden door. They went through, into a long corridor that ran the length of the wing. This middle part was essentially a large cage split into smaller sections. A heavy chain-link fence, stretched from floor to ceiling, faced the employee parking lot in the center of the U. A thick canvas curtain could be raised or lowered, depending on the sun and the weather.

The cats were in the cages that were backed up along the cinderblock wall to the left. There were twelve cages, originally for big dogs. The cats looked sleepy, sprawled out on the bare concrete, eyeballing Frank and Chuck through heavy-lidded eyes.

Two doors waited at the end. On the left, there was a regular wood door. To the right, the door was metal. Chuck turned left and opened the wood door, stepping into a storeroom filled with eighty-pound bags of cheap dog food on five pallets. An army cot, a folding chair, and a stained card table were tucked cozily in the far corner. "It ain't much, but there's a shower in the shitter up front . . . it's clean at least. And Sturm had us stock the fridge with plenty of beer." Chuck's face looked apprehensive, as if his feelings would be hurt if Frank didn't like the living arrangements.

"This'll be just fine."

"It's okay? Really?"

"Yeah."

"Sturm did mention there were some city boys who had a problem." Chuck grabbed a leather gun case from the top of the stack of dog food. Inside was a dull black pump shotgun with a barrel so short and abrupt it looked like an amputated limb. "Winchester. Twelve gauge. You got eight shells in here, double-ought buckshot. Any fuckhead makes you nervous, you just point this in their general direction and squeeze the trigger. Guaranteed results, I'm telling you."

Frank heard barking dogs, sharp, urgent. "There's still animals here?"

Chuck said, "Yes and no. Nothing official, no clients. Nobody's been around to see anybody. So folks just stopped coming. Either took their animal up to Canby or took care of 'em with a .22. You're hearing the dogs in the pound, animals that got left when folks moved on. Mr. Sturm and the boys probably got 'em all fired up."

Once through the metal door, the barking got ten times louder, the difference between hearing the fire department siren go off from miles away and being inside the station when it erupted; the sound seemed to have a physical quality that you could reach out and touch, like grabbing a handful of roofing nails and squeezing.

Although the pound was neither as grim or desperate as the zoo, it wasn't a place that Frank wanted to stay long. Instead of single, individual cages, the dogs had been thrown together in a single, large cage. The shit on the floor was almost a liquid, nearly three inches deep.

Frank counted eighteen dogs, ranging in size from some unidentifiable brown mutt just a hair taller than a tree squirrel damn near drowning in shit to a German Shepherd with nails over two inches long, fear and hate bright in his eyes. They were all barking at Sturm, who was crouched down at another back door, fingers splayed against the cage wires. Shit flew. "Look at that sneaky little pissant," he shouted to Jack and Theo, pointing to a bristling ball of black and white fur. The dog alternately hid behind the barking Shepherd, then would swim its way up through the pack, darting forward to snap at the air in front of Sturm's fingers, before slipping backward and hiding again behind the larger dogs.

Sturm stood up, waved at Frank, and readjusted his hat in the direction of the back door. Everyone followed and collected in a ragged circle in the gravel parking lot, everything silver, lit from the big stadium lights that flanked the vet clinic.

"Howdy, Frank," Sturm said.

"Howdy."

"How're the facilities?"

"Suits me fine."

"Good. We were just talking here about the qualities one would want in a dog. Jack here," Sturm tried to sum up Jack's description of his ideal dog. "Jack has just suggested . . . ah . . . aggressiveness, which, I think, everyone here would agree that that would be a certain . . . useful attribute, could benefit the owner." Everyone nodded. "So, Frank. What quality would you most prize in a dog?"

"Loyalty."

Sturm nodded at his son and the clowns. "Exactly. Loyalty. There ya' go. What'd I tell you? This man's an expert."

Jack shook his head. "Naw. But now, don't get me wrong. No offense, Frank. Loyalty's an admirable trait. Hell yes. But that ain't what you need when some shit has got your dog by the throat. You need inner strength. You need . . . fire, you need a goddamn dog that wants to live."

Sturm smiled. "And just what the hell is it supposed to want to live for?"

"Everything has a desire to live," Jack said. "Call it whatever you want. Guts. Sand. Believe the niggers call it soul. Goddamn toughness."

Sturm nodded patiently. "True, true. Hell, I ain't arguing with that . . . however, I believe that when an animal has a purpose, a, a *love,* then that will take them farther than simple survival instincts. If an animal has something to live for, hell, if anyone has something to live for . . . then they're gonna fight harder."

Jack spit into the tortured, baked mud. "I think it'll fight harder for itself than for any man."

"Then we're just gonna have to find out, won't we?" Sturm

clapped his hands. "None of them poor sonsabitches in there will fight for love. They been treated like shit." He shook his head. "Don't blame 'em one bit. If I was them, I'd say, fuck all you too." He took Theo's shoulder. "Forget that Shepherd. It's no good. Watch his posture. He's too excited, too much. Next time you see him, you watch him close. He don't know whether to shit or piss. No, he won't work. You just like him because of his size. I'm telling you, you watch that little black and white mutt. That's the one."

DAY SIX

Frank's mother was always spooning out a little wet cat food onto paper plates and leaving them in the alleys behind their apartments. Frank figured she was just fattening up the rats, but it seemed to make her happy to think that she was making a few stray cats' lives just a little easier. But rather than the alleys or the apartments themselves, Frank remembered the front doors the most. He'd be inside, listening to his mom argue with some asshole who had brought her home on the hope of getting something more than a goodnight peck on the cheek. The argument would escalate, and Frank would find himself huddling in an empty closet or under the sink, waiting until his mom would inevitably have to punch the sonofabitch. She'd slam the front door and lock it as best as she could. Then she'd find Frank and crawl into his hiding space—Frank would only hide in places where they both could fit—while they listened to the asshole kick and pound at the door, usually screaming vacant threats.

And when the other tenants complained, it was off to a new apartment.

So Frank wondered if his dreams were trying to tell him something when he woke up under his cot. Maybe it was just from sleeping this close to so many animals. He got dressed and checked on the animals. Most of them were now awake and hungry. They didn't make a sound, just watched him warily.

Out back, behind the barn, was a freezer. Sturm had stocked

it with fifty pounds of frozen lamb shanks, five-pound bricks wrapped in butcher paper and stamped with a red date. Most of the meat was over fourteen years old. Frank set out six packages, setting them on top of the freezer to thaw in the morning sun.

True enough, Frank found the fridge in the examining room stuffed full of beer, except for the bottom shelf. That was full of food. Bacon. Eggs. A roasted chicken, wrapped in aluminum foil. The freezer contained a selection of frozen food, mostly TV dinners. Frank cooked a couple of TV dinners and zapped up some coffee using an old microwave, and then took a long, ridiculously hot shower. He came out of it feeling better then he had in days.

Clothing had been left on a neat pile on the stacks of dog food. It fit fine, although Frank had to poke a new hole in the belt so he could cinch the jeans tight. He wore a long-sleeved gray cowboy shirt, Wrangler jeans, and black workboots. The clothes calmed him; he felt ready. Confident.

Sturm drove in around ten and waited for Frank to come out to the pickup. "Called an old friend last night," he said through the window, bottom lip full of snuff. "How're the girls?" He spit.

Frank shrugged. "Pissed."

Sturm laughed, cowboy hat bobbing like a cork in boiling water. "Think they'll be healthy enough for a hunt?"

"Depends on when you want to hunt 'em."

"You tell me."

Frank shrugged again. "Hard to say. They been starved for so long, don't know if the muscles'll come back. I mean, no point in hunting crippled animals. Maybe a couple of months, just to see."

"Wish I had a couple of months, son. Tell you what. You got

a week, maybe a week and a half at the most," Sturm said, tipped his cowboy hat, and took off in a cloud of dust, orange in the morning sun.

Frank spent the first few days taking care of the animals and reading everything about them he could find at night in the tiny office just off the operating room that was chock full of veterinary textbooks. Mornings, he mixed antibiotics, vitamins, and deworming pills into the food. For the next few days, he found fist-sized clumps of what looked like sluggish spaghetti in the animals' watery diarrhea. After the animals had eaten, he'd drag a long hose through the middle section, aim the nozzle through the chain-link cages, and wash their shit across the concrete into a waiting gutter. After three days, he was pleased to see that the stool was fairly solid. Most of the blood in the urine seemed to disappear as well.

After washing the cages, he'd push raw hamburger through the chain link, but he never opened the doors. He was careful to never look directly into the cats' eyes. Once in a while, feeding the cats made him feel uncomfortably like the zookeeper, and he'd have to back off for a while and grab a beer. Unlike the zookeeper, though, the cats, after a few days, would lick his palms, their tongues feeling like soft, wet sandpaper. The books told him their tongues were covered in tiny rasps that helped the cats lick meat off bones. He always kept his hands flat; despite the seemingly affectionate licking, he knew they'd chew off his fingers in a heartbeat. He had to resist the urge to name them.

In the meantime, he nailed up chicken wire in the barn, building a large cage for the monkeys. Their constant screeching and howling were getting on his nerves at night. He thought about pouring tranquilizer over their food and let them sleep for a few days. In the textbooks, he discovered they were spider monkeys.

The clowns brought over the rhino. Frank walked it carefully down the chute; it moved slowly, mechanically. Frank filled the largest stall with straw and hoped the rhino would like it, or at least feel comfortable enough to lie down. But once inside, the great beast just stood there, immobile and emotionless, like a lobotomized bull. Frank dumped an entire bale of alfalfa into the stall and couldn't have been more pleased when the rhino slowly lowered its head and started munching the green hay.

DAY THIRTEEN

As Frank lay on the narrow vinyl couch in the tiny office late at night, reading about the kidney functions of large cats, a severe, insistent buzzer vibrated throughout the hospital. He snapped the book shut and sat up. His first reaction was that the clowns were here, but they always just barged in through the back door. Curious, he made his way up to the front desk. There was a dark shadow behind the curtains in the front windows.

It was Annie. In the harsh orange glow of the bare bulb above the front door, she looked scared; her eyes were red and swollen. Behind her were two of her brothers, faces dark with fresh bruises and scrapes. Both grasped the handles of two wheelbarrows. The first wheelbarrow held Petunia. The dog lay on her side in a nest of old towels, breathing heavy, almost growling in and out; her front paws were held away from the body, stiff and covered with what looked like melted chocolate. The second wheelbarrow had been filled with knotted, twisted chunks of pine firewood. "I need your help," Annie said.

Frank didn't think twice. "Bring her in."

They wheeled the dog right into the waiting room, and both brothers carried her suspended in one of the towels back into the operating room. Frank switched on the overhead light and got a closer look. Petunia's front paws were charred black, seeping plasma. "What happened?"

Annie's little hands curled into fists. "These two cunts trapped her under the porch, knocked her sideways, and then

115

went after her with a lighter and a can of hairspray."

"Fuckin' thing shouldn'ta eaten my—" The brother didn't get a chance to finish. Faster than Frank could follow, Annie's arm shot out, whistling past her brother's head. He flinched, too late. Something bloody hit the examining table with a faint slap. Frank realized it was the brother's left earlobe as Annie neatly wiped the blade of her straight razor on the old towels.

The brother clapped his hand to the side of his head and looked like he wanted to say something as a thin trickle of blood meandered down his neck.

"Go ahead," Annie taunted. "Spit it out. Swear at me. Please. Next time it'll be your fucking nose."

He kept quiet. The second brother hung back, looking at the monkeys, the door, the green tiles on the floor, anywhere but at his sister.

Annie turned back to Frank. "Please help her."

Frank chewed on the inside of his cheek, wondering if any of the books in the back room talked about treating burns. He didn't want to appear clueless to Annie, so he said, "She's gonna need . . . rest, some antibiotics, and she's gonna have to stay off these front paws, give 'em a chance to heal." He met Annie's eyes. "She'll have to stay here. Maybe in a cage. She can't walk on these. We'll have to keep her quiet."

Annie nodded. "You do whatever you have to." Her bottom lip quivered and a fat tear squeezed itself out of her right eye and rolled down her cheek. "Please, just help her."

Frank had the two brothers hold the dog down as he slipped a padded plastic cup over the dog's muzzle. A circular rubber tube was attached to the cup; this was connected to a hose that ran to the wall. Frank had been reading about the halothane and isoflurane, anesthetic that was inhaled instead of injected, since he hadn't wanted to get close enough to the cats to slip a needle full of Acepromazine into their veins unless they were unconscious. He made a few quick calculations in his head, adjusted the vaporizer output on the wall, and fervently hoped the concentration wouldn't kill Petunia.

When her breathing and heart rate had slowed, he smeared aloe salve over Petunia's front paws. Toward the end, she fought through the haze of the anesthesia and snapped at Frank, but for the most part, the dog was remarkably calm, almost as if she understood deep down that he was trying to help. He injected her with antibiotics and encased the front paws in cotton and neon orange vet wrap. The brothers carried the now sleeping dog into the office where they placed her carefully on the vinyl couch.

"You two fuckheads wait outside," Annie told her brothers. "We're gonna have that little talk I promised. You run, and I swear to you one night, not too soon, just long enough for you to forget about it, but one night when you're sleeping, I'll creep in and cut your balls right the fuck off." Everyone in the room knew she wasn't kidding. "Get outside. Now." When the front door closed, she closed her eyes and another tear slid down her round cheek. "She was just in the wrong place at the wrong time," she said sadly. She blinked her tears away and tried to smile at Frank, but he felt like it was forced. "So how much is this gonna cost?"

"I . . . I'm not sure, exactly. Let's see how the treatment goes. Why don't we settle up when Petunia is better?"

"I don't like being in debt to anyone." She cocked her head. "You've been hearing about me. I can see it in your face."

"What? I haven't heard anything about anyone. Nobody's told me anything," Frank said. "Let's just see how Petunia heals." He put his hands flat on the table. "Then we'll talk payment."

"We'll talk payment then."

"Yeah."

"Okay then. We'll be talking, you and I." She gave a mischievous smile, but it looked to Frank like there was something else under the surface, still sadness maybe. Annie squatted in front of the couch, stroking her dog's broad, flat skull. "You take good care of Petunia. I find out you don't, I might have to go at your eyes with a screwdriver," she said without looking at him.

Frank believed her. "Yeah."

It was good enough for Annie. She stood, wiped her eyes.

"Come by anytime," Frank said. "Day or night." He wondered if that sounded too forward. Most of him was disgusted at the cruelty, but he had to admit that part of him was glad that Petunia had gotten hurt. It gave him an excuse to see Annie. "You know, see how she's doing."

"I will. First thing tomorrow."

Frank smiled. "We'll be here."

Quickly, almost without thinking, Annie grasped his elbows, stood up on her tiptoes, and kissed his cheek. Then, without another word, she left. Frank followed her to the front door and watched through the side window as the Glouck brother who still had both earlobes grabbed the wheelbarrow filled with firewood and stomped across the gravel, following his sister. The second brother, still holding his bleeding ear, reluctantly trailed along at a distance.

They left the lights of the parking lot and disappeared into the darkness of the field. Before long, though, Frank could see the first tentative flickers of a fire out in the star thistles. Frank got a beer and made himself comfortable, sitting sideways on the windowsill, watching the figures, letting his eyes adjust. When the fire had been burning for a good long while, Annie took a long branch and scattered the coals evenly on the ground around the fire and without any warning at all, whipped the thick branch at the closest brother's head. Frank couldn't tell if it was the one missing an earlobe or the younger brother. The blow knocked him face first into the star thistles and glowing coals, unconscious before he even started to fall forward.

The smell of burning skin mingled with the smell of rhino shit.

Frank turned away from the windows, feeling good, feeling fucking *great*. He grabbed another beer and headed back to his cot and .12 gauge. Outside, Annie had the second brother walk around in the fire pit barefoot, using the smoking branch as persuasion. Frank fell asleep to the second brother's screams and for the first time in months, he didn't dream.

DAY FIFTEEN

Annie wasn't the only customer to visit Frank. Two days later, the woman with the brittle red hair from the gas station rushed into the veterinary hospital, clutching a cat carrier. A coughing male cat, just shy of six pounds and twenty-two years, lay inside. The coughing jag subsided, and it hissed like a slow leaking tire. It was dying. Frank knew this. The woman with the red hair knew this. The cat knew this.

"Help him. Oh, please help him," she said.

But the cat wanted to die. It was ready. It needed to die. It shivered, breathing about seven hundred miles an hour for a while, followed by that long, low hissing leak that caught the attention of the lionesses out back when Frank took him out of the carrier.

At first, only the two lionesses closest to the back door noticed. They drew themselves upright and cleaned their shoulders, ears cocked. Then the others heard the familiar sound and one by one, stopped and went motionless.

Frank threw as much technical jargon as he could at the woman, trying to stall, anything, wishing the goddamn cat would finally just give up. After two minutes that seemed just a hair shorter than the last ice age, he tried to gently give the cat to the woman, saying slowly, "Why don't you hang onto him for a moment, and . . . well—it might be time to say goodbye."

But she couldn't say goodbye and wouldn't take the cat. She couldn't face the thought of losing her little man, and gripped the side of the table with her right hand, squeezing it hard enough Frank was worried that one of the purple veins across the back of her hand would rupture, filling the muscles and tendons with blood, slowly filling the skin until it resembled a pink Mickey Mouse glove. This cat was her life. It was that simple.

Frank started to place the cat as gingerly as he could on the table, but the woman shrieked, a short, sharp bark that escaped like a hummingbird out of her mouth. She clapped her left hand to her chin and shoved it down at her chest, held it there for the briefest moment, then plucked a towel out of the carrier and straightened it out on the table, so he wouldn't have to lay on the cold steel.

Frank put her cat on the towel and grabbed a sealed syringe and a 30 cc vial of Sleepazone. It looked like blue toilet bowl water and would stop the cat's heart instantly. The woman had her chin in her right hand before he said three words. She knew precisely what he was about to say and she wanted none of it. She demanded that Frank do something, anything to save her cat.

Admittedly, Frank didn't know much about common housecats. He had only really studied horses in school, but he knew that all the textbooks in the back room weren't going to help this cat. It was finished.

So Frank cradled the cat in his arms and talked to the cat and the woman in a low, calm voice. He talked about the cat's markings, the shape of the skull, splay of the claws, praising everything. The woman clasped her hands together, little trickles of tears mingling with black eyeliner and peach rouge rolling down the wrinkles in her face. The cat hyperventilated and leaked air.

It took nearly ten minutes, but the cat finally drifted into a sagging death in Frank's hands. And then the woman with the red hair really lost it. She backed away, skipping through the denial stage of death in about two or three eyelash flutters, and plowed right on into anger. A low, keening sound seeped out of her lungs as she tried to wrench the examining table out of the floor, dumped a roll of paper towels in the sink, and scooped a whole armload of vials onto the floor in a shattered mess.

Frank felt sorry for her. He really did. This cat was probably the only thing this woman had for a family, and now it was gone. As she crumpled on the table, cradling the cat, sobbing into the limp gray fur, Frank found himself listening seriously to a calm, reasonable voice inside that suggested just plunging a syringe full of Sleepazone into her ample backside. The medicine would hit her heart in less than a second, and it would be over. She'd sink to the floor, forever joining her cat in whatever heaven that allowed animals. At least then she'd be happy. No more sadness. No more death. Just an eternity together.

Frank actually broke the seal and had the syringe itself out before he realized that he didn't want to be responsible for another death. Killing her wasn't the best way to ease her suffering, although he'd be damned if he knew a better way. Instead, he found a small Styrofoam ice chest in the back, and together, they buried the cat out in the field of star thistles, near Annie's still smoking fire pit. It seemed to make the woman feel a little better, but Frank knew that once she got back to her empty house, the pain would be back with a vengeance, and again, he considered just gently easing her out of this world and into the next.

Before the idea really took hold, he urged her into her car, offering empty encouragement like, "He's in a better place now, and wouldn't want you to be sad," and "It's going to be okay. It really will get better." Both of them knew it was lies, but at least it got her moving. She drove away and Frank went inside for a beer.

The phone was ringing. It was Sturm. "How're my girls?"

"Better. They're moving around more, picking up on stuff. Eyes are clear. Stool looks good. So far, they seem to be responding quite well to the food."

"Good to hear, good to hear, 'cause come Saturday, I'm gonna need them to be, well—if not healthy, then active at least. We'll need four of 'em; one of 'em's gotta be the tiger. You think at least four of 'em'll be healthy? I want them to be able to run. Think they can run?"

"Saturday?"

"Yup. Got an old buddy coming into town. Known him for years. He's bringing some associate, and we're gonna have ourselves a good old-fashioned safari."

"Saturday then. I'll have four cats ready."

"Don't forget that tiger."

At night, Frank would sit in the office with Petunia, reading. At first, she would growl at him from her spot on the couch. But after two or three days, she let Frank sit on the couch with her and before long, she let him touch her back. Frank had lined the floor with newspaper, and replaced it every day. He kept the food and water dishes full and fresh. By Friday night, she was curling up on the couch next to him, throwing her shoulder into his thigh and sleeping as he read aloud about rabies vaccines and feline leukemia.

Annie never came by. Frank didn't know why. He didn't have her number. He wasn't even sure the Gloucks had a phone. Whenever he got the urge to drive on out to her house, he thought of the woman across the street at the gas station, and he couldn't face her again. Maybe he didn't do anything because he was afraid of that dead tree full of kids with BB guns.

To distract himself from waiting on Annie, he had been thinking about the vet office's role in the town. Found himself rearranging the vials of medicine on the stainless steel shelves in the examination room. Sweeping and mopping the floors. Thumbing through the clients' address book. Testing the radio. Writing down a proposal to spay and neuter the stray cats roaming the town. Lining up vials of vaccines for a rabies clinic.

Petunia squirmed and farted in his lap; she lay on her back, all four legs splayed against him and the couch, and it hit him like a bullet in the chest that he was dreaming. Here he was, squatting in one place like a goddamn elephant with constipation, when he was up close and personally responsible for the deaths of at least three men.

Closing the book softly, so as not to disturb Petunia, he knew he needed out of the country, out of this town, out of his skin. But the same problems were still there, waiting for him like a patient cat watching a mouse hole. He didn't know where to go. And wherever he went, the ten grand from Sturm would only last so long. He'd hidden the cash under the frozen meat in the freezer in back of the barn, just in case he had to get out in a hurry. He eased back into the couch, vinyl giving a squeaking sigh, grabbed the bottle of rum from the bookshelf, and unscrewed the cap with his thumb.

It tasted harsh and sweet and when he got to the bottom, he figured his problems could wait outside the door forever.

DAY SIXTEEN

Pine found him sprawled on the couch with Petunia in the morning. "Goddamn," he said. "You'll fuck anything."

Petunia growled at him.

Sturm had sent the clowns over to the vet hospital with a large horse trailer. Frank and Pine lined the inside with chicken wire, preparing it to haul the cats out to Sturm's ranch, listening to the monkeys chatter and screech at the two men. It took a while, mostly because the construction took a back seat to drinking beer.

Sturm pulled in, followed closely by a giant white SUV. The guy who got out of the driver's seat was big, as big as Sturm was short. He was near the end of his fifties, and looked like he might have been a football player in his day, but fat had grown off the muscles like a fungus and now everything kind of wilted off his large frame. He walked with a barely perceptible limp as if he was casually cheating at golf wherever he went. He looked like he'd swallowed about a gallon of red food coloring and tried to vomit it back up straight away, but it leaked out and soaked out through his face instead.

He shook Frank's hand with a hand big enough Frank thought the man might have been wearing a catcher's mitt. "Bob Bronson. How ya' doing."

It was like Castellari: Frank wasn't sure if the guy was asking a question or just stating a fact. Frank went with a generic,

125

"Good, good," but Bronson was already moving down the line, attacking the clowns' hands, beaming, saying, "Bob Bronson. Nice to meet ya," and "Bob Bronson. Good to see ya."

The other guy's name was Fairfax, and he might as well have been wearing a sign that said, "Lawyer." He wore clothing so new Frank wasn't surprised when he saw a long sticker on the back of his thigh, announcing to everyone that he wore a 54 waist, 28 length. His boots were so stiff that he winced whenever he took a step.

Sturm wanted to introduce the men to the cats, acting like a proud father showing off his infant daughter for the first time, so Frank walked everyone through a tour of the facilities, having fun with his new words and calculations. The real problem was administering the anesthesia to the animals. You couldn't just shoot them with tranquilizers every time.

"Why not?" Pine asked.

Frank didn't have an answer right away. He just felt it was kind of cruel to the cats, but he didn't want to give that as his real reason. "Lotta problems with that. You never know how much of the tranquilizer was administered for one. Two, there's always a strong risk of striking the animal in the bone, perhaps tearing cartilage. And if the subcutaneous tissue gets infected . . . well." He looked at all of them. "I think we all know what would happen then."

Everybody nodded sagely.

"Gentlemen," Sturm said, "I suggest we get this show on the road. My boy, Theo, will be hunting one of these fine animals this afternoon, and Jack and Chuck should be back by now. I've been promised that dinner will be served at eight o'clock sharp, and it's gonna be a goddamn treat, I'm telling you. I got just one word for you, just one word to start them taste buds." He sucked in a breath, looking around at the semi-circle of men. "Abalone."

"Algae?" Fairfax cocked his head.

"Abalone," Sturm said with uncharacteristic patience. "It's basically just a shellfish, spends its life on the same damn rock, just turning in a slow circle, eating algae and slime and shit. You've seen the shells, right? Lot of folks along the coast use 'em for decoration. But not many people have ever tasted abalone, and for good reason. Black market prices go for over ninety bucks a pound. Just wait 'til you taste it. I give them Japs credit. Nobody even thought about eating 'em here, but not them slant-eyed boys. They figured it out. You fellas just wait."

Sturm patted Theo's shoulder and said, "Now, you pick out which one you like. Look at their eyes," he murmured into his son's ear.

Theo took his time, walking slowly along the cages, letting his fingers trail along the chain-link fence. The cats watched him out of the corners of their eyes, tails flicking, acting disinterested. Theo stopped at the last cage, curling his fingers through the fence. The lioness inside, a large cat with tinges of black in her muzzle, growled low, almost inaudibly, and pressed her body against the warm cement, tail flicking back and forth. "This one," Theo breathed.

Sturm looked at Frank expectantly. Frank and Pine rolled the squeaking hand truck down the corridor, maneuvering the anesthetic tank closer. Frank handed the hose to Pine and cranked the two handles open. Pine held the plastic cup as close as he could to the lioness. All four heard the hiss of the gas emit from the end of the tube, but the lioness didn't move. The men at the far end stood still, trying not to breathe. After ten seconds, the tail flicking grew sluggish, and Frank saw the cat's muscles relax.

He opened the cage, moving slower than a watch's second hand. Pine turned his head away, pulled his "Bacon is a

Vegetable" T-shirt over his mouth, and tried to hold his breath. Frank crept inside, moving slow, slow. Pine started to work the plastic cup through the chain-link fence. Frank stopped, watching the cat carefully.

"Just fucking do it!" Theo yelled.

The cat flinched. Claws, nearly an inch long and sharper then a needle, erupted from its paws. Frank froze. The cat gradually relaxed. Frank moved forward, slowly, deliberately, took the cup from Pine, and gently placed it over the cat's nose and mouth. Soon, the cat's head rolled off to the side and before long, it was resting on the cement. Frank kept the cup over the muzzle, letting the cat breathe the anesthesia for a full two minutes, before he crouched down and injected Ace into the lioness's left back leg. The cat slumped even further, sinking deeper into the concrete. Frank removed the plastic cup and watched and waited. The cat continued to sleep.

He motioned to Jack and Theo and the three of them dragged the sleeping cat to the cage door. There, they lifted her onto a wooden dolly used for carrying heavy pallets of dog food back and forth along the cages. They wheeled the cat out the back door, across the overgrown lawn, to the waiting horse trailer. Once the cat was inside, sprawled awkwardly on a bedding of straw, Frank said, "She should be out, four, five hours at least. Give her another hour or two to wake up completely, and she'll be ready for a hunt."

"Perfect!" Sturm declared after checking his watch. "That'll be perfect. Goddamn. Couldn't of worked it out better myself." He shook Frank's hand vigorously. "Good timing. Perfect. Thank you for getting this hunt off to a splendid start."

"Yeah," Frank said.

"Okay then." He tuned to the clowns. "Don't know what the hell all you dipshits are standing around like slack-jawed morons. Snap to it. We got us a hunt to organize."

Frank wasn't sure what was left to organize, but he locked the back door to the vet office behind him, and jumped into Pine's truck. Everyone pulled out of the parking lot, slowly, slowly, as if it was a funeral procession instead of a hunt. Sturm led in his pickup, Bronson and Fairfax next, followed by Pine and Frank towing the horse trailer with the sleeping lioness. Chuck and Jack brought up the rear.

The convoy wound its way through town. Folks stopped whatever they were doing and stood at the edge of the highway, just watching the procession, as if they knew what was inside the horse trailer. The few people actually left in town proper all stepped out of their shops to witness the parade roll through downtown, watching the vehicles drive slowly away down the highway, shiny and sharp in the afternoon sun.

When they got to the Sturm ranch, Sturm drove right through his front lawn, through the pine trees that surrounded the lawn and the house, and out to the middle of the main field, a dry, dusty expanse that was ostensibly being prepared for next year, but it was obvious that the soil was quite dead. Pine and Frank parked, left the keys and the sleeping lion behind, and slowly walked back to the farmhouse, passing a bottle back and forth.

The hookers showed up at three. A little guy with a mustache big enough to demand its own hairdresser was driving. They all got out of a big blue minivan. The three women were short, lacquered, and all business.

"We pay you now?" Chuck demanded immediately, nervous and breathless, almost a threat.

The little guy shook his head, adjusted his razor-thin sunglasses. "No man. You pay the girls, you know, when you get down to it. Know what I'm saying?"

"Sure." Chuck nodded like he was an old hand at paying for sex.

The women didn't interest Frank. He tried, picturing them under him in bed, writhing and moaning, thought it was the right thing to do, to fit in with everyone else. But it was like trying to get fired up over a black and white picture of some old woman with tits as thin as wet mudflaps, hair growing out of her ears, and four teeth. Instead, he couldn't help thinking of Annie, back in town somewhere.

Maybe he should just take Petunia by the house. But Petunia had made it clear she didn't want to go anywhere. At the vet hospital, she had two, sometimes three solid meals a day, a cool place to sleep, and most important, someone who was always around to pet and talk to her. Frank knew getting Petunia into a vehicle and taking her home would be difficult. He hoped it wasn't because he was becoming fond of the damn dog. It was bad enough having a crush on the dog's owner.

Everyone gathered on the back deck, overlooking the wilting garden. Frank didn't stray too far from the keg, packed tightly in ice inside an oil barrel. But most everybody else stood in a tight circle around the women. The women all had tall glasses of Long Island Iced Tea, with straws and umbrellas and everything.

Sturm raised his beer. "Gentlemen . . . and ladies too," he said, leering up at the women, "a toast, if you please." Everyone raised their glasses. "First of all, my son."

Everyone drank. "Today is his first real hunt."

"Let's hope it goes better than his first fight," Chuck breathed to Frank and drank quickly.

Frank was more than happy to drink. He needed more, so he edged closer to the keg while Sturm rolled on. "Secondly, a toast to these fine, beautiful whores."

The men howled in appreciation while the women smiled

thinly and raised their glasses. Shockingly red lips found their straws and they drank quickly, sucking up the last drops. Theo fell over himself to refill their glasses. "That's right, goddamnit, that's right," Sturm continued, determined to ride the wave of their adulation. "And to our guests," he jabbed his finger at Bronson and Fairfax.

"And finally," Sturm said, quieter now, taking a seat on the railing. "To the prey." He fell quiet for a moment, letting it sink in. "We are men. We are men, last of a dying breed in a world that has failed to recognize man's need for instinct, for cunning, for . . . sharp teeth. We are true men. We are men that exist to hunt." He raised his glass. "To the prey . . . for without them, we are nothing."

"To the prey," the men echoed in voices that were swallowed by the wind, raised their glasses, and drank.

They gathered their guns. Rifles mostly, but a couple of shotguns could be seen. They headed out across the field in a wide line, eyes on the truck and horse trailer. The sun threw their shadows behind them, thin and impossibly long, like scarecrows marching across the field, eyes sparkling like their cars in the sun.

Sturm came riding out in an Army surplus open jeep. Theo was driving fast, and threw up a cloud of dust that hung in the late evening air like a blood red fog. Theo stood up in the driver's seat and rested his rifle—a thin, ancient lever-action rifle—on the windshield. It was a .405 Winchester and Theo's namesake had called this particular caliber "lion medicine."

The men clustered in a ragged semi-circle, all eyes on the trailer.

When Theo signaled that he was ready, Pine threw the bolt with a quick jerk and Frank yanked on the rope tied to the gate. But nothing happened as the gate swung wide in the swirling crimson dust. Theo fired anyway. The .400 Nitro Express shell sent the solid copper bullet ricocheting off the bolt at the top of the gate, splitting it wide open. The gate tilted wildly as it crashed into the dirt.

The recoil put Theo in the back seat of the Jeep.

A short laugh burst out of Chuck, but a sharp look from Sturm killed the rest in Chuck's throat.

Pine, the poor bastard that had had to open the gate, didn't think it was funny either, though for different reasons. The falling gate had nearly snapped his wrist, twisting his entire body sideways, and leaving him in the dirt. At first, he'd thought it was the lioness, busting out of the trailer and landing on the gate. But when he picked himself up and danced around trying to look everywhere at once, he finally saw the lioness, still crouched inside the horse trailer. Then he got pissed. "What . . . the fuck I'm gonna sonofabitch me that goddamn time it never happened mother-stumping fuck," he blurted in a machine-gun fire of hoarse words and came stomping up to the Jeep. "That was goddamn close."

"Settle down," Sturm said. "Bullet missed you by three, four feet."

Theo got out of the Jeep, ignoring his father and Pine, stalking the lioness. Everybody else took that as their cue; safeties were snapped off, bolts were thrown and locked, sweaty fingers caressed trigger guards. Theo slowly and methodically put each step in front of the other, as if he was creeping up on some strange house for a game of Ding Dong Ditch, and approached the back of the horse trailer in exaggerated slowness, rifle held straight up in front of him.

By now Sturm and Pine had stopped arguing, and were both hastily getting their own guns ready. Sturm carried a Ballard single-shot High Wall 1885 reproduction rifle, while Pine had his father's M-1 Garand.

Theo froze when he saw the lioness, still coiled in the back of the trailer, dry and dusty and frozen in place like the great Sphinx. Theo straightened, gently but firmly tucking the butt of his rifle into his shoulder, and waited. The lioness didn't move. Theo kept waiting, still as a stop sign at high noon. The dust sifted and fell over everything, leaching out of the air and onto any available surface. Theo coughed. The lioness only moved her eyes, watching the boy.

Theo coughed again and spit. Then he shot the lioness in her lower jaw. The big cat slammed into the wall, hind legs kicking in agony.

The Winchester's kick knocked Theo back a few steps, but he stayed on his feet.

The lioness wouldn't stop shaking her head, as if she could shake off the beast that had torn her dangling jaw loose.

"Finish her off this next time, okay?" Sturm said through lips drawn thin and tight.

It took Theo four more rounds to kill the lioness. He missed just once.

Blood collected in the horse shit at the bottom of the trailer and slid down the inclined floor, dripping out and collecting in a small puddle in the sandy soil. Theo walked back to the Jeep. Everyone climbed in and Pine started the truck. He drove back to the barn, following the Jeep.

They gutted the lioness and hung her upside down on a beam in the shade on the north side of the barn.

As promised, the abalone was served promptly at eight. The dinner was quite different than the town's potluck. A long table was brought out to the deck and draped with a white linen tablecloth. Genuine silver utensils flanked antique pewter plates. Candles were lit. The abalone, pounded flat, then breaded and fried, was served with pasta and sautéed tomatoes and green peppers. Pungent garlic bread completed the meal. The men left their beers on the deck railing and drank chilled white wine with dinner.

The sun finally sank behind Mount Shasta, cooling the temperature somewhat, but it was still like sitting in an oven that had just been turned off. There was no wind.

"Gentlemen," Bronson stood after eating five abalone and raised a toast to Sturm. "That was about as fine a meal as I've had in a long time." He pushed himself away from the table. "But . . . if you'll excuse me. Believe I've got some urgent business that needs my attention upstairs."

And with that, he escorted all three women into the house.

"He gets all three at once?" Chuck asked under his breath.

"Can you pay for all three at once?" Pine asked. "Then there ya go. Quit your bitching. You'll get your turn."

Cards were brought out. Cigars were lit from the candles. Frank was happy to sit back and watch. He didn't have any cash on him, and card games moved too fast for him. He couldn't count the diamonds or spades and with Jack dealing, he didn't stand much hope of winning anyways. Besides, he had a plastic two-liter bottle of Coke mostly full of cheap dark rum that needed his attention.

Fairfax walked around barefoot in the cool grass, giving his feet a break from the new cowboy boots.

Sturm folded his arms across his chest and pursed his lips at the card players. "This ain't gambling. This is luck. Gambling should hinge on skill, stamina, knowledge in some competitive test or challenge. Not random chance."

"Aw, you're just sore 'cause you got beat bad last time," Pine blurted. He'd drank his way through a twelve pack. Out in the yard, Fairfax laughed, a quick little hiccup, but everyone else froze, watching the table.

Sturm snorted, then finally chuckled. "Shit. You might be right."

The pimp with the mustache lasted five hands. Disgusted, he grabbed a drink and sat next to Frank. By that time, Bronson had come downstairs, face even redder than usual, grinning from ear to ear. "Whoooo-weeeee. I'm telling you, every one of them sweet young things could suck the chrome off a trailer hitch if you paid her enough. Deal me in, boys."

By eleven, the table was littered with cash, cigars, beer cans, empty wine bottles, and tumblers full of ice and whiskey and tequila and bourbon. Bronson carried a bottle of some kind of Scotch that no one had ever heard of. He gave each of the men a splash but kept the rest of the bottle to himself.

The pimp was telling Frank about the screenplay he was working on. "It's gonna be awesome, right? You ever see 'The Mack'?" Frank had seen a total of fourteen or fifteen movies in his life. "The Mack" wasn't one of them. "No? It's okay. Doesn't matter. See, it's about this fucking badass player, man, who has the baddest, finest women. Ten of 'em, you know what I'm saying? They're hoes, right, but get this, they're also these ultra-deadly assassins too, you know what I'm saying? Fucking international assassins, man. All over the world. Fucking and killing men. It's got that whole sex and death thing going on. The girls, they fuck the boys, then, then the kicker is that, they kill 'em, man, they slay 'em. With guns and knives and shit. The money guys like that. I've already got a guy in Vegas ready to hook me up with a producer. It's gonna be fucking awesome, with fucking explosions and shit, man, fucking sword fighting too, you know what I'm saying, man? And hard-core sex too, man. Gonna fucking go through the roof, you know what I'm saying?" He ambled over to the table. "You guys got any wine coolers?"

"I'm gonna pretend I didn't hear that," Pine said.

Sturm asked Frank, "Feel like taking a tumble in the sheets? It's on me. Theo's up there right now."

Frank said, "Maybe later."

Sturm clapped him on the shoulder. "You take your time. Enjoy yourself. You earned it, by God." He looked up at the dark windows. "Shit. I'd be up there myself, but this goddamn cancer, it's like God squeezed out a big old turd and left it in my head. Fucks with my equipment. Makes me wonder sometimes if you can still be a man even if you can't get your dick up." He suddenly cracked himself viciously in the temple with his knuckles. "Maybe I oughta get myself one of them Viagras." He considered it for a moment, then said, "Piss on it," and went through the sliding glass doors into the kitchen.

"Hey, Frank. Frank, right?" Bronson called out. He emptied the last few drops of Scotch into his tumbler. "Frank . . . Frank Buck. That's it. Mr. Frank 'Bring 'Em Back Alive' Buck. How's the jungle these days? How's the animal business? Them cats, they're something all right, when you're right up close. Sturm wasn't shitting me. It's not like watching 'em on TV, that's for sure. These cats, take your face clean off. Just clean off. Of course," Bronson said with a sly smile, "I certainly hope they put up more of a fight tomorrow."

"Maybe even make it out of the trailer," Fairfax said.

Theo came downstairs and was hailed with a drunken cheer. He ignored the men and stomped down the stairs into the darkness toward the barn and back fields.

"Well. Doesn't appear to be his night," Bronson said quietly.

"Shit, it ain't his year," Pine said, just as quiet.

"Wonder if he got the chrome sucked off his trailer hitch!" Fairfax said, a little too drunk, a little too loud.

"You got something you want to say?" Sturm said from behind the screen door, silhouetted from the kitchen lights.

Fairfax looked like he'd just swallowed an entire abalone, raw. "Ahhh, no disrespect intended, see, ahh, just having a little fun with the boys—"

"What? Don't know if I heard you rightly. No disrespect intended, but you think you can have a little fun with the boys at my boy's expense, is that it?"

Fairfax looked at Bronson, eyes wide and pleading, but Bronson just grinned and looked at the table.

In the sudden silence, they heard one of the hooker's voices, low and scratchy from too many cigarettes, "—little fucker. Not my fault he came in his pants. I tried to be nice. I did."

"Keep it down." The pimp's voice.

"Fuck you, pussy. You're supposed to be here to keep an eye on things. Make sure shit like this don't happen. Little fucker didn't have to hit me." The scratching click of a lighter, then a long exhale. "Rich little fucker."

Suddenly Sturm wasn't standing at the screen door anymore. The men heard his voice, clear as daylight. "Miss. I'm gonna ask you once. Put that cigarette out. No one smokes in this house. I mean it."

"I don't know who the fuck you think you are, you little freak, but I will not be treated like—" Her voice broke off suddenly in a faint crunch. And just as suddenly, it was back, twice as loud, "BATHTARD! You—"

Then a thud. A scream. Slamming doors. Sturm's voice, calm, even. "Get this stupid cunt out of my house."

A hooker came sliding into the kitchen on her face. Her mouth left ragged streaks of blood and fresh purple lipstick on the floor. Sturm followed, knotted her long, plastic, blond hair in his fist, and yanked her to her knees.

The pimp said, "Back the fuck off, dude. I *will* fuckin' kill you."

Sturm slammed the hooker's face into one of the cabinets.

"Do it then."

The pimp didn't look happy about it. He licked the sides of his mustache and mumbled, "Shit man. Now why did you do that for?"

Sturm did it again. The woman moaned, blood bubbling from her nose. "You got shit in your ears, faggot?"

The pimp took off his sunglasses, made a show of putting them in his pocket.

Sturm slammed her head into the cabinet a third time, this time cracking the wood.

The pimp popped his right foot at Sturm's chest in the blink of an eye, but Sturm was faster. He swung the hooker in front of him and so the pimp kicked her in the side of her head. The pimp resettled himself, and was just about to launch a series of kicks and punches that must have looked impressive in the gym, but Sturm broke the pimp's nose with his free hand. The pimp's head snapped back and blood actually hit the ceiling.

"Like I said, get this stupid cunt out of my house."

The two other hookers, who had been hiding in the hall, finally came into the kitchen, helped the pimp to his feet, and dragged the unconscious woman out the front door.

"You set foot in this town again and I guarantee you I will put a bullet in you," Sturm said from the front steps. The two hookers dumped their business associates in the back seat and were smart enough not to say anything, just slammed the doors. The minivan took off with a jerk and a cloud of dust and gravel. They didn't even turn on the headlights until they were safely down the long driveway.

Sturm pulled Frank aside. "Listen, do me a favor, would you? Would you go out and find my son, make sure he's okay? Maybe even talk to him. I'd ask one of the boys, but I think Theo's been through enough tonight. They're liable to give him a hard time, and you, well, I think you got enough sense to realize . . . well, hell he's at that age, you know. Don't want to listen to anybody, really, much less his father."

"Sure." Frank went down the stairs and stood at the far edge of the garden for a few moments, letting his eyes adjust to the darkness. A few minutes ago, his head had been swimming merrily along thanks to the fifth of rum. But now, standing out in the dark under enough stars to make a man go mad, he suddenly felt uncomfortably sober. His sweat felt cold and he shivered. The crickets were quiet. Even the mosquitoes had holed up for the night.

Truth was, he was scared. He didn't think he'd been this nervous since he'd had to talk to the cops outside the gas station. Theo was one goddamn cruel bastard. At least, with the clowns, you could see it coming if they lost their temper. With Sturm's son, you never knew what the hell he was thinking. Frank wouldn't put it past him to fling a pitchfork or something just because he didn't want to be bothered.

So Frank took his time and moved as quietly as he could. The barn loomed in front of him, dark as a tomb. He stepped inside the open door, skin on his neck crawling as he realized he must be silhouetted against the lights of the house. Once inside, he could hear nothing but Sarah contentedly chewing on hay.

He crept along the aisle, eyes straining in the palpable blackness. The fear grew. He couldn't help but wonder if Theo was watching him, stalking him. A tiny spot on his back, right between his shoulder blades, grew hot and tight, as if there was a laser sight pointed right at him. He whipped around, but the aisle was empty.

The horse stopped chewing and watched him warily for a moment.

In the sudden silence, Frank could hear something else. From out back. Out behind the barn. Where they had left the lion. A hushed grunt. Then, hissed between clenched teeth, "See? See? I told you, you bitch. I told you."

Frank swallowed. Sarah put her head down and tore off another mouthful of alfalfa. Frank moved to the far end of the barn, gently easing his boots through the dust. The hoarse grunts continued. "You. You. You."

Frank peered through a crack in the sliding door. Out in the grass, under the stars, Theo had his jeans down around his knees and was hunched over the back of the dead lion, fucking it. His white ass pummeled lion, making the big cat's corpse shudder with each thrust. "You. You. You." Theo said every time he slammed into the lion.

Frank had seen enough. He'd seen more than enough. He doubted that all the rum in Jamaica would erase the image. He tried not to run back to the house, acutely aware that if Theo knew he'd been seen, he'd probably kill whoever was watching him. When Frank got back to the garden, he forced himself to stop for a moment, collect himself, slow his heart, watch his breathing. He went back up on the deck, got himself a beer, and told Sturm he couldn't find Theo.

DAY SEVENTEEN

Frank dosed half a pound of ground lamb with Acepromazine and fed it to two more cats and the tiger early in the morning. They loaded the first of the lionesses and hauled her back to the ranch.

This time, it was Fairfax's turn. He'd managed to squeeze back into his new clothes. By now, everyone knew his boots hurt like hell. Pine stationed himself by the horse trailer, while Chuck was a good twenty yards away at the pickup, and they had some fun calling him back and forth, asking Fairfax to watch the lioness for a moment, then calling him back over to the pickup to ask him what kind of caliber he thought was the best. Fairfax never did figure it out. He just thought they were being nice to him because it was his turn, and so he just kept hobbling around.

Like before, Frank and Pine opened the gate and swung it back around while everyone else waited with their rifles back by the pickups. No one was ready. Everybody expected the lioness to simply sit there, like with Theo. But with a streak of tan fur, the lioness erupted from the trailer and was simply gone, as if the cat was bending the light somehow, slipping through the morning sunlight in a hazy mirage.

It leaped over the barbed wire fence and was halfway to the house before Fairfax had even gotten his eye through a scope. As soon as he caught a glimpse of the animal, he fired, jerking repeatedly on the trigger of the semi-auto like he was scratching

141

a nasty itch. But it was like trying to shoot a bumblebee out of your yard with a slingshot.

Bullets exploded into the back of Sturm's house, spiraling through wood siding, concrete, glass. Sturm shouted into the gunfire, but Fairfax either wouldn't stop or couldn't hear. Finally, Chuck and Sturm jerked up their rifles and fired. The lioness went down in the garden. The gunfire died.

"I got it! I got it!" Fairfax screamed.

"You didn't shoot shit, dickhead," Pine said. "Fuck, it'd be halfway to Idaho by now if it was up to you."

"What the hell is the matter with you?" Sturm ripped the rifle out of Fairfax's pudgy hands. "You. Stupid. Goddamn. Asshole. You're paying for all that damage, so help me God."

Fairfax stood stock still, mouth open, realization sinking in like concrete in his veins. He licked his lips a few times, but nothing came out.

Sturm glared at him. "You fucking stupid, or do you just not give a shit?"

"I . . . I . . . oh, good Lord."

The men tried to hold it in, but snorts of laughter escaped anyway, sounding like they were trying to suck snot from somewhere up near their brain. Sturm growled through his teeth, whirled, and flung the rifle as far as he could into the field. Frank figured Fairfax was lucky Sturm didn't just shoot him. Without another word, Sturm climbed into the Jeep. Theo started it up and everyone followed it back to the house.

They found Sturm on his knees in the dog pen, a little enclosure wrapped in chicken wire, set off in the back of the yard. Frank hadn't realized that Sturm even had a dog until he saw Sturm cradling the black lab's head. Frank immediately saw how a bullet had torn through the dog's guts lengthwise. Bluish gray intestines had spilled out in a wash of blood on the concrete.

The dog was still alive, breathing in low, keening sounds.

Sturm stood up, pinching at the bridge of his nose. He yanked his rifle out of the Jeep, shoved it up into Fairfax's chest, eyes searing holes in the lawyer's skull like a kid burning ants with a magnifying glass. "This is your doing. Now you finish the job, you sonofabitch."

Fairfax's fingers clasped the rifle against his will, but he knew better than to protest. He looked like he wanted to throw up. He stumbled over to the dog pen, put the barrel against the dog's head, just in front of the soft ear, closed his eyes, and pulled the trigger. Afterward, he couldn't move, just stood there with his head down, shoulders hitching once in a while. Bob Bronson went inside and pretended he didn't know him.

Sturm hurled a shovel at the pen as hard as he could. It hit the chicken wire behind Fairfax with a clang and he flinched. "You show my dog some respect and bury her deep out in the corner of the yard, over by the corn. Deep! You hear me, you fucking dumbshit? It best be deep, by God, or so help me, I'll shoot you myself." He turned back to the men. They were silent, subdued, respectful.

Sturm said, "Let's go hunt us a tiger."

When they got back to the vet hospital, the tiger looked like it was still unconscious. Still, nobody was in a rush to jump into the stall and find out. Instead, Chuck and Pine produced an oil barrel filled with ice and a beer bottles in the back of Chuck's truck. Frank gladly accepted a beer. It was ice cold and tasted almost sweet. A few minutes later, a few bottles of Jack Daniels got passed around. Frank filled his flask and passed the bottle on.

When the tiger hadn't moved in over twenty minutes, they picked it up by its paws. Nobody knew if it was male or female, nobody'd gotten brave enough to look close. They carried all six hundred pounds of cat out to the horse trailer.

Sturm had given Bronson the honor of hunting the tiger. But this time, he wanted to make sure that it was more of a real hunt and less like shooting fish in a barrel. So this time they went farther out, out in the foothills at the edge of Sturm's property, to a dry creek bed cut from the hill by winter storms. Over the last hundred years, the creek had wandered back and forth with impunity across the five miles of level valley floor. Where they had parked the trailer, the creek was nearly twenty yards across, filled with dead creek grass, brittle and draped close over rocks as if the grass remembered when water ran over the gravel underbelly of the creek. Now, in the brutal summer heat, the gravel was covered in a chalky white crust, burnt in the sun.

Farther up, the creek's banks rose sharply into loose, sandy soil, shrinking to only a fifteen-foot width. Pine backed the trailer up to where the creek narrowed, tires crunching on the white rocks.

Inside the trailer, the tiger didn't make a sound. Frank got scared that the Ace had done something permanent, and once Pine turned off the engine, he got out and peered through the slats. But the tiger was awake, and watching him back. It growled low, then suddenly sprang, snarling and ripping at the chicken wire.

Everyone except Fairfax, who was back at the house burying the dog, gathered at the back of the trailer. Sturm took a stick and drew a map in a sandy stretch; it looked like a long, S-shaped crude drawing of the esophagus, stomach, and large intestine.

Sturm told Bronson, "We'll drop you at this end here, up a ways, where the creek widens out." He jabbed at what would have been the stomach in the drawing with his stick. "That's where you wait. Then Pine and Frank'll release the tiger and send it your way. We'll be spread out up along the edge on top, just in case, but hell, in that narrow stretch, the bank's at least fifteen, twenty feet high. That tiger, he'll stick to the shadows in the ravine. He'll end up right in your lap. You just be ready, right?"

Bronson slapped the butt of his rifle and grinned. "Shit. That tiger won't know what hit it. Hope you're hungry, boys. That abalone was damn fine, but we got tiger on the menu tonight." He licked his teeth. "And if it's a male, then by God, I'm gonna eat the penis. Fella in Chinatown claims it'll turn you into a goddamn sex machine."

"Suppose the tiger doesn't head farther into the creek," Frank said. "Suppose it decides to head the other way. What then?"

Sturm mulled that over. Frank could see he wanted to dismiss that possibility, but after the last two hunts, he'd realized these goddamn big cats were unpredictable, to say the least. "Shit." He nodded. "Shit."

"Looks like we need a dog is all," Bronson said. "Tell you what. Frank here, he's the expert, why don't you drive the tiger up in there."

"What do you suggest I use? Foul language?"

Sturm snapped his fingers. "Rock salt." He went to the Jeep and started digging around in the tool box. "Get your shotgun." Frank's Winchester was resting in the gun rack of the pickup along with Pine's M-1. Sturm held up a fistful of .12 gauge shells. "Loaded these last year, after I caught a couple of them fucking Gloucks on my property. Just rock salt. Won't kill anything bigger'n a squirrel, but it'll sure sting like a sonofabitch."

"There we go. Problem solved," Bronson said.

"Yeah," Frank said, pumping the shotgun, spitting out the lethal shells. He didn't sound convinced. He put the shells in his shirt pockets, just in case, and reloaded the shotgun with the new loads.

Sturm handed Pine a walkie-talkie. "When we get in place, you let it loose. But not before I tell you, got it?" Everybody piled in the Jeep. Sturm drove this time.

Pine said, "Well. Don't that suck donkey dick."

"Yeah." Frank took a gulp from his flask and passed it to Pine. In this kind of sun, he'd found that an ice cold glass of fresh-squeezed orange juice with two fifths of Appleton Estate Jamaican Rum was better than just about anything. But today the raw Jack Daniels worked damn near as well. They crouched in the sliver of shade of the horse trailer and passed the flask back and forth for a while, not saying much.

The walkie-talkie beeped. "Let her rip."

Pine wouldn't look at Frank. "Good luck."

Frank checked for about the hundredth time that the safety was off and there was a fresh shell in the chamber. He backed slowly away, dull black shotgun heavy and slick in his sweaty fingers. Inside the trailer, the tiger was quiet as death.

Pine sidled along the trailer. Once there, he nodded at Frank, then kicked open the bottom gate, ripped the duct tape away from the top hinge, and let the gate fall open. He dropped to his stomach and wriggled backward under the trailer. Frank raised the shotgun.

The tiger exploded from the back of the trailer and went for him.

Frank aimed low, tracking the blur of black, orange, and white, and when the tiger was fifteen feet away, he fired. The blast sent a spray of stinging salt and sand up into the tiger's face. The cat immediately threw itself sideways, hissing and spitting. Frank felt sorry for the creature as it glared at him for a moment, seemed to consider trying for him again, then ran off, deeper into the creek, toward Bronson.

"That was goddamn close and I ain't shitting you at all," Pine hollered from under the trailer.

"Yeah," Frank said.

The walkie-talkie beeped again. "Tell Frank to make sure that tiger keeps going. Don't want it laying low in some bushes, got it?"

Frank jacked a new shell into the chamber and started across the white rocks, slowly following the tiger. The cliffs on either side grew taller and closed in. The shadows grew deeper, darker. White chalky crust gave way to damp sand and slippery, slick green algae, down where the sun never hit. Stiff, brittle bushes began to choke the creek bed. Frank clutched the shotgun, trying to look everywhere at once, watching for the tiger and Bronson. He didn't want to get eaten, but he sure as hell didn't want to get shot either.

When he reached the spot where the creek widened, he stopped, then crouched low, wedging himself into a tangle of bushes draped with dried moss and dead tree limbs. His eyes flickered back and forth, searching for movement. The wide spot, maybe twenty yards across, had been bisected with a rotting pine tree, a victim of the surging waters. The soil around the roots had washed away, and some years earlier it had toppled over into the creek. Now it was lying at a downward angle across a stretch of flat, smooth stones. Thick bushes dotted the crumbling cliffs. He couldn't see the tiger anywhere. He glanced up at the top of the cliffs, but couldn't see Sturm or Chuck or Pine or anybody else.

Thirty yards away, at the far end, Bronson clomped into view, his head just a turnip jammed into the shoulders of a safari jacket. The man couldn't sneak up on Sturm's dead Lab. When he reached the log, he straddled it and rested, wiping the sweat from his brow. At first, he held his rifle ready, slowly swiveling his head back and forth, scanning for the tiger. But as the minutes ticked by, Frank watched the man's patience erode like the dirt under the pine tree. Bronson set the rifle next to him and lit a cigar.

As Bronson exhaled the first plume of blue smoke, Frank saw the tiger. It had somehow materialized out of the bushes under the pine tree, up near the bank, and was now creeping down the rotting log toward Bronson; an undulating orange and black caterpillar, inching through the jutting, jagged branches with infinite patience.

Frank watched, frozen with fascination. Somewhere, way back in the dim shadows of his conscience, he knew he should shoot, shout, something. But he couldn't bring himself to move, because that voice, the same voice that urged him to put the red-haired woman out of her grief and misery, was now whispering, in biting, chopping words, that Bronson deserved whatever happened.

A half second later, it was too late for Frank to do anything anyway. The tiger, fifteen feet from Bronson, launched itself down the log and hit him like a locomotive going off a cliff. The force knocked Bronson flat, slamming him onto the smooth rocks; an instant later, the massive teeth crunched together at the back of Bronson's neck. His limbs flopped and shuddered, then wilted and lay still in an awkward pose that could never be achieved in life.

The tiger lifted its head and stared through the underbrush, locking eyes with Frank. It knew he had been there the entire time. It bent back to Bronson's body, clamped down on his left shoulder, and dragged him under the log, shaking the man's body like a German Shepherd breaking a rabbit's neck.

Frank let the tiger eat for a while. He figured the tiger deserved a taste of its kill. But he knew that Sturm and the others would be wondering what the hell had happened, and he sure as shit didn't want to be answering some tough questions. So he stood, taking his time, letting the tiger watch him, then fired, aiming at the rocks near Bronson's feet. Like before, the blast sent stinging flecks of salt and rocks up toward the tiger. It wriggled backward, leaped onto the log, and shot up it. When the tiger hit the top, it leaped, easily clearing the snarled mass of roots. It landed effortlessly in the dry grass at the top of the cliff and disappeared.

Frank pumped and fired again, this time at the cliff, just for the men listening. He ran across the gravel and climbed up the pine log, following the tiger as best as he could. He was halfway up when gunfire exploded into the pale sky. By the time he'd managed to work his way through the mess of roots, the Jeep was waiting for him.

"Where's Bronson?" Sturm demanded from the passenger seat.

Frank shook his head.

"Shit. Shit!" Sturm slapped the dash. By now, the tiger was just a speck, moving fast in an easy, loping run through Sturm's ranch. "C'mon!" he shouted at Frank. "Into the Jeep! Go! Go!" Frank scrambled up the loose sand and hopped in the Jeep with everyone else. Theo popped the clutch and roared off, following the edge of the creek, mimicking the twisting and cutbacks of the gash in the land with uncanny skill. Everyone just tried to hang on.

Theo roared across the field, through the backyard, passing a sweating, trembling Fairfax. He stood in a hole up to his waist, watching the Jeep with an open mouth. They hit the front yard and the long driveway and kept going, but it was too late. The tiger had slipped away. Theo kept going, tearing down the road.

In the distance, Frank recognized the giant satellite dish of the Gloucks' and the little gas station where he had first stopped and realized they were almost in town.

"Shit!" Theo said and slapped the steering wheel, imitating his father.

"Watch your language," Sturm said. "We'll get it. Everyone keep their eyes peeled. Can't be far."

Frank was wondering, if you were mayor, how you would explain losing a goddamn tiger in the middle of town after you intentionally set it loose, when he saw the big cat casually lope across the highway and slip into the Gloucks' backyard.

Pine saw it too. "There!" he shouted, pointing. Theo made the Jeep stand up and dance, shooting straight across the field, plowing straight through the tumbleweeds and starthistles. Frank had one moment take on a crystalline quality, frozen into eternity, as if he was outside himself, watching a still photograph as they burst through the aluminum gate. The metal popped with a surprised twang and the Jeep shot across the soft asphalt of the gas station. He caught a glimpse of the woman with the red hair behind the counter staring at the Jeep with an open mouth. Her expression was somewhere between terror and ecstasy.

Frank grinned as he realized that the hunters had just made the woman's day. Hell, seeing the Jeep tear across the valley, chock full of men and guns, chasing after a genuine tiger, that probably gave her enough fodder for an entire month's, maybe even a whole year's, worth of gossip.

They raced down the alley behind the Gloucks' house, but couldn't see anything. Behind them, the dead tree stood empty and abandoned, like a playground jungle gym after recess. The tiger must have been still running, still moving fast. Sturm sat rigid in the passenger seat, rifle upright at his left side. His right hand floated in the air, flicking in subtle, minute directions. Theo followed his father's gestures, making the Jeep gallop down narrow alleyways, sliding through intersections, following a striped shadow that flitted through the empty yards and barren streets.

The chase was eerily quiet. No one in the Jeep actually heard the engine or the squealing tires. They focused only on the breathing of the animal, watching it as close as they could through binoculars or their scopes, those hypnotizing stripes pulsing in and out.

The tiger bounded out into the afternoon sunlight and wide pavement of First Street. It stuttered to a stop, as if confused by the vast open space. It turned south, loped down the sidewalk in the shade, and paused a moment, slinking into the recessed entrance to the First Bank of Whitewood.

Theo hit the brakes with both feet and the Jeep slid to a stop in a squeal of burning rubber in the middle of Main Street. Sturm hopped out, ran low across the street, and crouched between two parked cars. Sturm held the Ballard single-shot tight across his chest, ready to snap it into his shoulder, hunting a real goddamn tiger through his hometown.

He rose and scurried across the intersection, moving northeast, and crouched behind the yellow *Sacramento Bee* newspaper box and the northwestern light post.

When the tiger saw Sturm, it was already too late. The tiger hissed, a low, awful sound, and bolted out of the entrance, instantly going down on its chest and stomach, tail falling limp when it hit the sunlight, as if it had given up. But instead of freezing and surrendering, the cat collected itself, drawing the legs in, getting down, suddenly springing forward, not fleeing anymore, but attacking, launching itself straight at Sturm.

Sturm was ready. He pulled the rifle in snug, tracking the cat for a half second. The tiger crossed the street in an eyeblink. Sturm exhaled, squeezed the trigger gently, and put a single

151

bullet through the tiger's chest.

It went down, rolling over itself and flopping to a stop in front of the post office. Sturm jacked the empty cartridge out into the gutter, slammed a new one into place. He watched the cat intently for nearly a full minute before he straightened, resting the rifle across the back of his shoulders. He turned back to the Jeep, a huge grin splitting the dark shadows under his cowboy hat, not much taller than the newspaper box next to him. "You boys get that BBQ fired up soon as possible. We got a tiger to grill."

And then it was all over, except for the picture taking.

They arranged the tiger in the middle of Main Street, laid along the middle of the street, facing east as if following the double yellow lines, rifles crossed over the striped orange and black back in an X of firepower. Sturm kneeled on one side, hand on the tiger's head between the ears, Theo on the other side. The clowns stood behind them, with more rifles resting on hips and shoulders, post office and bank off to the right, and the park off to the left.

Frank volunteered to take the picture, but Sturm insisted Frank needed to be right up front. "Hell, wasn't for you, we wouldn't be here."

They got the taxidermist to take the picture. He'd walked out of his storefront, arms already loaded with supplies. Apparently, he'd been watching the final moments of the hunt. He was an old guy, with long white hair, wearing clean overalls and a starched white shirt so stiff he probably just propped it in a corner at night. It was buttoned straight up to the top button at the neck, heat be damned. He had a beard and if anything, it was whiter than the shirt, just so wiry and twisted you'd think it was pubic hair.

First he propped a wedge of Styrofoam under the tiger's

chin, lifting the head so it looked as if the tiger was looking into the camera lens. Then he slid a few wooden matchsticks into the mouth, opening it slightly. A couple balls of sticky tar anchored the lips above the canines in a listless snarl.

"Say cheese," he said, his voice high and quivering, like the sound a handsaw makes when you hit it with a hammer. Everybody put on their best hunting face, as if they wanted to smile, but the business at hand was just too goddamn serious. The taxidermist snapped off three quick pictures and said, "Congratulations."

"Outstanding," Sturm said.

Chuck and Pine went to fetch Chuck's truck, parked at the fairgrounds.

Sturm stood over the tiger, cowboy hat throwing his face into shadow. He said to the taxidermist, "Let's butcher this old boy, I'm looking forward to tiger steaks, all right. But let's save the hide, them teeth too. Hell, I want the whole skull intact, if possible."

"Would you like the head preserved, so it can be hung upon a wall?" The taxidermist inquired politely, as if he was asking how Sturm wanted his shirts ironed. "Or I can leave the head connected . . . make a mighty fine rug."

Sturm shook his head. "No. I want the hide preserved, yes. But what I really want is just the skull, with the teeth intact, mind you, so I can keep it on my desk. No hide, no nothing. Just teeth and bone."

The taxidermist nodded and Frank was afraid that the beard might create sparks when it hit the starched shirt. The man said, "Of course. The teeth shall remain within the skull. I'll wire the jaw shut, and yes, you will have a very nice desk ornament."

Frank and Sturm dragged the tiger over to the Jeep. It took all four of them, Frank, Sturm, Theo, and the taxidermist, to manage to lift the cat up onto the back of the Jeep. They tied a rope to the back legs and anchored them to the roll bar, so the animal was nearly upside down, with the head and neck draped over the side. Sturm let Theo slit the animal's throat. Frank was glad they were taking care of the tiger right away; he didn't want Theo getting at this one out back behind the barn.

The blood was collected in a five-gallon bucket. When the blood slowed to a couple of drips a minute, Sturm lifted the nearly full bucket with difficulty, and spilled some over the side as he dragged it back from under the tiger's head. Using a rubber mallet, he pounded a plastic lid onto the bucket, and lifted it into the Jeep.

The taxidermist went to work. He pulled out a two-inch folding knife and slit the tiger's skin, from the direct center of the gaping throat wound down between the back legs to the anus without spilling any of the intestines. Some blood got into the fur, but not much, Frank noted with professional interest. Everything was still held inside, inside a wet sack wrapped in white webbing. The taxidermist gracefully sliced around the tiger's penis and lifted the bottom half of the entire sagging sack out of the animal. After another couple of drags of the knife up inside, he eased the whole sack out and dumped it into another bucket. Sturm knocked a lid on that one too.

Frank couldn't get used to the fact that here they were, butchering an actual tiger in the middle of Main Street, in the center of town, and they hadn't seen anyone else. Just the taxidermist. No one driving through town. No one pushing a stroller along the sidewalk. Nobody even poking their head out to see what the shooting was about. The town must have been emptier than he had first thought, and suddenly realized that he could be standing in the middle of a genuine western ghost town.

But then Pine and Chuck came back with an ice chest full of

beer and Frank stopped worrying about the rest of the town. Beer was passed out and the hunt was retold, over and over. Whenever Sturm tilted his head back to laugh, Frank couldn't help but notice how his open, curling mouth matched the scar on the back of his skull.

"Christ," Sturm snapped his fingers. "Damn near forgot. Chuck, you and Frank better go collect Bob. Won't be long before the buzzards and coyotes are all over him. Think you can find him again?"

Chuck followed the tiger's trail, back through town, past the Gloucks' and the gas station, back through the ranch. From there, he kept the tires in the two parallel lines mashed down through the field where the Jeep had come before. Chuck drove easily, left elbow cocked on the open window frame, steering with his fingertips, beer bottle in his right fist. He'd wedge the bottle in his crotch whenever he had to shift; this was a smooth, effortless motion, as if he'd practiced it a thousand times.

"Where you from again? Thought I heard Pine say Chicago," Chuck said.

"Not exactly Chicago. Born in Texas, then moved up to just south of the city."

"And now you're in California. Hell, you been all over. Me? I been out of the county once," Chuck said. He sounded proud, like he was thirteen and champion of the fights. Frank thought he had said country, until Chuck explained, "Went down to San Francisco once, on a field trip. What a goddamn shithole. Never had any urge to go back."

When they passed through Sturm's backyard, Fairfax was sitting on a pile of dirt, dangling his feet in the hole, staring at the corpse of the dog in the lawn. His face and bald spot were the color of a ripe tomato. He didn't look up or wave as they passed.

They came upon Pine's truck and the reinforced horse trailer.

"Can we make it all the way back there through the creek?"

"I don't think so. Gets pretty tight in spots."

"Then we'll have to pull him out the hard way." Chuck steered out of the creek bed and kept following the Jeep tracks. "So. You never said. What did you think of Annie?" He grinned, but the muscles behind the smile didn't have much of a handle on all that slack skin, so it was like two midgets trying to pull back a heavy felt theater curtain.

Frank shrugged, managed a small "Yeah," trying to make it sound casual. His jaw was clenched and his neck felt tight. "It was nothing," he added, letting his eyes go blank and dead.

"Nah. That girl ain't nothing," Chuck insisted. "She's something, all right. I spent more than I care to remember on that mouth. Boy oh boy. She'll—"

"There." Frank pointed, and down below was the dead pine.

Vultures were already circling overhead. Bronson's body looked like someone had gone after him for a long time with a dull axe. "Least he's in one piece," Chuck said. First, they tried to drag him back up the tree, but the sagging, heavy body, already slick with blood, kept rolling off the log whenever they had to go around a branch. Next, they tried dragging him up the sandy cliff, but the corpse was simply too heavy and the soil too loose.

"Fuck this," Chuck said, panting and blinking sweat from his eyes. "Wait here." He climbed back up the tree and a minute later, a rope came tumbling over the edge of the cliff. Chuck's wide face appeared at the top. "Tie that around his ankles or something. Something that won't come off. Not that I give a fuck, but I suppose it would be better if we didn't have to drag him up twice."

Frank knotted the rope around Bronson's expensive boots, then climbed back up to Chuck. The other end of the rope had been tied to the trailer hitch. They opened a fresh beer, and

Chuck simply put the truck in first gear and drove slowly straight out into the field. Frank kept an eye on the side mirror, and when he saw Bronson's flopping, rolling body, Chuck circled back around.

When they got back to the ranch, Sturm had just finished wrapping the dead Lab in a white sheet. Theo, Jack, and Pine stood back at a respectful distance, heads down, giving the man some time to say goodbye to his dog. Fairfax was on his knees, streaks of dried tears slashing through the dirt on his cheeks. Every once in a while, his back would hitch and shudder, but he'd force the sob back down. The man was probably counting the seconds until he could get the hell back to Sacramento.

But when Chuck dropped the tailgate and Fairfax got a look at Bronson's body, Fairfax's face looked like he'd just jumped in a tub of ice water. He popped up, jowls quivering, eyes blinking furiously.

Sturm stood as well, wiping his eyes with his thumb and forefinger.

"Oh, my God. What happened to him?" Fairfax pointed at Bronson, in case anyone was confused. "Do you stupid fucking hicks have any idea who this man is?"

"Watch your mouth," Sturm warned in a low voice. "That man was a friend of mine, that's who he is. Me and Bob been drinking and shooting since before you sucked on your mommy's teat."

But Fairfax wasn't listening. "You ignorant goddamn hillbillies. I cannot believe you let this happen."

"His own goddamn fault," Jack pointed out. "Should've paid more attention. He had a rifle. Wasn't like he was hunting ducks or something." Pine and Chuck nodded.

Fairfax blinked even harder, as if Jack had just unzipped his jeans and pissed all over Bronson's corpse. "You . . . you have

157

no idea how much trouble you are in. All of you."

And then, faster than Fairfax could blink, Sturm snatched the shovel off the ground and in one savage jab, thrust its blade into Fairfax's throat. Everyone flinched. The pitted blade sliced cleanly through Fairfax's heavy jowls and scraped along his jawbone with a sound like a claw hammer striking ice. Sturm didn't stop until the shovel hit the artery; bright, thick blood squirted out, coating the blade, the handle, and the lawn. Fairfax's knees wobbled and he waved his arms around like a toddler learning to walk. Sturm guided Fairfax sideways about five feet, until Fairfax fell into the dog's grave. The blade came free with a wet, squelching sound and Fairfax hit the dirt at the bottom with a solid thud. He feebly waved his hands around like a potato bug on its back for a few more seconds, but the movement gradually subsided as more blood soaked into the black dirt under his head.

The men gathered around the grave and watched his final movements. Sturm stabbed the shovel into the pile of dirt and flung the soft dirt onto Fairfax's face. Dirt filled the gaping wound, wide open mouth, and unblinking eyes. When the body was covered, they carefully lowered the dog's body into the grave, then each took a shovelful and gently sifted dirt onto the white sheet.

They finished filling the grave as the sun slid past the mountains to the west. Sturm left the shovel standing upright in the freshly turned dirt. "We'll make a cross later. For the dog," he explained, and looked to the darkening sky.

"Lord," he began. The others lowered their heads. "Please watch over this animal. She was a damn fine dog. Best hunting companion a man could ask for. All I ask is that you let her play in your fields, chasing rabbits and sniffing for pheasant. Try not to mind if she takes a dump near the back steps of your palace, as she was known to do from time to time. All in all, she was a good girl." Sturm swallowed, wiped at his eyes again. "She didn't deserve to go this soon. So please take care of her until I get there. I promise I'll look after her then." Sturm turned his head and spit. "And if it's not too much to ask, drop kick the sonofabitch who sent her to you all the way down to hell. I'm not trying to be sacrilegious here or anything, but I want to hear him screaming when I meet you. Amen."

Everyone else chimed in with an "Amen."

Sturm met their eyes. "Gentlemen, I'm afraid this ain't the only one we have to bury this evening." He nodded at Bronson's broken body. "Dumb as he was, Fairfax was right about one thing. We can't exactly take him back to Sacramento like this. He was a good friend, and we're gonna send him off into the beyond proper."

A few hours later, they were ready. Jack had filled the back seat of the Hummer with ammunition and black powder. They propped Bronson up in the passenger seat, with a hat over his face in case anyone on the road got curious. Jack drove the Hummer, following Sturm and Theo in the Jeep. Chuck, Frank, and Pine came up the rear in Chuck's truck. They headed south, winding their way up into the steep Sierra Nevada mountains. A hundred miles south of Whitewood, Sturm turned off the main highway onto a crumbling logging trail that zig-zagged up a ridge. By now, it was nearing ten or eleven o'clock, so Frank couldn't see anything. He had to keep swallowing to equalize the pressure in his ears, and realized the altitude must be very high.

Eventually, Sturm angled the Jeep at a right angle to the logging road, headlights fading away into nothingness. They joined Sturm at the edge of the cliff. Jack and Chuck dragged Bronson into the driver's seat of his Hummer and seatbelted him into place. Pine poured black powder over the shattered corpse, and left two full gas cans in the passenger seat for good measure. They duct-taped a fresh, unlit cigar in Bronson's mouth and propped his rifle at his side. Pine pulled a bottle of whiskey out of Chuck's pickup and they all gathered in a tight semi-circle and passed the bottle around for a while.

Chuck shoved a cassette tape into the player in his truck and a second later, the first strains of Kansas' "Dust in the Wind" drifted out of the open doors.

Sturm opened a tattered, leatherbound Bible and, using the glow from the headlights, read aloud, throwing his words off the mountain and into the darkness. "And I saw, and look, behold a pale horse; and the one seated upon it was Death. And Hell followed close behind him. And authority was given them over the fourth part of the Earth, to kill with a long sword and with food shortage and with deadly plague and by the wild beasts of the earth. Amen." Sturm snapped the book shut. "Goodbye, my friend. I'll be seeing you soon enough. Save a drink for me." He poured a bit of whiskey over Bronson's ruined face, screwed the cap on tight, and put it between Bronson's legs.

Sturm stepped back so Jack could start the Hummer. He left it in park, but jammed the rifle butt against the gas pedal, wedging the muzzle against the dead man's stomach. The engine rose into a whining snarl, anxious and upset at being held in check. Then, mindful of the flakes of black powder scattered across Bronson like ash, he lit the cigar. Without air being pulled through the cigar, it took a while, but the leaves finally caught. With a nod from Sturm, Jack jerked the stick into Drive. The Hummer shot forward into the night. The headlights tilted down, bounced, disappeared, and as they came back up, from underneath and behind this time, shining back up at the men gathered at the road, the Hummer's interior exploded. Blue flames curled out of the shattered windows and a second later, the gas cans went. The Hummer kept rolling end over end, a snowball of fire, now hundreds of feet down the rock-covered mountain. The temperature inside finally got hot enough to spark off the ammunition. Gunfire crackled into the night, temporarily overshadowing the music.

Everyone took a few steps back from the edge, wary of stray bullets. "Dust in the Wind" kept playing, echoed by the distant explosions below. All in all, Frank thought it was a nice sendoff, a genuine modern Viking funeral. It was kind of cool, really. Still, as he watched the lunatic grinning scar carved into the back of Sturm's head, bathed in the backwash of the headlights, he felt as if the hunts had been a failure. Two men were dead. Sturm's dog had been shot.

Sturm turned around. "Gentlemen, that was the finest god-damn funeral I ever attended. When it's time, I've decided I want to go out the same way. Same spot. Put me in my truck and send me down the mountain. Goddamn right. And hell, same music, whatever long-haired hippy band that was. But use more ammunition. I want God to hear me coming."

Day Eighteen

Sturm stopped by the vet hospital around noon. Theo was driving, but Sturm made him stay in the pickup for some reason. Frank opened the front door and watched Sturm slowly shuffle up the walk. Something was wrong. Sturm moved as if he couldn't trust his legs.

"I need to see them cats," he said.

Frank nodded. Sturm stumbled and Frank caught his arm. It felt like grabbing a piece of petrified wood. "Dammit," Sturm said. He seemed ashamed. Frank led him to the back where Sturm leaned against the chain-link cage.

"I think . . ." Sturm began, looking at the concrete. He brought his gaze up to stare at the lioness curled in the far corner. She ignored the men. "No. No. I don't have the luxury of thinking anymore. I don't have the time. I don't know if this is it or what the hell is happening to me. But I do know this. My boy needs me to teach him before I go. He needs some straightening out, that's for goddamn sure. All I got left is instinct."

Frank wondered what the hell Sturm was talking about.

"So I've made up my mind," Sturm continued. "And I need your help. I'm gonna go on instinct. You being a vet, you should understand instinct. The way an animal doesn't have to think, understand?"

"Yeah."

"I'm not running off like some whipped dog to die by myself.

162

That's no way to die for anybody. I'm gonna go out like a man and teach my boy how to live his life right."

Frank waited, still unsure where Sturm was headed with all this.

Sturm turned and stared Frank full in the face. His face cracked into a brief, thin smile. "You did well here, son. This was a hell of a thing." He faced the cage again. "This one, I don't want her fed today. I want her hungry. I want her mean." He licked his dry lips. "This'll be something folks will remember for the rest of their lives. You were right. This will be my legacy."

He pushed off the cage and headed for the office. "Jack and Pine'll be by later. Take that lioness to the auction yard and wait for me." He slammed the door behind him.

Men started arriving at sundown. It looked like the same crowd from the fights. Frank wondered how the word had gotten out. Maybe everybody carried cell phones. However they got the news, everyone seemed to know that something serious was up. There was no laughing, no yelling; the men acted as if they were at a funeral, talking in low, somber tones, keeping their eyes down. Frank couldn't shake the feeling that he had missed something, something big, this morning; like he'd slept right through whatever Sturm had been trying to tell him.

And since he didn't want anyone to know that he was in the dark, he kept his mouth shut and pretended to know exactly what was happening.

No one went inside the auction yard. Men clustered in small groups around pickups, once in a while casting a few sidewise glances up at the trailer on the hill. The clowns didn't move either, except to get more beer, although once in a while Frank caught Jack watching the highway toward town.

Soon enough, he saw a pair of headlights getting closer and closer until they flooded the parking lot in high beams. Without saying anything, the clowns rose to their feet. By that point, men had lined the driveway. A few of them removed their hats as Sturm's black pickup rolled past. Theo was driving. He parked right near the front doors and let his father out. Sturm climbed out. The tentative shuffle was gone. He moved like he expected the air itself to get the hell out of the way. He nodded at the men once, then again at the clowns on the hill. When Theo came around the pickup and joined his father, they walked into the building together.

The clowns chugged the rest of their warm beers, tossed the cans on the ground. "It's time," Jack said, almost whispered really, and rubbed at his eyes. His thumb and forefinger came away wet. Pine leaned into the trailer and grabbed the rifle Chuck had nearly used at the rest stop. Then they walked down the hill and joined the rest of the men flowing into the auction yard.

Inside, a tunnel had been built out of hog panels, leading from the livestock pens in the back right into the center ring. Frank and the clowns marched down to it. The men filled the place, quiet, respectable.

Pine took up a position in the front, chest against the fence, rifle butt on his hip. "Stick close," he murmured to Frank. Chuck stepped up to the ring on the other side of Frank, working his unlit cigarette back and forth across his mouth. No one sat. No one moved. No one breathed.

Until Sturm appeared in the doorway to his office, moving purposefully down to the ring. Frank heard the men exhale as one. Sturm climbed the gate and strode to the center. He was wearing jeans, cowboy boots, and nothing else except for a knife scabbard on his belt that held a Hibben Iron Mistress. The knife, a replica of the mythical Jim Bowie blade supposedly forged using ore from a meteorite, was over sixteen inches long, with a ten and a half inch blade that tapered down into a vicious point. The white, milky skin of his chest and arms stopped abruptly at his wrists, giving way to hands tanned as brown as dirt, as if he was wearing gloves.

Sturm slowly turned, meeting the eyes of every man in the room. When his eyes locked with Frank, Frank felt the impact reverberate down into his bones. Sturm went back to the edge of the ring and grabbed Theo by the shoulders in a fierce grip. He kissed his son on the forehead. Then he leaned back, staring into Theo's eyes. "Be strong. Be a man," he whispered through clenched teeth, then abruptly let go, and stalked slowly back into the center of the ring, shoulders back, head high.

He drew the Iron Mistress and tossed the leather sheath to Chuck. Out of the corner of his eye, Frank saw Pine crying. Silently. Motionlessly. Tears slowly rolled down the side of his nose. He refused to wipe them away, as if acknowledging his weakness would make it real somehow. If he simply ignored the tears, then it wasn't happening.

Jack had now come back and was standing next to the tunnel, hand on the gate. "Are you ready?" His voice cracked as he called to Sturm.

Sturm took a deep breath, lips tight, frozen eyes clear. He slowly brought the knife up in front of his chest, blade down and away, widening his stance, crouching down, ready. He faced the darkness of the tunnel. "Do it."

"It was an honor, sir. We'll never forget," Jack said as he swung the gate open.

The starving lioness padded silently and smoothly out of the tunnel. She stopped, pawed anxiously at the sawdust. But her eyes were on Sturm and her nose expanded, contracted. Frank knew the cat was hungry; she hadn't eaten fresh meat in nearly twenty-four hours.

"Go get it, Horace! Kill it!" someone shouted in a broken

voice, but that was all.

The lioness growled low, circling Sturm to the right. She never took her eyes off him. Sturm bared his teeth. The crowd seemed to recoil; this unexpected, brazen display of emotion from the man scared them.

Pine tracked the lioness with the .30-06, tears still rolling down his cheeks, collecting in the groove between his cheek and the top of the stock. Frank understood that Pine wanted to shoot the lioness more than anything in the world, but if he did, then Sturm was liable to shoot him.

The lioness leapt. Sturm leaped forward, meeting the cat, slashing wildly with the knife. The cat swung one massive paw and opened Sturm's skin from his left shoulder across his chest.

Sturm grunted and slammed the blade between the lioness' ribs and they both went down in a cloud of sawdust. There was some kicking, twitching. Dust billowed out and hung in the air like early morning fog on the river.

Pine leaned forward, finger tight on the trigger, eyes blinking away the tears.

Sturm rose out of the dust, blood sheeting his torso. Dust stuck to the blood.

The lioness stayed down. It kicked. Rolled. Sturm crouched immediately, swiftly reversing the knife with one hand, whirling the blade under his forearm, and slit the big cat's throat. Blood squirted out of the wound and soaked into the sawdust.

It was over.

Sturm faced the silent, shocked men. He raised his knife. Then the applause began, slow at first, but it didn't take long before the men were stomping and whistling, screaming his name. Frank was surprised to find himself clutching the top bar, shouting, screaming really, no real words, just a pure release.

Sturm took a hesitant step toward his son, and dropped to his knees. Instantly, Jack scrambled over the bars and knelt next to him. Sturm's white chest was now coated in scarlet dust. Blood sheeted the front of his jeans, down to his knees. It didn't look like it was stopping. Sturm shot his left arm out and landed heavily on his flat palm, but he refused to drop the knife in his right hand.

Jack's eyes found Frank, and Frank understood. He climbed into the ring and rushed to Sturm's side, carefully rolling him onto his back. Frank realized they should have been ready, should have been prepared with bandages, some kind of first aid. But no one had expected Sturm to live.

And still the men had not let up; the screaming and shouting was deafening, shaking the auction yard, filling it with an almost palpable force that squeezed Frank's head and doubled his vision as he looked down at Sturm's white face, his lips pulled back, baring clenched teeth under wild eyes that glowed with a feverish light.

Deep down, Frank realized something had shifted, reversed. Sturm could not be allowed to die, not now, not ever. And if Frank didn't save him, he'd find himself buried in a shallow grave somewhere out in the mountains that surrounded the town. So he placed both palms flat, pressing down hard, over the rip in Sturm's chest. Direct pressure, his mind kept repeating, direct pressure. Frank shouted over the mindless screaming of the men at Theo and the clowns, "First aid kit, now! We need bandages, lots of gauze, and a needle and thread! Now!"

Throughout it all, Sturm wouldn't let go of the Iron Mistress. He watched Frank with twitching, shivering eyes, but never said a word. Frank tried to move slowly, calmly; he was afraid that if he caused too much pain, moved too quickly and sharply, Sturm might bring that blade up and sink it in Frank's neck.

But in the end, Frank stopped the bleeding.

Day Nineteen

Chuck dropped Frank off at the vet hospital around four in the morning. Chuck waved and tore off, wanting nothing more than to fall into his own bed in the trailer out behind the auction yard. Frank knew there was nothing left in his flask, but he upended it anyway, swallowed spit, then tucked it away in his jeans. His body felt stiff and aching from sitting in a kitchen chair for most of the night, watching over Sturm. His eyes felt like they'd been sandblasted open. He ran his tongue over his teeth, wondered if he would have enough energy to scrape away the slick coat of filth before falling onto the couch.

As he lurched across the lawn, a lilting, mischievous voice from above said, "You boys never just have a few beers and call it a night, do you?" Frank looked up and saw Annie's strong brown legs swinging slightly from a thick branch about ten feet up. One flip-flop dangled from her big toe. The other was upside down on the grass. Frank winced when he thought of the possible needles in the lawn.

Frank was glad Chuck hadn't seen her. Annie popped a gigantic bubble of flesh-colored gum, peeled it off her nose, and threw it into the planter filled with the dried husks of dead bushes. "Been waiting for you. Busy night?"

Frank nodded. "Waiting to see your dog?"

"That too," she said, but didn't elaborate as she nimbly rolled off the branch and hung there for a moment, arm muscles taut, breasts full, baring her belly. She let Frank take her in for a mo-

168

ment, then dropped to the ground.

"Careful," he mumbled. "Needles." His brain, fogged from the Jack Daniels, the heat, and full of visions of Sturm baring his teeth and slashing at the lioness with the Iron Mistress, wasn't working right. The gears were trapped in tar. "Watch your feet. Needles."

Annie crinkled her forehead and looked at him with bemusement. She was used to dealing with drunks.

This wasn't going the way he had been hoping the last two weeks. Finally, he just said, "Let's go on in and see her." He fumbled for the keys while she worked her toes into the other flip-flop.

He got the front door open, and Petunia came barreling down the hallway, claws scrabbling on the linoleum. She stopped short when she saw Annie, hesitating only a half second before launching herself at the girl. Petunia hit Annie so hard she knocked the girl on her ass. The impact made Frank wince, but Annie just squealed in delight, closing her eyes and letting Petunia attack her face with her fat, wide tongue.

After a moment, Petunia backed off just enough to ram Frank's knees with her broad head, her other way of showing affection. Frank wanted to offer Annie his hand, to help her up, but it felt weird, like it was too intimate, too fast. Christ, he thought. He felt like some sixth-grader wondering how he should hold a girl for a slow dance.

If Annie felt uncomfortable, she didn't act like it. She simply reached out and grabbed hold of the front of his belt and hauled herself up. Petunia bounced around like a happy rubber ball, pleased as punch with her two humans.

"She sure seems better. Can I take her home?" Annie asked, scratching wildly behind Petunia's ears.

"I think so, yeah. No infection. She's getting around fine. Just—be careful. Hate to think of her getting hurt again."

"Don't worry. My brothers and I have come to an understanding. I don't want my dog to get hurt and they don't want
to be wearing their balls for earrings, so everybody's happy."

Frank didn't know what to say; he didn't want to end it,
didn't want to let her go. "Do you need a leash or anything?"

She laughed.

"Any dog food?"

"Nope."

"Okay. Well. She likes it when you scratch real hard at the
base of her tail—right on top of the hips here."

"I know."

"I've been reading to her. I think she likes that. Mostly medical, vet stuff, but I suppose it doesn't matter."

"Okay."

"Okay."

Frank squatted, pulled Petunia's head in close, rubbing the
top of her nose and stroking the loose folds at her throat. "Okay
then, little girl. You be good." He kissed the top of Petunia's
flat, broad skull and stood up. "Take good care of her."

Annie nodded, but her eyes were on the floor. She shifted
back and forth, stuck her hands in her pockets, then pulled
them out again just as quickly. Finally, chewing on her bottom
lip, she met his eyes. "Hey. Would you like to have dinner with
me tomorrow, I mean, tonight?"

"Yes. Yes, I would."

She smiled, that round face beaming, damn near glowing.
Frank almost squinted from the dazzling brightness and he
couldn't help but grin back.

"Good." She tried to tame her smile, pressing her lips
together, but the dimples in her cheeks gave it away. "Tonight.
At six. Okay?"

"I'll be there."

"I'll be waiting." And with that, Annie and Petunia left. Frank watched Annie's rolling ass, barely contained in her cutoff jean shorts, as she headed across the lawn. Petunia padded happily alongside the strong, brown legs. They walked down the middle of the empty street, silhouetted from streetlight to streetlight, until finally slipping into the darkness.

The hospital was empty and hollow without Petunia following him around. Frank went in and talked to the pound dogs for a while, but it wasn't the same. The immediate, insane barking kickstarted his hangover, hammering a throbbing headache to his skull with blunt nails. The big cats just stared him down with careful, precise eyes. They didn't hiss or snarl anymore. How was it, he wondered, he could understand exactly what the cats were thinking as they watched him, but he had absolutely no idea what the hell was going through Annie's mind when she invited him to dinner.

Frank took a hot shower and scrubbed himself raw. He fell onto his cot, but couldn't sleep. As the storeroom's walls and pallets took shape in the gray morning light, he thought of her dimples as she tried not to let the smile get away from her. Her belly. Those brown legs. That ass.

He stopped pretending to sleep when the phone rang at noon. It was Sturm. "We're having a meeting at my place. Appreciate it if you were there."

"Yeah, sure, of course." Frank panicked, thinking of his date with Annie at six. "When?"

"Be here in an hour. I can have one of the boys pick you up, if you'd rather not have that car out and about." Frank had hidden the long, black car in the barn, in a large, empty space next to the rhino.

"No, that'll be okay. Better for it, turn the engine over once in a while. How you feelin'?"

171

"Never felt better in my life. See you in an hour." Sturm hung up.

Frank fed the animals and himself. He took another shower in case he didn't have a chance before six, then drove out to Sturm's ranch. Jack, Pine, and Chuck were already there, sitting on the front steps, yanking off their cowboy boots. Inside, Sturm had the air conditioning going full blast. Frank's sweat instantly froze to his skin and everyone left damp footprints on the smooth wood as they walked through the house in their socks.

Sturm sat in one of the kitchen chairs while Theo carried the rest into the office. Frank peeled the medical tape off Sturm's chest and started to say, "Good thing you don't have much hair," but caught himself just in time. The wounds were clean and showed no sign of infection. Frank applied fresh bandages and everyone moved into the office.

They clustered around the desk. Frank was surprised to see a laptop; it looked out of place in the farmhouse, almost anachronistic, like John Wayne drawing a laser gun out of his holster. Sturm explained, "While all of us have been sleeping, Theo's been busy." He sounded proud, but almost relieved, as if his son had finally given him a reason to be proud. He nodded at the laptop. "Theo?"

Theo came forward, suddenly shy and hesitant, his movements the only sound in the muffled quiet of the book-filled room. He dragged his forefinger across the mouse pad and attacked the keyboard like a puppy going after a frog.

An image of the Twin Towers appeared, morning in New York, and the first plane came streaking out the sky from the right side of the screen and burrowed into one of the buildings. A title appeared above the towers, stark black. "DEATH LIVES IN US ALL—The Most Brutal Site on the Net." A menu faded in on the left side of the screen. "Videos." "Photos." "Links."

"Show 'em everything," Sturm said. "It'll curl your toes and pucker your assholes, boys."

Theo clicked "Videos." Another list came up, and Theo started at the top. The Twin Towers crumpled in fire and dust and smoke.

A paunchy, middle-aged guy in a suit stood behind a table in a nondescript meeting room, handing out manila envelopes. He was sweating and pale, trembling like he had a stomach flu. "This will all be explained in a minute—moment," he stuttered. His voice matched the color of his skin, cottage cheese that had been left out in the sun. It appeared to be some kind of last-minute press conference, but the camera angle didn't show anyone else. Finally, he reached the last manila envelope and pulled a large revolver from it.

There were panicked shouts, falling chairs. Someone shouted, "Wait!" and there was another hoarse, quick voice, "Don't!"

The man waved the gun around with a shaking hand and sputtered, "Please. Please, don't come any closer. Someone— someone could get hurt with this." And then, anxious to get it over with, he put the barrel in his mouth and pulled the trigger. Almost too fast to follow, part of his skull hit the wall behind him and he dropped like a cinderblock off an overpass. The camera tilted down, finding the man slumped against the wall. Blood suddenly erupted from his nose and mouth as if someone had quickly cranked on a faucet. His eyes were still open, sad and unblinking. The image went black.

"Jesus humping Christ. Ain't never." Chuck breathed. "Holy fucking shit. Shit!" Frank couldn't tell if Chuck was disgusted or excited.

That was just the beginning. The images were thick with death. They watched machete beheadings. Soccer riots. Helicopter disasters. Racetrack explosions that sent burning chunks of the cars into the crowds. Police chases. Bulls goring matadors; the clowns laughed like hell at those. Shootouts. Hot air balloon mishaps. An abortion, up close and personal.

The clowns acted as if they were watching porn, calling out in ecstasy "Oh fuck, YES!" when a cop stepped in front of a semi on a busy freeway and disappeared, leaving only the faintest red mist behind. One poor sonofabitch got sucked through a jumbo jet engine. People jumped out of a burning high rise in India and bounced when they hit the concrete. A mob in Africa literally tore a man apart with long knives and their bare hands.

They hit a stretch of animal attacks. Some misguided dipshit in Taiwan climbed over a zoo fence and tried to bless a couple of lions. He'd nearly completed the sign of the cross when one of the lions casually flicked a paw out and sent the guy spinning to the ground, probably wondering why his God had abandoned him. Another Asian guy, Frank couldn't tell what country it was, let his concentration falter for just a second, and a nine-foot alligator clamped down on his arm and just rolled and rolled and rolled, twisting that arm like a wet towel until it finally came off, right above the elbow. Frank wasn't the only one that flinched.

One genius tried to brand a horse. The horse gave a kind of squeezing flex, then, the next instant, the guy was gone as if he'd never been born. The website showed it again in slow motion. The horse kicked the dumb sonofabitch square in the chest and he flew backward out of the frame, branding iron spinning in midair. Even Frank got to laughing at that one. But he had to fight not to tremble. Sturm had the temperature down in the sixties, and to Frank, who had stepped out of the 107-degree heat, it felt like he'd just parachuted into the Antarctic in his underwear.

The cool air just made the clowns scratch a lot.

Frank wished he had his flask.

It was already three o'clock.

After the videos, Theo clicked through the collection of still images, mostly black and white crime scene photos. Shotgun suicides. Scissor stabbings. Mob hits. Then black screens with white words; jokes like "What's the difference between a truckload of bowling balls and a truckload of dead babies?" The next image was an infant girl in a white hospital shirt and nothing else impaled on a wrought iron fence with the text underneath. "You can unload one with a pitchfork."

One photo showed a giant dead crocodile, wetly gutted at the edge of a pier. It was night, coldly lit from the flashbulb. A slimy, blue human leg spilled out of the gaping stomach.

At the very end, there was the picture. And there they were, in the middle of the street with the tiger. It had been framed so you could see the park off to the left, bank and post office off to the right. It looked like these six men had chased a tiger out a safari photo in some particularly corrupt country and shot it dead inside a Norman Rockwell painting.

"Holy fucking shit!" Chuck screamed. "That's fucking awesome!" Pine blurted at the same time. Sturm ginned back at them.

Frank wondered how many people had seen this photo. He resolved to shave off his long hair the first chance he got. In the bottom left corner was a web address, black against the mottled pavement. It was too small to read, so Frank pointed at it.

Sturm nodded. "Wondered who'd find it first."

Theo rolled the cursor over to the number and clicked on it. This opened up several other windows. He went through them, tapping out passwords. The last window had a ten-digit number, nothing else. It was a phone number. "Somebody call that number," Sturm said.

Pine was the only one with a cell phone. He dialed. The phone on Sturm's desk rang. He picked it up and said, "Hell of a picture, ain't it?"

"It sure as hell is," Pine said.

"Shit, you'd think that was taken right here in America. Must be one of them faked photos you see on the Net from time to time. Can't be true. But hell," Sturm loaded his bottom lip with tobacco. "Wouldn't that be something. To stalk and kill an animal that exotic, that magnificent, on the streets and backyards of Small Town, USA."

"It sure as hell would."

"Chance to be thirteen years old again. Yessir. Can you imagine something like that, hunting and fucking just like you could when you were that age? But for real this time. Goddamn. This ain't no pussy canned hunt. No sir. This ain't for goddamn pansies who can't handle stalking and killing an animal. And it sure as shit ain't for those cocksuckers that don't have a problem shooting an animal tied to a stake. They try that around here, I'm liable to tie *them* to a fucking stake and start shooting. No sir. This is the real goddamn deal, hunting a genuine jungle predator. Hell I believe I'd pay just about anything for a shot at something like that. I tell you a figure I wouldn't blink at, I wouldn't think anything of paying ten grand for something like this. If the opportunity presented itself. Not for something that much fun."

Pine swallowed. "No. I wouldn't blink at all at a figure like that."

Sturm said, "Then I would suggest arranging for a trip say, around late August, somewhere around August 21." Sturm hung up.

He leaned forward. "This photo has been sent to a very exclusive group of gentlemen. Men who do not blink at spending ten thousand dollars or more to hunt anything they want." Sturm rapped the desk. "That ten grand? That's just to get here. The gentlemen are then free to gamble among themselves."

Sturm opened his large palms. "And naturally, in a situation such as this, it's only reasonable that the house deserves thirty percent of every transaction."

Everybody tried to quickly calculate the amount. Frank said, "We got six lionesses left. That cheetah." The amount got bigger.

"The monkeys," Chuck suggested.

"The dogs," Jack said.

"The rhino," Theo said.

Sturm nodded. "We got ourselves a chance to make some real money. But it ain't gonna just fall out of the sky. We have some work to do. First up. Walkie-talkies. I ain't got time to drive over half creation to find you." Theo handed the walktie-talkies out. Everyone got one, except for Frank. Sturm explained, "You stay at the vet's, so I know where to find you if I need you. The rest of you, you keep these charged and close. I expect you to answer quick if I call. Jack, you and Chuck head down to Redding. We're gonna need three, four big tents. I mean big. Big as you can get. And as much goddamn liquor as you can carry. You come talk to me soon as you get back.

"Pine, you go get as much ammo as possible. You need to leave immediately, so you can head back and unload at least a couple of times before our guests arrive. Hit Redding, then head over to Reno. Stop at every gun store, bait shop, and especially goddamn Walmart you pass. Go down I-5 and clean that valley out. We need every .12 gauge and rifle shell they got."

"You bet."

"And you, Frank." Sturm rolled his fingers across the top of the desk in a staccato burst. "Without them animals, this whole enterprise is nothing but a bunch of hicks with their thumb up their ass, trying to peddle a few silhouette targets. The Roman army had a special rank for getting their own exotic animals for the Colosseum games. Called 'em *venator immunis*. That's you. So you're gonna be my right-hand man in this. Them cats, they're an investment. A *serious* investment. We put their health first. 'Til the hunt, of course. But we will deliver what we promise. A chance to hunt one of the world's biggest and most lethal predators through the streets of a small town. I want them cats healthy as if God himself blessed them with his grace. And you're gonna do that for me. For us." Sturm stood up. "Gentlemen. We have thirteen days to whip this town into shape. There's a whole shitload of work to do, so I suggest we all get to it."

As they were leaving, the phone on Sturm's desk began to ring.

Frank got back with enough time to feed the animals and take another shower. Standing in the cramped bathroom, he eye-balled his reflection critically, said to hell with it, went out and found the clippers, and shaved his head. He wondered if he should wear his suit. In the end he decided against it, and went with jeans and a clean gray cowboy shirt. He wasn't sure where they would head for dinner, fairly certain that Whitewood didn't have any kind of restaurant or diner or café or anything like that, just a sliver of a cinderblock bar over by the railroad. That meant they'd have to drive to another town, and he wanted to look like just another field hand.

The dead tree was empty. Frank still parked where he'd watched the cop car park, protected by the satellite dish. The gas station across the street was closed and dark. The sun was setting and a persistent wind came down from the north. He felt almost cool as he stepped out of the car.

Smoke rose from the house as he came up the wide trail of baked bare earth that marked the path to the front door. Other than the smoke, the place was lifeless. Frank had been doing pretty good, wasn't too nervous up until then. He'd seen Annie take care of her brothers on at least two occasions, and he knew she could handle them without worries. But up until now, Frank hadn't thought of the mothers. He wasn't sure how this little date would go over at all, wasn't sure how they would react to a man taking their daughter out. He hadn't seen them since the night of the BBQ and carnival. He wanted to just say hi, get Annie out of the house, and take off.

The front door was in his face, daring him to either knock or get back in the car. He knocked. It opened immediately. Two brothers, twins, both around seven or eight, waited stiffly inside. They wore identical clothing, deeply bleached white shirts ironed into sharp angles, black bow ties that matched the black pants and plastic wing tips, a white bathroom hand towel over their right forearm. Their hair was neat and slicked back. One of them had a Band-Aid on his chin.

"Please come in, sir," Band-Aid said. Both were deeply respectful, deferential even, and kept their eyes downcast.

"Thank you," Frank said and walked inside. A giant, flat slab of oak dominated the center of the large room. Five chairs and place settings had been laid out. They looked lonely at the large table. The walls were the color of merlot, bisected by a wooden chair rail. A large wood cabinet with glass fronts sat in the middle of each wall. Various ceramic figurines were carefully arranged inside. Orange shag carpet covered the floor.

More brothers rushed around, each dressed identically. Only the black eyes, split lips, and scabbed knuckles separated them. A few were hastily dragging an old vacuum out of the room. A door waited off to the right; the floor gave way to tile, and it smelled delicious, mostly tomatoes and garlic. Two other doorways led to the rest of the house, in the corners of the far wall.

"Please, sir, have a seat." Band-Aid dragged out the chair

179

that faced the kitchen across the large table. His twin brother positioned himself on the other side of the chair. "Um, my sis— Miss Annie will be down in a minute. May I offer you a drink?" Frank sat down and before he could scoot it forward, the brothers shoved the chair at the table like they were football lineman driving a heavy training sled, almost pitching Frank out of the chair.

"May I offer you a drink?" Band-Aid repeated, nearly demanded.

Frank wanted alcohol desperately, but thought it might be impolite to ask. So he said, "Maybe a glass of water, thank you."

"Of course."

The brothers headed for the kitchen, always together, like they were Siamese twins, joined at the shoulder. Edie, the mother with the crazy eyeball, came out of the kitchen in their wake. She was wearing her usual limp dishrag of a housedress, but this time she had a white apron over it. It looked more like it had come from a hospital than a kitchen, but it was clean. She walked with long, determined strides, crossing the room like that tiger had bounded across the street.

Edie held out her hand and shook Frank's hand harder than Sturm, grinning so fiercely it looked like the crazy eye was squinting in rage. "So happy to see you again. I'm glad you have decided to take care of the animals in this town. We are all very pleased to have Petunia back with us."

"Thank you, that's—that's all right. Glad I could help her."

"Well." She wiped her hands on the apron. "Dinner will be served shortly. I must apologize for the tardiness of my daughter and wife. They wanted to look their best." She smiled fondly at the far door. It was closed. "I'm afraid I must get back into the kitchen." The thin, wicked grin was back. "My supervision is needed." She left the room as fast as she had entered and suddenly Frank was alone.

Frank could see that the place was banged up, but clean. The deep carpet was fluffy, and still faintly damp from last night's shampoo. The walls had been scrubbed and the table felt oily from the wood polish. Band-Aid came out of the kitchen with a tall glass of ice water. "If you need anything else, my name is Ezekiel." He stepped back and stood at the wall.

Another brother, this one maybe ten or eleven, with more scabs, Band-Aids, and scrapes than any of the brothers that Frank had seen, came out and lit the candles, four tall, twisted metal candle holders in the middle of the table. When he came around the table, Frank could see that this brother even had stitches, holding most of his left nostril onto the rest of his nose. This was Gunther, but everyone just called him Gun. He didn't look at Frank, but Frank felt trouble coming off the kid like a dandelion in an earthquake.

Annie bounced into the room, and Frank didn't even see the kid leave. All Frank saw was Annie's smile. He didn't even notice that she was wearing some kind of short dress until later, after dinner. Just that smile.

She kissed him lightly on the cheek and said, "Like your haircut," as he tried to push the chair back from the table in the heavy carpet. Before he could rise, she was past him and on her way down to the other end of the table. Two brothers materialized out of the kitchen, pulled her chair back for their sister, and shoved her toward the table.

"Thank you for having dinner with me," she said. "Would you like a drink?"

"Got some water, thanks."

"You sure you don't want something stronger?"

"No, thanks. I'm good."

"Well," she said, "you change your mind, you be sure to let Zeke there know. He'll take care of it."

"I'm sure he will. He seems very capable."

Annie laughed. "Yes he's that—capable. Last week Mom caught him with three rattlesnakes in his backpack. One, hell, it wouldn't surprise me around here. But three?"

Frank looked back at Zeke. "How'd you catch 'em?"

Zeke's eyes watched Annie. She nodded, said, "Go ahead and answer. It's okay this time."

"They like the paved roads out in the foothills, around dusk," he shot a look at his sister, making it clear he wished he was out there now. "They'll come out on the pavement, soak up the heat. Gets cold sometimes at night. They like the heat."

"How'd you get them in the backpack?"

Zeke looked at Frank like he was one of the biggest dumbshits he'd ever seen. "Grabbed them. They didn't crawl in by themselves."

The other Glouck mother, Alice, came out of the same doorway as Annie, in a long, black prom dress from the early eighties. It would have been tight on most women, but Alice was built like the Eiffel Tower, wide feet, thick ankles, narrow hips, smaller shoulders, and a tiny head. She moved in short, shuffling steps, chafed by the dress around her calves. Black lace gloves ended her skeletal arms, like two wooden matches, broken in half. Tonight, her hair was pinned up, and when she got close, Frank was startled to see that she was wearing a hint of makeup. "How lovely to see you again, Frank." She shook his hand, clasping it in both hands and petting it. "Our little Annie is pleased to see you—you do know that, don't you?"

Annie said awful quick, "Why don't we all have a seat. Maybe a drink?"

There was a knock at the front door.

"That must be our other guest," Alice said, but didn't let go of Frank's hand. One of the brothers ran to the door and yanked it open.

Sturm stood in the doorway, cowboy hat in one hand and a fistful of wildflowers in the other, the last gasp of sunshine filling the space above his head.

He wore jeans and a dark green cowboy shirt with the shoulders embroidered with scrolling, thick black thread. He'd gone to the trouble of wearing a shark tooth bolo tie.

"Please come in," Zeke said.

"Thank you," Sturm said and came inside. He moved a little stiff, but otherwise just fine.

"How lovely to see you again, Mr. Sturm." Alice finally let go of Frank's hand and worked her way over to Sturm. It took a while in that dress. "Flowers, how lovely." Her words came out in halting, stiff sounds, like they tasted unfamiliar. She took the flowers and said, "Let me get a vase. Please, please, have a seat."

Yet another brother appeared. "May I get you a drink, sir?"

"Sour mash whiskey. Two ice cubes. In a glass this wide," Sturm made a ring with his thumbs and forefingers. "And this high."

"Yes, sir." The brother tore off to the kitchen.

Sturm nodded at Frank. "Frank."

Frank nodded back, not surprised at anything anymore.

Sturm nodded at Annie. "Miss."

"How are you, Mr. Sturm?"

The same two brothers yanked his chair back and threw him at the table. "I'm doing well."

Alice came back with the flowers in a ceramic vase. She put them on the table between the candles. "How lovely." She sat down in the last empty chair. Her sons helped her up to the table. Zeke rushed up to Sturm with his whiskey, then stood rigidly at attention behind Sturm.

Silence grew across the table. Alice looked more and more

uncomfortable. Frank figured the Gloucks didn't entertain folks too often. Four brothers burst into the room, each carrying a bowl of minestrone. The soups were delivered at exactly the same time, quick and smooth; the brothers didn't spill a drop. They faded into the walls and Frank was impressed with the near professional conduct of the brothers. They worked hard.

"Please. Enjoy," Alice said.

Frank and Sturm murmured thanks. The soup was spicy, more vegetable than water, and delicious. Neither hesitated for a second spoonful. But as soon as everyone finished their soup, silence bloomed again.

Alice couldn't take it anymore. "Music! Would anyone like to hear music while we eat?"

"I guess that would depend on what kind of music," Sturm said.

Alice wasn't ready for that. "Well, ahhh, we have . . . classical?"

"We have classical music, Mr. Sturm," Annie said.

Sturm wasn't impressed. "Fine."

"We also have plenty of gangster rap," Annie said. "Would you prefer that instead?" Frank thought he heard a whisper of a laugh from the kitchen.

Sturm didn't dignify that with an answer.

"I have some serious black metal—Scandinavian death metal, you know?" Clearly Annie's favorite.

"I don't—I don't think that would be appropriate for the dinner table," Alice said.

The second course was brought out, giant ceramic tubs of some kind of pasta in a creamy white sauce, with broccoli. Like the minestrone, it tasted fantastic. Edie came out and asked, "You folks need anything?" and got a sharp look from Alice. "If you're looking for music, we've got some really cool disco albums around here." She started to softly sing under her breath.

"Please Edie, no ABBA. Not tonight." Alice helped Edie into the kitchen.

Annie's tone got more playful with Sturm, nicer somehow. "Let's see. I think we may have some country music around here. Old stuff."

"I always liked them singing cowboys, the early ones. Roy Rogers. Gene Autry. Not like that shit you hear on the radio nowadays. Just 'cause they wear a damn cowboy hat. Those people wouldn't know authentic country music if it came up and bit 'em on the ass."

Frank himself had a weakness for the Mexican tunes he had heard around the barns from twenty-dollar boomboxes choked with dust. The only Spanish he spoke was related to racehorses, so he figured the music had to be love songs. The lead singer sounded wounded somehow, but sang with a rolling melody like water over rocks in a desert creek. The band was almost always made up of trumpets, tubas, maybe a strange little guitar or two, and an accordion holding the whole thing together.

Frank kept this to himself.

Alice came back. "I'm sorry. She always gets nervous around company."

"She won't be like this around the guests, will she?" Sturm said. "I mean, maybe its best if Mrs. Glouck stays in the kitchen once we have company."

Frank knew Annie's feelings were hurt because she took her eyes off Sturm and for a second, couldn't look into his face. Frank had been wondering which mother was Annie's, but still wasn't sure. He heard Alice say, "Ah, I, well—don't think that will be a problem. I hope this won't interfere with our arrangement."

Annie cut in quick. "I think Mr. Sturm will understand this is a trial run, won't you, Mr. Sturm?" She'd looked back up and now stared across the table at him. Without waiting, she rolled on. "He'll understand that we have thirteen days to polish our services. We will get it straight. Tonight is a simple get-together."

"No dear," Alice said just as fast. "I believe the word was 'audition.' "

"Tell me, Mr. Sturm—"

"Call me Horace," Sturm damn near shouted.

"Tell me Horace, who exactly is this family's competition? Given the nature of your enterprise."

Sturm crossed his arms, leaned on them, knocked on the table. "Just making sure the food and service is at a professional level. Our guests have traveled the world, eaten at the finest restaurants, slept in the finest hotels. I'd hate to disappoint them."

"I think you'll find, Mr. Sturm, that your guests will be taken care of. There will be no complaints, I promise you," Alice said with an edge in her voice, an invitation for Sturm to disagree.

"I gotta be honest here, ladies." Sturm leaned back and turned his palms up, as if surrendering. "Everything I have seen and tasted tonight has been delightful. If I come across as some mountain man who's been out in the hills for too long, my apologies. I believe in being up front and honest. I have full confidence in this family's capabilities."

"See?" Annie said. "I told you Mr. Sturm—"

"I said, call me Horace," Sturm said and pulled an envelope out of his pocket. Inside was four pages of legal writing.

"—Horace would understand."

"How lovely," Alice said.

Sturm waved the brothers away and got up and flattened the papers on the table next to Alice's plate. He signed it, then let Alice sign. She signed twice. Sturm took the top two pages, refolded them, and tucked them away as he sat back down. Alice gave her copy to a brother and he took off.

And just like that, the ice was broken. Frank could feel everyone at the table relax, as if the house itself had exhaled. Alice and Sturm talked politics and weather. Frank caught Annie glancing at him now and again throughout the dinner, but her expression was indecipherable. He couldn't figure out what the next dish was, chicken parmesan maybe, but something was different. Sturm had to point out it was tiger meat. Frank didn't care. It tasted unbelievable.

Edie came out and tried to kiss Alice at one point, but Sturm didn't say anything. He just looked at his plate. The only other incident came just after desert, delicate little pastries filled with heavy crème. Frank didn't know how it started, just that there was a pop from the kitchen, and Gun slammed backward through the door, the front of his shirt on fire. He was pursued by two older brothers, who seemed to be more interested in making sure the flames burned off his face before the fire was extinguished.

Still, Gun fought back, punching and kicking, ignoring the flames searing his flesh. Eventually, he ripped off his burning white shirt and tried to use that as a weapon. Annie jumped to her feet and hurled the pitcher of water at her brothers, but it glanced off Gun's back and exploded against the wall. Edie burst from the kitchen and slammed Gun onto the floor. She kicked her toe under his shoulder and jerked him up, rolling him against the still damp shag carpet. That put out the fire.

She whirled and slapped both of the attacking brothers at the same time. They backed into the kitchen without a word. Then she got herself a handful of Gun's hair and lifted him off the floor and threw him at the kitchen door. He landed on the linoleum floor and slid into the stove with a crash.

Edie turned and said, "My deepest, sincere apologies. I knew it was a mistake to give him a job lighting candles. Should've never given him a lighter. You have my word, Horace, that this will never happen again." She vanished into the kitchen and slammed the door.

The house was quiet except for the muffled slaps and cries from the kitchen. The rest of the brothers had vanished into the shag carpet. Annie stood. "If you gentlemen will excuse me. I'll be right back. In the meantime," she snapped her fingers and two brothers reluctantly appeared. They quickly poured two whiskies and threw the glasses in front of Frank and Sturm.

Annie followed her family into the kitchen. "Stupid goddamn French fry licking—fucking morons—you too—" The door shut, reducing Annie's voice to hisses and barks.

"Well," Alice said. "My goodness. The boys, they like to roughhouse. Um, cheers." She lifted her glass at Sturm and Frank.

Sturm took his whisky, saluted Alice, and threw it back.

Frank decided it would be okay to drink. So he took a solid sip. It left a clean, pure burning path down his throat and rekindled the embers lying dormant in his stomach. His mood improved instantly.

Sturm waved his glass in the general direction of the brothers flanking the front door. They leaped to life and immediately refilled it.

Ignoring Alice, Sturm asked, "How're my girls?"

"They've been worse."

Sturm snorted into his whiskey. "Hell yes, son. I know that. Are they going to be ready to hunt?"

Frank took another sip and let it sit in his mouth for a moment, feeling the smooth sizzle of the amber liquid. He swallowed and nodded. "They'll be ready."

"That's all I ask." Sturm finished the rest of the glass and thumped it on the table. "Miss Glouck, this evening has been quite satisfactory. Well done. Give my compliments to the chef. Unfortunately, it is time for me to remove myself. I have a very full day tomorrow, as do we all." He gave Frank a meaningful look.

"Yeah." Frank emptied his glass, set it gently on the table.

Alice fought to rise quickly in her tight dress, as if she was afraid Sturm or Frank might stand first. "Well, thank you gentlemen for gracing us with your presence. It was lovely."

Sturm stood and nodded, "Of course."

"So . . . we will be waiting to hear from you," Alice said.

Sturm patted his pockets to reassure himself that the contract and his wallet were still there. "Soon as we get the tents set up, I'll let you know."

Frank stood as well, eyeing the kitchen door, but Annie didn't appear. "Thank you for dinner. It was delicious." He meant it.

Alice gave him a smile, a genuine one this time, unselfconscious, one that pulled her chin back in tight to her throat and exposed her crooked bottom teeth. It made Frank feel even warmer, fueling the whiskey fire. He felt almost safe. Alice stared right at him. "You come back anytime you want. You got a place at this table anytime, understand? You helped Petunia."

"That's his job," Sturm said. "He fixes animals that are broken." One of the brothers brought his hat. "Thank you again for a *lovely* meal." Settling the black Stetson on his white, bald head, he said, "Let's go."

Frank nodded, almost bowed, at Alice. "Thanks. Tell Annie I said goodnight," he said and followed Sturm out the front door. They walked through the deep shadow of the satellite dish eclipsing the streetlight. Sturm paused long enough to light a cigar. "That haircut. That's a whole lot better. Cleaner," Sturm said, popping his cheeks to draw air through the cigar. "Bet it feels better in this goddamn heat."

"How's the wound?"

189

"Frank!" It was Annie, silhouetted in the front door. Then, more calm, more composed, as she slowly came down the steps. "Running off without saying goodbye?"

Sturm grinned at Frank under the cigar smoke.

"Hold on, okay?" Annie said. "Just hold on. Don't go running off. Got someone here who wants to say hello." She went around the side of the house, and a few moments later, Petunia came bounding out, claws digging into the bare dirt, tail wagging furiously. She slammed into Frank and nearly knocked him down. Her tongue was all over his hands and she bounced like a kangaroo, trying to reach his face. Frank grabbed her wide head and bent over, crinkling his eyes shut and curling his lips inward, allowing the dog's wet leathery tongue to lick his cheeks, nose, and forehead.

Annie followed Petunia at a leisurely pace. "I think she's got the hots for you, you know."

"She's just a good dog, aren't you?" Frank said. "Yes. That's right. A goddamn good dog. Yes." Petunia seemed to agree, wiggling even harder.

"You in a hurry?" Annie asked.

"No. Suppose not," Frank said, scratching behind Petunia's ears.

"Then let's take Petunia for a swim."

Frank caught himself looking at Sturm for permission. Sturm just grinned back, puffing furiously on his cigar. Frank stood, and patted Petunia's skull. "Where?"

"Up at the reservoir. That okay with you, Mr. Sturm?" She'd caught Frank's look, and this seemed to be more to fuel Frank's embarrassment than Sturm's okay.

Sturm waved his cigar, smoke streaming in the orange light from the streetlight. "You kids go have fun." He walked back over and shook Frank's hand. "Don't worry. Go have fun. I'll talk to you tomorrow." Frank saw the hint of a wink, and felt

190

something flat and stiff in his palm, left from the handshake. He casually tilted his hand and saw a twenty-dollar bill, crisply folded in thirds, tucked into his palm. Sturm walked back to his pickup. "Tomorrow." He awkwardly stepped up into his pickup, like a handicapped child clambering into a playground spaceship, and roared off.

Frank started the car and turned the air conditioning on while Annie folded the front seat down, whistling for Petunia to get in the back seat. Frank thought of the quiet gentlemen's reactions to a dog in the back seat and smiled. And not just any dog, either; Petunia smelled like she'd swam across a few of the sewage treatment plant ponds to get home. Hell, if he could, he'd get Petunia to take a dump on the front seat before he got rid of the car.

Annie rode in the front seat and pointed directions while talking nonstop about her brothers. "Stupid goddamn fuckheads. They can't stop jerking off for fifteen minutes to settle on anything but sex—and if they can't get that—which of course they fucking aren't—then it gets to anger right fucking quick." She killed the AC and rolled down her window.

Frank hit a highway going up into the hills and stepped on the gas.

Annie lit a cigarette like she was shooting a gun into the wind. Petunia curled up in the back seat and went to sleep. "When they get into it, fighting, they're like goddamn dogs, all that frustration where they don't know whether to fight or fuck, so you just gotta treat 'em like dogs. Hose 'em off with cold water. Most of the time, that works. Most of the time." Annie inhaled the cigarette in six savage bites and lit another with the filter of the first one. "Turn here."

Annie slowed down, relaxing into the seat, taking it easier on the cigarette. "I'm sorry. Tonight was important, and those fucking morons fucking fucked it up," she said and put a hand on Frank's thigh. But the touch was brief, and then her hand was on to fiddling with the radio. "Fucking radio around here sucks. It sucks long and hard." With her particular emphasis on those last words, Frank couldn't help but wonder if she meant something else. Fed up with the selection, Annie switched the radio off. "Where you from?"

"All over."

"That much I guessed. Where were you born?"

"East Texas."

"Where's your family now?"

"All over."

"You visit with 'em much?"

Frank followed Annie's finger and turned into an empty parking lot. There was a half moon, just enough to reflect off the fifty-acre reservoir. He shrugged as he pulled into a spot and stopped. "Didn't see the point in driving all over to visit a bunch of cemeteries." He stopped the car, facing the lake, under a billion stars.

"Your mom?" Annie finished her cigarette, threw it out the window, but made no move to get out.

Frank gave a sad smile. "Cancer."

"Dad?"

"Don't know."

"My daddy's in jail. He's not a good man. I hope he never gets out."

"How'd he get there?" Frank was hoping she'd put her hand back on his thigh.

Annie gave her own sad smile. "He broke into seventeen campers and trailers across the Southwest, killing the husbands and any children, then raping and killing the wife. You probably heard about it."

"Jesus." Frank was sorry he'd asked.

"No, I'm fucking with you. He's in a jail, sure, but hell, he's just a dumb-ass. He went after armored cars—he'd stake out an ATM and follow the truck back. He nailed two trucks, cops nailed him on the third. Thought he had to be a tough guy and use a loaded gun. So he oughta be up for parole in twenty years or so. I take a bus and see him once in a while."

Frank turned off the engine and they sat in silence for a moment. "My daddy was a preacher. Can't exactly say he was a man of God. He believed in . . . well, he believed in the devil, one. That's for damn sure. And two, he believed in serpents. He was one of them snake handlers, always saying the Word of God was protecting him from bites. Didn't matter that he got bit twice in the face. He said that was 'cause of me. And mom, but mostly me. His fault for spawning me. God was punishing him."

Annie twisted around to look at Petunia and put her hand back on Frank's thigh. "You think she wants to go swimming?"

Frank didn't want to move, didn't want to give Annie any reason to pull her hand back, but he carefully turned his head and glanced into the back seat. Petunia snored softly, curled up in a tight ball, dead to the world. "I don't know. She looks awful comfortable."

"That's what I thought." Annie slid closer. "Kind of nice, just sitting here, looking at the water."

"Yeah."

"I know you've heard about me," Annie said without looking at Frank.

"What?"

"Let's stop pretending, okay? We do it all the time, with everyone, with everything that goes through our heads, so let's . . . let's just not do it tonight, okay? Not between you and me. It's demeaning. So, what did you hear? I know they filled you in. I want to know what they had to say."

Frank exhaled, long and slow, wondering if one of Annie's

cigarettes would help. He thought of something better. "Well. You're talking about the guys, the clowns, right?" He felt around under the driver's seat and pulled out the bottle of cheap rum he'd stashed earlier.

"Who else?"

"They're . . . they're big fans. Chuck is, anyway."

Annie smiled hugely. "Of course he is. But why? What did he say, exactly?"

Frank unscrewed the top, let the cap fall wherever it wanted. "He, uh, he said you were the best." He took a long, long drink.

"The best. Best at what?" Annie still hadn't moved her hand. Frank was sure he'd never been anywhere that had been so goddamn quiet. It was so quiet he could hear Annie's thumb and forefinger tracing little circles, smoothing out the denim on his thigh.

Frank took another hefty swallow, decided to get it over with. "He said that, for twenty bucks, you gave the best blowjobs ever." He immediately took another drink, then offered it to Annie.

She took the bottle with a knowing smile. "Good. Perfect. That's what I hoped he'd say." She took a drink. "Uggh. This is crap. Where'd you get this?"

Frank laughed, took it back. "It was cheap."

Annie lit a fresh cigarette, took it slow, enjoying the drag. She still wouldn't look at Frank. "The way I see it, no matter what you do, no matter what kind of job you want to get, it's all about marketing, you know? It's all about word of mouth. It's all about perception, see?"

Frank shook his head.

Annie said quietly, "I never gave anybody a blowjob. Shit. I'm still a virgin." She gave Frank a little grin that stopped his heart. "I just get 'em to pay for a blowjob, and then to say that they had one. You understand?"

Frank wanted to nod and say, "Yeah." But he said, "No."

Annie turned in her seat to face Frank, eyes alive with mischief. "It's simple. Men and their dicks. You play with their ego. See, I start slow. Maybe a little rubbing, through the pants, but the whole secret is talking dirty. You get to talking dirty to a man, I mean, really working it, really stroking his imagination, and hell, you're almost there. That's all it takes. Want me to show you?"

Frank's heart had almost started beating again when this stopped it dead. "Why don't you walk me through it first."

"You sure?"

"No."

Annie laughed. "Okay. Okay. Well, it starts slow, like I said." She started rubbing his thigh. "Then we go for a drive. Someplace private. Like this," she gestured out at the lake through the windshield."

"You been here before?"

"Maybe. So then I start talking about, oh, I don't know, about the night or the lake. Doesn't matter. The point is, I'm using words like *soft, wet, smooth*, for the place. Then I refer to them, using words like *powerful, hard, strong*. Things like that, you know?"

With each adjective or adverb, her voice became husky, slow, seductive. The rubbing of his thighs matched her voice. "Then my hand moves up. Hell, half the time I don't even have to unzip their jeans." Her palm slid up to Frank's crotch. He was surprised to find that he wasn't the least embarrassed about his aching erection, and took another swallow of rum.

"Then I just rub, slow, for awhile, talking to them the whole time. About what I'm going to do to them, about how much I enjoy it, how much I *need* it. I'll go into detail about how soft my mouth will feel, how much suction my tongue will give, how much I *want* them. Sometimes, that's all it takes. Sometimes, they last a little longer. So I use a rubber glove. Like a surgical glove. Didn't bring one with me tonight, though." Her hand paused on his belt buckle. "Thing with latex gloves though, you gotta provide a little extra lubrication, so I'd stick my hand down my pants, pretend to rub myself. All I had to do was act like I was enjoying it. Want me to show you?"

"Not if it's fake."

"You add a little spit to it," she mimicked licking her hand, "and yeah, sometimes you had to touch 'em." Her hand closed into a fist. "I just pretended I was milking a cow. Usually didn't take 'em long. 'Specially if I talked." Her hand unclasped his belt buckle with a smooth jerk.

"Then what?" he asked.

"Then what—what?" She pulled back and flicked the cigarette out of the window. "They came. I could usually talk them into wiping themselves with their shirts." Annie thought this was pretty funny.

"You never . . ."

"You've got to be fucking kidding me." She turned toward him, up on her knees, hands in lap, demure as a choir girl. "Put something like that in my mouth? Please. Especially with the hygiene around here. But the thing is, they can't tell each other the truth—they can't admit that they never got a blowjob. Hell, they think they're the only one that came before getting their dick sucked, and there's no way they want to admit it to each other. They don't want to be the only one that didn't come in my mouth. So yeah, they're out there telling each other that they got the best blowjob of their lives."

Frank didn't know what to say. He checked on Petunia. She hadn't moved. Annie blinked at him. His erection hadn't gone down. His scalp itched from being shaved. "Why are you telling me this?"

" 'Cause I want you to know that I'm not . . . well, I was going to say not a whore, but that would be lying, wouldn't it? I am a whore," she said, almost proud. "I just have boundaries."

"So why are you telling me this?"

" 'Cause I like you. And I want you to like me."

Frank took another long drink. The bottle was nearly half empty. "Look. I, uh . . ." The rum decided he should be honest. "Ahh, fuck it. I do like you. I . . . shit. Ever since I met you, I can't stop thinking about you."

Annie's face glowed in the starlight. "Please don't tease."

"I'm not. We both do things . . . things that we wish we didn't have to." He reached out and cupped her head, thumb just in front of the ear, the rest of the fingers stroking the back of her skull. He kissed her. Gentle. Tender. Her lips felt soft as clouds. He pulled back. "But you . . . stimulate cattle for reproduction." Frank gave her a cold, lopsided smile and Annie wanted to pull away from his touch. "I kill."

They sat in silence during the ride back. It wasn't uncomfortable, though. It was more a contemplative quiet, each lost in their own thoughts. Both realized that they had revealed more of themselves to each other than perhaps anyone else alive. This was a new experience, a strange sensation, being so honest, so open with someone else. It felt like struggling into a new skin. Something that didn't feel uncomfortable exactly, just different.

Frank stopped in front of the satellite dish. Petunia, awake by now, licked his ear. He turned to Annie. "I need to see you again. Soon."

She gave a secretive little smile, clasped his face with both hands, and kissed him deeply on the mouth. He felt the electrifying touch of her tongue, just a brief little stab, but it was enough to stick in his mind for days. Then, without saying a word, she slid out of the car, let Petunia out, gave a tiny wave, and disappeared into the house.

Frank finished the bottle of rum driving back to the vet office. He grabbed a beer and told the cats about his evening. He
wasn't sure if they were impressed or not, but he was happy. He
hadn't felt this good since the night of the town BBQ and
carnival. The nagging worm of doubt about who was telling the
truth was gone. Annie had shared her secret with him and he
was sure she was being honest. He couldn't say why, exactly.
There was something about the way she watched him most of
the time, direct, merciless; but she'd get shy every so often and
couldn't meet his eyes. Soft and hard. Sweet and sour. Yin and
yang. It was the contrast, that wonderfully wild seesaw of feelings that pulled him in. He didn't think she had enough control
over her emotions to lie.

He fell asleep on the couch, plotting out an escape to some
tiny seaside town in Mexico. He'd earned plenty of cash, and
Annie would come down later, only wanting to be with him, to
lie in his arms and listen to the distant surf. It was a fine vision.

And it seemed damn close to grab.

DAY TWENTY

Like the cheap rum, the fantasy had rotted the next morning, turning sour and sick in his mind. His head felt brittle, fragile, like his skull was too tight. He wanted to smash something breakable. Around six, the sensation of his head cracking apart like hardwood cooking in the sun drove him into the bathroom, where there was a bottle of aspirin on the toilet. He stumbled back to his cot where he slept dreamlessly until noon, when it took him at least ten minutes to realize someone was ringing the hospital's buzzer.

Frank drifted along the rows of cages, the eyes of the big cats like starving leeches on his bare skin. His tongue felt as if fungus had covered it during the night. The horizon swam and lurched in his eyes.

And when he saw the two deputies outside, his hangover got truly vicious, grabbing him by the ears and stabbing at the nerves behind his eyes and refusing to let go. His stomach spasmed and quivered, threatening to spatter half-digested tiger meat, pasta, and spicy vegetables all over the tile floor.

Through the bathroom window, standing on the toilet seat, Frank saw them waiting just outside the front door, hands on their hips, alternately watching the empty street and the door. They looked like they were trying hard to look bored, but the occasional cry or hiss from one of the hungry cats made their heavy-lidded eyes snap open in furtive movement. Then they'd glance quickly at each other, as if reassuring themselves that they were on the right track. Herschell Thibbetts still wore his mirrored sunglasses, anchored to his squashed, pinched face by a strap around the back of his head. Olaf Halford looked like he'd sheared his head that very morning. Neither one let go of the butt of their handguns.

Thoughts swam sluggishly through Frank's wounded mind. His first reaction was to simply bolt out the back door, snatch the cash hidden in the horizontal freezer behind the barn, jump in the long, black car and drive north. He was all the way to the back door, his hand curling around the doorknob, when he heard Herschell shout, "Mr. Winchester. Mr. Winchester, we know you are in there. That car of yours is back in the barn." Herschell hit the buzzer again. "Mr. Winchester."

The last shred of rational thought left in his head begged him to slow down and think. Driving north wouldn't help him much. Frank needed help, plain and simple. He could always try to run later, if it came to that. As long as he wasn't a suspect for the murder of some trucker. Or the murder of the zoo owner. Or, while he was being honest, one of the quiet gentlemen, the one he'd pulled into the tank with him.

He let go of the back door handle and stumbled over to the black phone nailed to the wall. He dialed Sturm's number, but Theo answered.

"Hey. This is Frank."

"So?"

"Your dad there?"

"Why?"

"This is important."

"Then tell me. And I'll decide if it's important enough to get my dad."

Frank resisted the urge to smash the phone against the wall. "I need to talk to your dad. Right now."

"He's not here."

"Where is he?"

"He's out."

Herschell or Olaf rang the buzzer again.

"Well, listen. This is Frank. I need to talk to him right now."

"He's out."

"Yeah." Frank punched the wall. "Listen, doesn't he have one of them cell phones or walkie-talkie things? Said so himself that this was serious work. Said these cats were the most important element in our business. I know you can reach him. Give me the number."

"Don't have it. So fuck you," and the line went dead.

Frank slammed the phone down hard enough to pull the top of the base away from the wall. Baby spiders, stung by the sudden light, crawled sleepily out from under the base, setting out for the nooks and crannies of the vet hospital.

Frank knew he didn't have a choice. He went back up front and opened the front door. He rubbed at his eyes and yawned with exaggerated gestures. "Morning."

"Good . . ." Herschell checked his watch. ". . . afternoon, sir."

Olaf Halford fixed his stare on Frank. "Wondering if we could come in and take a look around."

Frank said, "Sure," but didn't move. "What are you officers looking for? Maybe I can help you out."

"Some of the neighbors have expressed concern over the use of the facilities," Olaf said.

"Neighbors? Didn't realize I had any," Frank said, eyeballing the empty, dead houses down the street.

Herschell's smile was thin and forced. "This whole town is your neighbor, sir."

"And these concerns . . . concerned . . . ?"

"The illegal captivity and holding of nonlicensed animals."

"Well, this is a vet hospital. Didn't realize that sick animals needing my help needed licenses to be treated."

"We'd like to take a look around," Herschell said. The "sir" attitude was gone. "We can come back with a search warrant, if you'd like." Herschell's tone suggested that this would be a bad idea.

Frank knew it was useless to pretend anymore. "Of course, just curious, that's all. The animals are back here. Mr. Sturm had 'em brought in special." There was a distant hope that by mentioning Sturm's name, these deputies would understand he was simply following orders, same as them.

"Mr. Sturm is subject to the same laws regarding exotic animal captivity as anyone else," Herschell said, stepping inside. "If these are actually indeed his animals." Olaf followed, both removing their hats with their left hands. Their right never left the butt of the sidearm.

Stalling for time, Frank said, "I'm sorry. I don't understand."

"We've got these reports. From concerned citizens," Herschell said, standing solidly in the middle of the room while Olaf wandered around, looking nowhere and everywhere at once. Herschell held his hand up and snapped his fingers, a snapping, dry crack that stabbed Frank's brain like a dull ice pick. When he had Frank's attention, he said, "I think you know why we're here."

Frank shrugged. "I don't understand the nature of the complaints."

Herschell brushed past Frank saying, "I think you do," and followed Olaf through the door to the back of the office. He poked his head in the bathroom, the second examining room, and the back room filled with books. But this was a quick, cursory scan, making sure Frank didn't have any company.

Frank wondered if Herschell or Olaf had been with Annie.

"Seems like there's been a whole hell of a lot of different

animals in and out of this place in the last few weeks, not to mention the shooting in town, we want to know just what the hell is going on. We got the safety of this town to think about."

"Yeah. So you're looking for . . . ?"

"Besides the monkeys out in the barn? And that thing, whatever it is, some kind of retarded elephant?" Herschell opened the door to the cats. "And of course, these little darlins." He motioned for Frank to follow. Herschell stopped halfway down the cages, triumphant now that the game was up, fishing in the back pocket of his uniform. The cats shrank to the back of their cages, tails flicking, eyes darting.

He held up a sheaf of official-looking paper, skipped through a few parts with his index finger, and read out loud, ". . . here . . . 'for exotic specimen, including, but not limited to, lions, lionesses.' Both of 'em. In fact, 'both male and female for any other species named or unnamed, from henceforth within.' Tigers. Cheetahs. Any other kind of big cat. One big rhino. A barn full of monkeys."

As Herschell read on, Frank knew the cops had been through the hospital, had seen everything. They had already taken a good long look at all of the animals. They'd been in the back room. They'd been through his stuff. And just like that, Olaf brought Frank's shotgun up from behind him, bringing it up to that peculiarly soft stretch of skin up behind his ear, between his neck muscles and the back of the jawbone. The sharp coldness of the barrel hit his skin back there, strangely gentle, as Olaf's voice said, "And what the living fuck are you doing with a loaded firearm?"

Frank lifted his arms and spread his fingers wide. "Easy. Easy does it. I'm no criminal."

"Where you from, Mr. Winchester?" Herschell asked. Olaf pulled the shotgun back. But he remained behind Frank.

"I was born in East Texas. My mom and me, we lived all over

the Midwest, we—"

"Where you working now, dipshit," Olaf said.

"Ohio. Cleveland."

"Bullshit," Herschell said. "You seem a little on the slow side, so let me help you understand just how deep the shit is that you have just found yourself in. One," Herschell counted on his fingers, just to help Frank comprehend. "You got fugitive written all over you. Here you are, no identification, no nothing. You ain't from Cleveland, I'd bet my badge on that. Two. You seem to be running this vet hospital, but I'll be damned if I see any of your degrees or certificates or any other crap like that anywhere around. Even the head rat catcher over at the Dole sugar plant has got a certificate of somesuch. What do you got? Fuck all, that's what. But for whatever reason, you seem to be living here. And treating patients, I might add. Of course, from what I can tell, you ain't too good at your job. Last I heard, you killed a poor housecat. And that brings us to three and these animals here." Herschell tapped the cages with the official documents. "This is California, not some jungle village in deepest, darkest Africa." He shook his head. "You're in some serious trouble here and you're just too goddamn dumb to know it."

Frank didn't say anything. Herschell seemed disappointed.

"Fine. Fine. Here's what's gonna happen," Herschell said. "We're gonna take you down to the station, take a pretty picture. Then we're gonna send that picture out all over the country and I'd be willing to bet somebody, somewhere has a big time hard-on for you."

Olaf grabbed Frank's arms and Frank heard the distinct clicking and muted jangling of handcuffs in the small of his back. Real ones this time, not the plastic ones the quiet gentlemen used. There would be no breaking these with a screwdriver.

As if sensing the sudden tension in Frank's arm muscles, Olaf said, "Give me any trouble and them cats'll be licking your brains off the floor." The handcuffs locked into place like a pit bull's jaws.

They'd gotten Frank out to the cruiser and were just about to lock him in the backseat when Sturm's pickup bounced into the parking lot in a storm of dust. Herschell and Olaf exchanged glances.

Sturm ambled up like he was being social after church, bare-chested except for the wide swath of bandages strapped around his upper torso. The milky skin on his shoulders had started to glow red in the relentless sun. He had his black cowboy hat squarely over his bald head and the Iron Mistress swung at his hip. "Howdy boys. No trouble with my employee, I hope."

Herschell nodded. "I'm afraid so. This man has no ID, no license to practice veterinary medicine in California, no nothing. But we got all these animals, none of 'em native to this state, supposedly under his supposed care. Then there's the animal that got loose. Tiger, I believe. Operation of a firearm on a public street is a violation of County Code 43 and is punishable by a fine of not less than three hundred dollars and not more than six hundred dollars," Herschell recited in a flat, dull voice. "We'll have to take him down to Redding for this," he added and nodded at Frank. "I'd hate to think he was taking advantage of us. For the safety of the community, we're gonna take him in, see if we can't find out who he really is."

"Can't be too careful in these uncertain times," Olaf said.

"Oh hell no. Can't be too careful whatsoever," Sturm said. "And these are unfuckingcertain times, that's for goddamned sure. This man is an extremely valuable employee. I need his help. I need his help right now, today, in fact. And I'd hate to be inconvenienced in any way. You boys take him down to Redding, it might take a while to clear his name. I don't have that kind of time." Sturm tapped his head.

"I can appreciate that, Mr. Sturm," Herschell said. "But the fact is, we got ourselves plenty of violations happening here. We don't have a choice in the matter."

"Shit." Sturm rapped his knuckles across the hood. "This doesn't have anything to do with that permit I forgot to file, does it?"

"It might," Herschell said.

Sturm pulled a roll of cash bundled in a thick rubber band from his Carhart overalls. "Knew I forgot something last week. This permit we're talking about, I'll need it for the meeting of a gun club. How much was it again?"

Herschell eyed the roll. "Normally, we'd be talking a couple hundred. But this, this is different. These conditions, the large number of animals . . . I'd say we're looking at somewhere around four hundred, at least. Plus the fine of six hundred."

Sturm's fingers pinched off a thick stack of twenties. "Listen, I appreciate your willingness to take care of business out here. I'd hate to drag this downtown. Let's just take care of all them damn fines, citations, levies, taxes, and whatever else shit you want to charge right here and now."

Herschell took the cash and Olaf popped the handcuffs open. Frank rubbed his wrists and backed slowly toward the hospital. Somebody in the town, most likely the woman from the gas station, had sicced the cops on him.

Out in the petrified mud, past the back end of the vehicles, Herschell said quietly, "You sure about this, Mr. Sturm? I been in law enforcement going on thirty years now. I don't need a goddamn neon sign to tell me someone is bad news. And this boy is bad news, I'm telling you."

"He'll be fine," Sturm said. "I trust him."

Herschell shrugged. "Because of your . . . situation. So be it. That permit you just filed, that'll cover the next few weeks. You need anything, you let us know. Take care of yourself. You got our prayers." Herschell and Olaf solemnly climbed into the cruiser and shut the doors. Sturm waved. The cruiser slowly lumbered off across the parking lot and down the street toward the center of town.

Sturm clapped his hands together and blew past Frank. "How're my girls?"

Day Twenty-One

Sturm had Pine plant dynamite in a ditch tunnel under the highway for a roadblock. The thing that struck Frank was that there wasn't really a need to do much of anything to the highway. There was no traffic. There was nobody. Just the fields, a few sheep, the sun, and the men running around like ants building some kind of awful trap for a fat, unsuspecting bug.

But Sturm had a plan, and he didn't want any unexpected visitors during the hunts. He explained how it worked. If the town was expecting you, you were given a set of instructions. Instead of just taking the highway into town, you went back up the highway a ways until you came to a gate, secured with a heavy chain and combination lock. Beyond the gate was a road that looked like the parallel tracks of a dirt railroad through deep grass. It led around a swamp thick with cattails, up a little valley, and back down to the highway into town.

Sturm didn't want to blow up the bridge over the ditch just yet. He wanted it to be an event, a celebration. They left the trigger under a five-gallon bucket in case of rain, more of a distant hope than anything, and kept the dynamite waiting.

That night, Jack showed up at the vet hospital to pick up Frank. "Got a meeting," Jack said, cracking a beer as they pulled out of the parking lot. The sun was drawing closer to the western mountains, but the temperature was still 104 degrees.

They drove through town, and Frank could see that nearly

every window of every building had been covered with particle board and aluminum siding. It looked like the town of White-wood was preparing for an especially destructive hurricane. Jack explained it was for the hunts. No point in leaving the windows exposed for stray bullets.

The taxidermist wasn't taking any chances. He'd hung thick sheets of lead over his windows and front door. Instead of a hurricane, he appeared to be preparing for nuclear war.

A line of nearly forty pickups, all stuffed with what looked like junk at first, waited in town, starting at the park. Men stood in small groups, smoking and talking. They all looked up as Jack's pickup circled the park. Jack pulled into a U-turn, tossing his beer can out the window. He honked his horn a few times. Men got back into their pickups, and engines started up and down the line.

Frank asked, "Who are all these people?"

Jack headed south, back down the highway toward the back-hoe and dynamite. "Farmers, ranchers." He shrugged. "Folks that live—*used to* live around here. Mr. Sturm went around and talked to 'em. Those that were just renting, he kicked 'em off. Those that owned their land, Sturm bought it off 'em. Hell, he gave 'em more cash than these people have ever seen in their life. Everybody's clearing out, they're heading for greener pastures." The pickup rattled slowly through the empty town, windows blind with wood and aluminum.

The line of pickups followed, loaded with what looked like every possession the families could carry. The trucks' beds were stuffed with mattresses, washing machines, rolltop desks, oak cabinets, swing sets, televisions, children's bicycles, couches, sewing machines, water heaters, refrigerators, satellite dishes, and plenty of cardboard boxes. Often, the children themselves rode in the back, silent and sullen, wind whipping their hair. The back ends rode low, shocks compressed to their max, shuddering after every bounce, the kids automatically rolling with the stuttering progress of the truck. It looked like something out of *The Grapes of Wrath.*

"Why are they all leaving at night?" Frank asked.

"So the kids don't fry in the sun."

Frank nodded. It made sense. "I didn't think there were this many people in the town."

"Yeah, it's most everybody," Jack said, as if he knew most, if not all, of the people in the pickups.

Jack led the procession down the highway out of town. When they came upon the backhoe, lit in front by the headlights of all the pickups, backlit by the setting sun, Frank saw Sturm's pickup. Sturm himself was leaning against his pickup, arms crossed, black hat low, cold gray eyes watching and noting each pickup and family that passed him.

Jack pulled off the highway and stopped behind Sturm's truck. The procession passed, picking up speed once they had seen Sturm. Sturm never moved, never even nodded, never acknowledged any of the passing vehicles.

Jack and Frank watched for a while, then Jack headed back into town, passing pickup after pickup until finally there was nothing but the bare highway. He roared back into the empty town. "Goddamn. Look at it."

"So?" Frank asked. "Didn't Sturm own damn near everything anyways?"

"Well, sure. But the point is, they're gone. Say you're shooting at something." The pickup slid to a stop under the only stoplight in town, the one in front of the park, the same one the cops had ran Frank's first day. "Before, 'less you're back in the hills, you always gotta be thinking about your backdrop. Now," Jack belched, tossed his beer can out the window. It bounced and the hollow sound echoed throughout the streets. "Now, fuck it. You can shoot . . . without hesitation." He pulled his rifle out of the gun rack in the back window. "You don't have to worry about anything," he said, settling the rifle in his lap, barrel out of the open window. "Nobody's there."

Frank didn't think that anybody in this town believed in air conditioning.

Jack cracked open two new beers and handed one to Frank. Above them, the red light changed to green. Jack aimed his rifle down a dark street.

Frank took the beer, upended the one he had been holding. He finished it, squeezed the can, and crumpled it on his knee. "One sec." He opened the door, got out, put the fresh can on the roof, and unzipped his fly, pissing beer all over the green asphalt. His piss on the street turned golden, then the color of blood. Frank knew it was just the stoplight above him, but it still made him nauseous.

Jack fired, blowing a spiderweb of cracks through the windshield of a Ford pickup parked under a eucalyptus tree fifty yards away. Frank wasn't expecting this; he flinched and damn near choked the piss off in mid-stream. He felt like he might vomit, sick from the heat. The sound of the rifle shot faded into the bare asphalt, thirsty trees, and dark buildings and houses. There were no shouts. No telephones. No car alarms. No dogs barking. Just a quiet sense of vast emptiness.

Sturm waited for everyone on the front porch. He sat in a large rocking chair, toes of his cowboy boots just barely touching the planks in the floor, just enough to rock back and forth an inch or so. He rolled his head with each transition in motion, from one end of the inch to the other, emphasizing the barely perceptible rocking. He looked like a child, with the top of the chair, all carved swirls and bows, over a foot above his hat. He was bare-chested again, save for the bandages. Blisters had formed on his shoulders, the color of embers left in the BBQ. His pocketknife was out, etching complex patterns into his wooden cane. Originally, it was an unblemished, perfectly straight two and a half feet rolling up into a graceful half-circle handle, but was now tattooed like a Maori warrior.

Jack and Frank were the last ones to the meeting. Everyone else was waiting in their pickups, in an unspoken agreement to wait for Jack. Nobody would actually get out of their pickups yet; that would be breaking the rules. Stepping out of a man's vehicle, hell, then it's required you approach the owner of the property. That would mean facing Sturm, and Sturm didn't look ready to talk just yet.

Everybody respected Jack. So they waited for him, cleaning fingernails with pocketknives, squeezing blackheads on their forearms, smoking cigarettes, or just blankly staring at the fields.

Frank wasn't sure he had a handle on how many respected him. Even now, after three weeks in Whitewood, Frank still couldn't quite figure out whether the clowns were actually that stupid, or whether they were just fucking with him, stringing him along until they flat-out killed him.

Sturm didn't say anything to anybody except, "Follow me," and marched out to the barn. The barn, once open and hollow, was now choked with supplies. The empty stalls were now overflowing with boxes of all shapes and sizes, as if the dirt floor had suddenly sprouted a cardboard fungus overnight.

Sturm broke down the inventory soon as everyone was inside. He pointed to the first stall, stuffed with stacks of ammunition. "I opened fourteen credit card accounts under fourteen different names. What happens is, you buy too much ammunition with the same account, a red flag goes up. Then you got Mr. King Shit Federal Man sniffing around your financial concerns. Maybe asking the reason of your purchases. Well, I got news for him." Sturm cocked his index finger and fired off imaginary shots. "This is America, land of the free. And I'm brave enough to say fuck you. That's right. This is business. I will not pay one goddamn cent of any goddamn tax from here on in. This is my business. And you, my employees, you will not pay one god-damn cent for any fucking tax they come at you with. You will all reap the rewards of these hunts."

Sturm introduced the rest of the barn. It was stuffed with fifty-three boxes of liquor—mostly whiskey, bourbon, tequila, scotch, and gin—five Army tents, four giant generators, twelve lanterns, two portable showers, sixteen kegs of water, four axes, two cords of firewood, three gas BBQs, and enough knives, tables, chairs, bar supplies, and cigars to keep a small army comfortable for weeks. "And we got sheep in the corrals out back, case anyone gets excited." Again, nobody was sure if Sturm was making a joke or serious. Frank suspected that Sturm was joking, and didn't know how to deal with the lack of laughter. "Case you got the shits, we got approximately four hundred rolls of toilet paper. The portajohns'll be here in three days."

The rest of the stalls held tiki torches, mirrors and washba-sins for cleaning and shaving, furniture for the tents—couches, beds, tables, chairs—and on each of the tables there was bug spray and condoms for the hookers.

Sturm had led them around the barn, and now they were back at the door. "Any questions? Anybody think of anything we forgot?"

"I know we got the barbeques, but I don't see anything else for cooking," Jack said. "These guys, these hunters, they're rich old boys. Can't see them eating off the grill with their fingers."

"True, true. They ain't that type at all." Sturm smoothed out the dirt in front of him with the flat leather sole of his right cowboy boot. "Fact is, I've made an arrangement for an outside party to handle the food situation. You are to treat this party with the utmost respect and offer them any and all assistance if necessary."

"Just who is this outside party?" Jack asked.

"The Glouck family."

The clowns recoiled as if Sturm had just told them they'd be eating dogshit for dinner.

"Fuck them. Fuck all of them," Jack said.

"You questioning my decision?" Sturm asked quietly. He didn't wait for Jack to respond. "Anybody here questioning my leadership?" Sturm kept moving his foot in a slow, circular motion, smoothing the soft dirt directly in front of him. "If so, then let's have it out right fucking now. Any dick licker here got a problem with my decision? Speak up. Any employee of mine has himself a problem with the boss, the only man that signs every goddamn check in this county, then step up and say what you have to say."

Sturm kept the flat sole of his boot drifting effortlessly back and forth across the dirt, the sharp toe like the movements of a stalking rattlesnake. The dirt was smooth as the hood of his Dodge.

Sturm's foot was really the only thing moving within the barn. Even Sarah, down at the far end, had enough presence of mind to freeze, to breathe slow and easy so as not to attract the attention of a predator. Everyone was as still as the lion hide stretched tight against the corrugated roof, slowly cooking in the heat. Especially Jack. He'd seriously overstepped his bounds and he profoundly regretted his transgression. He kept the brim of his hat aimed at the ground, watching everyone out of the corners of his eyes.

Sturm's foot sank into the surface of the dirt like a semi tractor settling into a still pond in slow motion. He searched out every man's eyes. Jack was the last to look up. Looking directly at Jack, Sturm said, "But say it like a man. Be honest. Let's have it out. Right fucking now. Or, so help me God, you will either do your fucking job or I will hurt you."

Sturm waited about the time it takes to unlock and open your front door, then finally said, softer this time, the sandpaper grit of his voice much finer now. "I didn't like it at first neither. But you listen. You all know what I got in my head. Nobody knows how much time I got left. I am not a patient man. I am a man who needs things done." Sturm let that sink in for a moment. "The family will handle nearly all of the food—with only the exception of when we BBQ—but even then, the family is responsible for dressing and butchering the animals. And they handle everything else, the dishware, the tablecloths, the wait staff, the cleaning of dishes, pretty much anything related to the food. So let's have an understanding here. That family has their place. They understand that. Every ruling power has its serfs. You goddamn hotheads, you don't think. You don't use the mind God gave you. Beer, pussy, and fighting. That's it. Hell, I know. I been there. My boy, he's about to understand that. I'm asking you to trust me. Not just with this family, the goddamn Gloucks. Not just them. No, I'm talking about the future of this town. I'm talking about the hunts. Thanks to Frank here, we have ourselves a genuine opportunity here. So you are either with me, or you can get the fuck out."

Nobody said anything. Sturm walked over and ripped open a box. "That's it then. From now on, you listen to me. I'm goddamn running this show." He started pulling bottles of Jack Daniels out of the box, all smiles now, as if black clouds had passed over the sun momentarily, but now the light was back, sizzling and brighter than ever. "This calls for a celebration."

Everyone took a tiny, hesitant breath.

Sturm tossed bottles at the men. "We got ourselves a lot of hard work ahead, but you done good. Tonight, you earned yourselves a good time. Theo's got a keg on ice in the backyard.

Let's go outside and have ourselves a drink."

Two blocks east of the park in the middle of town, the First Lutheran Church of Whitewood stood guard over the corner of Fifth Street and Elm, a heavy, rectangular building flanked by two strips of dead grass. It reminded Frank of a fortress; tiny stained-glass windows were sunk into the thick concrete walls and it didn't take much imagination to picture rifles sticking out of the slits. Even the steeple was short and squat, plopped on the roof like a relative who'd had too much pork stuffing on Thanksgiving. The steeple was capped off by a wooden cross; the redwood timber, black from over a century in the sun, was two feet thick and over ten feet tall.

Four pickups congregated in the street below, headlights splashed against the granite steps and double oak doors. The men gathered on the steps, beer cups in hand. Pine and Chuck had thoughtfully loaded the keg into the back of Chuck's pickup. Chuck drained his cup, belched, and started taking a leak against the wall of the church.

Sturm watched this silently for a moment from the open toolbox at the back of his truck. He spit, then jerked a crowbar from the toolbox.

Everyone flinched as the crowbar bounced off the concrete wall next to Chuck in a burst of burst of concrete chips and sparks. The stream of piss dried up and died.

"Show some respect, dammit," Sturm shouted. "I was fucking baptized in this church."

Chuck carefully zipped up, ashamed. The crowbar had landed in the puddle of urine, so Chuck wiped it off on his jeans before he handed it back to Sturm who was stomping up the steps. "Sorry, Mr. Sturm. Won't happen again."

Sturm took the crowbar. "You gotta take a leak so goddamn bad, do it on the fucking lawn. Christ Jesus." He jammed the

216

tip of the crowbar into the gap between the double doors and shoved the other end sideways. The wood split and cracked with a sound like bacon grease popping. Sturm swung the doors wide and tapped the blade of the crowbar on the steps, knocking off the splinters.

"Theo. Get my chainsaw." Theo ran to the truck. Sturm eyed the men. "You wait here. Show a little respect, for God's sake." When Theo ran back, huffing and lugging the thirty-pound chainsaw, Sturm and his son melted into the darkness of the church.

There was an unspoken decision to wait down the steps at the back of Chuck's truck. More beer was drained from the keg. Boots scuffed the asphalt. Sideways glances were cast at the church.

"Gotta say, I dunno 'bout that fucking family helping us out," Jack said softly, trying to salvage a little pride. "Didn't think we needed any help. I wasn't trying to start trouble. I just don't fucking know about that family."

"Me neither," Chuck said, still smarting from the ass-chewing over taking a piss on the church. "Far as I'm concerned, they should have left town with everybody else. Hell, I got half a mind to go on over and burn their house down."

Jack shook his head. "Mr. Sturm says shit, I say how much, that's a given, but I honestly can't see what the hell he's thinking here."

"They had their shit together, that's for sure," Frank said, and instantly wished he hadn't. That was goddamn dumb. He should have paced his drinking better, shouldn't have hit the Jack Daniels that hard. He should have saved it for later instead, like he'd been doing the other nights.

"Who had their shit together?" Jack demanded.

Frank shrugged. "We had dinner over there last night. Me and Mr. Sturm."

"No shit?" Chuck asked.

"No shit."

"Why?"

Frank shrugged again, wondering how the hell to climb out of this hole. "You could say it was an audition. A demonstration, I guess. Very professional."

"Professional? Them? Bunch of fucking vermin." Pine said.

"Well. Food was damn good."

"So why weren't we invited?" Chuck asked.

From deep inside the church, the muffled whine of the chainsaw growled to life.

"I can understand Mr. Sturm being there. But how'd you happen to get invited?" Jack asked, resentment slowly creeping into his voice like the sleepy spiders crawling up the vet office walls.

"Hell, I know," Pine said. "It was Annie, wasn't it?"

Frank could feel the dynamics of the clowns shifting slowly, as if they were squeezing their anger, their resentment, their confusion out of their minds and pushing it toward Frank. They couldn't turn their emotions loose on Sturm, and so Frank became the target.

" 'Course it was. Fuck me. Of course. She gave you one for free, didn't she?" Jack said. His dry lips had split in three places. "Chuck told us all about it."

Frank felt the anger rolling at him, just gentle nudges at first, like rising waves pushed before a storm, but growing stronger. The whiskey and beer in his head decided he should push back. Just a little. After all, he knew something about all of them. None of their dicks had ever touched Annie's lips.

"Yeah. It was Annie. She invited me."

"I fucking knew it," Jack said, and drained his cup.

"Goddamn. You've been hitting that shit hard. Got any money left? Or she give you another one for free?" Chuck refilled Jack's beer. "You ain't gonna get all possessive and jealous on us now, are you? I mean, let's not forget, she's a working girl. Gotta let us have a piece, right?"

Frank had been practicing smiling in the mirror in the bathroom at the vet office. He'd get an image in his head, something disturbing, something awful, something like the animals trapped in their cages out in the desert zoo, or Sturm gutting the tiger on Main Street, or Theo fucking the lion, and work at forcing the muscles in his cheeks to stretch up and out. In the beginning, it looked like he was trying to shit a bowling ball. When he got better, it started to look like a truck had parked on his foot and he was too drunk to really notice. He'd refocus his eyes, shake his head, clutch the sides of the pitted porcelain sink, and grin at the mirror again and again and again.

The practice paid off. The clowns bought it. They hooted and hollered. But Frank didn't say anything; he let their imaginations do all the heavy lifting.

Sturm appeared in the church doorway, holding the chainsaw. "Damn thing's sunk into the wall. They sure as hell knew how to build 'em back in the old days. I'd need a goddamn tow truck to get it out."

"We can get you one," Chuck called out, wanting to make up for pissing on the church.

"Nah. Ain't worth it. I got a better idea. Watch your heads." He ducked back into the darkness.

Everyone turned back to Frank.

"Still," Pine pointed out. "What makes you so special?" He looked around the group. "I mean, it ain't like he's done anything half the fellas in town haven't done. So why were you invited . . . and we weren't?"

"Yeah, what is it makes you so special?" Jack asked.

The clowns clustered around Frank, pinning him against the

church steps, watching his smile close, his eyes closer. The anger was back, stronger now, the waves nearly knocking Frank off his feet. The practiced smile wasn't going to hold them off this time.

Again, instead of fear, Frank felt his own anger rise and crash into the waves like a clenched fist. He shrugged, one final time. "I dunno. All I can say is, she must of liked how I tasted. Well, that . . . and I made her come."

"Whoa." Jack's voice had become the temperature of morgue steel. "You're saying . . . you're saying you touched her."

The whiskey in Frank's head said, "Yeah."

A cracking, splintering noise made them all look up at the steeple. Sturm kicked out one of the louvered shutters and climbed out onto the roof, dragging the chainsaw behind him. "Anybody got any rope?" he shouted.

They shook their heads.

"We can go get some," Chuck shouted.

"Hell with it," Sturm yelled back. "Stand back." He inched his way up the steep roof to the cross, fired up the chainsaw, and without hesitation, sank the spinning teeth deep into the wood. He sawed into the base horizontally, cutting about two-thirds of the way through, then again with a downward angle. He knocked out the pie-shaped piece, then went at it from the other side. The immense cross shuddered and slowly toppled over to the right. It hit the steep roof, slid down it like an icicle, sliced off the edge of the roof, and soared off into empty space, arcing through the air upside down, until it hit the dead lawn with deep crack that the clowns felt in their bones. The bottom crashed down in an explosion of dry grass and dust.

"Good enough. We'll bolt that sonofabitch back together," Sturm hollered.

They waited until Sturm and Theo got back downstairs. It

took all six of them to carry the cross.

Sturm tore open the bag of quick dry cement with his teeth and dumped the gray powder into the wheelbarrow. Frank grasped the handles of the wheelbarrow and jogged with Sturm along the walkway between the house and garden out into the backyard to the bare patch of dirt.

Jack unspooled the hose from the garden and started to gingerly spray the soft gray powder but Sturm snatched the hose away and sent a river of water full blast at the cement, working it up and down, giving the cement a quick soak, but not overdoing it.

Jack pushed Frank out of the way and attacked the cement with a long-handled hoe, only this blade had two circles cut away in the middle, allowing the now liquid cement to seep through the holes. He swept the hoe back to him and shoved it away, over and over, as if trying to rip long, jagged strips out of a pool table.

Sturm barked out something that sounded like he approved, but it was lost in the scraping of Jack's hoe along the bottom of the wheelbarrow. Sturm turned the hose toward the grave and started soaking the ground. Frank found a shovel, the same one that Sturm had killed Fairfax with, and started digging as headlights appeared from around the house. Pine and Chuck carried the keg out to the grave.

The hole was four feet deep when Frank hit something soft. Black liquid dripped off the shovel blade in the flashlights. Frank figured that was deep enough and stopped digging.

Again, it took all of them to carry the cross out to the backyard and drop the bottom into the hole. Theo came out of the barn with several long two-by-fours, and used these to brace the cross upright while the men held it in place. Sturm feverishly shoveled wet cement into the hole.

One by one, they gradually let go of the cross, letting the two-by-fours maintain the balance. Sturm emptied the wheelbarrow, then got on his hands and knees and swept his palms over the wet, sticky cement, smoothing it out like with the dirt in the barn before. Frank saw a tear hang from Sturm's nose for a brief second before splashing down into the cement. Frank turned away, giving the man some privacy.

He sank onto the steps of the deck, and surveyed the backyard. The cross dominated the landscape, overpowering everything. It was simply too big, like a walnut tree in a field of dwarf pines. But Sturm seemed satisfied. It showed true respect for his dog.

Frank yawned, shook his head. "Well, gentlemen. I gotta get back and feed everyone." That, and finish the bottle of rum stashed under his cot. The bottle of Jack Daniels in Jack's truck could wait until tomorrow. He stood. Jack, Pine, and Chuck watched him with blank, dull gazes.

"Hold on. Want you to take a look at something." Sturm said in a thick voice. He led Frank through the garden again and back into the barn. But this time, he went straight down the aisle, past Sarah, and opened the back door.

Frank stepped out into a large, irregularly shaped cage. The ground was bare dirt, packed hard. A few bald tires were tossed in the corner; in the other corner was a crumpled, stained mattress. The sides of the cage were constructed of two layers of chicken wire, buried deep, bolted to steel anchors. The wire was stretched tight over a curiously curving and bulging framework. It took Frank a while for him realize the bars were actually the bones of old playground equipment, lashed together with chains and padlocks. The whole thing was interlaced with razor wire. Frank figured out they must have raided both the hardware store and the elementary school.

"Boys worked hard on this, I tell you that."

"Yeah. Looks like they locked this down tight."

"Think it'll hold?"

"Hold what?"

"Them two lionesses, back at your office."

"I thought they were for the hunts tomorrow."

Sturm laughed. "Shit, I got plans for them girls. Yessir. I would have shot them long time ago otherwise."

"I thought, well, thought that they were gonna be shot out in the fields. The clients were gonna—"

"No rich peckerhead dipshit is gonna shoot my girls. Not while I'm around. Fuck no. The clients'll have fun, don't you worry. They won't be complaining. They've got plenty to shoot at." Sturm grabbed hold of one of the curved bars and shook it. "No. What I need to know is, is this going to hold 'em? Those cats. They're not for the hunts. No sir. Those are my pets."

DAY TWENTY-TWO

The morning sun undulated into a white sky, sending temperatures into triple digits when Frank finally slipped away. He wheeled the long, black car away from Sturm's ranch, hunched over the wheel, joints in his neck and shoulders full of ground glass, everything coming through the tinted windows bleached and cracked, like bones picked clean and left to lie in the sun. When he realized he'd just blown straight through the highway intersection without stopping, without even slowing down, he decided he needed someplace to park.

He pulled off the road straight into an overgrown almond orchard, plowing silently through the three-foot grass into the center. Branches bursting with dry leaves and clusters of brittle almonds scraped the roof of the car. He killed the engine but left the keys in the ignition and slid down, relaxing into the corner of the seat and door, so that he could just see above the dashboard. He slipped into fitful sleep, too tired to even look for the bottle of rum under the seat. The shadows in the orchard were deep and dark and cool and Frank slept for six hours straight.

When he got back to the vet hospital, Sturm's truck was parked out front. Frank swore, and fumbled under the seat for the bottle as he pulled around back to stash the car in its usual hiding spot in the barn.

He took a few strong gulps of rum, opened the door to the

aisle that ran through the center of the barn, and found Sturm and Theo looking at the monkeys. Frank had gotten sick and tired of listening to the monkey's screeching and chattering all night every night, so he and Pine had lined the stall next to the rhino in yet more chicken wire. They sawed off a few thick limbs from the eucalyptus trees out back and nailed them crossways in the cage, giving the monkeys something to climb and hang off.

"Wasn't sure if you were gonna make it today," Sturm said. The blisters on his shoulders had deflated into slackened bubbles of dead skin.

Frank started to explain how he had nearly fallen asleep at the wheel, but Sturm cut him off. "Hope it doesn't happen again. These animals need you to look after 'em. That's what I'm paying you for, let's not forget that. Understood?"

Frank nodded.

"Good. Okay then," Sturm clapped his hands together and the monkeys jumped and scolded him in chittering screeches that echoed throughout the barn. Theo laughed and clapped his own hands. The monkeys flinched the first few times, but then got used to the sound. Theo took to kicking the wire to get a reaction from the monkeys. The rhino ignored them and calmly dragged more alfalfa through the bars of its feeder.

"Pick out a wild one," Sturm told his son. "We want one that'll give 'em a good run for their money."

"That one. The big one, up on top," Theo said, pointing and grinning, like he was choosing some exotic new toy.

Sturm turned to Frank. "Get it on out of there, then."

Frank got a scoop of dry dog food, undid the cage latch, and cracked the door open just enough to fit his arm and the scoop inside. He dumped the dog food into the trough and waited until all the monkeys had swarmed over the trough. From the far cupboard, he grabbed an apple and sliced it into wedges with Sturm's pocket knife. Sifting through the jumping mass of black fur, he found the big spider monkey Theo had pointed out, and carefully nudged it out of the rest of the pack with the toe of his boot. He kneeled quickly, bringing one of the apple wedges up to the monkey's face, instantly catching its attention. The furrowed brows popped open in excitement and the monkey snatched the wedge from Frank's hand. It attacked the sweet white flesh like a wood chipper going after Styrofoam. Frank didn't waste time; the other monkeys were clambering over him, reaching for the rest of the apple. He tossed most of the pieces into the corner to distract them, and grabbed the big monkey by the scruff of the neck.

He carried it outside, following Sturm and Theo. The monkey, fifteen pounds of sinuous, snake-like muscles, twisted and squirmed in Frank's hands, rolling its head and reaching for his arm with all four limbs as well as its tail. He gave it another apple wedge to keep it quiet.

Sturm had a wooden kitchen chair waiting on the lawn in the sun. Theo carried his father's heavy red toolbox from the back of the pickup over to the chair and thunked it down in the dry grass. He pulled a roll of twine from the toolbox and tied one end to the back of the chair. Looking up at Frank, he said, "Any day now."

"What's the plan here?" Frank asked.

"We're gonna make this monkey famous," Sturm said, fiddling with Theo's digital camera.

"Let's go," Theo snapped. "Hold it on the chair."

"You're just taking a picture?" Frank asked.

"What the hell else are we gonna do with it? Play checkers?"

"Knock it off," Sturm said. "Let's get this done. We still have tents to set up and a thousand other goddamn little things."

Frank could feel his insides clenching up as if he was afraid something might break loose and come washing down the insides of his thighs, blood pooling in his boots, but he knelt down and held the monkey on the chair. His scalp hurt, and he realized that the top of his shaved head was sunburnt. Theo looped the twine around the monkey's right arm and cinched it down tight to a chair leg.

The monkey made a sound like a cat in a pneumatic press, sending ice picks marching up Frank's spine.

Theo didn't pay any attention; he yanked the twine tight across the monkey's chest, tying it against the back of the chair. He repeated the process with the monkey's left arm, then criss-crossed the twine back and forth, securing the screaming, wriggling animal to the chair.

Theo grabbed a pair of ring pliers from the toolbox and a length of copper wire. "Which ear, dad?"

"Both. Easier to spot."

Theo threaded the wire into the pliers, positioned the pinchers over the monkey's right earlobe, and squeezed. The monkey, now the owner of a bright copper earring, shrieked and bucked against the twine, but couldn't move much; Theo had tied it down tight. After a moment, though, the monkey calmed down a little, just shaking its head violently back and forth, as if trying to dislodge a bug in its ear. Theo threaded another length of copper wire into the pliers and pierced the monkey's other ear.

Frank went to untie the monkey, but Theo stopped him with, "Slow down—we're not done yet." He stepped back, eyeballing his work. "Dunno how we're gonna get that vest on—we'd have to untie it," he called to his father.

"Hell with it, then. Just get the hat and boots."

Theo ran to the truck, came back with an old-fashioned bowler hat and a pair of children's cowboy boots. The monkey hissed at him when he tried to slide the boots over the long, finger-like toes. Theo just got hold of one of the new earrings and yanked upwards, saying, "Sit still, you little fucker. Sit!" He eventually got the boots over the monkey's feet, although one was on sideways. He jammed the bowler hat down over the monkey's skull, down to its eyes.

It glared out from under the short brim, fingers waggling like a bug's legs, tail whipping back and forth, and made worried chirps.

Sturm stepped closer, squinting into the viewfinder. He bent over, lowering the camera to get it level with the monkey's head. He rocked back and forth like a cobra for a few moments, trying to get the best angle. Finally, he said, "Say cheese," and took the picture. "You can put him back now," he said to Frank.

Frank took off the hat, the boots, got a good hold of the scruff of the monkey's neck like a wild cat, and broke the twine. After unwrapping the rest of the twine, Frank carried the monkey back to the cage. The monkey tried pulling on the copper rings, but quickly gave up when it discovered that they caused pain. After a few seconds, it seemed to have forgotten about them altogether and went scurrying up into the eucalyptus branches where it loudly warned Frank that he'd best not mess with it again.

When Frank got back out to the lawn, Sturm said, "Let's go see my girls." Frank followed him inside, leaving Theo to pack up the toolbox and chair.

Over fifty pounds of ground lamb had been thawing in the refrigerator. Each lioness required at least eleven pounds of fresh meat a day. Frank unwrapped each five-pound brick and dumped equal amounts of the pale meat into five-gallon buckets and carried them out to the lioness cages. Sturm knelt in front of his two lionesses, murmuring to them, curling his fingers through the diagonal openings in the wire.

"I wouldn't do that," Frank warned. "They'll take your fingers off if they want."

"Not my girls. Oh no. They're good girls, aren't you?" Sturm whispered to the lionesses. They regarded him with half-lidded eyes, tails sluggishly flopping about, slapping unenthusiastically at flies.

Frank worked his way down the corridor, dumping food into the cages, but when he reached Sturm's lionesses, Sturm stopped him with one finger. "No. No food. They're gonna go hungry. For tonight, at least. Tomorrow, it's gonna be up to them."

"I wouldn't let them go too long. They—"

Sturm stood suddenly, like a deadly serious Jack-in-the-box, popping up and stepping in uncomfortably close; Frank could smell the man's sweat. The frozen gray eyes drilled into Frank's soul. "I'm paying you for one thing, and one thing only. Your job is very simple. That's taking care of these animals until I deem it time for them to suit my needs. These animals are mine, not yours. They are mine to do with as I see fit. I've been sensing a little . . . hesitation in your work." Sturm stepped in even closer, the toes of his boots touching Frank's boots. "Suppose I wanted to shoot that monkey just now. Any problems with that, doc?"

Frank shook his head.

"Suppose I take a notion to cut off all them long fingers and toes with wire snips?"

Frank shrugged. "It's your animal. My job is to keep 'em alive until you see fit."

"Not just keep 'em alive, son. I want them taken care of. This is their last days. We have an obligation here. These animals deserve nothing but our respect. Thought I made that clear the other night."

"You did."

"So what's our problem here?"

Frank shook his head and said, "There's no problem here."

"I hope not. Then the next time me or my son tells you do something, you damn well do it, you got that?"

Day Twenty-Three

Sturm blew the ditch first thing in the morning. It was kind of anti-climactic, really. A whole hell of a lot of smoke spit out of each end of the drainage pipe, and some cracks appeared in the asphalt, but that was it.

"Goddamnit," Sturm said.

Everyone else expected a much bigger explosion. Frank, Chuck, and Theo were hunkered down behind the pickups parked a hundred yards back up the highway. Jack and Pine were off somewhere for Sturm. Smoke unfolded in the still air. Nobody said anything else.

"Shit, shit. Shit," Sturm said. "Chuck. Go park that sonofabitch in the middle of the goddamn highway. Park it right on top of the drainage ditch."

"You got it," Chuck said, and jogged down the highway, all that slack skin swaying and jumping. After a while, his figure got blurry in the heat rising from the asphalt that appeared a deep dark black under the morning sun, until it simply melted into the highway.

Sweat wormed its way down Frank's temple, and he pulled his cap off and wiped his forehead with his sleeve. He was pissed. Annie wandered through his mind, swinging those hips of hers, heavy breasts swaying, muscles gently contracting in her strong, brown legs. As always, he didn't know what the hell he was going to say. This was a waste of his time, being out here. A slow rage had been simmering in his veins all night, but he stood at the front of the vehicles with everyone else, facing the sun, and gave it his best practiced smile.

Sturm drank coffee, sitting on the front bumper of his truck. He tucked a pinch of Copenhagen snuff the size of a walnut into his lower lip. He grinned, black specks of tobacco seeping up into his teeth like tiny ants. He spit a gallon of black saliva at the dust as if it was a declaration of war.

Far down through the heat waves they heard a motor crank to life. It was the Caterpillar. And apparently, it was the signal Sturm had been waiting for. "Let's go," he said, and jumped into his pickup. Everyone followed.

They came upon the Caterpillar in the middle of the highway, tilted nearly sideways, caught in mid-lurch, haphazardly shoved at the sky as if it had twisted an ankle. The engine was silent. Apparently, Chuck had driven the backhoe onto the cracks in the asphalt, and the pipe underneath had collapsed, flinging him out of the tractor. He was off in the sand on the side of the highway; a thin line of blood trickled down his forehead into an eye socket full of blood. But it looked like he was too busy holding his left knee utterly still to worry about a bleeding scalp wound.

"Perfect," Sturm shouted. "Don't move anything. Leave it right in the middle of the road." He turned back to his son and Frank. "Frank, you and Theo set up those sawhorses. Make sure them lights are blinking."

"Which side?" Theo asked.

"Did your mother drop you when you were born? What side. Use your head."

Frank had already carried two of the sawhorses to the other side of the backhoe, so anyone driving into Whitewood would see the blinking lights and the orange sawhorses. After a moment, Theo followed him, and they arranged a straight line of sawhorses, blocking all traffic.

"Mr. Sturm?" Chuck sounded like he might burst into tears any minute. "I . . . I don't think I can walk. Can't see real good, either."

"Goddamnit." Sturm stood motionless for a moment, hands on hips, staring at the horizon. "This is most inconvenient, Chuck. You do understand that we have hunters arriving today." Sturm acted like an overworked parent scolding a toddler in the midst of throwing a fit. "Goddamnit."

"I'm sorry. I really tried—"

Sturm snapped his fingers. "Frank! Take him on back to the vet hospital. Fix him up. If it's real bad, then we'll figure out how to get him over to the hospital in Alturas."

Frank came around the backhoe and found a handkerchief in Sturm's pickup. "Here. Hold this to your head there," he held it out to Chuck. "Scalp wounds bleed like a bitch. You keep bleeding like that, you're gonna pass out." Frank thought all this was funny as hell, and he struggled to keep the laugh out of his voice.

As Frank pulled Chuck up and helped him limp across the highway to Chuck's pickup, he realized that it probably would have been a lot less painful to simply bring the pickup over to Chuck, instead of making him lurch at his own pickup as if they were being chased by that tiger. But hell, watching Chuck try to move was more entertaining.

The steady chugging of a diesel engine reached them. A square box grew out of the heat waves down the highway, coming into focus as a beige Winnebago.

The RV was so old they could hear the driver manually shifting down as it rolled up to the scene of the accident. It was towing an even older horse trailer, one that had been modified recently. Heavy bars had been haphazardly welded across any open space more than a foot wide.

Frank wondered what the hell kind of horse was inside.

The driver got out. He looked like a primitive voodoo doll made from horsehair; long and flowing in some places, short tufts of black bristles in others. Long, curly gray hair hung along the ears, brutally parted straight down the middle, as if it was a forest break, seared into the landscape by smoke jumpers. A black beard hung down past his ribcage. Apart from the sun-blasted forehead and the wrinkles surrounding his eyes, the only other skin Frank could see was the palms of the man. And the soles of his feet.

The driver was barefoot. The pavement was hot enough to sear pork chops, yet he acted like he was walking on cool evening grass. He wore black leather pants. A safari shirt. A safari jacket the color of an egg gone bad in the sun. With fringes.

"Y'all have an accident?" He had an accent, maybe Texas or some other southern state, all of the words smeared together in an easy drawl.

"Nah. We were just tickling this Caterpillar to hear it laugh," Sturm said. He faced the man from the other side of the highway crack, black boots wide, Carhartt jeans tucked into the boots, held up by red suspenders, hands on his hips, shoulders square, black Cowboy hat secure.

"Looking fer a Mr. Horace Sturm," the man said.

"You're talking to him."

The man smiled. "Name's Girdler. Talked to you a while back. Believe you mentioned something about a hunt."

"Believe I did, yessir."

"Well then, I'm ready for some shooting."

Sturm and Girdler drove the RV back up the highway to the locked gate, going the long way into town, while Frank drove Chuck back to the vet office. Chuck whimpered with every jolt and bump, barking out at one point, "Are you fucking trying to hit every goddamn hole?"

Frank hoped it wasn't obvious. "Hell no. Sorry."

Frank half-dragged Chuck into the hospital and left him on one of the waiting room chairs. He prepared a syringe of morphine and sunk it deep into the vein in the crook of Chuck's elbow, just to shut him up for a while. Frank thought about breaking the needle off in Chuck's arm, but figured that might be pushing things too far. Chuck gave a long, satisfied sigh, "Ah fuck yes . . ." and limply slid off the chair onto the floor.

Sturm and Girdler came in the back door, laughing and shouting as if they'd been pals for years. Sturm immediately grabbed a couple of beers from the fridge. Frank met them in the back examining room.

Sturm grabbed Frank by the shoulders, hugging him close, beaming, saying, "Like you to meet one of my most valuable employees. This is Frank, our vet. He's taking care of all our animals; hell, he knows these cats inside and out."

"Hi." Frank stuck his hand out.

"Howdy," Girdler extended his own paw; it felt like grabbing a leather glove wrapped in badger hair bristles. Up close, Frank could see that hair covered nearly every inch of Girdler's skin. The man had hair down to his cracked, yellow toenails; actually the hair surrounded the toenail, growing right down to the callused bottoms of the toes. Girdler's mother must have been raped by Bigfoot.

"Let's go meet my girls," Sturm said.

Frank held the door to the middle section open for Sturm and Girdler. Sturm strode briskly past the first four cats, simply saying, "These here will be available to hunt very soon. We're getting 'em healthy. Later, if you wish, you can have your pick. But these two, back here, these are my girls—Princess and Lady." Frank blinked, unaware that Sturm had already named his pets.

235

All of the lionesses lay in the far corners, but where the other lionesses seemed bored, if not downright sleepy, Princess and Lady were alert, anxious, as if a hot, vibrating wire had been laced through their spines. Sturm explained, "They haven't eaten in two days. Saving 'em for something special tonight. The evening's entertainment, you could say."

Frank expected Sturm to launch into the usual bullshit about his magnificent predators and the pure essence of nature and all that, and was surprised when Sturm asked Girdler, "Will this facility adequately address your needs?"

Girdler shook the corner post of the cages, noting how it was set into the concrete. The cats recoiled, folded into themselves, flat against the concrete. They didn't seem to like looking at the hairy man. Maybe it was his scent.

Girdler's tongue came out and found an errant lock of beard at the corner of his mouth, pulled it back in and sucked on it for a while. "Don't know rightly. Gonna be tight, that's for sure." He bit down on the lock of hair, chewed on it for a while, and spit out the pieces, like dark flecks of tobacco. "Maybe . . . if it was just a night. But hell. I may just be here a while. A week, maybe more. Providing you got plenty else to hunt."

"Oh we got plenty to hunt, that's for damn sure," Sturm said. "Your barrel'll melt 'fore you run out of things to shoot. If this place won't hold it, then hell, we'll just have to find something that will. And if we can't find something, then we'll just have to build something. That simple." He glanced at Frank. "Mr. Girdler's got his own animal to hunt." His voice got proud, awed. "Wait until you see it. Big as a goddamn mountain. A genuine grizzly bear. In my town."

"Kodiak, technically. Same damn thing as a grizzly really, just a tad bigger, from an island off the coast of Alaska," Girdler clarified.

Frank hoped the bear wasn't a relative of Girdler's. "Is it out in the trailer?"

"Yup. Got him doped up so he'll be asleep for a day or two."

"When he does wake up, we're gonna need some more tranquilizers. No question. How big is this animal?"

"Around eleven hundred pounds," Girdler said, pride coating his voice like warm syrup. "And over ten feet long."

"Then yeah, we'll have to figure some other place to keep it. No way it can stay here. It'll go through this chain-link fence in a heartbeat," Frank said. "We're taking a hell of a chance with keeping the cats here as it is."

"He's not dangerous, not really," Girdler said. "I've had him since a cub. I call him Bo-Bo," he said sheepishly, then got defensive. "Well, he was just the cutest damn thing. Bought him off a zoo in Kansas. They couldn't afford to feed him. Hell, I can barely afford to feed him. He eats 80 pounds a day in the summer, mostly blueberries and squash. He loves salmon. Thank the good Lord he sleeps most of the winter."

Sturm looked at Frank. Frank knew what he was thinking. They had just about cleaned out the meat from the freezer behind the barn, and Frank wasn't sure where or how Sturm was going to find more. He was wondering how in the hell they were going to scrape together 80 pounds of vegetables and berries. Forget salmon. The bear could eat lamb or hamburger just like the cats or it would go without meat. And that 80 pounds, that was just for one day. Sturm was wondering how they were going to feed this thing for a week or more.

"Bo-Bo's just like a big ole' puppy dog. Throw him in a corral. He'll be just fine."

"No disrespect intended here, but there's no goddamn way I can just let an eleven hundred pound grizzly bear wander around my town," Sturm said. "At least, not until you're ready to hunt."

Girdler pulled on his beard like he wanted to make sure it

was still attached.

"You sure you want to shoot this bear of yours?" Frank asked.

Sturm shot him a warning look, but Girdler said, "Sure as I'm standing here, son. Shit, I would've shot him long time ago, but I wanted him to get as big as possible for the hide."

"And the teeth," Sturm added.

"Hell yes. The teeth too." Girdler found some more hair to chew on. "Just couldn't bring myself to shoot him in the pen. Didn't seem right somehow. So when I heard about this particular hunt you folks got going here, I thought . . . well, this was just what I was waiting for."

Sturm finished his beer. "Then we need to find a place to keep it. Let's get my girls moved—I want them awake and hungry for tonight. Then we'll go for a ride. See what we can find."

By noon, Lady and Princess were sleeping safely inside their distorted, bulging cage that grew out of the back of Sturm's barn like a cancerous spider web. One door opened into the barn; the other into a large corral. Before they had left, Jack and Pine had drilled iron poles into the posts and lined the whole corral with hog panels, creating a square cage, nearly a quarter acre total, with walls over eight feet tall.

But this corral, this new cage, this wasn't for the grizzly. It had been built without Frank, so Frank could only guess that it was some kind of exercise yard for Sturm's new pets. Frank wondered if he should mention that eight feet of fence wouldn't hold the lionesses. Hell, if Lady and Princess had a mind to, they'd be over that fence in less time than it took for Sturm to spit.

Frank kept his mouth shut. Sturm probably already knew this, and besides, Frank was still pissed. And more than a little scared. He couldn't read Sturm, couldn't see how the pressure built. Yesterday still made him feel like a loyal dog who'd been kicked for no apparent reason by a previously kind and considerate owner.

He practiced his smile more and more.

Theo drove Sturm's pickup, windows down, one arm out the window. He took the trip slow and easy, as Sturm and Girdler were in the back, sitting on ice chests full of beer and ice. Neither one paid the heat any attention, just told jokes about niggers, politicians, beaners, fucking stupid Polacks, Kikes with their money, and dumb cunts. They'd laugh and fling their bottles at street signs, the few cars left, and the buildings.

Theo drove so slow there was no breeze. Frank wished Theo would roll up the windows and turn on the A.C., but Theo wouldn't even look at him, let alone speak to him. Even though the back window was open, so Theo could hear his father, the afternoon air slid over Frank's skin like a slug, leaving a sweaty slime.

First stop was the taxidermist, so Sturm could show off the tiger's hide.

Theo pulled up and parked in the middle of the street. Before the pickup had fully stopped, Sturm jumped out, hollering, "Didja know—" and stumbled. His boots stuttered along the asphalt and he fell heavily onto his knee and hip, like a chair leg had just collapsed on him.

Girdler laughed.

Frank flinched. He couldn't decide if he should run over and help Sturm find his feet, just like at the vet hospital, but if Sturm had actually gone and had too many beers, it might make him mean. And the last goddamn thing Frank needed was to piss off Sturm.

But Sturm just laughed too and found his feet in a rolling motion, said, "Didja know a chink girl's pussy is sideways, like their eyes," and laughed along with Girdler. Giggles burst out of Theo like snot bubbles.

The taxidermist shop smelled bad. Worse than bad. Like a freezer full of meat after the power had been out a week. Frank wondered if it was the taxidermist himself. He was wearing the same spotless faded overalls, the same rigid white long-sleeved shirt. Frank wasn't sure if this was simply the man's uniform, if he had a closet full of identical clothing, or if this was the actual clothes he'd been wearing a week ago.

He poked around the shop while Sturm and Girdler inspected the striped hide, and realized that most of the smell was coming from a large bubbling pot in the back, where the taxidermist was boiling the tiger skull.

The next stop was the town pool. When Sturm told Theo where to go, just north of the high school, Frank was surprised a town this size had a town pool, but didn't care one way or another. He was seriously considering jumping into the water, clothes and all, but when they unlocked the gate and went inside, they found the pool quite empty, just an echoing hollow husk of concrete, surrounded by a ten-foot chain-link fence.

"Think this'll hold a grizzly—sorry, a Kodiak?" Sturm asked, standing at the lip of the deep end, his voice booming off the blue-painted concrete.

The deep end was certainly big enough. Over 30 feet wide, the flat bottom gently sloped down from the shallow end, leveling out at fourteen feet beneath the pool deck. Stagnant, green water waited at the very bottom.

The problem was obvious to everyone. The bear could just walk up into the shallow end, a larger rectangle set at a right angle to the deeper part. They would have to construct some kind of wall; otherwise, the bear would simply stroll right up and tear through the fence like a fork through toilet paper.

The auction yard was next. Sturm led them to a large room with a high ceiling where they'd kept the original lioness that Sturm had fought and killed. It had one door. The floor was concrete, with two drains set into it. Tiles covered the walls four feet up, giving way to a series of small windows covered in thick wire.

"This'll work," Frank said. "This'll work just fine."

"You sure you don't have, I dunno, someplace outside?" Girdler asked.

Frank said, "We'll put some straw down for him, make him as comfortable as possible."

"Frank'll make sure your bear is comfortable," Sturm said. "He's a regular goddamn Florence Nightingale for these animals, believe me."

"It'll just be for a few days, right?" Frank asked.

"Guess so. Just wanted him outside, in the sun, for as much as possible . . . before the end," Girdler said. "It's a matter of respect."

"Of course," Sturm said, reaching up to pat Girdler's shoulder. "I understand respect." He was silent a moment, then said, "Let's get out of here and have ourselves another beer."

On the way back to the ranch, they stopped at the gas station. Theo stayed outside and filled up the truck. Frank wished the Glouck boys would fire some BBs and rocks at Theo, but the dead tree was empty.

"How's business, Myrtle?" Sturm said.

The woman with the shocking red hair shrugged in her kingdom of cigarettes and lottery tickets. "Kinda' slow, Mr. Sturm."

Frank stopped and waited just inside the front door, hands in his pockets, head down, bill of his cap obscuring his face. The place was even more cramped and hotter than before. Girdler hit the end of the first aisle, found a few beers in the cooler, and Frank realized that between the two coolers, in the left corner of the ceiling, perched a round, concave mirror like the Gloucks' TV satellite's younger cousin. Myrtle's curving face appeared in the distorted mirror, staring right at him. Hatred haunted the lines in her face.

Frank had killed her cat. It was that simple.

Sturm leaned on the counter. "That'll be changing soon. Can I count on you to be here?"

She took her glare off the mirror. "Of course. I'll be here, open 'til close."

Sturm nodded. "Good, good. Can I trust you?"

Myrtle looked as though Sturm had just asked her to drop her jeans and shit in the cash register. "I don't know quite what you mean, Mr. Sturm."

"What I'm getting at here is this. I've got men coming into town, they're gonna be needing gasoline and beer and liquor and snacks and all kinds of shit, and I need someone I can trust to run this place. I don't know the characters of these men. I don't know if I can trust them, so I need someone to keep 'em honest, do you see what I'm saying?"

Myrtle thought Sturm's question was as clear as mud. But she smiled and said, "Yes."

"So what would you do if some kid came in here, slipped a candy bar in his pocket?"

"I'd get up and stand in front of the door."

"Okay. He tries to run."

"I'd grab that little pisser by the back of his shirt or hair, whichever's easiest, with this hand," she said, demonstrating by vigorously shaking her metal stool that she sat upon, hour after hour. "And I'd get the merchandise with this one." She gave the stool a good shaking, and slapped it once.

"So what if two vehicles pull up, and the far one, the one you can't see, that vehicle pulls away without paying. What would you do then?"

"I'd be on the phone before they made it ten feet. I'd have the license number and a description of the occupants." She set the stool down. Crossed her arms. "I am a very observant employee, Mr. Sturm," she said, eyeballing the Glouck house across the street.

"Welcome aboard," Sturm said, and shook hands with Myrtle.

"I'll take all them beef jerkys you got," Girdler said, shambling up to the counter. "And these beers."

"Tell you what, Myrtle, you ring up this gentleman on my tab. Whatever he needs. This time." Sturm looked directly at Girdler. "From here on out, you pay your own way."

"Sure," Girdler said, cracking a beer.

Myrtle's fingernails kept track of everything Girdler carried. Frank opened the door for Sturm and Jack. When it closed, Frank saw Myrtle staring at him through the glass. Frank looked at the pavement. He felt bad. Again, but just for the barest blink, the voice, suggesting the solution to her pain. It could be over and gone.

He turned and went to the pickup. Before him, the Glouck house sat quiet, but smoke slowly rose from the kitchen. Sturm said, under his breath, "Crazy goddamn old bitch," and Girdler laughed. Theo slowly pulled away in the crackling heat and Frank blinked the sweat out of his eyes.

A big flashy Cadillac Escalade was parked in front of Sturm's house.

"Okay. We got customers. Look sharp."

The three new hunters waited out on the back deck, marveling at the giant cross in the corner of the yard. Frank could tell

243

right off that none of these three ever did anything without the other two behind him. He just knew these fuckers were executives somewhere, late twenties to early thirties. They probably worked together, played fucking golf, got their haircuts from the same barber, same goddamn fraternity. Frank suspected they didn't do much of anything at their work, neither making decisions or lifting something heavy. This would be one of their hunting trips, their version of an adventure.

They gave their names, but Frank immediately forgot and just named them Asshole #1, #2, and #3. He shook all their hands, smiled his smile, and immediately went out back to the lioness cage. He wanted to stop by Jack's truck for his bottle, but decided he needed to see the cats first. He went quickly through the deepening shadows and curled his fingers into the cage at the back of the barn.

The tranquilizers had worn off hours ago, and Sturm's girls were irritable and hungry. Lady was busy tearing ragged strips of hard black rubber out of the tires while Princess hulked in a corner, motionless except for her tail, which slapped at the flies. She hissed when she saw Frank, deep, vicious, and pissed.

"I know girl. I know. You'll eat soon." Frank's voice, smooth as fresh motor oil, was low enough that only the cats heard him. "You'll eat soon. Don't know exactly what you're gonna eat, but I know you're gonna eat soon. That's right, little girl. One, two hours, tops. You'll see. You'll eat."

Princess lowered her head, staring hard at Frank. Lady stopped shredding the tires and watched Princess, only occasionally glancing at Frank.

"You'll eat soon. I promise."

Lights burst on the corral, bleaching the color out of the dirt, the fence, the sky, leaving everything cold and bloodless. The cats each slid to the back corners of the cage, backs low, shoulders against the concrete foundations, as the light found them and sucked the color out of their eyes.

Theo ran up and jumped on the first bar of the cage, both hands wrapped around a video camera the size of a pack of cigarettes, glued to the lioness to Frank's right. Sturm came out of the dark and asked, "Which one?"

Frank wasn't sure if Sturm was talking to him or Theo, and was about to mumble something when Theo said, "Both of 'em."

"Well then, we're just gonna have to find out tonight then, won't we?" He turned to Frank, and before Frank could say anything said, "I know. I know. They gotta eat. And they will. Soon as we do. So come on back to the house. I gotta collect everyone and get 'em on out to the spread in the field."

A large army tent had been erected out in the pasture. Tiki torches illuminated the two tables set up in the front. One was six feet across; the second was considerably smaller. Glouck brothers in black jeans and white shirts and black bow ties walked stiffly from the tent to the table and back again, carrying and arranging the silverware, plates, candles, baskets of bread, bottles of olive oil, and pitchers of ice water.

Sturm took the seat at the big table and had the hunters join him. He started telling an elaborate joke. Frank sat at the smaller table with Theo and Chuck, clearly the little kids' table at Thanksgiving. The Gloucks poured water and took drink orders. Frank wasn't shy about ordering alcohol this time.

Theo stared at Gun with amusement and said low, under his dad's joke, "That's a nice tie you got there. Your mother sew it for you?" He called over his shoulder at his dad, interrupting. "Hey, Dad! Dad! Am I supposed to tip these boys or what?"

"Well, if they deserve it, then tip 'em. Yes."

"What if they don't deserve it?"

"Then don't tip." Sturm went back to the joke. "Anyways, so the nun says to the taxicab driver, 'Fuck yes, you stud you. Thanks for the ride. And oh yeah, by the way, I'm really a guy on his way to a costume party.' "

The three assholes laughed, slammed their hands down on the table, tilted their various drinks, and took long gulps. Girdler laughed too, but took slower sips out of a silver curved flask. Frank, finishing his glass and waving for one of the Glouck brothers, said, "Another. Thanks."

Sturm stood. "Gentlemen. Ladies . . . ?" he peered into the darkness. Someone near the house whistled. Frank saw her on the back deck leaning out against the railing, just a silhouette really, but that was enough to know it was her, more than enough. Sturm's house didn't just grow gentle curves like Annie. He wondered what the hell she was doing out here. Maybe she was helping her family out.

Maybe she was here to make some money.

"Tomorrow—for starters, you're gonna sight in your rifles. For those of you who have no idea what I'm talking about, we will assist you. This will be your only preparation for the hunts to follow, when your prey will not be so docile."

Girdler asked, "Absolutely. Then what will we shoot?"

"You all are hereby warned to be on the lookout for this dangerous gentleman here." Sturm unrolled an 8 1/2 by 11-inch paper. The big monkey sat locked to the chair, wearing western clothing, in a primitive cheap two-tone print. In wooden, western-style letters, the sign said, "WANTED" above the monkey's hat.

"I direct your attention to this particular detail here," Sturm pointed to the monkey's ears. "He's got brass balls and brass earrings." He pointed to the bottom of the sign, "REWARD: $20,000."

Sturm tossed the rolled-up paper down the table. "That's

right. Twenty thousand dollars. That's one bad monkey there. And he's loose. Goddamn King Kong. Somewhere in town. So be careful. It's a dangerous mission. So damn dangerous, I gotta be sure you're serious. This particular hunt, this ain't free. But the cost is next to nothing when you think about the twenty-thousand dollar reward on this outlaw's head." He stood behind his chair, only his shoulders and head visible. "So who's up for a little outlaw hunting?"

The main course was brought out. Theo asked Gun, "Hey, you wash your hands before touching this plate?"

Frank did his best to ignore Theo and just enjoy the food, but as soon as the plate was set in front of him, Theo grabbed it and switched it with his own plate. "There," he said. "Now you can enjoy their spit. I know they spit in mine, and I ain't gonna eat that shit."

The Gloucks' faces betrayed nothing.

Frank switched plates with Chuck, who was still enjoying the effects of the tranquilizers to worry about anything as unimportant as tainted food.

Theo didn't like it, but instead of pushing it with Frank, he poured his water on the ground and shook the empty glass at Ernie. "Hey. Hey, water boy. Gimme some water. Now."

Ernie picked up the water pitcher on the table and poured more into Theo's glass without saying a word. For now, his fear of his mothers was overriding his hatred of Theo.

"Shit. You might have a career in this, if you work hard," Theo said, took a drink, then poured the rest on the ground. "Now gimme some more."

Gun stiffly poured ice water into Theo's glass, like a robot whose joints had nearly rusted shut.

Frank did his best to ignore Theo; his mind wanted Annie. The curved shadows from the back deck were gone and the backyard was empty. He thought about excusing himself to go check on the lionesses, really just to look around and try and find her, but didn't want Sturm to see him leaving the table.

Gun made it all the way through dessert before snapping. Theo had had too much beer. He said, "I know you're half-coon, but even you can't be that goddamn stupid. I told you I needed another fucking napkin, so hop to it . . . nigger."

Gunther Ian Glouck was born at 8:56 A.M., after 37 hours of labor. Edie was the only parent who signed the birth certificate. She'd been seen with over fifteen men during the two-week window of his conception, men of all ages, races. She refused to give the men's names, refused to give any information. He was three years younger than Edie's next youngest and had learned very early that the only way to fight was dirty.

Gun snatched a fork with both hands from the stack of dirty dishes he was collecting, dropping the rest of the plates on the ground, and lunged at Theo. It didn't matter that Theo was four years older and outweighed him by fifty or sixty pounds, Gun's bottom teeth were bared, his eyes wild with fury. His left hand clawed at Theo's face while the right came up all sneaky, aiming to puncture the lower intestine with the fork.

Plates hit the dirt and shattered. Two Glouck brothers materialized out of the darkness, grabbing Gun and wrestling him to the ground.

Theo jumped up. "Let him go! C'mon you pussies! Let's do it!"

Asshole #2 started chanting, "Fight! Fight! Fight!" Assholes #1 and #3 joined in.

"Fifty bucks on the blond-haired kid, Sturm junior," Girdler blurted happily, waving a bill.

"C'mon, you fucking pussy!" Theo shouted at Gun.

Ernie had a knee in Gun's back. He turned and hissed, "Just

cool down, you—"

"Ernie." A mother's voice, sharp as a rifle shot, cracked out of the tent.

Ernie turned back to Gun, rocked back a moment, and then punched Gun in the back of the head. Gun twitched and lay still, either genuinely unconscious or smart enough not to move.

"That's enough, that's enough," Sturm said, rising to his feet, trying to get a better idea of what was happening down near the kitchen, since he wasn't tall enough to see over the table. "We're having a civilized dinner here. You can settle this later." Frank suspected Sturm was afraid of Gun beating the shit out of Theo in front of the rest of the hunters, and couldn't stand the shame of seeing his son lose a second fight to one of the Glouck family. A younger and smaller one too. "I've got other entertainment planned, something I believe you all will find much more interesting. I'll meet you gentlemen out at the back of the barn. Frank will show you the way. I'll be there before you've had a chance to refill them drinks."

Frank led the group back to the lioness cage, still peeled white in the lights. Princess and Lady pressed into the barn corners, eyes shut tight, tails still. Only their ears moved.

A Glouck kid, the one with the stapled earlobe, ran out and took drink orders.

Everyone looked at Frank. He watched them back. Didn't even bother to practice his smile. Asshole #2 coughed.

"Frank introduce you to the girls yet?" Sturm followed his voice out of the darkness, boots first, then black jeans, then a bare torso the color of a roasted almond, the grim slash of a mouth, and the black cowboy hat. The bandages were gone, revealing angry, pink scars. You almost didn't notice he was short until he came up to the cage and the top of his hat just barely rose above the shoulders of most of the men. "Well,

Frank don't say much, true, but he sure knows what he's doing with my babies. He's a goddamn Dr. Doolittle, no joke."

Frank found his peculiar smile and saluted the men with his drink.

Theo came out of the barn and into the light of the corral leading Sarah. The old horse fought him all the way, stutter-stepping forward, her head up, eyes wide, clearly terrified. Theo jerked her along like he was trying to yank a large goose that was trying to take off back to the hard-packed dirt.

Sturm took the reins, holding them at his hip, and kissed Sarah on the nose. The horse slowed down at once, the muscles sagged and relaxed. He whispered something low and sweet to her, got her to lower that long head even more, then kissed her between the eyes and rubbed her ears.

He led her out into the dark field for a few minutes, then brought her back at the far end of the fenced corral. He unsnapped three padlocks and led Sarah inside. He kissed her nose again, and stepped back, shutting the gate and relocking the padlocks.

"Turn 'em loose, Frank," Sturm called.

"What?" Frank shouted back.

"Turn 'em loose!"

"Who?"

"Who you think? Jesus Christ, boy." Sturm caught himself. He laughed. "I'm sorry, son. Didn't mean to lose my patience with you. I forgot you been touched, as they used to say. That horse kick to your noggin' there. There, there over by your hand there. Open that padlock. Swing it wide, boy."

And Frank finally got it. He figured out which padlock to unlock; it was a simple little thing really, a kind of gate mechanism, just grab it, push down, then pull back, and once he did, that would open a small, nearly hidden gate in the lion-ess cage, letting Lady and Princess into the larger corral, turning them loose on the horse.

Sturm hollered, "I got a fifty says my girls'll take this horse under a minute."

"You mean down or dead?" Girdler shouted back.

"Down."

Having smelled horse sweat, the lionesses had finally opened their eyes.

"Done. I got a fifty on this horse going a full minute and a half on all four feet."

"Okay then. Do it."

Sarah danced back and forth, looking for a clear way out, her movements growing increasingly sharper, more frantic.

"Open her up," Sturm shouted. "My girls got to eat."

Frank grabbed the metal, still warm from the heat of the day, pushed down and pulled back. The cats took a quick glance at each other and the rest of their cage and watched that horse-flesh kick at the dust in the white hot glare of the lights. They slowly curled apart and slunk along opposite walls toward the open gate.

"When are we starting the clock?" Girdler asked.

"It's already started," Sturm said.

"What's the time?"

"Where's your watch?" Sturm held up a stopwatch. "By my count, it's already fourteen seconds gone."

"Well all right then," Girdler said, checking his wristwatch. He'd been wearing it so long hair had grown up through the various holes and cracks in the leather band.

The lionesses watched the men at the fence closely.

Sarah kicked out, over and over. White lather from between her hind legs landed in the dust.

The cats' wide noses, those flat cliffs of finely etched black leather, flared open, vacuuming the scent, bolting it directly into the very core of their predatory souls.

When it happened, nearly forty-two seconds after Sturm started his watch, it happened fast. The lionesses hit the gate together, then split apart, bounding at Sarah from both sides. She turned to face Lady on the left side, kicking wildly at Princess, who leapt completely above the flailing back hooves, sinking her claws into the horse's back haunches, plunging great furrows into the old muscle, hanging there, letting the blood wash over the massive paws, snapping at the mane.

Lady went to the left, avoiding the bicycling front hooves, and as Princess hit Sarah from behind, Lady went for the throat. Her teeth snapped shut on Sarah's windpipe. A smaller animal would have been killed instantly, but Sarah was over eight hundred pounds heavier than any bush antelope; her spinal cord was still intact. Lady swung from Sarah's neck, dragging the horse down. The lioness' teeth tore out Sarah's right artery, and the horse went down, kicking and spraying blood.

The men cheered as Frank watched the fine dust sift over his boots.

"I got fifty-six seconds here," Sturm said. Everybody else chimed in their times, but nobody had over a minute.

Day Twenty-Four

The next morning, the heat was somehow worse in town, as if all the pavement, bricks, cinderblocks, and concrete, having absorbed so much for so long, were now more like hot coals, radiating a much deeper and stronger heat back out into the sunshine.

Frank kicked himself for forgetting his sunglasses back at the vet hospital. The last few days, in the full sunlight, he would have to shake his head once in a while, because his eyes would lose focus, and eventually everything in his vision would shatter in a blinding white light, and when the world refocused, the light was reversed, as if he was looking at a photo negative. The colors shimmered and melted into switching, like getting stuck between channels on a hotel television. So he'd shake his head until the picture snapped back into full color, keeping the lights and darks in the right places.

Theo rolled Sturm's pickup out of an alley running parallel to Main Street, behind the Holiday Market and its empty parking lot. He went painfully slow, just threw it in drive and didn't touch the gas. He turned into the street, moving slower than most people walk. Of course, the street was empty. Except for the engine, and Chuck's unrelenting conversation, the town was silent.

Chuck said, "I'm at this truck stop down in Reno, empty as all hell, sitting at the bar, chatting with the waitress. She was

253

interested, I know she was, 'cause she got me a chicken fried steak and eggs for half the price. And I'm eating, and gettin' cozy with her, when this guy walks in and sits down right next to me. Place is empty, but he has to fucking sit next to me."

Frank and Chuck rode back on the tailgate. Chuck's legs swung aimlessly back and forth under the truck. Frank's long legs would have been dragged along, so he was kind of walking along with the truck, taking long strides backward. He took a long drink, then passed Chuck his flask.

Chuck took it, saying, "And I swear to God, I can see him in the mirror, right? So in the mirror, he looks kinda' sick, but that's all, and when I turn to look at him, half his head is gone, from the nose on over, just gone." He slapped his palms together to suggest skipping a rock over water. "And I look back to the mirror, and he looks . . . well, not fine, no, but at least his head is all there."

A horse lead line was attached to the bumper. Fifteen feet down, at the other end of the line, was a ewe, dreadlocks of dry mud underneath, legs caked in gray mud, shuffling along, like a wobbly toy being pulled by a string.

Theo rolled across the crosswalk and into the Main Street intersection.

Chuck talked over the diesel engine. "And he turned to look at me, with that one eye left, and he said, 'Don. Don.' Then he got up and left."

"Why?" Frank was bored shitless, wondering when the hell Chuck would get to the point and take a drink. Then maybe he'd give the flask back.

"Why? Fuck, you listening to me? The ghost, man. What are we drinking here? What the hell's in this?" He shook the flask, spilling some of the whiskey. "You think I can get another injection of that shit? Haven't felt that good in . . . ever."

"I would. I mean, I'd like to. I would. But I can't afford it."

Chuck laughed. "Well. How much does this stuff cost?"

"I'm not sure. But I can find out."

"You got more back at the office, right? You know, any tiny bit. Hell, it don't take much. I can afford it. Hell yes—I can pay you! Jesus, don't worry about that. I got paid. So I got it." Chuck pulled a lump from his jeans and gave Frank a flash of his money, a tight roll of bills over three inches thick.

They rolled across Main Street. Frank was too busy looking at the pavement, pretending to remember how much he should charge, seeing that fat roll of cash in his mind, wondering when in the hell Sturm had seen fit to pay some employees and not others and barely trying to not listen to the voice raising the possibility of simply killing Chuck and that cash would be his.

So he didn't notice the school bus, farther down. Sturm, Theo, Girdler, one of the Glouck boys, and The Assholes stood in front of the bus, lined up along the crosswalk.

Everyone had a rifle.

Frank said, "Five hundred dollars. That'll buy you a damn good buzz tonight."

"You got it." Chuck peeled off five bills and slapped them into Frank's hand, as the pickup finally rolled through the opposite crosswalk.

As the sheep crossed the center traffic line, the crack of a single rifle knocked Frank's eyes into the swirling photo negative mode again.

The sheep was yanked off its feet and to the side, as if a giant invisible hook came out of the sky and caught it just behind the shoulder blades, catching on the bones and slamming it to the ground.

A cheer went up. Sturm raised his rifle.

Frank was so shocked he stood up, eyes locked on the dead sheep, nearly black in his eyes, now being pulled along by the lead line. The pickup rolled out from underneath him, unfelt and unheard. He suddenly looked up, and seeing the hunters aligned along the crosswalk, connections were made. He figured out that someone, probably Sturm, had shot the ewe. He went to sit back on the tailgate and fell on his ass.

The hunters roared.

Theo hit the gas, and tried to drag the corpse into Frank.

Frank jumped up and hopped over the sheep as it slid underneath him, painting the street like a sponge soaked in blood. Frank dusted himself off, and waved back at the hunters. Theo turned in a big circle, dragging the ewe around Frank, pounding on the roof, honking the horn, and generally having himself a good time. Chuck clutched at his belly, laughing all the while, his head swiveling around like a half deflated balloon of casing atop a sausage as he squinted through tears at Frank. "Sorry man, but that . . . that was fucking funny shit right there."

Theo turned around and stopped. Chuck jumped off, shaking his head and giggling. He unbuckled the dog collar and joined Frank back on the tailgate. Theo took off, leaving the dead ewe in the middle of the side street.

Riding the tailgate back, Frank's smile was more or less in place. After a while, he thought that if it hadn't been him, it would have been pretty funny. And it wasn't too long before he thought the whole thing was pretty funny, until they turned back into the alley.

He'd forgotten about the rest of the sheep. Twenty-five or thirty of them clung together like wet oatmeal in the shade behind the supermarket. The fence was simply a roll of chicken wire stretched from the back wall out and around two dumpsters, forming a square.

Theo kept the pickup moving until Chuck was level with the corner of the fence. He jumped off, went up to the wall, and unhooked one end of the chicken wire. He grabbed a sheep, another ewe, by one ear, and threw the collar over her neck. He let go of the ear and grabbed the other end of the collar before the ewe could back away. He cinched it tight, buckled it, and dragged it out of the pen.

And that's how it went. Theo would drive slowly out across Main Street, towing a sheep, and somebody down by the bus would be shooting like hell. Sometimes the shots would kill the sheep instantly, blasting it sideways two or three feet. By early afternoon, there was a thick trail of clotted gore the color of crushed pomegranates, covered in flies. Blood sizzled on the pavement, scarred with hundreds, maybe thousands of bullet strikes. The air smelled of blood and gunpowder.

For three hours, in the worst of the early afternoon, even the flies wouldn't go out into the sun. They would cluster in curious stripes along thin strips of shadow that marked each tree limb, eating, shitting, fucking, and marching forward through the gore with the relentless snail's pace of the sun.

Sometimes the shots weren't even close, and Sturm had to step in and kill the ewe before it crossed Main Street completely.

Sometimes they'd blow the ewe's head off and the collar would slip through the ruined skull and skitter along the sticky asphalt like a child's pretend pet. Theo would stop the truck, back up, and Frank and Chuck would have to wrap the collar around part of the carcass, so they could keep dragging it along, and let the shooter continue blasting away at the target.

When this happened, it was really a two-man job. Most of the time, the neck was useless. Once in a while, if the sheep was skinny, they could buckle the collar in the hollow over the spine just in front of the back hips. That didn't happen often. Instead, Frank usually had to lift the sheep by the front legs, while Chuck hacked away at the tendons and ligaments where those back hips were connected to the spine, slashing his way into the sheep so he could sink the collar deep into the wound, around the hips of the sheep, and buckle it securely.

Frank always got nervous during these times, standing out in the street, hoisting the dead target, right in the middle of the shooting range. The shooters were undoubtedly drinking heavily, and you never knew when some drunk sonofabitch might just decide to take a shot at the sheep when Frank had it in the air, just for fun. The sun hammered down like a blunt nail into his eyes. Sometimes, when Frank's eyes would blink over into seeing negatives, the blood looked like semen.

By noon the pile of sheep was as big as one of the dumpsters back at the sheep pen. By two, at the end of it, the pile nearly covered the street. Theo had to drive up onto the sidewalk, just to get around it. And they worked for hour upon hour in the blood and bullets and live and dead sheep.

Blue smoke rose above the town like smog.

Until finally, the last sheep was pulled slowly across Main Street. Theo must have been on his walkie-talkie, because everyone unloaded on the ewe. It exploded in a bright red mass of blood, bones, wool, innards, and brains. The collar slipped away, caught one of the front legs, and dragged what was left of the carcass away like a half-digested bird skeleton through cat vomit.

Theo killed the engine and silence bloomed again. Frank and Chuck sat on the tailgate, staring dully at the pavement. Neither moved. The blood had crusted into a color of crushed red peppers on their clothes and skin, as if they'd been at ground zero inside a slaughterhouse. The flask had been empty for hours.

The hunters stowed their rifles back into the cases and ambled slowly down Main Street, rubbing their shoulders, talking loud over the ringing in their ears, and kicking the spent shell casings, which littered the ground like confetti after a ticker-tape parade.

Everybody was pleased as punch.

"Fine job, boys. Fine, fine job. I'd say our guns are good and sighted in," Sturm said. Frank didn't care if he was supposed to say something or not, or even if Sturm was talking to him and Chuck or the hunters or the sheep. All Frank wanted was to get back to the vet office, where he could wash the blood off and crack open a fresh bottle of rum. He practiced his smile amidst all the back slapping and yelling and joking but, really, he just wanted out of his clothes, out of his skin.

"Gentlemen," Sturm called out. "Lunch is two blocks west. And beer." He was slurring his words, but Frank didn't think Sturm was drunk. Not yet anyway. This was different. Frank wondered if the tumor was doing the talking like the day when Sturm faced the lioness.

Frank shook the last guy's hand and found Sturm waiting for him and Chuck and Theo. "Superb work, gentlemen. Simply goddamn superb." He speech sounded normal, and Frank wondered if the suddenly dead tongue would come back. "You boys come on back and eat 'til you bust, got it?" Sturm surprised Frank by tossing a bottle of Jack Daniels at him. Chuck got a bottle too.

"Well then. Get going, you two. You earned it, by God," Sturm said, eyeing the vast pile of corpses. "Theo. Like a word with you." Sturm went around the pickup and climbed into the front seat with Theo. Chuck was already halfway down the block, heading for the food.

Frank scratched at the blood and blisters on his head and followed.

The Gloucks arranged tables along Third Street, bordering the east side of the park, in order to catch the afternoon shade. They loaded the tables with sliced meat and long loaves of bread. Steak-cut French fries with the skins still on. There was a whole table devoted to BBQ sauces alone, at least forty or fifty of 'em. Giant tubs of mayonnaise and mustard and ketchup, all soaking in ice. They'd raided the grocery stores down in Redding armed with several thousand dollars and damned near cleared the first few out.

It looked to Frank like they were prepared for more people, a lot more.

Everything sat in rapidly melting ice. The family had gone to the local supermarket for only two things during the chicken wire fence construction: the ice machine and horizontal freezer. It had taken the entire family to accomplish this, but now they had the ice machine running nonstop, filling it with water from the garden hose.

Three picnic tables were clustered in the shade down on the south side of the park. A shooting bench had been placed apart a ways, out in the sun; a large locked toolbox sat on top.

The hunters ate like they hadn't seen food in two or three days.

Frank gave up looking for any kind of soap and simply plunged his hands into the ice water surrounding a bowl of honey mustard to clean them. The water calmed him right down, as if he just slid on his back out across a frozen lake at night. It felt so good that he splashed it back into his face, and more across his scalp. This was met with great enthusiasm and everybody tried it.

Frank got a plate and eyed the meat. Before he got any food, he got a freezing cold can of Milwaukee's Best Ice beer. Ice water and sweat ran down the cracks in sheep's blood on his face. The beer tasted so good that he finished it and went for three more. These went into hip pockets. Then he got some

French bread slices, took another beer, and drifted through the tables in the shade and made his way around to the north side of the park, and sat in the shade on the running board of the old fire truck, away from the festivities.

"OK, like your attention please," Sturm's voice came floating out across the park. Except for the men, the park was unnaturally still, as if nothing lived in the limp tan grass and brittle leaves. "It's time to hand out some guns."

The men cheered. Frank opened another beer, slumped against the wheelwell, and listened to Sturm unlock the toolbox. "Have to introduce our referee first. This here's Wally Glouck and he did a damn fine job keeping score."

Later, Chuck told Frank that Sturm had gotten all the men to pay for the chance to shoot and win guns, something like five grand apiece. The pistols were handed out according to cost, most of the guns, all of 'em handguns, came in around two to three grand at the most. Girdler took third place and won a German Luger. Asshole #2 beat Girdler, but just barely. He got a nine-millimeter Beretta.

Sturm took first, winning a pair of beautiful Old West Colt .45 bright silver revolvers, like a TV cowboy's gun. Scrollwork was etched into the barrel and the intricately carved handle. Chuck said that Sturm knew he was going to win; he wanted the twin six-guns from that dealer, and went and bought the guy's entire collection out, for a low, low price. With that amount of cash and no paperwork, the collector couldn't refuse. He kept the cash and hired a few guys to burn his house down. The other guns weren't worth near as much; basically, the clients had paid for Sturm's guns.

"This very afternoon," Sturm said, "you all are going to have a chance to hunt that goddamn monkey you all saw on those wanted signs. So don't go wandering off just yet. Remember, there's a goddamn twenty grand bounty on its head. I have it on very good authority that he's gonna make his escape in this very park—and just to make things interesting, he's gonna be bustin' loose with all his monkey buddies. That's right. I promised you some shooting, and it's shooting you're gonna be doing, by God."

Frank cracked open another beer.

"But—but here's the only rule. You can only hunt with the pistol you won here today. That's the only rule."

The guy who won the .22 groaned; so did Asshole #3. He'd won a snub-nosed .38, which was accurate all the way up to about three or four feet. Everybody else laughed.

Frank found himself in Sturm's cab as they drove to the vet hospital. "First off," Sturm said, "you have to realize a couple of facts. One. We don't have enough cash to pay the winner of this particular operation. Two. We don't pay these boys off, then this whole operation is bust. You add that up, son, and you'll come to understand that if we don't win here, you don't get paid. You understand that?"

"Yeah." Frank understood all right, but he wondered where the hell all of Sturm's cash had gone. Sturm had gone down to Chico a few days earlier and cleaned out his bank account, bringing back at least five Army duffel bags full of bills. Frank got the feeling that it was bullshit, that all that was really going on was that Sturm simply didn't like to lose.

"So here's the deal." Sturm laid out the facts.

When they got to the hospital Frank cracked open another beer and led everyone into the barn. Sturm pointed out the monkey. "There's the little fucker. See his earrings? Okay then. You're gonna watch us load all these monkeys, every last one of 'em, into that truck. Then you're gonna follow us to the park. There, you'll have a chance to get your guns ready, and we're gonna let these monkeys loose."

Getting the monkeys into the horse trailer wasn't tough. They backed the trailer up the side of the barn, pried off a plank, and Frank coaxed all them, including the wanted monkey with the earrings, into the trailer with a pile of dried apricots. Sturm made a big deal of locking the gate with a chain and a padlock, presumably to prove that there would be no cheating. He gave the key to Girdler to hold.

Chuck and Frank jumped into the cab. Then, with Sturm following directly behind Chuck's truck, the Assholes next, and Girdler at the rear, the convoy pulled slowly out of the gravel parking lot. As they turned left onto the highway, Chuck said, "Go," dropping the pickup's speed to just a crawl. Sturm made the turn slightly tighter, angling his truck so he was partly blocking the view from the Escalade and the Winnebago. Frank stepped out of the pickup and crouched, waiting until the running board of the horse trailer had reached him, hopped on, and crawled inside through the front window.

He had a pair of pliers and ten minutes.

He had kept some of the dried apricots in his pocket and pulled them out now. The movement of the trailer spooked the monkeys, but they quickly surrounded Frank, making grabs at his fistful of dried fruit. He located the big monkey with the earrings and held an apricot. Just before the monkey could snatch it away, Frank dropped the fruit, and in the split second the monkey's attention was diverted, he grabbed the back of the monkey's neck and went to work. The hard part was avoiding the nails at the ends of the fingers and long toes. Sturm had warned him about getting any cuts on his face; he didn't want Frank showing up at the park with any fresh wounds to spark suspicion. The left earring was the easiest, because Frank could handle the pliers with his right hand. The right ear took a while, but Frank had just finished when he heard Chuck start honking the pickup's horn, pounding out a rhythm.

This was Chuck's signal that they were nearly to the park. Sturm started hitting his own horn as well, and pretty soon, both the Escalade and the Winnebago horns joined in, the mechanical bellowing echoing down the empty streets. The horns had a sort of formal effect, heralding the arrival of the hunters.

Chuck made another left, slowing down as much as possible, and Frank slithered out of the front window. He scurried up to the cab and hopped inside. Chuck pulled out of the turn and circled the park, turning into the alley in the center of the block on the park's south side.

Sturm had all the hunters line up along the north sidewalk, facing the bank, while Chuck backed the horse trailer back across Sutter Street. This way, the hunters would be turning and shooting into the late afternoon sun, just to make things more interesting.

Girdler returned the key and while Frank and Chuck drew back the bolts and got ready to drop the gate, the hunters loaded their handguns. Sturm said, "As winner of the last competition, I'm sitting this one out. It's all yours, boys. Get your guns out."

Everybody already had their pistols and revolvers ready.

Sturm raised one of his new pistols. "But before there's any shooting, understand this. There's rules here. We can't have our own men under fire. You get five seconds. Understand me? You'll watch as the monkeys get loose. There will be no shooting, none at all for a full five seconds. I'll be going by my watch here. Anybody fires, anybody—and I'll shoot them myself."

Chuck and Frank propped the gate shut with 2-by-4s, and didn't waste time hopping into the cab. They crouched low in the bench seat.

Sturm held up the other revolver as well, aiming both arms, arms straight, elbows locked, at the bank across the street. The pearl handles shimmered and flashed in the sun.

Sturm fired. Chuck floored it. The bullets punched the bank sign; the sign buckled inward slightly, but the damage was small, like someone getting playfully hit in the gut. A few pieces of glass the size of quarters hit the sidewalk. Everyone snapped their safeties off and jerked their guns up, itching to turn around and shoot, as the trailer door fell open and monkeys scampered through the cloud of dust and dead grass. The truck tires gripped first grass, then sidewalk and a quick jolt of grass again, finally bouncing down onto pavement.

"Three seconds," Sturm hollered. Nobody knew if he meant that three seconds had passed, or if there was three seconds left.

Chuck's truck made it to the alley and started gaining speed. The horse trailer bounced once as the hitch hit the center of the road. Most of the monkeys immediately went for the trees, but some stayed in the trailer, looking for the dried apricots that Frank had wedged between the loose slats in the floor.

"Set," Sturm shouted.

Hammers clicked back.

The monkeys shook dust into the air as they clambered into the dead trees.

Sturm turned his pistols to the bank sign again, yelled, "Shoot!" and kept squeezing the trigger until he was empty.

The hunters turned and fired, nearly as one, an explosion of gunfire that reverberated through the town and went rolling out through the pasture and fields until dying in the ravines and creeks and hills.

Girdler had thought ahead. Where the Assholes had laboriously spent half an hour carefully shoving shells into brand new bandoliers, he'd simply dumped all his shells into the hip pockets of his safari jacket. He'd fired and reloaded a thirteen-round magazine four times before Asshole #3 could pinch six shells out of the bandolier to reload just once.

Dead and dying monkeys fell out of the trees like rotten fruit.

Chuck and Frank pulled around the block and parked alongside the lunch tables. The tubs of ice were just tepid bowls of water, now alive with wasps. Frank got low and tried to come in under the wasps and ended up getting stung twice as he groped for three warm beers. He danced away, crushing one wasp in the crook of his neck, and another against his chest with a beer can. A couple followed him for a while, but gave up when Frank dumped two beers in his pockets and shook up the third one, but instead of spraying it at the wasps, Frank cracked the beer open into his mouth and then spit beer at the insects. He was glad that all of the hunters were too busy shooting monkeys to see him. Chuck didn't see Frank either, because he was too busy going for his shotgun in the back window of his truck. Chuck pumped it quick and announced he was gonna join the hunt.

Frank retreated to the shade of the fire truck. Behind him, the shooting gradually tapered off. Girdler and Asshole #1 ran out across Sutter Street, firing at the rest of the monkeys that had scattered down the alley, but the heat of the day made them walk back to the park, gasping and sweating. The rest of the men kicked through the monkey carcasses, arguing over who shot which monkey.

The low, purring sound of a luxury car rose slowly above bickering. Frank bolted upright, convinced, for just a second, that the quiet gentlemen in one of their long, black cars had finally found him.

But the Mercedes that rolled up Main Street was pale blue, not black. It turned left on Third Street and parked next to the tables. The man that got out wasn't as short as Sturm, but was quite small nevertheless. He wore a white linen suit with a matching white hat and some kind of red ascot and carried a tiny dog close to his chest, like a fragile egg. The dog had huge, bulging eyes and some kind of fluffed mane, like some hairstylist's idea of a toy lion.

"I em lookeeng fah Meestah Hoooreece Stahmmmmm." It sounded like the stranger's voice was coming out of his nose, and every syllable ran together, as if enunciating the crisp notes of each word was simply too much trouble. He tilted his head so far back Frank was surprised that the white hat didn't topple backward into the street. It was an odd accent; definitely French, but he wasn't from France. Maybe Quebec.

Sturm ambled up to the man, not quite eye-to-eye, more like eye-to-nostrils. Sturm now wore his new pistols strapped into a glittering silver-studded gunbelt and holsters. "That's me. What can I do for you, Mr. . . . ?"

"Meester No-hweee."

"No-weee?"

"Meester No-hweee, yes."

Frank already hated the guy. Only an asshole would wear a fucking ascot in this heat. The little dog yipped and struggled within Noe's arms. Frank couldn't even call it a bark. He thought back to the little dogs he'd treated as a vet student and none of them were any damn good.

"Hush, Maxeemus, hush."

"Well, Mr. Noe. What exactly can I do for you?"

Mr. Noe smiled. "I am here to hunt, yes?" he said simply, looking at the dead monkeys strewn across the brown grass.

Something cold nuzzled Frank's palm. He looked down and found it was Petunia's nose. She stared up at him, her thick stump of a tail wriggling frantically. "Well, I'll be damned. How are you, you big girl you." He crouched down and let Petunia lick his face, scratching her haunches, her chest, her ears with both hands in long, slow strokes. "What are you doing here, huh?"

"She missed you." Annie smiled down at him, all aglow in a scandalously short babydoll dress and cowboy boots. She'd come up behind Frank while he was watching Mr. Noe and his little rat, Maximus. "She thought she should come visit."

"Did you now," Frank said, massaging the loose folds of skin around Petunia's neck. The dried blood on his head and neck itched.

Annie sat down next to him on the fire truck's running board, and he could smell something sweet, not perfume exactly, more like she'd washed her hair in honeysuckle. Her tan skin glowed in the shade. She patted his thigh and he was glad they were out of sight from the hunters.

Frank was trying to think of something clever to say, something maybe even downright romantic, when Mr. Noe's dog, all four pounds of pop eyes and bristling fury, came around the corner, strutting through the dead grass with his sharp nose and sharper teeth, and caught sight of Petunia.

But instead of flinching and barking, as Frank expected, he pranced right on over, and now Frank could see quite clearly that Maximus was indeed quite male, as his penis suddenly erupted like an embarrassingly red and swollen cocktail straw.

Before Petunia even knew Maximus was there, the little dog was on her. Frank didn't even have a chance to stop scratching her ears. Maximus rose up and launched his pelvis at the base of Petunia's wriggling stump of a tail. Petunia jerked sideways at first contact, somehow swiveling with her front shoulders, kicking her hindquarters into space; she brought her sledgehammer head around faster than Frank's eyes could follow, and crushed Maximus's skull in one chomp. It sounded like hitting a shotgun shell full of #9 shot, when you've got it in a wood vice and you're bashing away at the primer with a ball peen hammer, all dry and crackling.

Petunia wouldn't let go. If anything, she sunk her teeth even deeper, locking those jaws into place. She shook the tiny dog's body viciously, like she was trying to water the lawn with his blood.

"I guess Petunia wasn't in the mood," Annie said.

"Was she in heat?" Frank asked. For some reason, this seemed important, as if it might be some kind of shelter in the face of the inevitable storm.

Petunia tossed the little sack of bones and skin into the air, then pounced as soon as it hit the grass. She shook it again, just for the hell of it, and proudly brought it over to Frank and Annie, dropping it at their feet. She sat back and panted at them, mouth open in a toothy grin, bloody tongue lolling wildly.

"Oh, oh, you're fucked." Theo peered around the back end of the fire truck. "You are fucked but good. Dad! DAD! That Glouck dog just killed Doctor No's dog!"

"Maxeeemussss!" Mr. Noe shrieked and wobbled in front of his dead dog. But he couldn't bring himself to touch the corpse. Petunia rolled her eyes toward him, decided he was harmless and had no food, and turned her attention back to Frank and Annie, that stump of a tail just a blur. Mr. Noe's horrified stare went from his dog to Petunia and back to what was left of his dog. He rose and slipped backward through the knot of hunters crowding around the two dogs.

"For a dead dog, he sure is excited," Girdler said, nodding at Maximus's erection.

Sturm's icy gaze slid over Frank and Annie, noticing everything. "Just what in the hell happened here, Frank?"

Frank shrugged. "I guess Petunia was in heat . . . and the little dog here thought he'd help himself . . . and well, Petunia wasn't . . . ready."

Sturm stared at Annie. "What's that dog doing here?"

"She's with me," Annie said, voice sharp and definite.

"Well," Sturm said, "this is one major fuckup, that's for god-damn sure. I'm gonna have to give Mr. Noe some kind of a discount . . . where is he?"

"Here he comes," Asshole #3 said. "Looks upset. Where'd he get that rifle?"

Mr. Noe shouldered his way through the cluster of hunters, brandishing some kind of stocky European rifle with a banana clip. He jerked the bolt back and let it slam home. Everybody suddenly gave him some room to move; it was like Mr. Noe exhaled, and his breath blew everyone back five feet.

"Now just hang on here now—" Sturm began.

Mr. Noe pulled the rifle to his shoulder and the barrel found Petunia.

Frank was on his feet, fist around an unopened can of Milwaukee's Best Ice, and as Mr. Noe's finger settled over the trigger, Frank flung the can at Mr. Noe's head. Twelve full ounces of cold beer encased in whisper-thin aluminum cracked into Mr. Noe's forehead and his rifle spit out a bullet that took out the side mirror of the fire truck instead of Petunia. Mr. Noe's head snapped back and this time, his hat did fly off.

Annie smacked her open palm across Petunia's hind end and hissed, "Home! Now!" Petunia was disappointed, but she waddled away.

Mr. Noe shook his head, blinking rapidly. He found a white handkerchief in his coat pocket, fluffed it out, and pressed it to the red half-moon on his forehead. His small eyes found Frank. "I think, Meester, you make a very big mistake."

"Yeah," Frank said.

"I think, Meester, that I will shoot both you and the dog, yes?" Mr. Noe said, reshouldering his rifle.

"You do what you think you have to," Frank said.

Mr. Noe pivoted, aiming at Petunia in the street. The hunters parted like the Red Sea, giving him a clear shot. Frank was all out of cans, so he simply whipped one of his long arms out and snatched the rifle from Mr. Noe's hands. He jerked the banana clip out, aimed up at the sky, and fired off the remaining round.

"You aren't shooting that dog today," he said, tucking the clip into the back pocket of his jeans. Frank advanced on Mr. Noe, his eyes glowing with an unnatural light from deep within his bloodcaked skin. "Understand, I'm sorry about your dog. It's tough to lose a pet, I know. But your dog asked for it. Now, I'd be happy to bury your dog. I'll show it the respect you demand. But I'll be damned if you're gonna shoot her dog." He handed the empty rifle back to Mr. Noe.

Mr. Noe stared uncomfortably at this man who looked like he'd just crawled from inside of a gutshot elephant and took the rifle gingerly, keeping it well away from his white suit.

"Okay, Frank, okay," Sturm said. "It's been a long day already. Why don't you head back to the hospital, get yourself cleaned up? You'll feel better."

"C'mon, Frank," Annie said, taking his arm. "Let's get you home."

She led him across the street. Sturm said something quiet to Mr. Noe, then called to Frank. "Frank. Hold up. Frank!" Sturm trotted over to them. He glanced at Annie for a second, but Frank couldn't read the expression. "Listen," he took Frank by the waist, since he couldn't reach Frank's shoulders, and led him into the center of Main Street. "Listen, I, ah, don't worry 'bout this. With this client, I mean. We'll get his money." He steered Frank on farther, down to the intersection. "I'll take care of it. Don't worry. You just worry 'bout them cats, okay? You make sure Lady and Princess are in the best of health, okay? That's all I'm asking for." He glanced at Mr. Noe. "I'll take care of Mr. Dipshit here. You just go on back to the office and get cleaned up. And keep them cats happy."

Sturm stopped at the crosswalk white line. Frank took three more steps and looked back. Sturm scuffed his boot against the pavement. "And just as important, I also just wanted to apologize for my behavior the other day, when me and Theo were getting a picture of the monkey." Frank stopped and listened. "Didn't mean to come on so strong. Sometimes my temper really gets a hold of me and I don't know if it's cause of the tumor or what, but it seems like when it happens, all I can do is spit fire. You're doing a fine job. Keep it up. Now, you take that bottle and go on back to the office and have some fun."

"Me and Petunia, we're lucky, you know."

"Why?"

Annie still had her arm linked in Frank's, and now she took his hand, interlacing her fingers within his. They were walking south along the highway, toward the vet hospital. The sun was still at least an hour away from the horizon, but Frank couldn't feel it anymore. Maybe the dried blood acted as some kind of extra-strength sunblock. The Jack Daniel's was nearly gone.

" 'Cause we met you, dumbshit."

"I don't understand."

"You stopped him."

Frank shook his head. "Nah. I just distracted him."

"No. You stopped a man from shooting my dog. I owe you."

Frank shook his head again. "Shit, if it wasn't for me, you wouldn't have been there." He coughed out a chuckle. "Shit, if it wasn't for me, *he* wouldn't of been there. Hell, I'm the one who brought all this to your town."

Annie didn't answer. They walked in silence, past the quiet streets that branched off the main road. "Maybe so," she said finally. "But this town was dead long before you showed up.

Now, for the people left, for my family, there's a chance to make something of themselves. There's a chance to make some money." She caressed his shoulder with her free hand, picking away at the dried blood.

"I don't know. Sturm doesn't seem to be in much of a hurry to pay me. Has he paid your family yet?"

"Of course."

"All of it?"

Annie thought for a moment. "Well, no, I guess not. He dropped off the down payment, and we used that for supplies."

"When's he supposed to pay the rest?"

"I don't know."

"What if he doesn't pay your family?"

"He will," Annie laughed nervously. "Would you try to cheat *my* family?"

"No. But I'm not dying of cancer, either."

They walked in silence for a while.

"All I know is that there's an awful lot of cash coming into this valley," Frank said. "And I don't know if Sturm is gonna share."

They reached the vet hospital. Instead of going in, she uncoiled a hose, turned the water on, then drank deeply. She turned to him, letting the water hit her chest briefly. "Oops." The thin cotton greedily drank the water, transforming the fabric into a transparent sheen. "You wouldn't happen to have some kind of tub around here, would you?"

Frank didn't take long. "Think there might be something in the barn. Let me check." Sure enough, buried deep in a pile of junk in the stall next to the rhino, was a metal tub almost three feet deep. He dragged it out to Annie. She had him put it in the middle of the backyard, in the direct sunlight, and washed it out.

She said, "Now strip."

Frank was too tired, too drunk to argue. He peeled off his sticky shirt, and slid his jeans down to his ankles while Annie aimed the stream of water into the tub. Barefoot, but still wearing white underwear, Frank took another swig of whiskey. "In," Annie said, and flattened her palm against his chest and forced him backward into the tub.

The water sent sparks through his brain. It felt gloriously cold. Annie grinned and worked the end of the hose along his skull, washing away the flakes of dried blood. She hooked the hose under his knee and let the water continue filling the tub. She handed him the bottle and said, "Drink up. I'll be right back."

She went into the vet hospital, leaving Frank alone with his bottle and the hose, shooting fresh, freezing water into his bath. He finished the bottle, deliberately blocking out the day, focusing solely on the field of star thistles and the jagged mountains. He finished the bottle, screwed the cap back on, and let it float around in the tub with him.

Annie came back out with a fresh grin and a bar of soap. She had Frank lean forward so she could work the lather into the short stubble that covered his scalp. "I liked your hair better when it was longer," she said. "But I can understand why you cut it." Her strong fingers firmly worked their way up his skull and he shivered. "Sturm told me you had some folks upset with you."

His vision slipped into liquid darkness. "Sturm told you that?"

"Yeah." Her slippery smooth fingers moved down to his shoulders, gripping and squeezing.

"When was this?"

"I dunno. The other day."

The water felt warm all of a sudden; his vision sparked back over, and the quick sun was too bright. "What were you talking to him about?"

"I dunno. Stuff."

"You talk about me?"

"Already told you. Yes."

"What did he say?"

"He said you were a goddamn genius with all these animals. Idiot savant I believe is what he said."

"Anything else?"

"No."

"You sure?"

Annie sat back and wiped her forehead with her forearm. "What are you getting at here, Frank?"

Frank looked back at the mountains. "Are you here 'cause you like me . . . or did Sturm set this up?"

"Oh for God's sake, Frank. I like you. Of course I like you. Thought we'd been through this."

"But did Sturm tell you to come back here with me? Did he pay you to come back here with me?"

She stopped rubbing his back and flicked the soap off her fingers. "Who cares? I'm here with you. That should tell you everything you need to know."

"No. That's not . . . did he pay you to be here with me today?"

"Christ, Frank. I'd be here whether he paid me or not."

"So he paid you."

"Yeah. Fuck, I wasn't going to turn down money. It was cash, you understand."

"Yeah."

"Listen to yourself. It was a chance for me to be here. And he said he'd pay me, got that? So not only would I be here with you, I was going to get paid for it. Fuck, I wasn't going to turn it down."

Frank closed his eyes and sank down to his lips in the water. "Go home."

"Just relax. I—"

"I said, go home. Get the fuck out."

"Fine. Fine. Okay, tough guy. Enjoy your bath."

He heard her wipe her hands on her dress, hesitate for just a moment, then heard the cowboy boots striding purposefully through the overgrown lawn and out to the street and just like that, she was gone. He fought the urge to call her back. Fuck her. FUCK her.

He eyed the Jack Daniels bottle bobbing around in the bath and wished it wasn't so empty. He had a couple of beers in the fridge, but they wouldn't work. They'd just make things worse. But the pills he took from the trucker, they were just waiting for someone, they were waiting for someone with a need. Someone with a purpose.

Frank stood up in his bath and dropped the underwear. It was the first time he'd been naked outside since the night the quiet gentlemen had made him walk up those stairs to the alligator tank. Today, it felt good. He stepped out of the bath and pissed in the driveway.

Off in the distance, he heard shooting. But it never got closer.

There were two kinds of pills in the baggie. Strikingly vivid pale blue pills, the color of ice in the sun, and green and white capsules. Frank tore off a sheet from the prescription pad and folded the paper into quarters. He cracked one of the green and white capsules open and poured the white powder into the creases. He eyeballed it for a while, holding the folded paper up to the light, as if deciphering the chemical breakdown.

Frank scowled. He set the paper down and tossed one of the brilliant blue pills into his mouth and washed it down with beer. He poured the white powder back into the green capsule as best as he could. That one and the rest of the pills went back into the baggie. He slapped a long piece of duct tape across the baggie, opened the cupboard under the sink and wedged the tape and baggie up into the sink molding, in the narrow space between the edge of the counter and the front of the sink.

He took his beer back to his room and got dressed. On his way out front, he stepped into the small room at the back of the vet hospital. The pound. Although the dogs jumped to their feet, all wide eyes and wider mouths, thinking it was feeding time, they didn't bark. They were used to him by now. Some even wagged their tails. He'd cleaned the concrete weeks ago, and now hosed it out at the end of each day. He kicked open the back door and emptied the bag of food on the ground. Then, before he could really slow down and think about it, he snapped open the lock and swung the door wide.

The dogs blinked uncertainly in the bright sunlight until the tiniest dog, the one that darted forward through the legs of the bigger dogs to snap at intruders, trotted confidently through the open door, crossed the small room, and bounced over the threshold. The rest of the dogs boiled through the open door and ran into the back parking lot, barking excitedly. A few paused long enough to gobble at the dry food on the ground, but the sheer intensity at being outside seemed to override any hunger in most of the dogs.

He went back up front, grabbed the last beer, and went out to sit with the rhino for a while. He took it slow with the beer, just listening to the crickets, the dogs' distant barking, and the rhino's breathing.

The slow-motion rhythmic pulsing of the rhino's flanks nearly hypnotized him, when all of a sudden, time caught up with him and it seemed to be gaining speed. Lightning bolts started sparking through his limbs. He managed to slow down enough to reach slowly out and gently stroke the rhino's head, the space between the ears.

The rhino closed its eyes.

DAY TWENTY-FIVE

The next thing Frank knew, he was lying on the couch in the waiting room with an unbelievable headache. It was the first time he'd felt a truly vicious hangover since the accident, but he didn't think it was from the alcohol. He sat up and a thousand nails pounded into the glass of his mind. Waves of bleach stabbed at his eyes, his nose, his heart. The hospital had been scrubbed raw; he could eat off the floor.

He decided he needed alcohol. Immediately. He fought through the haze of chemicals like he was running through tear gas to the back door. It opened to a blast of heat and he stumbled out into a mess of mosquitoes swirling about in the early evening stillness. He swatted at a couple and felt more land all over his bare back, but at least it was better than breathing bleach. As he caught his bearings, Frank finally realized he'd been awfully busy.

The lawn had been mowed. A handful of dogs watched him from the shade under the tree in the side yard. A large cardboard square, wrapped in several garbage bags stretched tight over it, covered a cracked window. He wandered out to the barn. The monkeys were full of fruit and happy. He had even reinforced several sections of chicken wire. The rhino's stall had been mucked out, giving the rhino a thick, luxurious bed of fresh hay. The rhino chewed contentedly on a mountain of oats.

He found a half-full bottle of rum under the seat in the long, black car and collapsed into the driver's seat and tried to sort everything out. The situation with Annie was well and truly fucked, but he should have known better. Did he really think that she would quit using sex, or at least the suggestion of it, for cash? It wasn't like they were going to run off together and live in a cozy little house with a fucking white picket fence.

If nothing else, at least he now knew the effect of the pale blue pills. He finished the bottle and felt a little better, but not much. He decided he would shower, find something to eat, and head out to the ranch.

Driving out there, he got nervous, and pulled into the gas station. The sign had just been turned on, pale against the twilight sky. He needed gas, yes, but this little place was also the only place open in town, the only place to get any alcohol. The clowns had moved whatever was left in the liquor store up near the park into the gas station. The last time he'd been here, he'd been with Sturm, and Myrtle had made a point of ignoring Frank. This would be the first time he'd be alone with her since the night her cat died.

He'd thought about trying to break into a house instead, see if there was alcohol left, but he figured there wouldn't be anything left behind. Especially alcohol. Facing down Myrtle was quicker.

As he unscrewed the gas tank, he watched her reflection in the driver's side window. Encased in her reinforced plastic shell, she stared at his back. Frank slammed the gas nozzle into the long, black car and waited, making a point of ignoring her.

Gallons and dollars thunked along, and with a prickling of hair on the back of his head, Frank realized he had his back to the Glouck house.

He stood and stretched, working his shoulders, and glanced surreptitiously at the house. The dead tree was empty. The yard was still. Smoke did not rise from the kitchen vent. The gas pump shut off with a deep clunk. He put the nozzle back into its holster and went on in the store.

It was as hot as always. Myrtle had suddenly come across some important paperwork; her head was down, attacking the order form with her pen. Frank went straight to the alcohol, a stack of boxes shoved into the near corner, leaning against the bulletproof glass.

He picked out a bottle of whiskey, a bottle of vodka, and three bottles of cheap rum. He lined the bottles up on the counter and waited.

She made him wait a while. Finally, she looked up and added up the bottles, stabbing the prices of each bottle into an angry adding machine that spit out a strip of paper like a machine gun. "Thirty nine ninety-five." The words were delivered in such a flat monotone the adding machine might as well have been speaking.

Frank slid two twenties through the slot. She took both bills and snapped them into a cash register drawer, kept loose under the counter. Then she went back to her paperwork.

"You owe me a nickel," Frank said.

Myrtle checked the cash register. She took her time. Sure enough, she owed Frank five cents. She flicked a nickel through the slot. But she still wouldn't look at him.

Frank drove for about a mile before he couldn't take it anymore and simply stopped in the middle of the highway. He fumbled through the bottles on the passenger seat and managed to find one of his bottles of rum. He cracked the seal and took a long, long swig. He shut the engine off and listened to the crickets for a while.

Off to his left, the sun had disappeared completely behind the mountains, but there was still a little light left in the sky, enough to see the scraggly fence posts on both sides of the highway stretching away into darkening hills. The rum pooled and warmed his stomach, massaged his mind. He rubbed his newly shaved head, still not quite used to the short bristles of black hair.

Headlights hit his rearview mirror. Hard. High beams, most likely.

The sudden flash of lights gave him a start, despite the soothing rum. He started the engine, jerked it into Drive, and put the gas pedal on the floor. The long, black car surged forward, picking up speed. Fence posts slid past, fast and faster. He realized he didn't even have his own headlights on yet.

He turned them on, juggling possibilities. The headlights behind him probably belonged to new hunters. But just for a second there he wondered if it was more quiet gentlemen in another long, black car. No. There was no way they could have found him. He didn't think he could be recognized in the photo on the website. Not this fast, anyway. It might be the cops, Olaf and Herschell. He hadn't seen them around much, but ever since the day at the vet hospital, he'd been keeping an eye out.

He pressed down on the gas even harder. The headlights were gaining.

He was going so fast he damn near missed the turnoff to Sturm's ranch. He locked up the wheels and slid past the driveway in a blue, acrid cloud. He jerked the gearshift into Reverse. The headlights crested the rise behind him and the highway around him began to glow. He savagely stomped on the gas, downright panicked now, and the car jumped backward. Back into Drive, turning into the driveway lined with palm trees, he told himself he was being fucking stupid. He had the protection of Sturm, didn't he? Those cops couldn't touch him.

He slowed, watching the flickering headlights as they rushed down the highway. They slowed as well, and turned into the driveway behind him, filling the car with orange light. He hit the gas again, roaring through the palm trees. When Sturm's house came into view, the front littered with SUVs, he exhaled and realized he had been holding his breath.

Frank slid to a stop behind the Assholes' white Cadillac Escalade and jumped out, forgetting the bottles. He crouched low and ran along the fence line out to the barn. There, in the deep shadows, he waited, struggling to catch his breath. Off to his right, the back yard was softly lit with lanterns. He heard laughter and the clink of dishes. It looked like it was dinnertime.

The headlights reached the house and a deep, vibrating airhorn sounded, once, twice, three times. It seemed celebratory. The vehicle slowed, and Frank could now see it was a tractortrailer lit up like a Christmas tree. It wasn't the quiet gentlemen; it wasn't the cops. Jack and Pine were back.

Jack shut off the big engine and climbed out. Sturm came around the corner of his house, followed by Theo and the rest of the hunters. Pine opened his door, but stayed in the cab, just swiveling on the bucket seat and propping one leg on the doorframe.

"Well?" Sturm asked.

"Thirty-seven," Jack said.

"Outstanding," Sturm said. "Any problems?"

"Fuck no. Worked slicker 'n shit. Hell, I think most of them people woulda' paid us to come haul 'em away. But I can understand. You would not believe how much these suckers can eat. Good thing we're back, 'cause we're fresh out of meat."

Sturm turned to the hunters. "Well gentlemen, I hope you all are ready for some real shooting, and I ain't blowing smoke up your ass. The main course has arrived. So here's the plan. Come dawn tomorrow, you have your rifles ready." He walked out to the truck and gestured grandly. "You have just been delivered some of the deadliest big cats in the world."

Everyone funneled through the gate in the front yard and took a look at the truck.

Frank figured he'd better go see what all was in the truck too. Sturm saw him immediately. "Howdy, Frank. Where'd you come from?"

Frank jerked his head back to the barn. "Checking on your girls."

"And how are they doing?"

"Fine."

"They like their new food, don't they?"

Frank wondered what the hell Sturm was feeding the lionesses now. "Looks like it," he said. Later, he found out that Sturm hadn't killed off all the sheep in town. Not by a long shot. There was a pen way out in the pasture and he kept five or six in there at a time. Every night, just before dinner, all the hunters would gather along the tall fences that surrounded the cats' corral, and Sturm would lock a ewe inside, then turn Lady and Princess loose. The show wasn't as spectacular as watching them go after Sarah, but the hunters couldn't get enough.

"What's this?" Frank asked.

Sturm clapped his hands together like a child. "Didn't want to ruin the surprise," he said. "Take a look. We're in business now, by God."

Frank got closer, and before he could even see the cats, he somehow felt the impact of all those gold stares, striking him from all sides, all at once, as if he was being enveloped in a thick blanket and punched by unseen figures. The cats had been packed tightly into a two-level cattle truck.

One of the Assholes had found a long stick and was jabbing at one of the cats through the round holes in the side of the trailer, giggling as the lioness hissed. The game didn't last long; there was a quick snap, and the Asshole pulled back the stick, now half as long.

Mr. Noe snorted and moved away, taking short, precise steps. Frank watched him out of the corner of his eye, waiting until the little man became nothing but a white blur in the darkness.

"Never would have thought there was this many cats out there in private hands, not in a million years," Sturm told Frank as he approached the truck. "Apparently, everybody wants just cubs. That's what brings in the audience. Cute little baby lions, chasing each other around. Maybe even give folks a chance to pet 'em when they're young like that. But hell, just like anything, them cubs grow up quick. People lose interest. Stop spending money." He shrugged. "It's a goddamn shame, really. They get sold. Goddamn cheap, too."

"We're gonna need a hell of a lot more meat."

"You got that right," Sturm said.

Jack led Frank and Sturm around to the other side of the trailer. Three wolves shared a cage. A mountain lion's eyes flashed and burned in the blast of Jack's Mag-lite beam. "Up front, we got hyenas. Mean little fuckers," he said.

"This is just the start," Sturm said. "We got more en route this very minute, private owners bringing in their own animals, so in the morning, you and Chuck, you go grab as many of them sheep we left in town as you need. Keep 'em in the freezer at the office."

"We're gonna need a place to keep all of these. There's only seven empty cages at the vet's."

"It's taken care of. We got the auction yard all set up. You'll have to stop out there and feed 'em. You're gonna have yourself a full day tomorrow, that's for sure." Sturm grinned, teeth bright in the moonlight. "Missed you last night at dinner. Have a good time?"

"Yeah."

"What happened?"

Frank didn't want to think about last night, much less talk about it. "Nothing. I had work to do. She went home."

"She went home, huh? Look at me." Sturm grabbed his arm and stared up into Frank's eyes. "She just a whore to you, or there something else going on?" He glanced at the knots of men and lowered his voice. "C'mere." He led Frank out toward the barn.

When they were far enough away not to be overheard, Sturm asked quietly, "Is there something going on here that I need to know about?"

"I don't know what you mean."

"You got feelings for this girl? You two got some kind of relationship going on here?" His frozen eyes bored holes in Frank's skull. "Shit," he said, answering his own question. "You listen to me and you listen hard. That girl, she's nothing but a fucking whore. You got that? She sucks dicks for cash. You understand what I'm telling you here? She don't care about you. She cares about what you've got in your wallet. That's all. And hell, she's a goddamn Glouck." He spit. "That family, they're nothing but trash. That's it. Worthless goddamn trailer trash. They got no morals. No nothing. Ain't hardly human beings." He brought up a fist and popped his index finger out in Frank's face. "You stay the hell away from her, got it? I'm gonna let her hang around, just so our guests can blow off some steam. Ever since we had that incident last time some working girls were here, I can't get any more to come all the way up here. Word's out, I guess. So I'm gonna let her be. But she is off limits to you, understand?"

"Yeah."

"It's nothing personal, son. I'm just trying to look out for you is all. You look like you could use somebody to look out for you. You'll thank me later, down the line, once you find a nice girl and settle down. Trust me. Later on, you'll thank me."

DAY TWENTY-SIX

They collected thirty of the dead sheep, butchered five, and put the rest in the freezer. Chuck offered to help, but Frank waved him off. He preferred to feed the cats on his own, so he could take his time, talking to them in a soft, almost crooning voice.

Most of the new cats had grown up in captivity, and knew nothing beyond life in a cage. People had always been sources of food and water and pain and fear, but something about Frank, his slow, easy movements, his smell, his low, soothing voice, something made them trust him immediately. They allowed Frank to scratch their ears, closing their eyes and milking the bottom of their cage in pleasure, stroking the floor, extending and retracting their vicious claws as they alternated paws. Some even licked the palm of his hand.

The hyenas snarled and bristled and snapped at each other when Frank tossed bloody bones into their cage. The wolves were quiet and still as death. They made no move to eat anything until Frank had retreated, taking his clanging bucket with him. The mountain lion paced and ignored the meat.

He found an old boom box in the office upstairs and tuned in a scratchy radio station of slow, sad Mexican songs. The music drifted through the cavernous auction yard and Frank whistled along.

Frank had to resist the urge to step into the Kodiak's room and scratch the bear's head, just behind the ears. He tried to just look at the four-inch claws, imagining what they could do to flesh, how they could shatter bone and split muscle, but his gaze kept sliding back up to the shaggy face with its loose jowls, wet nose, and soft brown eyes. Bo-Bo thrust his massive head at the bars in the tiny window and snuffled, craving attention. Frank's resolve crumbled, and he lightly stroked the broad, flat nose through the bars.

More hunters showed up. So many that Frank gave up trying to keep track. He got used to seeing unfamiliar pickups and SUVs rolling through town. A trailer park had sprouted in Sturm's back field, and bonfires sent black smoke into the sky. Gunfire crackled day and night.

They shot eight cats that first day. Ten the next.

Chuck and Jack would string a live sheep upside down from one of the lone oak trees out near the edge of the fields, where the foothills began, and stick it a few times with a pocketknife, just enough to get the animal to bleat and kick and bleed. Then Frank or Pine would swing the gate of the horse trailer wide, turning loose whatever big cat was next. The lioness always locked on the struggling ewe and went for the helpless sheep. Sometimes the hunter would shoot it before it reached the sheep. Sometimes the cat would leap and tear the sheep from the tree, and the hunter would shoot the cat as it tore through the wool. Sturm was always ready with his rifle, just in case. But usually, it only took the hunter three or four shots to finish off the lioness. Sometimes more, depending on how drunk the hunter was.

If the ewe had been torn off the tree, Frank would drag it back to the trailer and use the meat to feed the rest of the cats. If it was still hanging there, they'd leave it for the next cat. They'd take a few pictures of the hunter and his dead cat, careful to frame the landscape so that if the hunter wanted, he could claim he shot the cat in Africa. The taxidermist would twist a thin wire around the neck of the animal and have the hunter sign the affixed tag. Then, they'd load it into the taxidermist's pickup and he'd take it back to his shop.

Chuck would drive back and they'd pick up the next cat and it would start all over again.

The Gloucks set up a thriving business selling sandwiches, burgers, sausages, deep fried burritos stuffed with eggs and meat, all remnants of the hunts, from a little stand in their front yard. The family got any leftovers from the dinners and such that Sturm served his hunters. He provided the dinner, and sometimes breakfast for the clients, but for the rest of the day, the hunters were left to fend for themselves. Girdler took to cooking lion steaks on a campfire beside his Winnebago. Sometimes, Frank saw hunters barbequing meat on their own little portable gas grills.

Four new men shot eight more lions, several hyenas, and a wolf.

Trash and animal bones littered the highway and the streets of Whitewood. Sturm sent Chuck around to all of the barns in the valley to collect any three and four wheelers left behind. Chuck found fifteen. Sturm gave all of them to the Glouck boys, and had them drive around carting two or three trashcans and keep the town clean. After that, every once in a while, Frank would see a flock of young boys tearing through the fields or the town, like a juvenile gang of Hell's Angels Garbage Men.

And through it all, Frank saw cash slapped down onto hoods and tailgates. They gambled over everything. Mostly shooting accuracy. And they'd shoot at anything. That was a big part of the fun, shooting at whatever they felt like in town. Ever since Sturm had unloaded on the bank sign, everyone wanted to shoot up the place. They'd shoot at business signs, windows, telephone poles, street signs, mailboxes, bones in the road, anything. Sturm even arranged a ride through town in the school bus. The hunters stuck their rifles out of windows, shooting at anything and everything that caught their attention. The abandoned vehicles drew the most fire. Everybody was trying to hit the gas tank, but nobody could make a car actually explode.

They shot more cats. Another wolf. The mountain lion.

Most of the cash went to whatever hunter won, and sometimes, Sturm just flat-out couldn't take losing and would have to step forward and shoot and win the bet fair and square. But most of the time, he stepped aside to let the hunters gamble among themselves, but even then, ten percent always, always went into leather saddlebags that Theo hung over his shoulder.

Each night, when the hunts were over, Sturm would collect Frank from either the auction yard or the fields, and take him back to the vet office to get cleaned up for dinner. Theo sat in the middle, saddlebags between him and his dad. Frank would give his report on the remaining animals, and Sturm would toss him a bottle. Then, after a shower, Frank would drive himself out to the ranch for dinner.

Once, they stopped at the house for a fast change of clothes; a lioness had sprayed urine all over Sturm's thighs. "Get that cash settled before anybody shows up for dinner," Sturm told Theo in the driveway. "Frank'll help you."

Theo looked like he didn't want Frank's help, but he didn't say anything. Frank followed him to the barn. They passed stall after stall of ammo, camping supplies, and beer kegs. A dusty tarp covered what appeared to be a pile of junk in the last stall. Theo jerked the tarp back, sending a cloud of dust billowing into the still air, and revealed an upturned dining room table, a jumble of rusted garden tools, some kind of primitive bicycle exercise machine, and a massive, horizontal freezer. An ancient air conditioner rested on top of the freezer.

It pained Theo to speak. "Grab that end," he said, indicating with his chin the air conditioner. Frank helped him lift it off the freezer. They set it down next to the exercise machine. Theo opened the freezer's lid, and inside, nestled tight, was a gunsafe. It was the color of wet concrete, almost three feet wide, and nearly five feet long. You could only spin the combination wheel if you unlocked it with a key, which Theo produced from the saddlebags. "Turn around," he said. "This ain't none of your goddamn business."

Frank turned and almost flinched as he found Sturm standing silently behind him. Sturm didn't say anything, just put a finger to his lips. The meaning was clear as the sky outside. This is a privilege. You don't breathe a word about this to anyone. Frank nodded, and let his eyes drift up to the lioness hide still tacked to the roof.

Behind him, Theo dumped the cash into the gun safe and slammed it shut. He spun the combination, twisted the key, and closed the freezer lid. Frank took his end of the air conditioner and they put it back on the freezer. Then it was just a matter of dragging the tarp back over all the rest of the junk. As a final touch, Theo took a coffee can, scooped up some of the dirt in the aisle, and sifted it carefully over the tarp. When he was finished, Frank honestly couldn't tell that the tarp had been moved at all.

"Let's go get some dinner," Sturm said.

Day Thirty

The Gloucks found two new long tables at the fairgrounds to accommodate all the new hunters. Frank, Theo, and Chuck still sat at the rickety card table at the end of the head table. Tonight, dinner was fairly basic, nothing fancy. Frank wondered if Edie and Alice were running out of recipes. The waiters brought out chilled goblets of shrimp cocktail, followed by lioness steaks, sautéed zucchini and garlic, baked potatoes stuffed with sweet onions, butter, and sour cream. Frank found out later that Sturm had forbade any kind of rice, especially wild rice, to be included in the meals.

The original hunters, Girdler and the Assholes mostly, seemed to have adopted Wally Glouck as their personal mascot ever since he had served as a referee for the sheep hunt. They'd call him over, joke with him, give him sips of their highballs, and slip him bills when they thought the mothers weren't looking. He'd usually be quite drunk by the end of the night. Edie and Alice never said anything, but they went through his pockets before they sent him home.

One hunter, Asshole #1 in particular, was awful fond of pulling Wally close and slipping a twenty-dollar bill into the front pocket of Wally's black jeans. He'd give Wally his glass, letting the fourteen-year-old take a sip. Sometimes, Asshole #1 would even tip the glass further, forcing more of the amber liquid into Wally's mouth. The hunters would laugh, Asshole #1 laughing the hardest, as Wally coughed and grinned at the attention. Asshole #1 would pat Wally's lower back and send him on his way to refill his drink.

Sturm watched all this but never paused, never hesitated in telling a story or a joke.

But this night, something was off. Whether Sturm was irritated at missing hitting the front left tire of a Toyota at four hundred yards in early morning fog or he'd finally had enough of Asshole #1's behavior, no one knew. He watched Asshole #1 pour his drink down Wally's throat, watched as Asshole #1 whispered something in Wally's ear as he slipped a bill into the boy's front pocket, maybe letting his hand linger a bit too long.

Sturm finished his joke, nodding at the laughter, and stood quickly, letting his hands fall to the handles of his new cowboy revolvers. He never went anywhere without them anymore. He strode the length of the table as the laughter died and jerked one of the revolvers out and shoved the barrel into Asshole #1's right eye. He pushed hard enough that Asshole #1's head cranked back until the entire chair toppled over. Sturm rode him all the way down, keeping that barrel sunk deep into the guy's eye socket.

All conversation and laughter died.

Asshole #1's head slammed into the ground and didn't bounce. Sturm clicked the hammer back. Still standing, but bent nearly double at the waist, forcing Asshole #1's head into the bone dry soil, he said quietly, "I been watching you. Been watching how you touch that little boy. I think you're a sick goddamn fuck. You're lower than a fucking worm. The only thing stopping me from putting a bullet through that fucking twisted mind of yours is the sliver of chance that I might be wrong, that you're just drunk, that you're just a big, dumb, friendly sonofabitch. I don't think I'm wrong, but here's what's gonna happen. You are gonna get up and get your shit and drive like hell and hope to hell I don't come looking for you. You got that?"

Asshole #1 was too afraid to nod, too afraid to blink.

Sturm drove the gun barrel deeper. An involuntary grunt escaped Asshole #1's lips. "I said, do you understand what I'm sayin'?" Sturm asked through gritted teeth.

"Yes. Yes," Asshole #1 said thickly.

Sturm abruptly pulled his revolver back and stepped off Asshole #1.

Asshole #1 scooted toward the house and stood up, stumbling backward toward his tent. He was smart enough to keep his mouth shut as he blinked rapidly and tried to wipe the dust off the back of his head. Thick tears seeped out of his right eye. ". . . completely wrong . . ." was the only thing he said before ducking around the side of the house.

Sturm's voice cut into the still air. "I am truly sorry, gentlemen, that something like that . . . I can't call that twisted little evil shit a person, let alone a human being."

"I ain't never seen him do anything like that before," Asshole #3 shouted, a little too shrill. "Hell, just met that fucker, really. He's lucky I didn't shoot him myself."

Asshole #2 was too busy looking at his plate and shaking his head to say anything one way or the other.

Sturm nodded slowly, as if making up his mind. "So here's the deal. Let us put our trust in God, that he alone in his wisdom and eternal grace will iron everything out. Amen. Everyone here," Sturm saluted them with his glass, "has landed themselves a genuine lethal killing machine." Everyone took a drink. "Sometimes two or three. At the moment, we have how many cats left, Frank?"

"You counting Lady and Princess?"

"No."

"Seven."

"Seven." Sturm looked at the twenty or so hunters before him. "Guess how many sheep we got?"

"Plenty?" Someone asked hopefully near the kitchen tent.

"Plenty," Sturm said, laughing. "You're goddamn right. Any time you fellas want to see what your bullet will do on living flesh and blood, you let me know. It ain't exactly like shooting a lethal killing machine, but it ain't bad for shits and grins. I'm saying we got seven cats left. It's goddamn time we give these lethal killing machines a chance to do what they do best. Tomorrow, gentlemen. Tomorrow. Until then, good night." Sturm tipped his cowboy hat at the hunters and pulled on a long-sleeved shirt as the sky grew darker. "Frank, Theo, Jack. Like a word, inside."

Frank felt the last bite of lion steak catch in the back of his throat. Theo, on his right, stood immediately, holding his plate as he rose, shoveling food into his mouth. Zucchini fell on the table, Frank's plate, and the ground. Theo kicked his chair over, dropped the plate upside down on the table, and followed his dad.

Jack was already waiting up at the back door, holding it open when Frank got there. Frank stepped into the air-conditioned bliss and knew without asking that they were meeting in Sturm's office. Frank and Theo sat, while Jack found a book, leaned against the bookshelf, and started reading.

"Fuck me," Sturm said, sinking into his chair. He took off his cowboy hat and threw it on the vast desk. "Never thought I'd come across something like that pervert in my time. No goddamn chance. Jesus Christ." Sturm looked like he wanted to spit on the floor for a second, swallowed, and coughed. "Still, it's done." He thumped his thumb against his Copenhagen can, put a healthy pinch into his bottom lip, and leaned back. "Jesus. Frank. We got seven left. What shape are they in? I mean, they ain't half dead, are they?"

"Not too bad, no. Six are solid. They're eating, pacing, stool looks good. They're sharp. The other one, well, she's fighting something. She's on antibiotics, but hell, I don't know."

"Six. Okay. Good." He leaned forward, large hands flat on the desk. "What I have to say next stays in this room. Understood?" Frank got the feeling that even though Sturm glanced at Jack and Theo as well, Sturm was really only talking to him. Frank nodded and Jack said, " 'Course." Theo just looked bored.

"We're gonna see if we can't wring a little more cash out of these boys. I know for a fact that a couple of 'em are ready to head home tomorrow. Hell, they shot their cat, why shouldn't they? Well, Theo here had an idea, and a damned good one at that." Sturm's icy eyes found Frank. "You oughta see their faces when Lady and Princess go after a sheep. Like a bunch of little boys on Christmas morning. I'm telling you, they can't get enough of it."

"You want to have the rest of the cats go after more sheep?" Frank asked.

"Hell, we're gonna do that anyway, with Lady and Princess. No, Theo thought of something better. Something a little more entertaining. How're those dogs doing?"

"What dogs?" Frank asked, knowing goddamn well what Sturm meant.

"The pound. Those strays at the hospital."

"What about 'em?"

"How's their health? How much fight they got left?"

"Plenty. Enough to get loose."

Sturm knocked on the desk once. "They got loose?" He leaned to the side, and spit into an old-fashioned brass spittoon.

Frank nodded and spread his hands, willing his face to sag just a hair more, letting the left corner of his mouth get in the way of a couple of the words, just a bit, just enough to remind

Sturm that Frank had problems. "Part of the wire was coming loose in the corner, and I guess I didn't notice. Guess they forced it even more, got loose."

"All of 'em got through some little hole," Theo demanded.

"Yeah."

"How'd they get through the door?" Sturm asked. "They get out of their cage, that's one thing. But they should still be inside that room. How'd they get out of the second door? Or did they get into the hospital itself?"

"No, they got out through the back door there, out to the employee parking lot. It was open when I got back there."

"When was this?"

"Two nights ago, I think." Frank didn't have to say that he wasn't the only one with access to the vet hospital. Everyone, Sturm and Theo, Jack and Joe, even Chuck, had keys to the vet hospital. Frank had come back to find the front door unlocked, even wide open, a couple of times.

"Did you leave the door open, Frank?"

Frank shrugged. "I really don't remember leaving it open. Hell, I never hardly use the back door there. I use the other one, off the front office."

Sturm knocked on the desk again, like he was waiting for someone to knock back. "Well. They scatter?"

"Not yet. I been feeding 'em."

"Fuck son. Why didn't you just say so?" Sturm spread his arms and raised the muscles above his eyes, not really eyebrows anymore, more like a couple of fat nightcrawlers under a thin stretch of skin. "So when were you gonna tell me about this?" He waited.

Frank's words came out halting and stiff. "Things have been kind of busy. I wasn't prepared for that business with the monkey. Give me enough time and we can prepare something properly. I need a bit to think some of these things through.

What would you like to do with the dogs?"

The nightcrawlers relaxed and Sturm's arms came to rest on his desk once again. "I want to pit three dogs against the most vicious lioness you can get. On the auction yard floor, tomorrow night."

"Is there gambling?"

"You bet your ass."

"Who's gonna win?"

"We are. Here's how it's going to happen—that girl, she's gonna take on one dog for round one. Two dogs for round two. Three for round three. And so on. Until that round when there's just two many damn dogs and that's it. You're gonna make it look like she can go strong 'til round five, but it's gonna end in round four. You ain't still here 'cause of your good looks, son. So you tell me. What do you need?"

Frank was quiet for a while. "I don't know if they'll fight. The dogs and the cat."

"Son, I can make any of these animals do any damn thing I want. You watch. They'll fight. We got mace and pepper spray and cattleprods and pitchforks. We got all kinds of persuaders. You add all them together and you got yourself a real humdinger of a fight all right. No, that I ain't worried too much about. These dogs we got, these dogs from the pound, they ain't much for fighting. I figure that cat, if provoked enough, it'll tear 'em apart. No, they're just practice. We're gonna see how fast that cat can take care of 'em tonight. Say, ten?"

Frank said, "Yeah."

They caught six of the pound dogs. Five were the biggest dogs left, but the sixth, the tiny mutt that darted forward to snap and bark, Sturm wanted that one special. They locked the dogs in the horse trailer and took them up to the auction yard.

The last time Frank had been in the main room of the auction yard was back on the night Sturm had fought the lioness. Now it was encircled with long sheets of chain-link fence; the top was covered as well, again with stretches of chain-link fence, held up by four poles, providing about five and half feet of clearance inside. Sturm could walk around in the center ring standing up straight, but Frank had to hunch over.

They turned the cat loose in the auction yard floor, and kicked the dogs into the cage, one at a time. At first, the cat ignored the dogs, pacing constantly and hissing once in a while. The dogs were smart enough to avoid the cat. But when all six dogs were finally in the pit with the lioness, Sturm got impatient and had Chuck hose the lioness with pepper spray while Jack jabbed at the dogs with a pitchfork.

It didn't take long. Sturm had been right. The lioness went through all six dogs like a swather through a wheat field, leaving the floor stained with blood. The little dog was smart enough to stay well behind the bigger dogs, but the lioness snaked through air like some kind terrible eel, snapping and lunging, tearing the guts out of clumsy flounders, until only the little dog was left. It circled the floor, looking for any kind of break in the fence. The lioness didn't hesitate and crushed the dog's skull like Petunia had done to Mr. Noe's dog.

Sturm sat down on the lowest bench and asked, "Think we can make it happen in four? I want these fuckers betting, understand? I don't want it to be obvious."

Frank scratched his head. "Depends on the dogs. What's she fighting?"

"Mostly pits. Retired fighters. Old champions. Owners who want to see their dog go out in style. Maybe a few Dobermans, one or two Shepherds. Guy might be bringing a goddamn Mastiff."

Frank shrugged. "They're gonna have to be tough. I mean,

real tough. This one, she's a fighter. She'll kill the first few easy. After that . . . I don't know. Hard to say."

"Well, you just do your best. But hell, that's just tomorrow night. We're gonna make our real money the night after. Tomorrow night is just a taste, something to whet their appetite. I want all these dipshits to drive back down to Reno or wherever the hell they're flying into, and I want these boys to call as many as these rich fuckers they know, and have 'em bring as much cash as they can carry. We'll get three, maybe four solid days out of it. Maybe more. Depends if a few calls I made earlier today work out."

"Cats fighting dogs?"

Sturm spit. "No. That's just the opening round. I want to see what two, maybe three of these cats would do when they face that Kodiak."

DAY THIRTY-ONE

The next morning, Frank found pieces of Asshole #1 stacked neatly inside the freezer. The clothing had been removed. Asshole #1's head stared up at him from inside a plastic freezer bag. His mouth was open, eyes almost shut, as if caught in the middle of a sneeze.

He'd been shot in the right side of the head, leaving a crumpled hole the size of a bottlecap in the left temple. Pine told Frank all about it; he'd been hiding in the backseat of the Escalade with a nine millimeter Smith and Wesson semi-auto, and was planning on just putting the gun to Asshole #1's head, telling him to just drive slow and easy out of town, but Asshole #1 took off before Pine could get up off the floor. So Pine waited. He didn't want to shoot the dumbshit and be stuck in an out-of-control SUV. Asshole #1 slowed and stopped at the mouth of the driveway; he couldn't remember which way to turn on the highway to get out of town, and was halfway through stabbing at the onboard GPS when something spooked him. Instead of just picking a direction and getting as far as he could, he went for the cell phone. Soon as he flipped it open, Pine simply sat up, jammed the barrel against the Asshole's right ear, and fired.

Pine and Chuck hid the SUV in a barn and were thoughtful enough to butcher the body for Frank, leaving it in easy to handle pieces. Feeding Asshole #1 to the lionesses put him in a good mood all day.

It was going to be a long couple of days so he took a nap around noon. Afterwards, his head felt clear, clean. He sat in the yard a while with a few beers on ice. When the shadow of the tree had completely crawled off onto the lawn and onto the building, leaving him squinting and sweating in the sun, he took a shower, put on a clean shirt, got his shotgun, climbed into the long, black car, and drove to the auction yard.

He parked in the back, next to the Sawyer clowns' trailer, and kicked his way through empty beer cans to the back door. Hunters had been gathering all day, drinking, smoking, gambling, and shooting. Now, around three in the afternoon, everyone was huddled in whatever shade they could find, sitting at the picnic table under the trailer awning or slumped against the tires of their trucks. Out in the fields, a couple of men were tossing beer cans into the air and blasting away with antique shotguns.

A high, whining sound, like a tooth being filed down with a power sander, grew as four of the Glouck boys flew into the parking lot on their ATVs. Ice chests were strapped to the back end of the first three ATVs, full of cold sandwiches and colder beer. The fourth carried a little gas grill to reheat burritos and cook plump, oblong balls of aluminum foil. They set up shop in the corner of the highway and the auction yard driveway and sold out of the aluminum balls in fifteen minutes.

These little footballs, slightly larger than a brick and nearly as heavy, had been named "Campfire Surprise." Frank had been reluctant to try any, but the hunters loved 'em. Basically, they were filled with leftover meat, raw potatoes, onions, garlic, plenty of butter and spices, some frozen peas and corn; you buried one in the embers of a dying fire for a half an hour to forty-five minutes, then slapped some sour cream and hot sauce on top and dug in.

New men had brought dogs all day, keeping to themselves in the southeastern corner of the parking lot. They were young, younger than Frank, and drove low, flashy cars. They kept their dogs in the cars, letting them out one at a time to sniff the others' urine and shit and leave their own contribution to the party. The dogs, mostly pit bulls, were beat all to hell. Scars everywhere. Over half only had one eye. Entire jowls were missing, leaving the teeth and gums and sometimes the bottom of nasal passages permanently exposed. Southern Comfort and blunts were handed around.

Chuck had been letting them lock up their dogs in individual stalls. Frank went inside and counted twenty-nine dogs. Sturm was very particular about who he let into town, and imposed a fairly strict guest rule, so there weren't many more men than dogs.

Frank gave all the dogs water. He let the owners feed their dogs if they wanted, then pushed everyone back outside and locked the door behind them. He got his clipboard and went to work.

Around six, the lot was half full. Combined with the dog owners, Frank guessed the audience would be around fifty, maybe sixty men.

Sturm pulled into the parking lot, got out, took a look at the trash, and shook his head. "Hey!" he called over the cluster of three Glouck boys, up on the bank of the highway, sitting on their ice chests. They glanced at Sturm and ignored him, clearly on their own time.

Sturm's pumpkin face of a scar bobbed as he yelled across twenty-five yards of gravel, "Okay. You're young, so you get one more chance. I expect you to be down here in three seconds. One."

One Glouck kid smirked at his brothers. One spit. The third, Gun, picked at a scab on his knee.

Sturm slammed the backrest of his truck's seat forward into the steering wheel. The rifles were tucked neatly away behind the bench seat. He grabbed his .30-06, wrapped his left forearm around the leather sling, and pulled it snug into his shoulder. Frank had enough time to crack open a beer before Sturm squeezed the trigger.

The lower half of Gun's ice chest exploded and he fell backward into the cloud of dust, plastic, ice, and water. The other two didn't waste time getting up. They took a look at their nine-year-old brother, each other, then the ground, and came trotting over. Gun swore viciously under his breath in at least two or three languages and followed his brothers.

"Next time I tell you something, you best listen." Sturm worked the bolt quickly, spit one shell out onto the dirt, and reloaded. He slid the rifle back into the scabbard. "That was your first and last warning," he said, slamming the door. "Next time it'll be your skull I crack. I will open your head and let the light of God inside."

They nodded, but wouldn't take their eyes off the ground.

"Good. I hope I'm making things clear here. Now," he gestured at the litter. "This place better goddamn sparkle before I come back out. Start with that casing right there," he said, pointing at the spent shell. "Your family and mine have a contract. You will do your job or so help me Christ you will suffer the consequences."

Everyone followed Sturm through the back door and into the pens.

Frank and Chuck went down the center of the aisle to the

lioness cage. Sturm turned and walked backward slowly, addressing the men and the dogs. "Take a good close look gentlemen. You're gonna be wagering on these canines very, very soon. You'll place all your bets through the office upstairs."

Girdler sat outside Bo-Bo's room, whittling away at some stick; he watched the dog owners with amusement. He looked like he desperately wanted to be asked what he was doing, but nobody said anything. Sturm ignored him.

The aisle stretched away from them, to either end of the building, with stalls on both sides, thirty in all. They had built a chute that ran from the lioness cage to the auction yard floor.

Everyone got a good close look at the cat that had been chosen for the fights that night. Frank was hoping that one of the dog owners would kick the cage or spit on the lioness, just to piss Sturm off, but the dog owners just flung quiet insults at the cat.

She stared at the men, coiled tight on the blanket and wooden pallet Frank had put in the corner farthest from the door, right next to the gate that opened out to the chute. She never blinked, never moved a muscle except for the flicking tail. "You sure this thing ain't stuffed, and that tail is some kind of machine?" one of the hunters asked.

The taxidermist spoke up, his voice loud and scratchy in the dusty air, like a worn needle settling into the groove of an old record. "If I had indeed preserved that creature, as you say, it would be the proudest moment in my career. What I achieve in my work is nothing but a crude mockery of this, this beautiful specimen here."

The lioness yawned. The teeth were something to see.

"Exactly," Sturm said.

After the tour, everyone walked down the chute, through the auction yard floor, and out through a special gate, arguing about what dogs were the most dangerous and how long the lioness would last. The dog owners kept together and claimed the far left side, under the chalkboard. Frank and Chuck waited at the mouth of the chute, on the backside of the one wall of the auction yard that wasn't seats.

Once everyone had gone through the floor and settled into place in the bleachers, Sturm stood way back in the chute, letting the anticipation build. He turned to Frank, talking low and fast. "I want that lioness to last at least four rounds. You got that? I want her to finish that last one strong. Then we'll get 'em in the fifth. I want it to look like she can go seven, eight easy. Got it?"

"Yeah."

Sturm went down the chute and out into the cage, raising his hat. The men erupted. The sound barreled around the auction yard main floor and bleachers, rattling the tin roof. It rolled into the back barn aisle like thunder, pricking every dog's ear, making the lioness hiss.

Sturm was dressed the same as the night he faced down the lioness. Boots, jeans, and a cowboy hat. He took off his hat and banged against his knee a few times, knocking off the dust. Under the blinding sodium vapor lights, every detail seemed magnified. Sturm's head was deeply tanned from the forehead down; his skull was an off white, like an Easter eggshell that had only been dipped into the dye halfway. If you got close, you could see black dirt beginning to collect in the wrinkles and crevices of his scar across the back of his head. The scars on Sturm's tan, hairless chest now looked like five great furrows of ash.

He raised a hand to get everyone's attention. "Gentlemen. Gentlemen. Now, I promised you something special here tonight." He let himself out through the gate at the far edge. "You've all seen them dogs. You've seen that cat. In just a few moments you're gonna be putting your money where your mouth is—but right now I'm going to have to take just one more moment of your time, before we open the betting." He padlocked the gate shut. "Tonight, that cat will take on as many dogs as it takes. But tonight, tonight is just the appetizer." Sturm climbed up the edge of the cage and propped his boot on the cover, bouncing the whole thing slightly. "Tomorrow night, well, that's the main course." He spit onto the bare dirt floor of the pit. There was no sawdust this time. No blood would be hidden. "Tomorrow night, three of them cats are going to fight a goddamn grizzly to the death."

For a split second, it was quiet enough that Frank could hear a dog licking itself three pens back. Then the men exploded.

The next thing Frank knew Girdler was passing him, the Kodiak on a dog leash, lumbering placidly behind him. They passed under the wall, and the shouting got even louder. Girdler soaked it all up. It was just a taste of his moment in the sun, when he got to prove to everyone that he was a goddamn genuine mountain man, and that bear was truly lethal.

Bo-Bo didn't look lethal. He looked sleepy. His lower lip hung away from teeth the size of .45 shells, wagging sluggishly from side to side as he loped along on his curiously pigeon-toed stride. If it wasn't for the great gashes his four-inch claws left in the dirt, he almost resembled a gigantic, shaggy teddy bear. Girdler walked him leisurely in a circle around the cage and back up the chute.

Frank and Chuck stepped well back and gave the man and bear plenty of room. Girdler walked his bear down the aisle like he was taking a horse for a walk and went back to Bo-Bo's special quarters.

Sturm got everyone simmered down enough to yell, "That's tomorrow." He let that go for a second, then yelled, "Tonight!"

and turned his cowboy hat upside down.

Jack came down, carrying a mason jar filled with twenty-nine of Sturm's checks. V-shaped slices of each of the dogs' ears had been stapled to the checks. Each check was blank, just waiting to be filled out and signed by Sturm, just for bringing their dogs to the fight. Jack dumped the jar into Sturm's upturned hat as Sturm said, "We're gonna draw these names out at random. Soon as the names are read, well pretty soon after, the house'll issue its odds."

Of course, it was all a show. Jack had the whole sequence memorized. Frank had taken a good long look at each of the dogs and ranked them according to the most dangerous down to the least. Jack memorized the dogs and spent a few minutes in the back, arranging the checks into the seemingly random order, twisting them into a tight circle, then fanned out the ends, so it looked like it was just a big wad of knotted-up paper. When he dumped them into Sturm's hat, it just turned them right side up, so they would be easier to read.

Jack reached into the hat, pretended to search around for a bit, and pulled out the first check. He handed it to Sturm. Sturm read the result and held up the check for everyone to see. "Desperado! Desperado!" For the first round, Frank went for a dog a little on the slow side. Not too weak, but not too strong either, compared to the other twenty-eight dogs. He wanted to see what the lioness would do with a dog with still plenty of fight left, at least compared to the pound dogs.

A stocky guy still wearing sunglasses and at least a couple hundred dollars on each ear and a thousand on his fingers came down. He took the check from Sturm, folded it once, and tucked it into his back pocket. A few of his buddies shouted encouragement in Spanglish at him. He went through the office upstairs and down a flight of wooden stairs into the aisle behind the scenes. He went down the aisle, got Desperado, and waited.

The dog knew damn well something was up, and began to growl.

Frank slammed the chute gate open and stomped his foot, just once. The lioness shot out of her cage. Chuck hit her with pepper spray and kept spraying her through the chain-link fence until she hit the auction yard floor. She circled, hissing and spitting and rubbing at her burning eyes.

Chuck and Pine snapped a handle originally used for a shovel over Desperado's collar and led the dog, a half-blind pit that limped slightly, away from his owner into the chute. The dog didn't want to go down into the pit. He growled louder. A quick jab from the cattle prod helped him along.

The cat didn't need any encouragement. It wasn't much different than the practice session with the pound dogs. The lioness, already primed and conditioned, went after Desperado immediately, before the cattle prods could come out. The dog tried to follow the cat with his good eye, but when the cat came at him from the left side, where Desperado's eye was nothing but a ragged, terrible wound, as if a fine steak had been gouged at with a sharp spoon. The lioness ripped the dog's body back and forth, snapping the neck faster than Asshole #1 could pop open his cell phone. Desperado was dead inside seven seconds.

The men were impressed. More money was laid down.

The lioness flung the corpse at the back of the pit, near the chute. She shrank into a spot between the dog owners and the hunters, up in the front, refusing to look at the body. Chuck dragged the dead dog out with a long gaff, originally designed for hauling 100-pound tuna out of the ocean.

Jack read two more names. "Scorpion" and "El Perversio." Based on how fast the lioness had killed an experienced fighter, Frank chose one of the strongest dogs, Scorpion, and a dog near the bottom, El Perversio. Scorpion had both eyes, most of his muscle; El Pervesio had three legs. The entire process was repeated, all the way through until the cat killed both dogs. She was smart, and went after Scorpion first, holding El Perversio off with her left paw. That fight lasted fourteen seconds.

The lioness was panting, so Frank opened the chute and placed a five-gallon bucket half-filled with water on the floor and stepped back. The cat came forward, sniffed, and lapped at the water. Frank studied her and decided to gamble. The cat had to die in the fourth round, yet Sturm wanted the hunters to believe that she could just keep killing dogs all night long, so Frank had to make it look realistic. He chose three of the healthiest and most vicious dogs. They weren't the biggest, but he knew they would be some of the toughest. He rested his beer on the fence, holding it loosely with his right hand, fingers slowly working in code. His eyes remained on the cat. Six. Nineteen. Twenty-seven.

Jack, who was seemingly looking at Sturm the entire time, nodded. He pulled out the checks and read the names aloud. "Shadow of Death. Pansy. Tr—" But before he could finish, Pine tore up into the stands and knocked one guy on his ass. Pine must have caught the hunters making a bet between themselves.

While the first hunter struggled to push himself up from in between the bleacher seats, Pine alternated between jabbing the second hunter in the chest with his index finder and driving the first hunter on his back deeper into the narrow gap between the benches. When Pine finally let the guy up, the hunter was spitting blood.

Nobody had any objections to placing all bets through the house after that.

Jack repeated the first two names and read "Trigger" for the third round. Frank knew the cat would kill all three, she was that tough, but it would be a good fight. The dogs would undoubtedly get a few good licks in, maybe tearing her open a little in the process. With all the blood on the auction yard floor, Frank figured it would be tough for the hunters to get an accurate fix on the cat's condition.

The dogs were released, and the lioness took on all three at the same time, one with her right paw, one with her left, and the dog in the middle with her teeth. Pansy, the dog under her left paw, got loose and circled around the back, snapping at her back legs. Pansy got hold of the lioness's dew claw just above her back left foot, and nearly tore it completely off. The dog sank its teeth into the meat of the cat's leg, just under the knee. The lioness whirled, Shadow of Death still hanging limply from her jaws, and broke Pansy's neck with one swipe. Trigger was kicking in a slow circle, dragging his intestines through the dirt.

Girdler, who had been keeping track with his watch, hollered, "Two minutes, forty-three seconds!"

Frank immediately saw that she left a track of fresh blood every time she took a step with that back left paw. No one else could see it, the chain-link fence was too constricting, and there was simply too much blood on the auction yard floor. But Frank knew it was over. This was fresh; there was an unmistakable sheen under the lights. But like cats everywhere, she hid any outward evidence of the wound and never altered her rolling, sinuous walk. This was an instinctive trait, hiding any weakness or sickness from possible predators. So no one suspected. No one knew. It would help.

"She's wounded," Frank said. Nobody listened. But that was okay. It was his job to make things realistic, so he took a chance that this bunch would be ready to brush off his warning. "I said, she's wounded."

Sturm watched him. "Heads up," he hollered. "The vet says she's wounded. I don't see it. Anyone else see it?"

Frank didn't point out the location. He wrote it down on a twenty, and wedged it into the edge of the cage. "When it's over, you check and see what I put down. You'll find the wound on her. You can see the blood already."

"That's fucking dog blood," somebody in the crowd shouted. He stumbled down the bleacher steps to the cage. "I'll fucking bet you that goddamn lion is gonna chew through the next four dogs faster you can say shit. That bitch is mean." He jammed a cigarette into his mouth, held a lighter to it, and inhaled. But the act of taking a deep breath jarred something loose, and he coughed up a thick tether of phlegm that unfurled in one long wave, the back end still clinging tenaciously to the side of his tongue. The other end stuck to his bottom lip and chin like a dead jellyfish. Either the guy didn't notice it or just pretended it didn't happen, he took the cigarette back out of his mouth as if he'd forgotten what he was doing, got out a twenty, stuck it in the cage. "Fucking believe it. I'll take that bet. She'll kill them dogs deader n' shit." He stuck the cigarette back into his mouth and finally got it lit.

"Sir, you do understand that Frank is telling you flat out that that lioness, that beautiful specimen down there, that she's not going to make this round, and you still want to bet?" Sturm asked the guy, but he was saying it loud enough so the crowd could hear.

"You're goddamn right," the smoker yelled.

"I'm telling you, that cat is finished," Frank said.

"Go fuck yourself, retard." The smoker wiped his chin. A chorus of insults rained down over Frank as hunters rushed to leave cash at the cage.

Plenty of men wrote their names on twenties and stuck them in the crevices of the cage. Frank yelled back. "Bunch of piss-brain morons."

"Look who's talkin'," someone else yelled back.

Frank knew he'd take some shit for his gamble, and getting insulted was a necessary part of the plan. But this was more than he'd expected. The men saw it as the perfect opportunity to air all their jokes and names in an open place. They unloaded on him. It was unnecessary. He got pissed. "Look, I'm telling you. She's not going to make it. The wound is connected to a major tendon back there—that back leg goes, that's it. It's over."

"Hey, he got enough to cover this?" the smoker asked Sturm. Nobody paid the slightest attention to Frank, except to have fun at his expense.

"It's covered," Sturm said. He checked his watch. "One minute 'til the betting window closes." When the minute was up, a green hedge of cash had sprouted along one side of the fence. Sturm nodded at Frank.

Frank went back to the mouth of the chute clenching and unclenching his fists. That just sealed it. That cat was not going to finish this round one way or another. He bent over the water bucket, lifting it with his right, and helping guide it toward the small flap with his left. Conscious of his audience, he concealed a short, squat syringe with a modified plunger in his curled left hand. Instead of a needle there was just a wide snout of plastic and a cap. The cap was connected by a short piece of thread to his little finger; the syringe was connected to a horse catheter that ran up his arm and across his shoulders, filled with enough morphine to keep Chuck busy for the next year or two. If Chuck had seen Frank surreptitiously squirting all that morphine into the bucket, he might have wept. He pushed the bucket through the small gate while sliding the syringe up into his sleeve at the same time.

The cat sniffed the bucket as before and began to drink. Frank held off starting the round until the cat had lapped up her fill. It would take a while for the morphine to seep into the bloodstream through the stomach lining, much longer than injecting it into veins, but at least, when the time came, when the dogs finally got her down and her throat and belly were exposed, it would be as painless as possible.

Chuck gave her another blast of pepper spray just to piss her off and Frank turned the dogs loose. They swarmed down the narrow chute, and backed the lioness up against the far side of the floor. Men screamed and shook their fists. One dog got too close, and the lioness swatted at it, but that left her side open, and two more dogs lunged for her back legs, jaws snapping and popping in quick succession, like a string of firecrackers.

The lioness held them off for a while, killing one dog, but Frank could start to see that her reflexes were slowing. Finally, the biggest dog, a pit built like an anvil and accustomed to killing anything that moved, clamped on the cat's right front paw and rolled into her, knocking her flat. The other surviving two dogs went after her face and she fought them off, best as she could, as the giant pit bull scrambled up and tore at her inner thighs.

Fourteen minutes later, she stopped trying to move and Sturm stood up and declared it finished.

Afterward, when the men were gone, Jack laughed and shook his head as he opened the cage and let Frank out. "Would you just look at the balls on this one!" Chuck and Pine dragged the lioness out the front door to Sturm's pickup. Up in the stands, Sturm kept his attention on his folded hands.

"Frank," Jack explained patiently, "the whole point of throwing a fight is to make money off it, true. But if you're throwing it, don't try and convince the gamblers to keep their money. Or, God forbid, they bet with you. You follow?"

Frank nodded, plucking bills off the cage. Every tenth one was kept in a different bundle.

Sturm laughed at Jack, then came down for his ten percent. He said, "Well, well. This is all fine and I understand. First time you grew a pair and all that. Fine the first time. And as it happened, it worked like a charm. Them dumbshits went for it. You made some more money. Good." Sturm tucked his cash away and glared at Frank. "But if you think you'll ever, ever get away with that shit again, understand this. I will shoot you, no warning, nothing, I ever see you doing that. Anybody else around here starts questioning why you are somehow knowledgeable about the outcomes of fights, then you are putting our financial income in jeopardy, and I can't have that. You're on probation."

"I didn't th—" Frank started.

"You didn't think," Sturm said. "I know already. Problem here is, the more I think about it, I don't much appreciate your general attitude. I expected more from you, son. I would have thought you would have had all this figured out by now. You did once work at the racetrack, right? You were responsible for some things that left those horses dead. Or have you forgotten?" Sturm crossed his arms, waiting for an answer, demanding one.

"I remember," Frank said.

"Then I would think that you would be coming up with all of this yourself. For a goddamn horse killer, you sure are a squeamish sonofabitch." Sturm let the words hang in the suddenly quiet air. He spit. "Aw hell. That's okay. Good for you. Hell, you told 'em. Told 'em not to bet." He started to laugh. " 'Ya'll are a buncha' dumb fucking cunts.' Exact words." The clowns started laughing as well, popping the tension like a knife in a balloon.

They followed Sturm out to the parking lot. It was now clear of any beer cans. Sturm did his best to find any litter at all and trotted all over the place, but couldn't spot one piece of trash. The place was otherwise empty; the hunters had gone back to their campsites.

Frank and the clowns clustered around Sturm's pickup, staring into the bed at the body of the lioness. Underneath that was a bed of monkey corpses. The hunters had been pissed that the monkey with the earring had gotten away, so Sturm promised he'd drop all the monkeys at the taxidermist, who would then go through each one, looking for any evidence of pierced ears. Problem was, some of the heads were half gone.

Frank cracked a beer. "We're gonna have problems with that bear. He won't fight. Not like you want him too."

"Nah. It'll work the same," Chuck said, leaning over so far that his chin and both wrists rested on the pickup, up near the passenger side of the cab. "We'll just blast him with the pepper spray. That'll get him goddamn set and prime." He yawned. Jack stood next to him, but kept his eyes on the far-off campfires, listening closely to the distant gunfire. Frank was alone at the tailgate. Pine and Sturm flanked the other side. The side of the pickup came up to Sturm's Adam's apple. Theo's shadow peered out from inside the cab, listening through the open back window. Chuck finished his yawn with a flourish. "Worked just dandy with the cat. Besides, Girdler said it would fight. 'It'll fight hard,' " he drawled, his imitation of Girdler dead on.

Frank shook his head. "Girdler is simply too fucking dumb to realize the bear is like that with everyone. He's a big old puppy dog. The cats will kill that grizzly faster than the dogs tonight."

"So we don't feed it," Sturm said.

"Girdler already did, when the old girl in there was killing seven dogs here tonight," Frank said.

"That sonofabitch," Sturm said. "We're gonna have to watch him." This was directed at Jack. "He's liable to go apeshit he sees what's gonna happen to his pet."

"That's the problem right there," Jack said. "He still thinks its his."

Sturm spit. "Fuck. Thought we had an understanding all

worked out. Why didn't you tell anybody that he was feeding it tonight?"

"I didn't know the bear had been sold," Frank said.

"Fuck. I guess, technically, we never got around to telling him." His attention turned back to Frank. "No, that's not why I'm telling you this. That bear is going to kill a bunch of them big cats over the next few nights. All I want you to do is make sure that damn bear wins until I say so. Hell son, all I'm asking you to do is make it look halfway fair, but hell, as long at that bear wins until the third, the fourth night if it'll hold out, then we're all gonna make some very serious money. As long as nobody finds out the damn thing's name is Bo-Bo."

"Look, it wouldn't matter if that bear hadn't eaten for a month. He simply isn't going to last. You put that thing up against hell, one of them pound dogs, and it'll shit itself. It'll be dead tomorrow night."

"Well then. That's why you're here. You're the expert."

"We'll go in there, spend all night going to work on that bad boy if you want," Pine said, always ready to hurt something. "Make sure it'll fight good and hard."

"No. Not this time. I got a feeling Doctor Doolittle here's got a point." Sturm gave a hint of a smile at Frank. "That's why you're gonna make that thing fight tomorrow. I got confidence in you, son," Sturm said as he climbed into his truck. "See you gentlemen tomorrow."

Nobody said anything to Frank. They looked at the horizon, mumbled excuses, and left. Frank drove back slowly, nursing his bottle. He didn't see the point in hiding the long, black car anymore, and left it outside in the parking lot at the vet hospital.

He stood for a long time in front of the sink. He got down on his knees and pulled the baggie free. It came loose with the sensation of pulling a long, fresh scab off your knee. The noise was very loud in the vet hospital, echoing inside the small space under the sink. He put the bag in the butter drawer in the refrigerator, finished the bottle, and went to bed.

DAY THIRTY-TWO

Sturm thought the bear had to weigh at least a thousand pounds. Frank's guess was closer to nine hundred. The Kodiak was still massive, like a VW bug covered in rolling muscles and sparse fur, but it looked to Frank like he might be getting a little thin. Maybe the lack of hibernation had caught up to his metabolism.

Frank, Sturm, Chuck, and Jack looked down at the bag of pills on the examining table. "I think four of 'em will put that bear right where we need it," Frank said slowly. "Any more . . . I'd hate to give it a heart attack. Be a hell of way to end the fight."

Frank had called Sturm first thing in the morning. Early. Just to let Sturm know that he was working. "I got these pills. Got 'em offa trucker. I took one and it knocked me sideways for at least twenty, twenty-two hours."

Sturm was silent for a moment. "How many are left?"

"Six of the speeders, and five of the unknown ones." Frank had put ten pills aside earlier, hiding them back up under the sink, just in case.

"Okay. Okay. I'll see you later. In the meantime, you make sure the rest of them lions are ready to go tonight."

"Okay."

"Oh, and son, you did the right thing telling me this." He hung up.

Sturm came alone to the vet hospital an hour later. Chuck

318

and Jack were already there, getting the trailer ready to haul the remaining cats over to the auction yard.

Sturm picked the baggie off the table and shook it, peering at the pills. "You think four'll do the job."

Frank shrugged. "It's a guess. That's all."

"What'll they do to him?"

Frank shrugged again. "Can't say. They're definitely a stimulant. I'm hoping they'll make him stronger. Meaner. For a while, anyway."

"How are you gonna dose him?" Jack asked.

"Hide the pills in his food."

"What's Girdler feed that damn thing?" Sturm asked.

"Whatever sheep parts we got left over at the end of the day. Walnuts. Almonds. Peaches. Oranges. Whatever he can find in the orchards. Fish, too."

"Fish?"

Frank nodded. "Three, four a day."

"Oh yeah," Chuck said, going through the fridge. "He goes up to the lake. He drinks all night, you know, with us. So he goes up there at dawn, goes fishing. Catfish mostly. Sometimes trout. Crappie. Whatever. He keeps the fish on ice while he sleeps."

Sturm was pissed. "That freeloading sonofabitch. Taking fish outta' my lake." He spit. "You said, how many pills, four?"

Frank nodded.

"We're gonna give him five pills," he said.

"I'll crush 'em up now."

Sturm turned to Jack. "Go find this fuck. Find him and tell him I'd like a word. Sonofabitch thinks he's going to take advantage of me, he's got another thing coming."

This time, the lot was full. The hunters must have called all of their friends; Frank counted over fifty pickups. Sturm opened the auction yard early, just to get the betting underway. Most everybody was inside when Girdler came walking down the highway in the twilight, face streaked with charcoal and holding a burning branch.

Sturm, Jack, and Frank were waiting outside the front doors. Sturm had instructed Frank to keep the back door locked. "Fuck the fire codes," Sturm said. He wanted only one way in and out of the building.

Girdler got close. He waved the branch at the sky, sending a flock of sparks toward the first glimmers of stars, then tossed the branch onto the gravel. He strode up to the front door and Sturm could see tracks of tears cutting through the smears of charcoal.

"It ends tonight," Girdler said.

"Is that so? You haven't been up in the hills chewing on peyote or some other hippy shit, have you?" Sturm asked.

"It ends tonight," Girdler repeated.

"Heard you the first time," Sturm said.

"So it'll end. Tonight. Right here. Now."

Sturm spit. He took his time, cleaning out the snuff. He pulled a new can from his jeans and thumped it with his thumb. "No. We got plans for that bear. He's gonna fight for a few nights, at least. Gonna kill more than a few cats. Make us all some money."

Girdler shook his head vigorously, long hair flying. "No. You can't put him through that . . . that torture. He dies tonight."

"I don't know what kind of shit you got in your ears, but I'm gonna assume you didn't hear me. That bear in there, that's no longer your property. Your opinion don't mean two shits around here."

"Please, listen to me—"

"I ain't listening to anything but the sound of the bell that starts the round. You want to, you come in and lay down that

cash you just earned. You don't, then you best hop in your goddamn RV and keep driving. Don't you dare look in your rearview mirror 'til you're out of the state."

Girdler blinked soot out of his eyes.

Sturm waited. "Your decision. I got business to tend to." He
marched into the auction yard. Jack gave Girdler a moment as
well, then followed Sturm. Frank kept his eyes on the ground;
he didn't want to look at Girdler's face.

Girdler fingered the two bricks of cash, one shoved in his
right pocket, the other in his left. He looked to the burning
branch, but it had gone out, and nothing was left but a thin
trickle of smoke. The roar of the crowd as Sturm came into
view made the doors reverberate.

Girdler grabbed Frank's wrist. "Will you help me? Please?"

Frank looked into Girdler's eyes. "No," he said, shrugging off
the man's hand and going inside.

The sound hit Frank first, like a physical blow. The arena was
packed; everyone shouted and screamed and clapped. Men
sprayed beer over themselves. They ate beef jerky. Popcorn.
Smoked cigarettes. Cigars. Spit chewing tobacco on their boots.
Almost to a man, they carried bottles of some kind of hard
liquor, along with a bottle or can of beer. And everyone,
everyone had their rifles.

Sturm got 'em quieted down enough to shout, "One thousand
pounds of teeth and claws!" and the men roared again. They
practically threw cash at Theo up in the office. Sturm shook his
hat, "You men are privileged to see this, this offering to our
God. The blood that spills is in His honor. He will drink the
blood that soaks that earth."

Nobody seemed to know exactly how to respond to that so a
few bowed their heads and a few clapped. Frank didn't
remember that particular passage from the Bible from his

father's sermons, but his father would have liked it. Frank suspected the only place it existed was written across the tumor in Sturm's head.

Sturm shouted, "Fifteen minutes 'til the betting window closes!"

Frank stepped into the cage and watched as Girdler came in the front door and made his way up the steps to the office window.

Girdler slapped both bricks of cash on the ledge. Frank didn't have to hear the conversation to know he was putting all of his money on the cats.

"Twelve minutes," Sturm hollered. He went up to the office and stepped inside. Girdler followed him before Sturm could shut the door. Frank took a long look around, making sure none of the shit that the men had been throwing at the cage had slipped through the chicken wire, then walked up the chute.

He let himself out of the cage and into the back aisle and took a long look at the bear. Bo-Bo was fast asleep, flat on his back, legs splayed, leather footpads the color of milk chocolate in the light cast from a string of sparse bare bulbs. Frank gave Pine a hard look.

Pine shrugged. He was sitting on a rickety office chair with wheels that he'd carried down from the office earlier. "Watch," he said, jabbing at the bear with one of the long cattle prods. Bo-Bo just lazily slapped it away. "I been shocking him for the past half hour, solid. Got it cranked up to the max. See? See? Shit. Too much fucking hard work." Pine sank back into the chair and the bear's breathing evened out and it wasn't long before he started snoring. "Didn't want to go any farther, you know? Didn't want to get carried away, not before the fight."

Frank said, "It's time to get carried away."

"Fuck yes!" Pine said, clapping his hands together like it was Christmas. He yanked a bowling ball from a storage locker across the aisle and lobbed it into the cage. The ball bounced, thunked into the side of the bear, and settled against the fence on the right. The bear jerked away from the blow and shook the sleep out of his head, making a surprised, barking cough.

"Time to play, Mr. Bear," Pine said.

Bo-Bo snorted and rocked back and forth, keeping a careful eye on the ball. Now that he had the bear's attention, Pine reached into a small cooler next to his office chair and pulled out a ball of ground mutton the size of a softball. He held it up, making sure Bo-Bo was paying attention. Pine kicked the door open and tossed the ball into the cage. The meat had been laced with all five pills, ground down into a powder finer than talcum.

Bo-Bo ambled over and ate it without hesitation.

"Ten minutes!" Sturm's voice echoed throughout the entire auction yard, amplified a thousand times over the loudspeakers. For a moment, everyone heard Girdler's voice, high and thin, "This ain't—" and then a brief, ear-splitting whine of feedback, then a solid click. The loudspeaker system went quiet.

The back door to the office upstairs banged open and Sturm stomped out. Girdler was right behind him. "You've got to listen to me," Girdler begged. "Please. Please don't do this."

Halfway down the stairs, Sturm spun and grabbed Girdler's beard and jerked the bigger man over the railing. Girdler went over sideways, legs kicking, arms flailing. He only managed to knock Sturm's cowboy hat off before slipping over completely. A few feet down, he hit the storage locker, rolled off, and landed heavily on his back in the aisle. Sensing a fight, the remaining dogs began barking.

Sturm followed his hat down the stairs. "Warned you once, hippy." He dusted the hat off, put it back on. "You keep pushing, you're just gonna get hurt worse."

Girdler grabbed hold of one of the cages and pulled himself up. He laughed, but it sounded desperate. "I've been watching you, little man. Little bantam rooster, strutting around. You like to hit people when they ain't ready. Then you step back and let your boys finish the job."

"You saying I don't fight my own battles?" Sturm asked.

"That's exactly what I'm saying, you little turd. Come on. You got the balls, come on then." Girdler pointed at Pine. "Tell this asswipe to step back and let's see just how tough you really are."

Frank knew it wasn't that Girdler had questioned Sturm's ability to fight that made Sturm slowly take his hat back off and hang it on a nail. No, it was because Girdler had called him "little." "Pine, you keep out of this. Frank, you too. Dumbshit here thinks he's a big shot, won't listen to sense when he was warned fair and square, well then, guess he needs a lesson." And without any more words, Sturm launched himself at Girdler.

His abnormally large fists popped through the air like a pair of sledgehammers. Girdler had just enough time to get his forearms up and in the way; all he could really do was focus on blocking Sturm's punches.

Sturm slipped one past and his left fist caught Girdler in the throat.

Girdler made an *urking* sound and fell back against the bear cage.

Sturm immediately slammed his left fist into Girdler's solar plexus.

Vomit spewed out of Girdler like a water balloon full of green bile and meatloaf landing on a thorn bush. Several gobs spattered across Sturm's skull. This just made him more pissed off and he hit Girdler hard enough in the chest that Frank heard something crack.

Girdler lurched off to Sturm's right and stumbled over the office chair. Both of them went down. "Treehugger," Sturm hissed and stomped on Girdler's hand.

Girdler screamed, but Sturm kicked him in the face a couple of times, breaking the scream off like a violin string snapping in mid-note. Girdler tried to roll over, gagging blood. Several of his front teeth had broken off and were imbedded in his bottom lip.

Bo-Bo ignored all of this and settled back onto the pallet, yawning and pawing at himself, scratching at his belly.

Sweat and vomit glistened on Sturm's skin under the naked bulbs. But he wasn't even breathing hard. "Some folks, you tell 'em something, they listen. But other folks, you talk 'til you're blue in the face, telling 'em what's what, and they still just don't get it."

Girdler crawled toward the bear cage.

Sturm pointed to the office chair and told Pine, "Set that up right here. I want this dumbshit to have a front row seat. Frank, there's some duct tape in that locker over there."

Pine and Sturm grabbed Girdler's shoulders and threw him onto the chair. Sturm took the roll from Frank and slapped the end across Girdler's chest and wrapped it around his back, again and again, taping him to the chair. Pine duct taped Girdler's feet to the chair base, so they could roll him around easily.

The sound of the tape ripping away from itself reminded Frank of tearing the baggie out from under the sink. He checked the clock. The pills should be working by now. But Bo-Bo was still lolling on his back and looked like he might doze off any minute. Frank patted his chest, feeling for the sixth and final blue pill in his shirt pocket. If the bear didn't start to show signs soon, Frank would have to somehow slip him the last pill, but he sincerely hoped it wouldn't come to that.

Girdler whimpered something, but it was hard to tell what he was trying to say through a mouthful of broken teeth.

Sturm patted Girdler's shoulder affectionately. "That's right. Glad you see things my way now." The fight didn't seem to have taken anything out of Sturm; it just fired him up even more. He checked his watch. "Holy shit. Time's up." He gestured toward the cage. "He gonna be ready?"

Frank shrugged.

"We're counting on you, son. That bear dies out there tonight, it's on your head."

Sturm's voice came booming out of the loudspeakers. "Two minute warning, gentlemen! Get your bets in now!"

Pine was bored and idly spun Girdler in circles as he appraised the bear. "I dunno, Frank. I don't think your pills did shit."

Frank shook his head. "You think we can get Sturm to stall for a while?"

Pine just laughed.

Sturm's voice came over the loudspeakers again. "Window is now closed! The fight is ON!" He thundered back down the stairs. "Them cats ready?"

Frank glanced over at the three cages and the pacing cats. "Yeah."

Sturm stopped in front of the bear cage, stuck his hands in his pockets, and rocked back and forth for a few moments. "You think that bear's ready?"

"No."

"Me neither. But it's showtime. You better figure something out." Sturm started down the chute. "Soon as I shut that gate out there, you let this big boy out. Then you got thirty seconds and I want all three of them cats coming down this chute. Got it?" He locked eyes with Frank.

"Yeah."

Sturm headed down the chute. Frank knew that he had no time, no time at all. He pulled the last pill and found a hammer in the locker. He put the baggie on the cement and rolled the head of the hammer over the pill, grinding it down until it was as fine and smooth as flour.

A roar made the walls shake. Sturm was out in the auction yard floor.

"You gonna feed that to him?" Pine asked. "I don't think it's gonna do much now, you know?"

Frank shook his head. After sifting the powder down into a corner, he twisted the plastic, creating a plump little triangle, and tore the rest of the baggie away. "Do what you got to do, but get that bear up and moving."

Girdler made another noise, deep down, but Frank and Pine ignored him.

Pine pulled a pitchfork from under the stairs and plunged the tines into Bo-Bo's back thigh. The bear jerked away, uttering a surprised yelp of pain. Pine stuck him again.

Frank swung the gate open and clicked it into place, sealing off the cage while simultaneously opening into the chute. He crouched and waited, the triangle of powder tight in his sweating fist.

Pine jabbed at Bo-Bo a third time, and rather than face the source of pain and swipe at the pitchfork, the bear retreated, just as Frank had feared. Bo-Bo was no fighter. The cats were going to rip him wide open. Panicked now, the bear slammed his massive shoulders through the narrow gap, and in the split second it took for him to squeeze through, Frank brought up the triangle, letting the plastic fall away, and blew the powder into Bo-Bo's nose and brown eyes.

For a moment, the bear just flinched and blinked, his fear of the pitchfork overriding his confusion. Bo-Bo padded down the chute quickly, anxious to get away from Pine. But then that great shaggy head shook once, twice. He stopped. A spasming quiver worked along his spine as if he had just stepped on a live wire, shooting 110 volts through his bones.

The Kodiak howled, a sound that shook the dust from the cages and made Frank's heart stop. Bo-Bo reared up, smashing through the top of the chute like he was breaking through the thin ice of a frozen lake. Paws bigger than hubcaps tore strips from the sides of the chute and the whole thing threatened to collapse. He twisted, and started coming back the other way and if anything, that awful, screaming roar got even louder.

Frank leapt onto the closest cage and scrambled up as fast as he could. Inside, the lionesses had curled into a corner, her hissing moan lost under the bear's terrible bellow. He heard Pine blurt, "Oh fucking hell," just as the grizzly sent the gate crashing into the dog cages across the aisle.

Pine needed a distraction, so he gave Girdler a kick that sent the duct-taped, bleeding man spinning across the aisle in his office chair. The bear, drowning in a mindless, furious frenzy, swiped at Girdler and sent the man and his chair sliding sideways across the cement, leaving a trail of blood like the sheep back on Main Street. The bear followed and pounced, seizing Girdler's skull between his teeth and clamped them together, working those jaws in a slobbering froth of saliva and blood.

When the grizzly finally looked up, there wasn't enough left of Girdler's head to put in the plastic baggie of pills. Bo-Bo's shoulders spasmed again, and he whirled, swatting at unseen demons. Frank hooked one leg over the rafter and pulled himself even higher.

Gunfire exploded from inside the chute. Sturm, marching up to the where the shredded chicken wire blocked the chute, had both revolvers out, blasting away at the bear. Frank couldn't tell if any bullets hit Bo-Bo, but it was enough to send the bear loping down the aisle.

The Kodiak, in this state, literally could not feel the bullets, but the noise of the gunfire echoed like a thousand dreadful storms through his mind, spiking agony through every cell. He ran back to his room, but the door was shut. He smacked the door with the top of his head and bellowed.

Sturm fired again and again, aiming for the knees. He didn't want the Kodiak to go running out into the night. Men followed up the chute and everyone carried a gun. They filled the aisle behind Sturm.

Bo-Bo turned, and gunfire erupted, knocking the bear back against the door. Blood flew, spattering the walls and cement like an abstract painting. The bear shivered, falling on shattered knees, and finally died. The men kept shooting.

Frank reached out to knock on the Gloucks' front door before he could change his mind. He'd slipped away in the chaos after Bo-Bo's escape attempt; he didn't want to face Sturm. Frank had a feeling that things were starting to get out of control, just a little, as if he was back on the carnival ride, the Wheel of Screams, and it wouldn't stop, it just kept going fast and faster and Frank could feel his grip starting to slip.

Frank knocked again. The light above the door flickered on and he felt like bait under the sudden glare.

The door opened and Gun squinted out. "What?" he demanded.

"I need to talk to your mom," Frank said.

"Which one?"

"Doesn't matter."

Gun shut the door and left Frank standing in the pool of light. His night vision was gone and he couldn't see a damn thing beyond the concrete steps. Even the gas station sign across the street was off. He'd hid the long, black car among the shadows of the station.

Again, he wondered if he was doing the right thing.

The door opened again. And there was Annie.

She was wearing shorts and a Judas Priest tank top and a hint of a smile. "Yeah?"

"Just, ah, thought you and your family should know. The grizzly got loose. Could be anywhere." He needed an excuse to see Annie and figured the Gloucks wouldn't find out until tomorrow that the bear had been killed inside the auction yard. "I'd keep everyone inside. At least tonight."

"Is that why you came by? To warn us?"

"Yeah."

Annie let the silence grow, then said, "Not to apologize for the other day?"

Frank let a hint of his own smile out. "No."

"Okay. Thanks." She started to close the door.

"I know where the money is," Frank said.

The door stopped. Annie's eyes peered out from the crack, watching Frank for a moment. The light was suddenly shut off, leaving Frank in momentary complete darkness. He just waited.

"So what?" Annie asked softly.

"You still interested?"

"Maybe." A pause. "You interested?"

"Yeah."

"Why?"

"I got a feeling that I won't be getting all the money I'm owed."

"So you think stealing it is a good idea?"

"I figure I deserve it."

"So where is it?"

Frank let a hint of his own smile out.

Annie crossed her arms and smirked. "Fine. When you planning this?"

"Soon." He turned and walked back to his car.

"Hey," Annie called after him. "You gonna apologize for the other day?"

Frank opened the driver's door. He looked back at Annie, silhouetted on the front steps. He smiled fully this time, nothing hidden. "No," he said, and got in the car and drove away.

DAY THIRTY-THREE

Surprisingly, Sturm hadn't been pissed about the bear's escape. On the contrary, he had been delighted. "Got me a genuine killer grizzly—no, no, a goddamn killer *Kodiak*," he shouted over the phone at sunrise. It sounded like he'd been up all night. The skull and teeth were going on his desk, right next to the tiger. "Get to the yard soon as you can. Got someone I'd like you to meet."

Frank fed all the cats at the vet office, then packed fifty pounds of meat into an ice chest in the trunk of the long, black car and drove through town. He felt like he'd lived here his entire life. He could dimly remember the night out in the desert, when he was trying to break the plastic cuffs, but the memory was so distant it might as well have happened to someone else. His mother still lived within his memories in vivid, precise details, but the images of his father often flickered into images of Sturm, like overlapping radio stations.

When he got to the auction yard, he found a new truck, some overhauled refrigerated vehicle, parked in front. The engine was shut off, but the cargo cooler wheezed laboriously under the midmorning sun. Sturm and another guy were standing in the shade at the back of the truck; Sturm raised a hand as Frank drove past and parked.

Sturm said, "Like to introduce you to Billy . . ." Sturm obviously didn't know the guy's last name. "Well, he's brought us something special."

Billy reminded Frank of a squirrel that had lost a fight with a riding lawnmower. He was mostly bald, except for a braided foot of hair where the hair grew at the top of the back of the neck. A long, stringy goatee erupted off the end of his chin; there was no hair above his lip. A couple of sores at the left side of his mouth looked like they might be infected and his upper teeth probably came from a toy vending machine that waited near the exit doors in a supermarket. Whatever was left of the bottom row, that was all his, no question.

He grabbed Frank's right hand and shook it like he was trying to rip it loose. Something about the guy's grip felt stunted and curiously lumpy, but Frank couldn't have pulled his hand away if he had tried. He was too busy trying not to breathe air contaminated with Billy's breath.

"Heard all about you, that's right, friend of the animals and all that. Well, any friend of animals is a friend of mine. Them cats are in damn good shape—feeding 'em meat, right?" Billy answered his own question. "Right." He finally released Frank's hand.

Frank backed up slightly, eyeballing a row of fresh beer bottles, ice still clinging to the glass, lined up along the truck's bumper.

Billy followed his look, and handed Frank a beer. Frank couldn't help but notice how mangled his hand was, like it had been slammed in a pickup door a few times and the tailgate too, just for the hell of it. A few fingers were gone, Frank couldn't actually tell exactly which ones—only a few nubs peeked shyly around the sweating bottle. Billy's thumb looked suspiciously like a big toe.

"Much obliged," Frank said.

"Betcha," Billy said. "Always got some on hand, since I gotta keep the truck cold anyways."

Frank nodded, as if this made perfect sense. He figured maybe Billy had a dead animal on display and he needed to keep the corpse frozen. When Frank was around nine or ten, his mom took him to the county fair and he paid fifty cents to walk into an air-conditioned semi-trailer and see a big plastic-looking shark behind sheets of rippled glass that were supposed to be ice. Still, the shark had been huge, and Frank had stayed for hours, squinting through the ripples, trying to see the shark better. Finally, the truck owner had to kick him out.

"Go on, son," Sturm said. "Ask him what's in there."

Frank looked at Billy. "What's in there?"

Billy smiled. The top row of teeth looked like it had frightened the bottom row into rotting and melting away. He leaned into a quick spiel. "A genuine dinosaur. Right in front of your eyes. Guaranteed. Biggest reptile you've ever seen. It eats crocodiles for breakfast. Deadliest predator to stalk the Earth. Spanning the ages all the way back to the dreaded Paleolithic era. Which is before the Jurassic Park era, just so you know. It is nature unleashed in all her raw fury. Behold . . ." Billy snapped the latches at the back of the truck open and swung the thick door wide. "The awesome power of the Komodo Dragon."

The dragon stared coolly out at Frank and flicked its tongue at the wall absentmindedly. Frank hadn't been expecting the thing to be alive. But it made no move to dart to the back end of the trailer, content only to lethargically move its eyes. Frank touched the metal interior and it was cool, but not freezing, like a knife that had been left out all night.

"I keep it cold so he stays calm," Billy said.

Frank realized Billy and Sturm were waiting for his reaction.

He said, "That's a damn big lizard." And it was true. The Komodo Dragon easily stretched across the eight-foot trailer, even with the head curled around slightly and a solid three or four feet of tail along the opposite wall. The head and neck looked like an uncircumcised penis that had gotten surly one day and grown teeth and a tongue.

The claws, incredibly, were even longer than the Kodiak's. These were thinner. Sharper. Meaner.

"The spit alone will make you sicker n' hell," Billy said. He held up his mangled hand. "When it was just a pup, sonofabitch got hold of my hand here, and I kicked it in the head, got it off. Didn't think it was so bad at first. Hell, just poured some tequila over it. Shit. Inside of two days I woke up, found myself in the emergency ward. That shit fucked me up but good. That monster, he ain't nothing to fuck around with."

"You gonna shoot it?" Frank asked Sturm.

"Hell no," Sturm said. "Jack and Pine are picking up a motherhumping white Siberian tiger as we speak. I don't need to tell you that that's one of the rarest goddamn animals on the planet right now. And," he lowered his voice, "story goes, it's the same tiger that went after that faggot magician few years back."

"No shit?" Billy asked. "I heard they had to put it down."

"Supposedly, they switched it with a tiger that was already dead."

"I'll be damned," Billy said.

"Tonight, we got ourselves a regular rumble in the jungle; this damn dinosaur is gonna go toe-to-toe with that tiger in the bottom of the town pool."

When Frank came over the slight bridge that traversed the dry creekbed that cut across the north end of the valley on his way back to the vet hospital, he saw Mr. Noe's Mercedes parked on his side of the highway. It was late, and the nearly horizontal rays burned the back of the Mercedes into a slippery white fire. Frank's first instinct was to just hit the gas instead of the brakes and just crash right into the fucker. But he managed to at least take his foot off the gas, and coasted up on the other car.

Mr. Noe stood in the sunroof, aiming his rifle at something in the empty irrigation ditch. He fired, twice. Theo, in the driver's seat, glanced at the rearview mirror. By then, Frank was close enough to see Theo's eyes narrow as Theo caught sight of the long, black car.

Frank drifted over into the oncoming lane and stopped directly across from the Mercedes. Mr. Noe turned to look, gave a little bow, and then turned and fired a third time. Something cracked inside of Frank's head and filled him with unease. This was all wrong. These two fucks weren't just shooting pheasants or raccoons. He shut off the car and got out.

Mr. Noe waved and dropped back into the passenger seat and Theo made the little car leap forward and by the time Frank had crossed the dotted yellow line in the center of the highway, the Mercedes was twenty yards away and gaining speed.

Frank didn't bother to chase them. He kept going on to the irrigation ditch.

Petunia was down there.

She'd been shot three times. One bullet had passed through her chest, one through her fourth row of nipples, and one had shattered upon impact as it struck the outermost, center muscle in her thick jaw, sending shards of itself along her skull, into her eye, her throat.

Frank jumped into the ditch and said, "Easy girl. Easy." Petunia whirled and snapped at the direction of his voice, shredding herself even further. "Easy. Oh, please. Just . . ." Petunia dragged herself toward him in a barking frenzy, spraying blood with every horrible crunch from her ruined jaw. Frank finally made himself shut up by clasping a hand over his mouth. He crouched and watched until he couldn't help but try and silently reach out to gently touch the uninjured side of her neck.

She ripped herself at him and chased him out of the ditch.

Frank stumbled back to the highway. He looked toward town,

where the Mercedes had headed. Fighting the urge to follow, he grabbed a bottle from his car and went to watch Petunia either pass out or die.

Half an hour later, when Frank finally dared to get in closer, he wasn't sure if she was unconscious or dead. She didn't react when he gathered her in his arms and carried her to the long, black car. He put her on the front seat, cradling her head in his lap as he steered with one hand on the steering wheel, the other on the dog, and talked to her the whole way, telling her about all the squirrels she would chase when she got better and how pretty she was and how he was going to take care of her and how Mr. Noe and Theo were going to be hurting worse than she was real soon. But when he finally got her back to the office and up on an examining table, Petunia was dead.

Frank sat on the floor for a long time. Then he carefully washed her and stitched up her wounds. He closed her eyes. He eased her tense muscles, moving the legs gently, letting her relax. He put her tongue back inside her teeth. He laid a white sheet on the floor and wrapped it around her more carefully than a new parent tending to an infant.

He put Petunia in the back seat of the long, black car, but before he left, he unlocked all three outside doors to the vet hospital and let them stand open. He shut the freezer off and left the lid open. The ten thousand went in the trunk, under the spare tire. Then he went along the row of cages and unlocked all of them, letting the doors swing open by themselves. The cats watched him without moving.

"Go on. Get the hell out of here," he told them.

He drove to the Glouck house. The girl that had been hanging in the dead tree his first day in town was out front, sitting on a wooden see-saw, as if waiting for someone to play. He'd overheard the mothers calling her Amber.

"Where's your boots?" she asked.

Frank took Petunia out of the back seat and gently laid her in front of the satellite dish. He turned to Amber. "Your sister here?"

The front door slammed open and Annie came running out. She had seen the figure wrapped in the white sheet. Strong, tan legs faltered and slowed as she got closer until she finally simply stopped moving forward. She clapped a hand over her mouth. Tears filled her eyes, spilled out, and ran down her cheeks. "Why?" was the only thing she managed to get out before a sob choked her throat and stopped any more words.

Frank didn't say anything. His vision grew blurry. It took him a moment to realize that his own tears were flooding his eyes. He couldn't remember the last time he had actually cried. He hadn't even shed any tears when his mother was buried. Something tore, deep inside of him. It sounded awfully like the duct tape under the sink. It kept ripping, shredding some thin membrane down in the darkness. The voice hissed in approval and urged whatever had been sealed inside to squirm free. He shook, his knees buckled, and he collapsed onto his haunches, hands and face numb.

Annie stepped closer and knelt beside him.

"I'm sorry," he whispered. "I'm so sorry. I couldn't help her."

Annie took his face and kissed his tears, her own hot tears spilling down her cheeks, mingling with his.

A great, agonizing wail grew in Frank's chest and he felt that if he didn't let it out and scream for every animal he ever hurt or killed, for all of the animals in his miserable life, his entire body would explode in pain. But he choked it back, rocking back and forth on the Gloucks' front lawn.

Annie held him close, sobbing into his ear.

Frank heard nothing but the anguished cry of the Kodiak, the horses, the big cats, all of them. And underneath it all, the voice. The voice, saying it's about goddamn time. Enough is enough. You've been the goddamn grim reaper to the animal world for too long now, and it was time to end it. To end it all.

Annie grabbed the back of his skull and kissed him.

The pain floated up into the sky and dissipated among the stars.

He looked into Annie's eyes and saw compassion. Kindness. Love. He took a deep breath. She wiped his tears away. He reached out, curled his hand around her ear, slipping her hair back. Her eyes never left his. He pulled her close and kissed her, hard. He tasted tears mixed with saliva.

He lowered his head and touched his forehead to hers. "The money? It's all in a gunsafe, hidden in the barn. It's in a stall in the back, inside a freezer. You got that?"

"I—"

"It's heavy, but you'll figure it out. I know you will." He kissed her again. "Remember, it's in the barn. In a freezer. In the back." The edge in his voice was sharp enough to shave steel. "Tonight is gonna be your only chance."

Annie ran her hand across his prickly scalp. "What are you going to do?"

Frank was dimly aware of one of the mothers, standing silhouetted in the doorway, Annie in front of him, staring into his eyes, and the body of Petunia in the sheet. He stood and walked away.

Instead of climbing in the car, he passed the front grille and kept going. The gas station had closed for the night. Frank didn't care. He walked up to the front door and kicked in the glass. He ducked under the metal push bar and grabbed the entire case of rum. When he came out, Annie was still watching him.

Frank put the box in the passenger seat, and for a moment, he wanted to say how sorry he was for everything, but instead, he finally just started the car, slammed the door, and drove into the darkness.

He saw the lights of the town pool a mile off. After parking in the driveway of an abandoned farmhouse, he walked the rest of the way. If things went bad, he didn't want to come running out of the pool and have to jump in his car. It was too slow. He wanted to slip away in the dark and get back to the office quietly.

Men stood in little knots on the front lawn, smoking, drinking. Rifles and shotguns lined the bike rack. No weapons were allowed in the pool. Chuck was charging ten bucks just to get inside. When he saw Frank, he visibly flinched. "Where you been, man? Sturm's pissed as all hell. You better get inside and take care of it." Chuck looked like the conflict might make him throw up. He changed tactics. "Say, what was that stuff you gave me? I was just wondering. The other day," he added and said nothing else.

"Yeah."

"I was just curious, you know, what it was called."

"You need some more?"

"Well, yeah, now that you mention it . . . but I was . . . you know, I was just wondering what you called it." Chuck snapped his fingers and pointed at a big guy in a leather duster that had been trying to slip past him. "Ten bucks—you, Mr. Universe there—ten bucks, pal." The big guy reluctantly gave up the cash, then hurried on inside. "So. What's it called again? I wanted to look it up," Chuck asked, taking a wad of cash the size of a softball out of his front pants pocket and tucking the money into a leather saddle bag under his stool.

"I call it, 'Frank's Surprise.' "

"Oh yeah?" Chuck looked disappointed.

"I'll have some for you tonight. Same amount, same price. Tomorrow morning at the latest," Frank said and that seemed to cheer Chuck up a little.

The first few notes of the national anthem lurched out of the loudspeakers, and everyone took that as the signal for the fight and started inside. Frank let the current carry him into the cinderblock walls. He swept past the front office, the entrance to the changing rooms and toilets, and the shower, until it threw him against the shallow end.

To the left, Chuck and Pine had done a good job sealing off the deep end. Chicken wire, reinforced every four feet with a stout pole anchored in a five-gallon bucket of cement, stretched across the shallow end. Men climbed down the three-foot ladders and lined up along the fence, wanting to see the fight up close and personal. Black, brittle leaves were scattered across the dull white paint like dead scales against a fish's white belly. Most of the men lined up along the edges of the deep end.

A stainless steel box, at least six feet long and four feet high, hung on the edge between the low and high diving boards from a series of ropes and pulleys. The box was nearly solid, with only a single row of holes the size of quarters along the top; it was tilted at such a steep angle that the line of holes pointed up at the high board. A separate rope led to a catch on the gate.

Fourteen feet below, the bottom was covered with six inches of murky water, choked with algae. And even that water was disappearing fast. When Frank, Sturm, and Girdler had visited, the water was around two feet deep. Next week there would be nothing but algae, spread thin and dying under that relentless sun. Week after that, dust.

Someone threw a bottle into the deep end. It shattered and Frank saw the previously hidden Komodo Dragon tear away from the corner up near the shallow end and zigzag across the thin pool of water, moving faster than Princess and Lady going after a sheep. It circled around in the corner under the high board and sank back into the water.

Sturm hit the record as he burst out of the doorway of the front office, sending the needle skipping and tearing across the vinyl.

The guy was looking up at the speakers and joking with his buddies and had no idea Sturm was about to come down like a hammer striking the primer of a shell. Sturm went in low and jerked the guy's boots out from under him with his left hand while grabbing hold of the guy's belt with his right and pushing down. All the guy really felt was his legs get yanked from under him and the gritted surface of the pool deck smash into his face, shattering the cartilage in his nose, cracking the bone above the eyes, and breaking his upper two front teeth.

Sturm was so mad he jerked one of his pistols out and shot the guy's hand. "Throw another fucking bottle!" he hollered, letting everyone around the pool hear him loud and clear. He clicked the hammer back in the sudden quiet and aimed at the back of the guy's head. "What's that? What?" Sturm tilted his head.

The guy whimpered something.

"You're sorry? You fucking ought to be." Sturm eased the hammer up and put the pistol back in its holster. He stepped up to the edge, let his voice bounce around the hollow concrete. "Anybody else feel like interfering with this fight? This establishment has rules, and anybody thinks these rules don't apply to him, then he'd best be thinking hard about this decision. In fact, he best be thinking about it so hard he leaves. Right fucking now."

Frank trailed Sturm at a distance as men crowded the edge, climbed up on the roof of the front office, hung off the two lifeguard towers. The clowns sat along the high board, the best seats in the house, except for the shallow board, which was reserved for Sturm and Theo only. Frank slowed, watching faces, clothes, gestures.

And there was Mr. Noe, still in his white suit, one leg hooked around the ladder bars by the deep end's lifeguard tower, taking pictures with a cheap, disposable camera.

Frank wished he hadn't left the shotgun in the car.

Sturm climbed up on the low diving board and everyone cheered. He let the applause build, then nodded to Jack. Frank figured he must have missed all the speeches, because Sturm wasn't wasting any time. Jack swiftly pulled the gate up, releasing the tiger. It came out backward, clawing at the smooth metal of the box in a blur of white fur. But it couldn't catch hold, and slid along the wall all the way down, splashing into the water, turning the white coat quite green.

The Komodo watched the tiger for a moment, tongue sliding greasily in and out as it tasted the air, and turned back to clawing at the wall. The tiger scampered out of the water and coiled itself at the edge of the shallow end, near the chicken wire. After that, the two animals refused to look at each other.

Frank didn't want Sturm to see him, so he kept his head down and worked his way around behind Sturm. Men shouted, screamed at the tiger and the Komodo Dragon, but neither animal moved much. Frank overheard someone say, "I've seen better fights at my son's school, and he's in fucking third grade."

Frank eased his way around the diving boards, avoiding Jack and Pine, who were lowering the tiger box and dragging it back away from the edge. Billy was right there, saying, "Maybe it's still cold. Shit, I dunno."

"Thought you said it was mean," Pine said.

"Oh it is, you betcha. But this, this I dunno," Billy said.

Frank hung back, near the fence, and rounded the corner.

Mr. Noe was still taking pictures. Frank slid between men until he was directly behind the white suit. He let his eyes flicker up to Sturm, who was busy stomping back and forth on the low diving board. Frank knew Sturm was looking for him, wondering how in the hell to get these two animals to fight. Frank didn't care. The only thing that mattered was hunched over in front of him, clicking away at the bottom of the pool.

It was easy. He waited until Mr. Noe leaned out one more time to take a picture, peeled Mr. Noe's hand off the ladder handle and simply pushed at the same time. Gently. In the small of the back. Mr. Noe's center of gravity shifted unexpectedly, and almost in slow motion, before he realized that he was too far out, before his balance had a chance to sound the alarm bell, he slowly toppled over and fell.

He shrieked, an anxious, desperate bleat. Frank wished he had seen the man's eyes when he had finally realized that he was about to fall into the empty pool, but Frank was already slipping backward through the cluster of men.

Mr. Noe, for some reason, held onto the camera the whole way down. He landed on his shoulder in the water and the flash went off. The impact cranked his head sideways and forward; if he'd hit a slightly different angle, if his head had gone backward instead of crushing his chin into his chest, and the fall would have snapped his neck instantly. But Mr. Noe wasn't that lucky. His ribs collapsed into his collarbone and his pelvis settled over his face, leaving his bony legs jutting limply into space, like trees that had snapped in half in a high wind. They flopped back and forth, eventually slapping against the edge of the wall, not five feet from the Komodo Dragon.

Frank caught Sturm staring at him.

The men laughed, cheered. Everyone had simply assumed that Mr. Noe had leaned out too far, and lost his balance, but Sturm knew better. Frank met those ice-cold eyes for a moment, and shrugged. Sturm nodded imperceptibly, telling Frank that they would be speaking later.

The tiger's ears swiveled and froze as they locked onto Mr. Noe, and it collected itself, lowering the front shoulders and tensing its rear haunches.

The Dragon's tongue shot out, retracted.

Mr. Noe struggled to lift his head out of the water with his good shoulder, the left one, since the right shoulder and upper arm had been broken in the fall, just enough to grab a breath. He pushed himself around and managed to wriggle over to the edge of the water. He still hadn't seen the Dragon yet, and this brought him even closer, to within a yard of the giant lizard.

"When's the last time that lizard of yours ate anything substantial?" Sturm asked.

"Last week," Billy answered. "Fed it a pig for a showdown in San Jose."

But no one else moved. No one wanted to be seen as interfering in a fight.

The Komodo, making no sudden movements, moving almost lazily, clamped half-inch teeth on Mr. Noe's upper arm, puncturing the triceps and biceps like wood screws through jello, and jerked him sideways.

Mr. Noe's shriek echoed around the bare cement walls and into the sky. His right arm splashed uselessly in the water as the Komodo Dragon dragged him deeper in the water. It sank its claws into his chest and pulled at the left arm. Mr. Noe's scream came out in bubbles as the teeth shredded the muscles from his upper arm down to his wrist, like ripping off a wet sock. It bit down harder and pulled, taking the middle finger as it tore the flesh away.

The tiger crept forward.

The dragon went after Mr. Noe's armpit. His legs scissored frantically, like a fly whose wings had been pulled off. The Komodo held him down and kept tearing at the soft flesh under his arm. Bloody swatches of the white suit floated in the algae. After a while, the legs stopped moving.

The tiger finally settled down and just watched the Dragon eat.

Frank wished it had lasted longer.

After the Komodo Dragon had gorged itself on Mr. Noe, there wasn't much left. A few scraps of ragged muscle and bone left in a trail, with a few larger chunks inside the pelvis and the skull, but not even enough to bury him in a child's coffin. The Komodo Dragon was an especially efficient killer and scavenger, and broke off chunks of bones and joints and swallowed them without any trouble at all. It kept Mr. Noe's ribcage and backbone with it as it skittered along back to its corner, ignoring the white tiger. When it had become obvious that nothing else was going to happen, the men had drifted away on their own.

Sturm watched the Komodo Dragon and Siberian white tiger for a while. The tiger had moved in and taken the pelvis and leg. Most of it was mostly just bone and ligaments; the Komodo had focused primarily on the other leg. But there was some tissue left, stubbornly clinging to the bone down near Mr. Noe's toes, and the tiger happily settled into place and gnawed on the bones.

"Where were you?" Sturm demanded. Except for Sturm and the clowns, the pool was empty. Billy and Theo waited near the pool entrance.

Frank had stayed. Sturm had seen him, and Frank didn't see the point in hiding; he knew he wouldn't make it out of the valley without one of the clowns or even Theo tracking him down and shooting him in the back. Frank stood. "I was tending to a wounded animal."

"And what animal was that?"

"Petunia. The Gloucks' dog."

"The Gloucks' dog."

"Yeah. She'd been wounded. I thought it was my job to take care of wounded animals. After all, I am the vet in this town."

"Let's go for a ride," Sturm said.

They went out to Sturm's pickup and Theo handed his father a blanket. Sturm wrapped it around his shoulders, and climbed up into the pickup bed. He settled into a La-Z-Boy and gestured for Frank to climb up and sit on the wheelwell. Jack followed Frank and Theo slammed the tailgate. Theo hopped in the front, started the engine, and drove slowly through town.

The town now knew it was dead. Bullet holes pierced every bare window. All the streetlights had been shot out. The few cars still left on the streets were riddled with more holes than a colander. They passed a pile of blackened husks of hyenas, still smoldering in the intersection of Third and Main Street. The strip of dried blood from the sheep appeared almost purple in the headlights.

"You ever read much about the ancient Egyptians, Frank?" Sturm asked.

"In school. Long time ago," Frank said, resting his elbows, scanning the town on his right while keeping an eye on Jack and Sturm.

"You ever read about how they buried kings?"

"In the pyramids. The tombs."

"Exactly," Sturm cried, delighted, as if Frank was a dog that just learned not to piss on the floor. "And what did they put in there with them?"

"Treasure," Frank said. If Sturm wanted to play a game, Frank would play along.

347

"Yes! All of it buried, supposedly forever. But not just wealth, slaves too. And animals. They took everything with them on their journey across the river of Death. Everything. And they weren't the only culture throughout history. Look at the Indians. They were buried with weapons, tobacco, everything they needed once they reached the other side." Sturm reached out to the cool rushing air, cupped a little of it, let it drift threw his fluttering fingers. "This town, this is my tomb. And all of this, this destruction, this sacrifice . . . it is mine."

Frank looked up at Sturm. "Are you saying that you are taking all of this," Frank let his fingers flutter in the air for a quick moment, coming dangerously close to the edge of mocking Sturm without actually going over. "Everything, over with you?"

"Yes."

"Then I'd say you oughta have your head reexamined." Frank gave his crooked grin.

Jack punched him once. It was fast. He was smart, and came in under Frank's left jaw, where the vision wasn't the best, snapping Frank's head back so far he almost fell out.

Frank spit blood; Jack's punch had pinched the left side of his tongue between his teeth.

Jack sat back just as quickly. "You mind your manners. You weren't born here. You don't know shit."

"I thought you might understand, having been so close to death, yourself," Sturm told Frank. He sounded genuinely hurt. "To get that close, to peer into the abyss . . . well, it makes ideas that you may have once sneered at seem suddenly possible. Maybe even hopeful."

Frank didn't say anything. He was done playing. He wasn't worried about himself. Pain didn't matter anymore. The only thing he was doing was keeping Sturm and the fellas occupied, giving Annie and her mothers a chance to get out to Sturm's barn and take the whole damn safe.

Theo stopped at the southern edge of town, where Main Street officially turned back into Highway 61. Frank's long, black car was parked on the side of the road, Pine behind the wheel and Chuck in the passenger seat.

"Son, I'm afraid I have no choice." Sturm stood and looked at the stars while Theo let down the tailgate. "I hereby terminate this contract we have here. Your services are no longer needed."

Frank slowly climbed down, followed by Jack, joining Pine and Chuck in the wash of the red taillights. Sturm looked down at Frank. "I think you're smart enough to understand a few things here. I don't have to let you go. Shouldn't be a big surprise that Theo wanted to feed your ass to the cats, after what you did. Fact is, nobody here wanted to leave you alive."

Pine and Chuck looked at the ground, but Jack met Frank's stare with an intensity that dared Frank to challenge him. Theo jumped up and sat on the tailgate, next to his father's feet, and happily swung his legs back and forth. He nursed a beer; he didn't like the taste, but wanted everyone to see him drinking.

"But, for some goddamn reason," Sturm continued, "I like you. You got yourself a gift there. Never seen anybody handle animals the way you did. But on the other hand, never seen anybody with a talent for dealing out death quite like you. You were one handy motherfucker to have around for an operation like this. But you fucked up and cost me money. Let your emotions get in the way. You embarrassed me tonight. So you got two options here. You can leave, and never come back. Or you can stay here and suffer the consequences."

"What about my money?" Frank asked.

Pine stepped close and jabbed Frank in his lower back, just above the right hip, a vicious, powerful, unseen punch that sent tendrils of curdled pain shooting through Frank's groin. Frank took a half step to his left, recoiling from the blow, and Jack brought his fist around in a swinging, roundhouse blow, driving his knuckles into the soft tissue under Frank's left ear.

Frank went to his knees.

Now they could use their boots as well. Frank fell sideways and curled up, protecting his face and head with his arms. He pulled his knees into his chest and pressed his heels into his haunches as hard as he could, covering his balls with his feet. His body shuddered under the onslaught of punches and kicks, but most of Frank's mind had retreated down into the darkness, hiding out in the raw, wild place that had been sealed and secure until it had been ripped open when he kneeled in the dirt yard with Annie. He thought of her now, and his only wish was that she had gotten the safe out of the barn and was taking the whole damn thing far, far away from this town.

Sturm let the clowns kick at Frank for a while. "Jack was right. You weren't born here. This land is my land. This land is my family's land. It sure as shit ain't your country, son. My great-great grandfather worked his way out here with the goddamn chinks on the railroad. He saw how much this valley had to offer, chased the fucking Indians out, and my family has been here ever since. And will continue to be. Long after my bones are gone, long after this town has dried to dust and blown away, the ground will replenish itself, and when Theo returns as a man, all of this will be his."

He realized that Frank wouldn't or couldn't make a sound. "That's enough." He jumped down off the pickup and lifted Frank's chin. One eye was swollen nearly shut. Blood ran from his hairline. Frank's lips had been split like overripe tomatoes. "This was for your own good, son. It was your own damn fault. Understand this, I spared you. I'm giving you a chance. Leave. Now. You got a full tank of gas. Hell, I'll even leave that box of liquor with you, just so you understand there's no hard feelings. But let's make one thing very, very clear. You get to thinking you're man enough to come back here, you'll force me to pull the trigger. So help me God, you'll be down at the bottom of the town pool with Dr. No back there, keeping that goddamn lizard company."

Frank spit blood on Sturm's boots. His tongue found a few alarmingly loose teeth. He took a deep breath and winced at how his ribs seemed to be stabbing into his lungs. Still, he found enough strength to sit upright and look Sturm full in the face with his good eye. "What about my money?"

"You just don't give up. Sometimes, that's admirable. Sometimes, it's just fucking stupid," Sturm said. He stood. "Theo. Bring me that envelope on the dash." He looked down at Frank. "Boys didn't want me to give you this. They wanted to split it between themselves."

Theo came back with a manila envelope and handed it to his father.

Sturm knelt down, tapped the thick envelope on Frank's skull. "There's two months of wages in here. However," he said, slapping Frank in the head, hard. "I subtracted payment for not fulfilling your duties. If I were you, I would consider this amount to be extremely generous, given the circumstances." He tossed the envelope into Frank's lap and stepped back. "You've got a full tank of gas. Use it. I'd head north, I were you. Get yourself a job on a ranch somewhere and just enjoy breathing."

Pine and Chuck moved slowly toward Sturm's truck, clearing the way to the car for Frank. Chuck was still trying to get his breath back. Theo flung his beer bottle at Frank. The bottle shattered on the pavement, flinging foam and glass into Frank's face.

Frank blinked slowly, making sure there was no glass in his eyes, and moved his body even slower, checking that nothing had broken from the beating. His muscles felt like he'd fallen into a harvester. But he could move, the bones still held together. He stood, met Sturm's eyes, and without bothering to count the money, turned and walked stiffly to his car.

The only sound he could hear was his own boots scuffling along the pavement. The skin at the back of his skull crawled over itself to get away from the impact of a bullet that could come at any time. Frank figured that this was the moment when he would find out if Sturm was going to really let him go or simply have a bit of fun and shoot him. And if Sturm went ahead and shot him, well, Frank told himself that that was okay. He'd kept them out here long enough. To die now, instantly, that wouldn't be so bad. He wouldn't even know it happened. It would be over and done with, like snapping his fingers. Lights out.

It was all he'd ever wanted for his animals.

But his heart wasn't listening to the calm, reasonable voice. It thudded urgently away, skipping over itself as it ricocheted around his ribcage. Like the skin along his back, now squirming down his spine like a twitching toad, it wanted away. That part of him just wanted to crawl into a hole and hide.

In the end, they didn't shoot him. Didn't even threaten it. Frank walked back to the car and as he dropped into the driver's seat, he saw the men hadn't moved. They simply watched as he started the car, backed up across the highway, and headed south, down to the detour.

Frank kept his foot on the floor and watched them in his rearview mirror until the blood red pinpricks of Sturm's taillights disappeared. Nobody waved goodbye.

He found the turnoff, and drove through the fields, slower now, looking for a place to hide the long, black car. He crossed over the irrigation ditch and followed the twin tire tracks that snaked along the edges of the foothills. He found a spot, twenty yards off the dirt lane, up a dry wash. The mud had been baking for months, and was now harder than concrete. A couple of oak trees flanked the creek bed, filtering out the starlight.

He backed the car up and shut the engine off and just listened for a while. Frank didn't think that anyone would actually follow him, just to make sure he left; Sturm had seemed awfully sure of himself. After a few moments, the crickets in the tall, dead grass gradually filled the silence with their creaking, throbbing calls.

He wondered how long it would take Sturm to get back to the ranch.

He wondered if Annie and her family had gotten to the safe.

He wondered if he would hear any gunfire.

To distract himself, he tore open the manila envelope. It felt thick, and he thought there was a chance that Sturm had upheld his end of the bargain. He pulled the stack of bills out and flicked on the interior light. His fist was full of goddamn singles. He quickly killed the light, and counted by feel. If they were all singles, and it certainly looked that way in the quick flash of light, then he had been sent on his way with about three hundred lousy bucks.

"You sonofabitch," Frank whispered. Three hundred wasn't enough to get to Washington, let alone Canada. Three hundred bucks wasn't shit. He stuffed the cash back into the manila envelope and shoved it under the seat. The car suddenly felt close, suffocating, as if the seat, ceiling, and steering wheel were all crushing him.

He swung the door open and climbed out. His body, stiff from sitting still, screamed at him to stop. He stumbled sideways and fell into the bank of the creek. Pain squatted over every nerve in his body and warned him in no uncertain terms that he wasn't allowed to move again for a long time. He agreed wholeheartedly and promised the pain that he was in no hurry to go anywhere anytime soon.

So he relaxed into the bank and watched the stars crawl sluggishly across the sky. The high-pitched roar of some big cat silenced the entire valley for a while. The crickets knew they were safe, and started calling to each other after a few minutes. An owl hooted in the gnarled oaks above him. A mosquito whined in his ear and without thinking, he slapped at it.

A fresh wave of pain jumped through his shoulder, ricocheted through his neck and chest, and settled somewhere in his gut. Everything hurt. But he figured if was going to be in pain, he might as well make it count. He crawled back over to the car and popped the trunk. Sure enough, the box of rum was still back there, but they'd taken his shotgun. And the ten thousand.

They hadn't found the rest of his pills, though, taped to the underside of the front bumper. He decided to save them for later and put them in his pocket. He grabbed a fresh bottle of rum, fell into the back seat, and stretched out. He propped the bottle upside down against the back of the passenger seat so he wouldn't have to move much, and nursed from the bottle until he fell asleep.

DAY THIRTY-FOUR

Frank woke up and found a lioness sticking her head in the window and sniffing down at the bottle of rum and his head. The lioness pulled back and Frank exhaled. Without thinking, he tried to push himself up. Agony marched through his joints, and just then, the lioness stuck her head into the other window down by his feet. He hadn't realized he'd left both of the windows down.

Frank forced himself to relax. If she sensed fear, heard his beating heart, her predator instincts would kick in and she would tear him apart in the back seat. He tried to slow his breathing down, willing his stomach to rise and settle slower, slower. And then he realized that he'd pissed on himself sometime in the night and hoped there wasn't blood in the urine. The lioness would smell it. She inhaled, three times, deep, and looked at him, then pulled itself out of the window and disappeared.

Frank decided he needed a drink. And a change of clothes.

The extra suit was underneath the box of rum. He wasn't concerned about wrinkles.

He left the jeans and the shirt in the trunk, but kept the bag of pills. He cracked open a fresh bottle, jammed a pill in his mouth, and drank. He figured it was smartest to just leave the car and walk. The sky was lightening quickly now and he could see the strangled branches of the oak trees. The stars were nearly gone. He stuck two more bottles into the suit pockets and walked slowly down to the dirt track, wincing in pain with each step.

He found Chuck's pickup blocking the narrow bridge over the creek. By then, the rum had eased some of his pain, and he was able to creep quietly up to the cab. He heard Chuck's snoring even before he looked inside. Chuck was sprawled out with a .30-30 and a half full bottle of tequila. Theo's .405 Winchester was in the gun rack in the back window.

Sturm must have sent him out here to stand guard, either to make sure that Frank didn't try and come back or to make sure anyone new coming into town had been invited. Maybe both. Frank's first instinct was to simply keep going and leave Chuck snoring peacefully. Avoid trouble.

But then the voice in his head spoke up, and Frank listened carefully. He took another look at the inside of the cab. It was a mess. Empty beer cans covered the floor. Wrinkled and faded photos of some sickly woman fondling a horse's penis had been taped to the roof. Stained, crumpled napkins and used paper plates covered the dashboard. The trash nearly covered the red leather sheath of Chuck's hunting knife with a fixed six-inch blade.

He went around to the driver's side, reached in, grabbed the knife, and tucked it into the small of his back. He watched Chuck a moment, watching the chest rise and fall with the sound of some small animal drowning in mud. Frank took another drink, a long one, and put the bottle on the hood. He was starting to feel the first tingle of speed as it spread through his system, simultaneously calming the pain and urging the muscles to look sharp. It made him impatient. He slammed the bottom of his fist against the horn.

Chuck jerked awake at the noise, dropping the bottle and clutching the rifle.

"Mornin', sunshine," Frank said.

"You ain't . . . I don't . . . what time is it?"

"It's early."

"Shit. Don't tell Sturm." Chuck rubbed his eyes and yawned. "Wait a minute—you're supposed to be gone." His eyes swept the cab. "You ain't supposed to still be here."

Frank offered Chuck his bottle of rum. "Yeah. But I got to hurting pretty bad, and decided to just rest a while, have a drink, you know? You boys didn't exactly hold back when you were kicking the shit out of me."

Chuck looked like he wanted to apologize and take the bottle, but he knew that Sturm would be pissed. He shook his head. "You gotta get the fuck out of here, man. Sturm finds us, no joke, he's liable to kill both of us."

Frank nodded, took a drink. "Yeah. Might kill me, I suppose. But you? Why?"

But Chuck just shook his head. "Jesus Christ. Get outa here, okay? Don't make me shoot you."

"Now, Chuck. Think about it. Hell, I wanted to, I could've taken your rifle and shot you dead. Right?"

Chuck shrugged, reluctantly nodded, and tried to bite back a yawn.

Frank said, "Right. So relax. Shit, I can't wait to be on my way. Just saw your truck here, and though you might like some medicine before I leave for good."

That got Chuck's attention. "What kind of medicine?"

Frank smiled, and it almost made it across his whole face. "*Your* medicine. You know. Frank's Surprise."

"Wait, you got some out here? What, were you taking it with you?"

"Sure. You never know." The chemicals from the pill were seeping into Frank's muscles, his joints, his mind. The sun hadn't quite broken over the horizon just yet, but the lines of the truck, the stubble on Chuck's cheeks and chin, the pattern of tires left in the dirt, all of it, it settled and shimmered into crystalline clarity. "Come on, I'll show you what I got. Then I promise, I'm outa here."

Frank left Chuck and walked to the back of the pickup. He unlocked the tailgate and slammed it down. Frank set his bottles on the tailgate and made a show of patting the suit, looking for the drugs. Chuck came out of the cab, wary, holding his rifle out. He joined Frank at the back of his truck.

Frank said, "Here we go," and slapped the baggie of pills on the tailgate.

Chuck bent over. "Uh, that ain't what you gave me before."

"It isn't? Shit." Frank looked up, into the deep, dark, blue sky, suddenly alarmed. "Fuck is that?"

Chuck followed his gaze.

Frank stuck Chuck in the throat with his knife with his right hand and yanked the rifle away at the same time with his left. He stepped back and left the blade imbedded in Chuck's neck.

Chuck grabbed his pickup for support, knife handle jutting out of his neck at a perfect ninety-degree angle. His mouth gaped open, as if he couldn't believe Frank had just pulled something so sneaky. But then his expression changed, as if he wasn't surprised anymore, just worried. He tried to breathe and couldn't. The skin that hung loose off his face grew red, then white, then blue. It was almost patriotic.

Chuck's hands went to his neck, but he couldn't find the handle, couldn't coordinate his fingers to close at just the right time. Finally, he managed to grab the damn thing and jerk the knife out of his neck.

There was surprisingly little blood.

Chuck exhaled, a sweet, blissful sound, despite the neat, inch-long wound, pale and so far bloodless, like a young woman's prim lips, pressed tight together like she'd just seen something truly obscene, such as the pictures at the top of his cab, for the first time. He damn near smiled with relief. The promise of fresh, cool air was close enough to grab and simply inhale.

Frank was glad that Chuck felt better, but as Chuck relaxed enough to draw his first breath, Frank got out of the way. A great gush of blood erupted out of the wound, blowing open the thin edges.

"Fucker," Chuck whispered, and dropped.

Frank rolled the body into the truck bed and slammed the tailgate. Chuck had close to six hundred dollars in his front pocket. Frank took it and the trucker hat. He tore out all the pictures in the cab as he followed the dirt track as it curved through the hills. It must have been somewhere around five o'clock in the morning.

He passed four SUVs clustered around a campfire. A few men were up, wiping sleep from their eyes. Frank thought a moment, felt the maniacal energy striking sparks where it brushed up against the self-loathing and hatred he carried with him. He put on Chuck's hat, roared up the camp, and shouted at the men, "You fellas better get moving. Sturm is coming, and he's pissed." Without waiting, he pulled in a U-turn, hit the gas again, and tore off.

A mile back down the road, he crossed the creek and wrenched the wheel sideways, effectively blocking the dirt road on the far side of the bridge. He pulled Chuck's body out of the back and propped him up in the driver's seat.

Frank took the .30-30 and the .405 Winchester, slinging the rifles over each shoulder. To the south lay the valley, too open. To the west, rice fields. To the north, a grove of oaks, but it didn't have much cover. That left east, where a hill, dotted with a few more oaks, rose into the sunlight. Frank started up the hill, loading the .30-30, moving slow. His pockets were heavy with rifle shells.

Forty yards up the hill, he found a level spot in the shade and laid the rifles out before him. He got comfortable, leaning into the trunk. He took a long drink of water. This was the deal he had made himself, a sip of rum for every ten sips of water. He pulled Theo's .405 up to his shoulder and propped his elbows into his knees and put the crosshairs on the bridge abutments.

He heard the growl of engines, closing in. The men had bought it. Frank wasn't the only one scared of Sturm. The lead SUV drove across the bridge, right up to Chuck, and honked indignantly. Three more followed, all moving fast, all crowding onto the bridge, rats fleeing a sinking ship.

Frank settled the crosshairs and shot the driver of the last SUV in the head. The man's skull exploded like dynamite in a watermelon, spraying the cabin. The bullet blew the passenger seat headrest out of the window. The passenger flopped forward as if kicked in the head. The headless corpse of the driver gripped the steering wheel feverishly while both legs stomped down, urging the Mercedes forward, slamming into the second SUV, a giant yellow Hummer.

The men in the lead, those closest to Chuck and his pickup, somehow decided that Chuck was shooting at them and decided to shoot back. They both reached into the back seat and flailed at their rifle cases. The guys in the Hummer backed up, and for a while, it looked like the larger vehicle just might push the Mercedes out of the way. Until Frank shot the driver. This time, it wasn't so clean. It was low, and punched through the yellow door, taking out the driver's hips. It was still enough to blow him sideways out of his chair. The two passengers jumped out of the Hummer.

Frank rubbed his sore shoulder; it felt like he'd been kicked by a horse again. He had left the rest of the .405 caliber bullets back in the truck, so he picked up the .30-30 and shot the two men that jumped out of the Hummer. They were trying to hide behind the Mercedes, but since Frank was higher, he just shot the tops of their heads off. By now, the two guys in the lead car had figured out that someone else was shooting at them, and had deserted their SUV, shooting in all directions. Frank shot the first guy in the thigh, spinning him into the creek; the second got a bullet in the back. Gunfire rolled and crackled through the creek, but nothing else moved.

Frank listened for any more sudden engines, but there was nothing but the wind. After a while, the insects started back, the shrill clicking in the weeds. One of the men started to moan. Frank wasn't sure if it was the guy that had been shot in the leg, or the one he got in the hip. It didn't matter, not really, as the men couldn't crawl far, and in just a couple hours, maybe less, certainly by nightfall, these woods would be crawling with hungry predators.

Frank walked back to Chuck's truck and reloaded the .405. He'd only gone through ten or so bullets. It wasn't much of a hunt at all. The deaths of these men wouldn't bring back Petunia, the cats, the horses, or any of the animals. And he couldn't say if he felt any different, one way or another. But it was the least he could do.

He patiently moved all of the vehicles off the bridge, yanked Chuck's body out of the truck, leaving it by the side of the road, and tried the engine. The engine started, despite all the bullet holes. He drove back across the bridge, ignoring the blood and meat coating the inside of the cab. The flies were already thick. Once across, he parked and blocked the bridge again with all three SUVs.

Frank drove into town.

The fires in the streets were nearly out, leaving charred bones and black ashes scattered across the pavement.

He drove past the vet hospital. The parking lot was empty.

The Glouck house was silent. The gas station was closed, glass still on the concrete. The auction yard was just as quiet. Frank stopped at the park and found it empty. He sat for a while, thinking it over. The urge to run, to flee, that same urge from the alligator tank, was back inside of him, fed by the drug, twice as strong and ten times as ugly. He didn't so much fight it, but channeled the energy into rage, letting the fear fuel the anger.

He drove out to Sturm's house.

The pill wanted him to drive Chuck's truck straight up the driveway and smash through the front porch and start shooting. But Frank didn't want to get there and find out that Sturm wasn't home. And if he got shot, there was a good chance the animals still left in cages would starve to death. Frank figured that if he was going to finish all of this, then that meant turning the animals loose first. He decided that this called for a little caution and passed the driveway, parking in the same orchard where'd he spent the night two weeks earlier. He took the .30-30 and the knife and slipped through the trees and tall grass, circling around Sturm's ranch.

The trailers and tents were still set up, but they looked abandoned. He couldn't see Sturm's pickup. He darted across the open ground in a low, crouching run at the corral in the middle of the field and opened the gate for the sheep. But, being sheep, they simply huddled against the far fence and wouldn't come near him. Frank left the gate open and crawled through the stiff dead grass to the corral behind the barn.

He opened the gate, then circled around the barn to the distorted, bulging cage. Lady and Princess watched him with sleepy eyes. They'd been feeding regularly, and so they were happy, content, and sluggish. Frank pushed down and slid the bolt back, letting the cage door swing wide. The cats just watched him.

Frank ducked into the barn. He jogged around the aisle and lifted the tarp over the horizontal freezer. He decided not to try and move the air conditioner, though it took all of his strength to lift the hood just enough to see inside. "Shit," he breathed.

The gun safe was still inside.

He scratched his head violently. The pill wanted to go kick down the door and shoot Sturm in his bed. That way, he could come back and get the safe anytime he felt like it. But killing Sturm wouldn't be as easy as sticking a knife in Chuck's throat. There was a damn good chance Sturm would shoot back. Frank reminded himself of all the animals still left locked away at the auction yard.

So he lowered the lid and slipped out of the barn, heading back to Chuck's truck. Lady and Princess hadn't moved. That was okay, though. They'd get the idea, soon as the sheep figured out that the gate was open and went wandering around the pasture.

Frank started at one end of the auction yard and moved fast, popping latches and swinging the cage doors wide, bouncing from one side of the aisle to the other. Frank left the big doors at the back open, and sunlight spilled inside, beckoning the animals.

The dogs, big cats, a few wolves, and one lone hyena mostly watched the other animals with caution before they crept out of their cages. Once the animals were out, they snapped at each other a few times, but most of them simply ran for the sunlight.

Frank stepped out of the auction yard and turned quickly, walking along the wall toward the parking lot. Two wolves burst out of the building, headed for the clowns' trailer, and disappeared into the fields. Several lionesses slunk out, heading along the wall away from Frank. The exodus was slow at first, but more and more animals plunged into the sunlight and left the auction yard behind.

He strolled across the parking lot over to the lone car. He knocked on the driver's side window. The window rolled down. A voice, groggy and pissed, said, "Fuck's your problem? What?"

Frank stuck the .30-30 into the open window and fired. Someone else inside screamed. The passenger door popped open and the other dog owner sprinted across the gravel toward the building. Frank shot the guy in the leg. The man twirled like a ballet dancer and landed hard on his side in the gravel. He saw the back doors yawning open no more than ten yards away, a possible sanctuary, and crawled over and slammed the doors behind him.

Not all of the animals had left, though, and the guy had just locked himself in the building with the rest of them. Frank got a kick out of that; he waited until he heard screaming and then reopened the doors and left them open. He climbed back into Chuck's truck, reloaded, and drove back down into town.

Frank peered over the edge of the deep end of the pool and saw that the Siberian tiger was gone. They'd either taken it or it had been able to jump clear over the fence or scrabble up one of the walls, down near the shallow end. The Komodo Dragon was curled in his corner, surrounded by Mr. Noe's bones.

Frank climbed down into the shallow end and unlocked the fence from the ladder, and dragged the concrete blocks back, clearing a pathway for the Komodo Dragon. That long tongue shot out and it tasted the air, looking from Frank to the shallow end. It broke for the new exit, moving fast, faster than Frank had expected. He didn't bother running for the ladder, just hoisted himself onto the deck and scrambled to the front gate. He risked a look back. The dragon's head appeared at the edge. The vicious claws scraped concrete. It wouldn't take long for the giant lizard to be roaming the streets.

Frank left the front gate open, climbed into Chuck's truck, but then noticed a pickup and camping trailer in the parking lot. It wasn't Billy's; Frank was hoping to run into the Komodo's owner. He pulled into the lot and stopped next to the campfire. A steel coffee pot burbled happily to itself as it rested on a blackened grate over the coals. It smelled delicious. But with all the chemicals surging through his system, Frank decided he didn't need any caffeine. He knocked briskly on the trailer door.

The door opened. A hunter stepped out onto the steps, scratching the four-day stubble on his chin. "Morning," he said, looking down at Frank and rubbing the sleep out of his eyes.

"Morning," Frank said. "Afraid I have to take a look at your hunting licenses."

"Hunting license?" The hunter turned into the trailer. "Greg, you know anything about any licenses?"

Frank couldn't hear Greg's reply. The first hunter turned back to Frank. "You're looking for what now?"

Frank shot the hunter in the chest. The guy went down hard on his ass, legs sticking out of the trailer. Frank stepped over him and found Greg rolling off the bed, bloated white flesh spilling out over his jeans as he struggled to pull a handgun from a leather holster. Frank shot him in the jaw. Greg spun sideways and left a spray of blood against the yellow fridge.

Frank slung the rifle over his shoulder and picked up Greg's handgun. Greg waved his own hand a little, but Frank ignored him, concentrating on the pistol. A 1911 Colt .45 semi-auto. Frank liked it immediately. Compared to the rifle, it was small, compact. It took a while, but he figured out how to release the magazine. It held seven rounds.

Greg tried to get up. He was doing a damn fine job too, despite having half a jawbone and only one lower cheek, when

365

Frank slapped the magazine back into the gun, yanked the slide back, and shot Greg in the stomach.

It was a practice shot, and it worked beautifully. Frank admired the lethal efficiency, the simplicity of the handgun, the feel of it jumping in his hand like something alive, while Greg fell against the table, landing on his ruined jaw. Greg made a sound like a rat getting its tail caught in a garbage disposal and dropped heavily back to the floor. Frank stepped over him and poked around a little and found a full box of shells. He slung the holster over his shoulder and put the box of shells in his suit pocket. Greg was still rolling around on the floor, but he was slipping into shock and wouldn't be going anywhere anytime soon.

He heard a pickup door slam outside.

Frank stepped on the first hunter's chest getting out. A third hunter was running for the road. He must have been sleeping in the pickup. Frank decided that, as much as he liked his new .45, this was a job for the .30-30. He stuck the handgun into Chuck's jeans, pulled the rifle in snug, tracked the running man for a moment, and shot him in the base of the spine.

The third man flopped onto the single rope of chain that separated the parking lot from the highway and twitched erratically, like a worm hung over an electric fence. The guy was making a high-pitched keening sound, and it hurt Frank's head. He walked over and shot him a few more times with the .45.

Something out of the corner of his eye made Frank look up, bringing the Colt around, ready to fire. But there, not more than twenty yards away, he saw the Gloucks' four-wheel drive station wagon, slowly rolling to a stop. Edie was driving, Alice next to her, Annie in the passenger seat; a handful of kids were stuffed into the back. They all stared.

Frank stuck the pistol in Chuck's loose belt and tried to smile as the pill walked him over to the car. He caught a glimpse of himself in the car windows and something disgusting uncoiled in his chest and he thought he might throw up. He looked like some careless butcher with a hungry tapeworm; flecks of blood, tissue, and bone were splashed across his suit and hands and face. The chassis of the station wagon was so high off the pavement he could look directly into their faces without bending over.

Annie stared through the bug-spattered windshield at the corpse on the fence and wouldn't meet his eyes. Her expression told Frank that she didn't care about anything, but he knew that wasn't true because her legs were half-crossed, knees crushed against each other, calves rigid as she pushed up on the balls of her feet, fingers hanging onto each other for dear life. She felt Frank watching her, and tears spilled over the corners of her eyes and slid down her cheeks.

Alice raised a trembling hand. "Is that who . . . who killed Petunia?"

Frank thought it might make them feel better. "Yes."

They were silent for a moment. "We're going up to the lake to bury her, Frank. Would you like to come?" Alice asked.

"I can't," Frank said and focused on Annie. "Last night. I told you. Why didn't you take the safe and leave?"

"Leave to where, exactly?" Edie asked. "This is our home."

"I don't think it's your home anymore."

"That's not for you to decide," Edie said.

"I don't think you understand. Things have changed. Sturm—"

"We've dealt with Sturm for years. We can handle this."

"Yeah, but once Jack and Pine and Chuck find—"

"You leave Jack and Pine to us, Frank. They're family."

"What?"

"Annie didn't tell you? Jack and Pine don't like to admit it, but they're still our sons, even if they don't come around much anymore."

Frank remembered Chuck telling him not to bring up Annie around Jack and Pine, their resentment over not being invited to dinner, and their unrelenting hatred of the Glouck family. Now, looking at the mothers, the resemblance was faint, but it was there. Jack was Alice's son, and Edie had had Pine. Looking back on everything, it made a weird kind of logic, but Frank had a feeling that if things got bad, real bad, if it came down to it, the clowns would take Sturm's side over their own mothers. Being a family clearly meant more to Edie and Alice.

"You had no business volunteering Annie to go get that safe," Edie continued. "We didn't raise our children to be thieves. No, this is still our home, and it will be our home for a long, long time. We're not looking to push Sturm into a fight." She looked at the dead man on the fence and shook her head. "Our dog is gone. That's enough. No more. You seem like a good boy, Frank, but you've gone too far. You should clear out before things get worse."

Annie touched his hand. "Goodbye, Frank. Please take care of yourself." And with that, Edie put the car in gear and they pulled slowly away. The few boys and Amber in the back, knees drawn up around the shrouded figure of Petunia, watched Frank with wide eyes.

He went back and sat in Chuck's pickup. His head was starting to throb and he wondered if he should take another pill. Maybe Edie and Alice were right. Maybe he should just leave. This was their home. He had a little cash, not much, but enough that he wouldn't have to spend the first few nights in the car. He could head west, see the ocean. He had a full box of rum in the trunk, after all. It might not be so bad, just sit on the beach and watch the waves for a while. He'd caused enough damage this morning. If nothing else, the remaining animals would most likely be shot, and wouldn't be forced into fighting for their lives. Their deaths would be quick.

He watched the sun climb higher and made up his mind. He would go back to the long, black car and drive away and never look back. It was over. He had done enough. The Gloucks knew where the gunsafe was if they didn't get paid. It was up to them now.

He twisted the key and stomped on the gas. Something about the animals nagged at him, like an infected tooth, but he couldn't figure it out. He had done everything he could. He had turned them all loose. Sturm would have his hands full with over a dozen cats, a tiger, a few wolves, one lone hyena, and a goddamn Komodo Dragon running loose through town. If Frank's luck held, he would make it back to the car without anyone seeing him and he could leave this valley forever.

Frank was nearly out of town when it hit him like a punch in the gut.

The rhino. He'd forgotten the rhino.

Last night, he'd turned the cats loose from the vet hospital, but hadn't thought to go out to the barn. Goddamnit. He punched the steering wheel, pissed at his own stupidity and thirst for rum. It had gotten in the way. He pulled the truck in a wide U-turn and shot back into town, back to the vet hospital.

The rhino was gone.

The gate stood open, a few handfuls of grain scattered across the floor. "Shit," Frank said, gritting his teeth. The drugs were really kicking his heart into high gear now, marching double-time through his limbs, making him flail and shiver and jump. He scratched his scalp with trembling hands and paced up and down the barn aisle.

The sudden urge to simply grab the .45 and start shooting at anything, everything, seethed through his veins, just unload his rage and guilt on the barn, the vet hospital, Chuck's truck, the trees, the sun. But that wouldn't get him anywhere.

As much as he tried to tell himself that all he had to do was jump back into the truck and drive out to the long, black car and he would be free, he knew, deep down, that this was different. No matter how many bottles of rum he had, it wouldn't be enough to blot the memory of the rhino's warm breath on his hand. It wasn't like the horses. Not that the rum had helped his nightmares much.

It didn't matter that the rhino was damn near dead to start with. He was responsible. And if he didn't try, that wrinkled gray beast would haunt his nights for the rest of his life. "Shit," Frank said again.

He went outside and stood in the sun. It wasn't even ten o'clock yet, but already the air was hot enough to singe his skin, his eyes, his lungs. Sweat boiled out of his pores, trickling down his temples and back and collecting in the insides of his elbows and knees.

He turned in a slow circle, wondering which way to head. Sturm's ranch was probably the most logical place to start, but he sensed that it would probably be the last place he would have a chance to look. Sturm might be there, and even if he wasn't, the place was undoubtedly crawling with hunters with guns.

So on the chance that the rhino was somewhere else, he decided to circle the town, check out some of the other fields where'd they been shooting. Then maybe swing by the auction yard again. If he got lucky, he would find the rhino and be on his way.

But as he drove into town, he wondered what the hell he was going to do if he found the rhino. It wasn't like he could take it away with him. Shit, it wasn't like he had really helped any of the other animals out, not really. They were going to die, just the same. If you wanted to get right down to it, it was his fault these animals were here in the first place.

Frank had just unscrewed the cap on a fresh bottle of rum when he came upon a bunch of pickups at the town park. He slowed down, pulled Chuck's hat lower over his face, and got a better look. Six or seven hunters gathered around one of the picnic tables out near the sidewalk. A bunch of small-caliber rifles were laid out on the table. Theo walked along the bench seat on the other side of the picnic table, throwing his arms out in grand gestures and laughing.

And there was the rhino, tied to a tree in the middle of the park.

Frank hit the brakes. He pulled in next to the pickups and shut off the engine.

Theo's voice drifted in through the open windows. "Fuck, it's easy, ya' bunch of pussies. Fifty bucks a bullet. That's it. Just fifty bucks. You decide the target. Head or heart. It's your call." He had seen Chuck's truck, assumed it really was Chuck, and just ignored him.

"We been shooting for half an hour," one of the hunters said. "It ain't going down."

Theo snorted. "I s'pose you're the kind of pussy that goes to Vegas and whines when you don't hit the jackpot after giving a slot machine one pull. You never fucking know. Could be your bullet's the one that cracks that skull. Or punches through that heart. Or it could be that the fucker finally just bleeds to death and you happen to have had the last shot. That's the kind of game this is." Theo checked his watch. "And in, oh, thirteen minutes, the price of the bullets go up to a hundred bucks a pop."

The last hunter to shoot said, "Take your time, boys. Look at it, it's not going down."

371

"Fuck you, Todd," another hunter said. "That sonofabitch is ready to fucking drop any second. Oh hell, here." The hunter handed Theo two hundred. "Gimme four bullets."

Frank felt icy fingers claw at his insides.

The thin crack of a .22 split the air. A tiny pop of rough hide and blood burst out of the rhino's head. It swayed, blood running in swift rivulets along the wrinkles, but did not go down. The hunter fired again, at the same spot. More blood. The rhino still stood.

Frank squeezed the .405's barrel until he heard his knuckles crack.

The hunter fired two more times, but still couldn't kill the rhino. "Who's next?" Theo cried. "We've gotta be close now. Could very well be the next shot is the one. Any bullet could do the job. You just never know. Just fifty bucks for another," he checked his watch, "seven minutes. Then we're up to a hundred bucks a pop. Come on you cunts, you drop it, you win it all."

The hunters checked their wallets, argued with each other, and watched the rhino. It stood in the full sun, gray hide the color of ash, head down, eyes closed. Bullet holes the size of peas were clustered in two main areas, in the chest just behind the front leg, and in the head, under the ears. It had taken over fifty rounds of small-caliber bullets, and somehow, it was still on its feet. Frank could hear its wheezing, agonized breathing from thirty yards away.

Theo was in the middle of saying, "If nobody has the balls to step forward and do some shooting, then—" when the heavy blast of a serious game rifle rolled through the park and something punched the rhino. It stumbled sideways, and slowly, gratefully, sank to its knees, and rolled onto its side. It took one more breath, and then lay still.

Theo jumped on the table. "Who the fuck used a bigger gun?

You just made a big fucking mistake, you—" And then he saw Frank, coming across the dead grass, face pale and gaunt and streaked with dry blood, moving in uneven, quick steps, like a grim spectral shadow that had slapped on some flesh and blood and went walking among the living for a while.

Even Theo didn't know what to say for a moment. But he recovered quick, shouting, "You just wait 'til my dad—"

Frank shot him in the knee with the .30-30.

The impact blew Theo's leg out from under him and he went down, landing on his chest on the table of guns. Frank kept moving forward, slinging the rifle over his shoulder and pulling the .45 out of his jeans. None of the hunters moved. Until Frank shot the closest man in the face. He shot another before the first hit the ground. The other hunters scattered, squirting in all directions like water from the giant wheel sprinklers out in the fields. Frank shot two more with the .45. The last hunter was nearly across the street when Frank jammed the handgun back into his jeans, unslung the .30-30, and shot the hunter in the neck. The man went down, arms and torso on the sidewalk, legs in the gutter, and didn't get up.

Still, Frank followed him across the street and shot him in the head, just to make sure. He methodically walked back to each hunter, shooting every one in the head with the .45, until he was back at the picnic table and looking down at Theo. The boy had rolled off the table and lay whimpering in the grass, clutching at his thigh, just above his knee. Tears squeezed from his eyes and ran back toward his ears.

"Oh please, please, please don't hurt me," Theo whispered. "I'm sorry, I'm sorry. I promise, oh please . . . oh please . . ." He rolled slightly back and forth, recoiling from the pain. "Please . . ."

Frank tilted his head and regarded Theo for several long moments. He eyed the .22s on the table and set the .30-30 down.

He selected a Ruger .22-.250, released the box-like clip, and grabbed a box of shells.

Theo kept begging. "Please, please call my dad. Please. He'll take care of everything. He'll give you all the money. Everything. Just please . . . please . . ."

The clip locked into place back inside the rifle and he drew back the bolt, snicked it back closed. He shot Theo in the same bloody, ragged knee. Theo screamed, a raw squeal that swirled up and around and died in the dusty leaves. Frank shot him again in the thigh. And again in the crotch. Theo's scream hitched, catching on itself, like long hair caught in a motorcycle chain and dragged into the wheels at eighty-five miles an hour, until he was only making a series of "Uhhh, uhhhh, uhhhh" sounds. Frank shot him in the stomach a few times, just for the hell of it.

Theo's white face stretched tight over an open, silent mouth.

Frank said, "That's the kind of game this is."

Theo writhed in slow motion in the dead grass. His screams were too weak to carry across the street. Frank thought about running, jumping in Chuck's truck and racing back to the long, black car. But the rest of him didn't want to run anymore. Despite the drugs rocketing through his system like an out-of-control roller coaster, he was terribly, terribly tired.

Frank paced while he waited. Theo's guttural moans just made him itch to fire a few more bullets into the little shit. Frank figured he'd better save his ammo. Not only would he have Sturm to deal with, but also Jack, Pine, and the rest of the hunters. He went through all of the pickups, gathering guns. He left the rifles on the table alone; the calibers were simply too small for any serious gunfights. He stashed rifles around the park, in the trees, under the picnic table, around the fire engine.

But just as he was wedging a shotgun between the folds of

the fire hose, he froze, and stood stock still for several moments, as if he had gone into some kind of trance. The drugs had left his body alone for a moment, and ricocheted around his brain instead, firing off signals.

He unscrewed the cap to the tank and found it bone dry. If there was a fire, this particular fire truck would be useless. The keys were still in the ignition. He took one last look at Theo, surrounded by the corpses of seven hunters. Sturm's son had stopped screaming and was now grabbing the picnic bench and trying to pull himself into a sitting position.

Frank started the engine. It wasn't smooth, but it ran. He let the engine warm up a moment, grabbed the shotgun from the back, and walked back over to Theo. Frank was getting impatient, and Theo wasn't bleeding to death fast enough. The last thing he wanted was for Sturm to come along and give first aid to his son. He rested the barrel of the shotgun on Theo's knuckles, pinning them to the wood, and squeezed the trigger.

Frank put the fire truck in gear, and drove out of the park. He rolled down Main Street, gaining speed. He wanted to hit the siren and lights, but figured that might draw more attention before he was ready. He was pleased with his plan, and didn't want anyone screwing it up before he had a chance to have some fun.

Myrtle was faithfully waiting in her plastic box inside the gas station. Frank drove right on in and left the engine running. He grabbed the nozzle and dragged the hose up to the top of the tank, stuck it in, and locked the nozzle handle, filling the empty fire engine water tank with gasoline. He turned and waved at Myrtle's shocked face.

As the gallons of gas splashed into the tank, Frank reloaded the shotgun. It didn't have the comforting feel of his own Winchester, but it would do. He kicked open the door. The broken bottom half was sealed in cardboard. The bells tinkled, and Frank wondered who in the hell would need a warning; the place wasn't much bigger than a large closet. It wasn't like you could sneak inside without the attendant spotting you. Frank put on his best smile. "Howdy."

Myrtle's pinched face got even more severe, as if she was trying to squeeze her eyes, nose, and mouth into one single organ. She said, "I don't know what exactly it is you think you're pulling, but you are not getting out of here without paying for that gas."

Frank said, "Put it on my tab. You call Sturm?"

"That's none of your damn business."

Frank brought up the shotgun. "Let's pretend my business is testing just how bulletproof this plastic really is."

Myrtle swallowed. "Fine. Yes, yes, I called him."

Frank said, "Good," and squeezed the trigger.

The shotgun instantly blasted the clear plastic into an opaque spiderweb of cracks and tiny holes. But the plastic held. Myrtle shrieked and flinched, flinging both hands in front of her face. She glared out at Frank. "You sonofabitch. I'll have Sturm cut your balls off, you lying, cat-killing sack of shit."

Frank gave her another grin and pumped the shotgun.

She whirled, unlocked the door, and ran. The last time Frank saw her, she was running down the highway, slippers slapping the asphalt, arms waving, red hair bobbing like a lit match.

Gasoline started to run down both sides of the fire engine tank. Frank took another drink from the bottle of vodka and climbed back into the driver's seat. The vodka didn't have the sweet, seductive bite of the rum, but he could feel the chill bloom into warmth as it hit his stomach. It would do. Before the rest of him could talk himself out of it, he plucked another pill out of the baggie and washed it down with vodka.

The distant whine of ATVs rose above the clunking gas pump and Frank realized that he'd only seen about five or six Glouck boys in the back of the station wagon. That left at least eight boys or more somewhere in town. The engines slowed and stopped and Frank knew they were at the park.

He hit the accelerator, pulling away without bothering to take out the nozzle, turn the pump off, or screw the cap back on. The fire engine roared down the wide street.

His original plan was to hose down the park and the rest of the surrounding buildings with gasoline and wait for Sturm to show up. Then, with a match or even a few bullets through the tank, he could take out everyone within a three-block radius. Hell, if he could, he'd burn the whole fucking town. Just turn everything into a fiery holocaust.

But the arrival of the Glouck boys had changed his plans.

The fire engine handled like a fat woman slathered in cooking oil with the shifting weight of the gasoline in the tank. The sun stabbed into the cab. Frank blinked and felt his eyes slipping again, flipping over into photo-negative mode. But this time he was ready. He fumbled for his sunglasses. He glanced up, saw the street, in blinding white light, and had just slipped on the glasses on when he heard gunfire.

He hit the brakes, feeling the truck surge and jump under him. Using a combination of the brake pedal and the emergency brake, he managed to slow down without sliding over the road too much. More gunfire.

He saw the trees in the park. Felt, rather than heard, booming shotguns, interspersed with the purposeful cracks of two revolvers. And finally saw Sturm as a ghostly figure striding through a desolate landscape, shooting smaller shapes. Jack and Pine trailed along behind, finishing off the Glouck boys, making sure there were no survivors. Jack had a shotgun, and stopped every few seconds, shooting wounded Gloucks. Pine had a machete, and hacked away at anything that moved.

It took Frank a few seconds to comprehend that they were killing their own brothers and stepbrothers.

Sturm heard the fire engine, turned to it, and fired. A hole appeared in the windshield and Frank felt something thump into the seat, inches from his right shoulder. Frank hit the clutch and the emergency brake at the same time.

Sturm fired again, and another hole appeared. But this time it smashed through the window behind Frank's head with a dull whistling rush. He must have been out of bullets because he put his revolvers back into the holsters and put the picnic table between him and the fire engine.

Frank hit the gas. The truck yawed and pitched and Frank fought her the whole way, sliding through the grass. Frank crunched the gearshift into first and popped the clutch. The truck launched itself through the picnic table after Sturm.

For a split second, Sturm was a fearless matador without a red cape, facing down a pissed-off three-ton vehicle. Calm, like he was going out for a Sunday stroll with the dog, he moved to the left, and Frank tracked him. And when Frank knew he had him, he eased off on the gas but Frank wasn't expecting the tank full of gasoline to slam forward, pushing the cab before it in mindless fury, throwing the steering all to hell. Sturm simply stepped aside.

The fire engine smashed into a two-foot thick elm tree with the sound of dry thunder, the back end bounced with the impact, and for a moment, under a burning midday sun, everything, even the dust in the air, was still.

Frank heard voices. The words didn't make sense. He thought he was sitting upright in the fire engine cab, but all he could see was some smooth, curving piece of metal and the dry leaves under a bleached sky.

He had been thrown into the dashboard and had his head stuck somehow between the steering wheel and instrument panel and the door, staring up through the windshield. He untangled himself and sat upright as much as possible. The seat and the dash had suddenly gotten much closer. He didn't know if it was the first or second pill or the crash but suddenly, he was feeling decidedly calm. Relaxed, even. Blood, both fresh and dry, streaked his face. He'd somehow ripped his shirt. But nothing much hurt anymore.

He got out and stepped into a flood of gasoline. The crash had broken something loose, but hadn't sparked. Steam hissed from a crumpled radiator. The nearly sweet stench of gasoline hung heavy in the air, stinging Frank's eyes and nose.

Ten feet away, Sturm mechanically reloaded his revolvers, using speed loaders. He slapped the cylinders back into place and spun them, then turned to Frank. Pine was way off to the left, keeping well away from the tank. He cut the air around him in short, swift strokes with his machete, as if the blade was thinking for him. Frank couldn't see Jack.

But he could see a lioness, slinking from between a couple of abandoned houses, nose twitching, eyes locked on the corpses. Frank let his gaze wander for a moment and saw another lioness, a wolf, and even more animals. They were drawn by the smell of death to this park. It was as if the park was calling to all of these animals, drawing them in, like some kind of magnet.

Sturm said, in an even, emotionless voice, "Fuck's wrong with you, son?" He cocked one of the revolvers and brought it up.

Frank reached into his pocket and came out with Chuck's matches. "Shoot. Go ahead," Frank said, striking a match.

Sturm hesitated.

"I mean it," Frank said, watching the small flame.

"Why'd you come back, son? This ain't your home," Sturm said.

"Drop 'em, right fucking now. Or I'll drop this." Frank pinched the burning match between his thumb and forefinger and held it out to the side, directly over the pool of gasoline. "We'll all go up. This whole fucking town."

"Why? I took you in. I showed you nothing but love," Sturm said.

The match went out.

Frank went to strike another, quick, but something hard and heavy and dark exploded in the back of his head and the last thing he knew, he was pitching forward into the lake of gasoline, unlit match and matchbook falling from his fingers.

Frank tried to breathe, tasted blood and dirt and gasoline.

It hit his lungs like Drano attacking a clot of hair in a sink. He whipped his head out of black water, sucking in a ragged, searing breath, and found that he had been facedown in the middle of one of Sturm's rice paddies.

Frank knew this was it. He was beyond kidding himself. But surprisingly, he realized that he was okay with the idea of death. It didn't bother him as much as it had. In some ways, death was liberating. The worst had happened. And now that it was here, it was a relief. This life would be behind him and he would be held accountable for it. Frank just hoped it was quick.

The sun hung directly overhead, burning away the shadows. The water lay flat and smooth, except for bones that littered the edge of the water; sheep ribcages curled into the muck. Among the rotting carcasses, other rough, segmented humps lurked. He squinted in the scalding sunlight.

One of the humps moved. A segmented tail swept lazily through the muddy water. Just above the surface, cold green eyes watched him. Something gripped him deep inside and squeezed unmercifully. Sturm had known, seen Frank's fear when he watched Frank's reaction when they climbed up the metal stairs. And so, just in case, weeks ago, he'd sent Jack and Pine back to the zoo to haul away one more load.

The sun hammered down into Frank's eyes, sizzling into his skull, and he lunged forward, giving in to the screaming urge to run. Something clenched at his neck and yanked him back. He grabbed at it; a dog's choke chain, padlocked to another length of chain wrapped around a T-post that had been driven deep into the soil. Only a foot or so of the post rose above the water. He tested it. He might as well been trying to pull Sturm's Lutheran cross out of the yard with a four-foot length of twine and some spit.

As ready as he'd thought he'd been for death, this was different. This wasn't simply death. This was something far worse. Panic clawed at his skull. He kicked at the post and wished he had been wearing shoes.

It wasn't just the shoes. He was completely naked. He squatted, dropping back into the water, drew his knees to his chest, and scanned the horizon. To the south and east, nothing but more of Sturm's fields.

To the west, thirty yards behind him, Frank spotted the silhouettes of Sturm's truck, the refrigerated Komodo truck, the police cruiser, and Jack and Pines' pickups parked along the edge of the highway.

In front of Sturm's truck, a row of lawn chairs had been lined up along the water. It looked like some surrealist's vision of Da Vinci's last supper, arranged in front of truck grilles. Sturm was in the center, flanked by Theo and Pine. Jack lounged on the other side of his brother, playing with several pistols on his lap. Olaf and Herschell sat next to Jack. Olaf drank Coke out of a glistening bottle with a straw. The taxidermist and Billy waited on the other side of Theo.

Theo was quite dead. He had been propped up next to his father, sunglasses shrouding his blank, dry eyes. His right hand was gone, a shredded stump of flesh that began at the wrist and ended with a few splinters of bone; blood seeped out of his ruined groin. Sturm kept touching his son's shoulder, dribbling sips of beer into Theo's open mouth. He patted Theo's hair, caked and matted with blood. The gesture was affectionate, loving; it didn't look like Sturm knew his son was dead.

Billy, the owner of the Komodo dragon, jumped out of his chair and flung a beer bottle at Frank. "Goddamn you. I had you drowning in the next five minutes. Fall back down, boy!"

Sturm whispered something out of the side of his mouth to his son, waited a moment, chuckled at the answer.

For the most part, they left Frank alone. There was no jeering, no gambling, no singing, no screaming, and no shooting. They all seemed content to simply wait and watch.

Frank kept one eye on the men and the other on the alligators. He stayed low in the water, knees straddling the T-post, and worked on unwrapping the chain, uncoiling it and yanking it at his chest.

Two hours later, the first alligator got close. It coasted in just under the surface, using its legs occasionally to steer the seven or eight feet of cold muscle, gliding along like a submarine full of teeth.

It got to within five feet before Frank sobbed and the panic took hold. He tried to attack the reptile, kicking and screaming and sobbing and slapping at the water. He had two feet of chain loose by then. The gator whirled away and shot away into the far corner of the rice field.

The men laughed and applauded.

Sturm put his arm around his son's shoulders and finished his beer.

The sun crawled across the sky.

Four alligators went at Frank the next time. By then, he had nearly three feet of chain loose, and whipped it at the gators like he was popping a wet towel. He drove them off, but an hour later, he watched as every gator he could see got closer in slow, lazy movements.

Heat waves shimmered off the water, attacking the air with shards of light.

Frank splashed water on his face and chest, eyeballing the sun. He squatted again, now holding a chain loop almost five feet in length. He scooped up a handful of mud and smeared it across his scalp, his face, his shoulders.

He couldn't help himself and swallowed a few sips of water from his palm.

Sturm watched Frank the way a housecat will watch a rattlesnake, waiting, learning, full of hunger and reluctant respect. He bent down at the water and splashed some over his skull, imitating Frank's movements, smearing mud across his face. Frank watched him right back.

Sturm unzipped and pissed in the rice paddy. Some of the others looked like they had to take a leak, but weren't sure if they were supposed to, worried that this might be some kind of important ritual. Sturm zipped and unsheathed his Iron Mistress. He dipped the blade in the water, held the blade to the sun, then sliced Theo's shirt open. He touched the edge of steel to his own chest, drawing blood, and in a precise and methodical manner, cut into Theo's chest, cracking the ribcage and prying his son's heart out.

Sturm held it out and sprinkled blood into the water, as if blessing the land with a sacrifice. He took a bite out of Theo's heart and tossed it into the rice paddy. Jack and Pine silently wrapped Theo in a sheet, and put him in the back of Sturm's pickup. Sturm pulled his chair closer to the edge and sat, watching Frank.

Conversation bubbled up, like vultures going back to a dead squirrel after a truck had passed. An alligator took the heart.

Frank vomited. He knew it was from drinking the water from the rice field, and it was his own damn fault. He retched again. It foamed around his shins and haunches. He didn't know if the drugs were still affecting him anymore, and just as he began to lose faith in the pills to either kill him or give him a fantastic burst of energy, the whisper of the drugs wearing off was enough to corrupt the waves of energy that he imagined floating up through his chest and head, and he felt the fire go out as if someone had turned a knob, killing the BBQ burner.

Frank tried to scare himself, to shock himself into an adrenaline overdose, something to clutch at the strength in his limbs. He sank to his knees, too exhausted and hurt to stand anymore, forcing himself to see it as it would happen, feeling the gators go after him like a pack of pit bulls ripping at a three-legged cat, twisting and tearing him until he was pulled apart like taffy, all while the men watched.

The gators closed in, their tails sweeping great swaths of dead rice stalks in the creamy mud. Frank gripped the chain tight, tighter, cried out, and slashed it at the first couple, but the others came in from the side. He kicked out, using his heels and elbows. Teeth snapped on bubbles and steel.

Two gunshots, flat and quick, ripped across the water.

It was Alice. She had a worn Remington semi-auto .12 gauge, moving quickly through the mud. The Glouck station wagon waited behind her, on the east bank. They had clearly come from Sturm's, and Frank knew they had found their boys. Alice got closer and shot two more alligators. Fifteen feet from Frank, she stopped to reload.

Pine jumped up. "Are you aware that these animals are private property?"

Alice shot another gator. "You oughta be ashamed of yourselves." The reptiles stopped stalking Frank long enough to attack their dead kin.

Sturm stood. His voice boomed across the water like the shotgun blasts. "Ashamed? Ashamed of what? I'm ashamed abominations of nature such as yourself still walk the earth." He drew his pistol and shot Alice in the hip.

She spun, firing the second round into the white sky, fell into the water on her wounded side. Bobbing up, water still running off her face, she tried to take a breath and Sturm shot her in the shoulder. Her mouth was still open when she flopped back into the shallow lake.

Frank lunged for the Remington.

Alligators came out of nowhere, clamping down on Alice's hand, her knee, her feet, her head. They twisted and rolled until the water exploded in a churning vortex of mud and blood. A tail slapped the shotgun away.

Even over the thrashing water, in the baked silence of the valley, everyone could hear Edie's howl. She floored the station wagon and the motor growled as if matching her scream. Tires spun in the dust and she raced around the rice paddy.

Sturm waited until Edie turned the final corner onto the highway, then yanked out both pistols and fired at the windshield. Glass popped and cracked. But Edie kept coming, faster and faster, gobbling up the highway. When Sturm was out of ammo, he dropped the pistols, turned to the men, said, "Finish it," and unsheathed the Iron Mistress. He fixed his eyes on Frank and started into the water.

The men began to shoot, careful and slow at first, then

quicker, the firing becoming more dense, becoming a single deafening blast, the gentle squeezing of triggers becoming frantic twitches as the station wagon roared down the highway like a tornado thrown by God.

Edie slammed into the row of the pickups and everyone stumbled into the water to get out of the way. The station wagon rocketed onto the driver's side door, glancing off Pine's pickup, and rolled over upside down, half submerged in the water, where it finally stopped in a cloud of dust and steam.

Sturm was almost running when he got to Frank. The ten and a half inch blade sliced through the air. Frank smacked the length of chain across Sturm's forearm, knocking the fist and knife away. Sturm whipped the knife back up, but Frank was already rolling his wrist, spinning the chain back at Sturm. Frank had nearly a foot and half over Sturm in height, and this, along with the chain, gave him an extra two and a half feet.

The folded chain caught Sturm in the jaw, snapping his head at the huge sky. Still, like in the arena, after fighting the lioness, Sturm held onto the knife.

The men crept closer to the upside-down station wagon. Besides the cops, only Jack and Pine were armed. Jack had a pistol, and Pine carried his M-1. For a moment, they heard nothing but the hiss of steam from the crumpled engine. Then Edie blew a hole through the back window with a shotgun, blasting a bigger hole in Jack's chest.

Everyone scrambled.

Edie kept shooting, as fast as she could point and pull the trigger of her side-by-side double-barreled shotgun. She could fire twice and reload in less than a second. Olaf went down and didn't get back up. Another blast folded the taxidermist in half. Herschell leapt behind his cruiser. Billy dove into the back of

Sturm's pickup, landing on Theo's corpse. Pine slammed the bolt home on his M-1 and unloaded on the station wagon.

He squinted through the steam and gunsmoke. He heard Edie reloading. As if that reminded him, he ripped out the clip and feverishly forced more rounds into it. But Edie was faster. She fired, taking out Pine's left leg.

He toppled face first into the mud, dropping the M-1.

Edie scuttled out of the station wagon like some arachnid Jack-in-the-box and snatched Pine's rifle before wriggling back inside. Silence bloomed again. Her voice cracked with emotion as she called to her son. Her firstborn. "My boys. . . . How could you . . ."

Pine said, "Please—"

Edie shot him in the head with his own rifle.

Sturm bared his teeth and rushed at Frank.

Frank whipped the chain around and took a step back and slipped in the mud. In that faltering second Sturm rushed at him, landing on Frank's back. The knife plunged at his stomach. Frank caught Sturm's wrist with both hands, but Sturm snaked his left arm around Frank's neck, squeezing at the carotid artery, trying to get Frank to black out as he clung like one of the spider monkeys.

Pools of darkness grew in Frank's eyes. He hung onto Sturm's wrist and slowly toppled backward. They hit the water and Frank slammed Sturm into the rice stalks and mud.

Sturm hung on.

Frank flattened the little man into the soft, wet earth.

Sturm bit him, at the base of Frank's neck, in his right trapezius.

Frank relaxed, letting go of Sturm with one hand, and simply guided the blade up and let Sturm slit his own forearm. Frank ripped himself out of Sturm's grasp as the little man jabbed the knife at his face. He found Sturm's false teeth still embedded in his neck. He tried to slap them away, to tear them out, but they were stuck fast, like a starving tick.

Edie rolled out of the car, Pine's M-1 slung over her shoulder, a shotgun held in front of her. She stayed low and worked her way up the bank on her back, sidling closer to the police cruiser.

Herschell got brave and stuck his head over the trunk, fired a few times at the station wagon. When nothing happened, he edged around the bumper, gun up and ready. He didn't expect to almost step on Edie as she lay on her back glaring up at him. She fired, and a deluge of #9 shot exploded up through his groin, his gut, his face.

Edie was on her feet before Herschell hit the pavement. She reloaded and held the shotgun up to her right shoulder, good eye glaring down the barrel, the pale, unblinking other eye staring fixedly on the late afternoon sky. She advanced on Sturm's pickup.

Billy shrieked, "It wasn't me—" Edie shot him twice at point blank range.

Sturm circled, mouth oddly puckered without his teeth. Frank pivoted in place, eyes locked on Sturm. Frank drifted to the south, then broke into a clumsy run, darting past Sturm the other way. He dropped, pretending to reach the end of his chain, landing sideways in the water.

The closest alligator was ten yards away, mouth open slightly, black water spilling through the lower teeth. Sturm rushed at Frank.

Frank drove his foot into the older man's sternum. They both heard something crack. Sturm slashed at Frank's leg. Frank kicked out with his other foot up and caught Sturm under the right armpit, knocking him into the air.

Sturm dropped the Iron Mistress.

Frank scrabbled at the mud. He grabbed at something that felt somehow both cold and hot at the same time. Jerking his left hand out of the water, he saw his fingers wrapped around the Mistress's blade. Blood ran into the water.

Sturm grabbed for the handle. Frank dropped the blade, and got hold of the handle in his right hand underwater. He drove it straight up, through the soft flesh of Sturm's bottom jaw, up through his mouth, into his nasal cavities.

Sturm smacked his sunken lips and bare gums and drooled blood. Frank saw how the blade had split the tongue in half lengthwise. Frank refused to let go. Sturm's hands slapped at Frank's arms, still some fight left, but it was leaving soon.

Frank leaned in close. "When you die . . . you aren't going to heaven. You will not see your son. Ever. Again. You will never see these animals. They will not serve you in the afterlife. There is no afterlife for you. There is only the long emptiness. That is the truth. Do you understand?" Frank used the knife handle like he was controlling a puppet and nodded Sturm's head for him. "Good."

Frank ripped the Iron Mistress away.

Sturm took one solid, confident step forward, just to let anyone watching know that he was okay, that he was in control, then the mud grabbed at his boot and he went to his knees. Something underwater snapped at his leg and yanked.

They tore him to pieces.

Edie settled into one of the lawn chairs and simply watched him.

Frank couldn't see her expression. He stood straight, tugging at his choke chain, but it was too tight. He fingered the padlock, and knew it was hopeless. There was no way to break it or the chains. He still held the Iron Mistress, but it was useless against the steel. He looked back to Edie, but she hadn't moved, and a grim certainty descended upon him.

Frank realized that she hadn't made up her mind to either help him or kill him. She was just going to sit there and wait and watch and see if he could make it out on his own.

He held the chain limp in one hand, Iron Mistress in the other. Exhaustion didn't creep up softly and seduce him; it ran him down and stomped on his head. Frank collapsed into the water. Water filled his mouth and he vomited again. He dry-heaved, somehow crawling backward. His bare foot slid against the Remington.

He shot two of the closest alligators. He fired again and missed. He squeezed the trigger one more time and heard the dry snap of an empty shotgun.

He pulled himself over to the T-post and used the butt of the shotgun to start digging. He worked at it until his muscles screamed, his back twitched in agony, and his hands bled. The sun was nearly touching the horizon when Frank finally wrenched the fence post free with a small squelching sound.

He fell backward and stared up at the gathering twilight as if he'd never seen the sky before. He felt movement in the water and knew he had to keep moving. The other end of the chain had been padlocked to the fence post, so he ended up carrying the T-post. Halfway to the bank, his legs gave out and he had to crawl the rest of the way. It took at least half an hour. He inched out of the water, and collapsed in the mud in front of the chairs.

Edie's voice said softly, "My Alice is dead. She's dead because she went out there to help you." Frank rolled onto his back and stared up to the black chasms of her shotgun muzzle, inches from his head.

Frank tried to speak, but his mouth wouldn't work. It didn't matter. There was nothing to say. Edie didn't move. Tears slid down her high cheeks and fell from her chin, spattering silently on the shotgun, rolling slowly down the center of the two barrels and dripped on Frank's forehead. She exhaled through her teeth.

Frank closed his eyes.

They both heard the far-off whine of an ATV. Several of them. It was the rest of the Glouck brothers, the ones that had helped bury Petunia. The four-wheelers roared up the highway to the pickups.

Frank heard the shotgun clatter to the pavement.

When he opened his eyes, Annie was staring down at him. The sun was nearly gone, sending light flat across the land, lighting her face in soft, glowing warmth. Her eyes were red. A coldness had settled within them, and Frank thought she might just pick up the shotgun and shoot him and be done with it. But instead, she squatted down, gently patted his head like he was a good dog, and walked away.

Frank managed to lift himself up into the cab of Sturm's pickup when he heard the big cats snarling and snapping over the bodies. It was much later. Cold stars blanketed the sky. Strange howls and cries rose above the crickets.

The Gloucks were gone.

Frank fumbled with the glove box and found the First-Aid kit. He splashed disinfectant over his hand and used up the entire roll of white tape wrapping his fingers. He slumped back on the bench seat and slipped into sleep as he listened to the animals fight over the meat.

DAY THIRTY-FIVE

Everything hurt. Frank sat upright, squinting into the hideous sunlight. A few lionesses rested in the shade under the pickups, tails slapping absentmindedly at flies and mosquitoes. He slid over into the driver's seat and found the ignition empty. Even through the throbbing pain, Frank knew if he stayed in the cab, he'd be dead of dehydration before the end of the day.

None of the big cats moved when he cracked the door open. He stepped gingerly down, pavement already hot under his bare feet. He realized he was still naked. There was nothing else to do, so he walked, still carrying the damn chain and fencepost. He skirted around the rice paddy and headed back through the fields to Sturm's house. None of the animals bothered him. He figured they'd eaten well the night before, and didn't feel the need to stalk and hunt prey now.

The sky was alive with vultures.

He went into the house first, straight to the kitchen sink, and stuck his head under the faucet, gulping water until he vomited again. The fridge was full of meat. He grabbed an apple from a bowl on the counter instead. Then he went upstairs.

None of Sturm's clothes came even close to fitting. Finally, he found a T-shirt and a pair of sweats in Theo's room that came down to mid-calf. Theo had a pair of flip-flops that covered most of Frank's feet. He poured Listerine over his hand, and put fresh bandages over the slices in his flesh.

Sturm kept his liquor in the living room. Frank grabbed a

bottle and went out and sat on the deck. The morning sun threw the shadow of the Lutheran cross over the entire backyard. Frank finished half before heading to the barn. There, he found a hacksaw and went to work on the choke chain.

Later, he checked on the stall at the back of the barn. It still looked the same. Dust everywhere. He toppled the air conditioner off the freezer and let it crash to the floor. He froze as the sound reverberated around the barn, wondering if Princess and Lady were still around. But after a full minute ticked past, he figured they were either gone or weren't hungry. He opened the freezer.

It was empty. The gun safe was gone.

Frank let that sink in for a moment, then carefully closed the freezer door. There was nothing left to do, so he grabbed two bottles of rum from one of the stalls and went out to the driveway to sit on the front porch. He settled into Sturm's rocking chair and had been rocking for almost fifteen minutes when he saw the saddlebags hanging over the porch railing. He couldn't remember if they'd been here when he first got to the house or if someone had left them here when he was in the barn.

The bags were full of cash. Frank looked toward town, as if he'd find answers. Instead, he just saw a thick column of smoke, probably rising from the park. The gas in the fire engine had finally caught. Or someone had put a match to it. He wondered if it would spread to the rest of the town. Swallowing some more rum, he slung the saddlebags over his shoulders and started walking to the long, black car.

ABOUT THE AUTHOR

Jeff Jacobson's stories have appeared in *Doorways Magazine, Read by Dawn Vol. 1* and *3*. His other novels include *Wormfood,* published by Medallion Press. He teaches Fiction and Screenwriting at Columbia College Chicago and lives near Chicago with his family and far too many animals. His website is jeff-jacobson.com. Stop by and say howdy.